PENGUIN

NJA

Born and raised in Bethlehem, Pennsylvania, ROBERT COOK
was educated at Princeton, Zurich and Johns Hopkins and taught
English medieval literature at Tulane University in New Orleans
for twenty-seven years. In 1990 he moved to Reykjavík to serve
as Professor of English Literature at the University of Iceland.
He has published on English medieval literature and on the
Icelandic sagas, and together with Mattias Tveitane edited *Streng-
leikar* (1979), an Old Norse translation of twenty-one medieval
French lais.

WORLD OF THE SAGAS

NJAL'S SAGA

Translated with Introduction and Notes by
ROBERT COOK

PENGUIN BOOKS

PENGUIN BOOKS

Published by the Penguin Group
Penguin Books Ltd, 80 Strand, London WC2R 0RL, England
Penguin Putnam Inc., 375 Hudson Street, New York, New York 10014, USA
Penguin Books Australia Ltd, 250 Camberwell Road, Camberwell, Victoria 3124, Australia
Penguin Books Canada Ltd, 10 Alcorn Avenue, Toronto, Ontario, Canada M4V 3B2
Penguin Books India (P) Ltd, 11 Community Centre, Panchsheel Park, New Delhi – 110 017, India
Penguin Books (NZ) Ltd, Cnr Rosedale and Airborne Roads, Albany, Auckland, New Zealand
Penguin Books (South Africa) (Pty) Ltd, 24 Sturdee Avenue, Rosebank 2196, South Africa

Penguin Books Ltd, Registered Offices: 80 Strand, London WC2R 0RL, England

www.penguin.com

This translation first published in *The Complete Sagas of Icelanders (Including 49 Tales)* III, edited
by Viðar Hreinsson (General editor), Robert Cook, Terry Gunnell, Keneva Kunz and
Bernard Scudder. Leifur Eiríksson Publishing Ltd, Iceland 1997
First published in Penguin Classics 2001

037

Translation copyright © Leifur Eiríksson Publishing Ltd, 1997
Introduction and Notes copyright © Robert Cook, 2001
All rights reserved

The moral rights of the translator have been asserted

Leifur Eiríksson Publishing Ltd gratefully acknowledges the support of the Nordic Cultural Fund,
Ariane Programme of the European Union, UNESCO and others.

Set in 10/12.5 pt Monotype Janson
Typeset by Rowland Phototypesetting Ltd, Bury St Edmunds, Suffolk
Printed and bound in Great Britain by Clays Ltd, Elcograf S.p.A.

ISBN-13: 978-0-140-44769-9

www.greenpenguin.co.uk

Contents

Acknowledgements

Special thanks are due to Sverrir Tómasson and other learned scholars at the Árni Magnússon Institute in Reykjavík, to Icelandair, to Professor Jón Friðjónsson of the University of Iceland, to Guðrún Ingólfsdóttir, and to my copy-editor, Elizabeth Stratford. So many others have helped me in one way or another that in mentioning the following I beg indulgence from those I may have temporarily overlooked: Carol Clover, Gerda Cook-Bodegom, Helle Degnbol, Susanne Eisner-Kartagener, Davíð Erlingsson, Henry Frey, Galina Glazyrina, Terry Gunnell, Fritz Heinemann, Viðar Hreinsson, Ármann Jakobsson, Örnolfur Thorsson prepared the maps, genealogies and glossary, and Jón Torfson the index of characters. Bernard Scudder, Robert Kellogg, Helga Kress, William I. Miller, Hermann Pálsson, John Porter, Christopher Sanders, Marianne Kalinke, Andrew Wawn and Yelena Olegovna Yershova.

Introduction

Njal's Saga is by far the longest of the forty family sagas written in Iceland in the thirteenth and fourteenth centuries, and over the years it has proved to be the favourite. The saga teems with life and action, with memorable and complex characters from the heroic Gunnar of Hlidarendi, a warrior without equal who dislikes killing, to the villainous, insinuating Mord Valgardsson, who turns out to be less dastardly than we first expect. Unforgettable events include Skarphedin's head-splitting axe blow as he glides past his opponent on an icy river bank, or Hildigunn's provoking of her uncle to seek blood revenge by placing on his shoulders the blood-clotted cloak in which her husband was slain. In *Njal's Saga* we read of battles on land and sea, failed marriages, divided allegiances, struggles for power, sexual gibes, malicious backbiting, revenge, counter-revenge, complex legal processes and peace settlements that fail to bring peace, not to mention dreams, portents, prophecies, a witch-ride and valkyries. Behind all this richness lies a well-crafted story of decent men and women struggling unsuccessfully to control a tragic force propelled by persons of lesser stature but greater ill-will. Just as in the Norse poem *Völuspá* ('The Seeress's Prophecy') the gods met their doom (no mere twilight) at the hands of brute giants and monsters, after which a new and peaceful earth arose, so do the terrible events of *Njal's Saga* lead finally and at great cost to a dignified resolution bearing the promise of a better time.

BACKGROUND

From the time they adopted the Latin alphabet in the eleventh century, the Icelanders have been prodigious writers and record keepers. Among the many genres that have been preserved is a group of annals, begun around the year 1200, most of which contain, usually under the year 1010, the simple entry 'Nials brenna' (the burning of Njal). Another work, which dates back to the twelfth century, *The Book of Settlements*,* a detailed account of the people who settled Iceland in the late ninth century, reports this about a man named Thorgeir: 'His son was Njal, who was burned to death in his house.' Some versions of *The Book of Settlements* add 'at Bergthorshvol' and the number of men (varying from seven to nine) who were burned to death. Snorri Sturluson, the great thirteenth-century writer and man of affairs, ascribes a half-stanza in his *Edda* to 'Brennu-Njáll' (Njal of the burning) and *The Saga of Gunnlaug Serpent-tongue* reports that the general assembly held after the burning of Njal 'was one of the three most heavily attended Althings of all time'.

Thus a number of sources which pre-date *Njal's Saga*, in several of the genres of medieval Icelandic literature, testify to the fact that around the year 1010 the buildings at a farm named Bergthorshvol in the south of Iceland, on a marshy area dotted with hillocks and bordering the ocean, were set on fire and burned. Inside were the farmer, a man named Njal Thorgeirsson, and some others. The references to this burning make it one of the best documented events of the so-called 'saga age' in Iceland (930–1030), and there is no reason to question it as historical fact.

Another prominent event in *Njal's Saga* (or *Njála*, to use its popular nickname) is supported by external sources. A stanza in the twelfth-century poem *Íslendingadrápa* by Haukur Valdísarson records that a man named Gunnar defended himself against an attack by a certain Gizur, and managed to wound sixteen men and kill two. This event is also mentioned in *The Saga of the People of Eyri* and in *The Book of*

---

* For full details of this and other sources see Further Reading.

Settlements, and it seems safe to conclude that this too was a historical fact.

These two events, the attack on Gunnar at Hlidarendi and the burning of Njal at Bergthorshvol, constitute the two principal climaxes of *Njal's Saga*. There is a huge gap, however, between the bare saga-age events and their elaboration in the prose masterpiece we have before us, written around 1280. As with the Homeric epics and the *Song of Roland*, well-remembered historical events were passed down through several centuries of oral tradition and finally shaped by the hand of a master story-teller and writer into a *non*-historical work of art. The author of *Njal's Saga* was not trying to write history, but to create his own dramatic fiction, using events and persons known to him but going far beyond them with his own inventions and interpretations. There was a man named Njal who was burned to death in his home around the year 1010, and a man named Gunnar who was killed by men who attacked his home around 992 – but they are not the Njal and Gunnar of the thirteenth-century *Njal's Saga*.

In Icelandic the word 'saga' means both 'history' and 'story', and if *Njal's Saga* represents inspired story more than remembered history, it does not exist in isolation, is not a beginning or an end in itself. It is the longest, among the latest, and arguably the best of a group of forty sagas written anonymously in Iceland in the thirteenth and fourteenth centuries about people who lived there in the tenth and eleventh centuries. Among these 'Sagas of Icelanders' (also known as 'family sagas') there is a remarkable consistency, owing largely to the long period of oral transmission. For one thing, many characters overlap from saga to saga, and are mentioned as well in *The Book of Settlements*. The family of Hoskuld Dala-Kolsson, introduced in the first chapter of *Njal's Saga* and prominent in the first half of the saga, is the principal family in *The Saga of the People of Laxardal*. The lawspeaker Skafti Thoroddsson (first introduced in Ch. 56) appears in other family sagas as well as in historical works, as does Thorgeir the Godi of Ljosavatn, who played a key role in the adoption of Christianity. Many other characters in *Njal's Saga* are known from other Sagas of Icelanders, including rulers of Scandinavia like Harald Grey-cloak, Hakon Sigurdarson and Olaf Tryggvason of Norway, and Earl Sigurd Hlodvisson of Orkney. The multiple appearance of characters is so common in early Icelandic literature that the notes to this tradition occasionally record that a certain character, for example, Gunnar's brother Kolskegg, does *not* appear in other sources. This may seem gratuitous information, and it is certainly no guarantee that the character is non-historical, but in some cases it may suggest that a person has been deliberately invented, either in the process of oral re-telling or by the late thirteenth-century author.

A second way in which the Sagas of Icelanders display consistency is their use of a common body of narrative motifs. Scandinavian kings and earls appear frequently because it is *de rigueur* for a promising young Icelander to establish his credentials by visiting foreign rulers and making a favourable impression on them, whether by composing a poem of praise or excelling in games or defeating the king's enemies. The triumphant journeys abroad of Hrut (Chs. 2–6) and Gunnar (Chs. 29–32) are two among many such in the corpus. Other motifs common to *Njal's Saga* and other Sagas of Icelanders are the refusal to sell (as in Ch. 47), the horse fight, the broken shoelace, quests for support, dissemination of important information by itinerant women or other unnamed characters, the use of spies, and, last but not least, the goading woman who incites a man, usually a kinsman, to take blood vengeance for a slight to the family's honour. Such common motifs, together with the time and place (Iceland in the tenth to eleventh centuries), the subject matter (primarily feuds and their resolution), character types, standardized descriptions of battles and feasts, common thematic concerns and the general social setting, make the Sagas of Icelanders a homogeneous literary genre.

The social setting is so consistently presented that we can think of it as a third major defining feature of the Sagas of Icelanders. Recent saga scholarship with an anthropological and sociological focus has in fact demonstrated that although the sagas are not to be trusted as history in the narrow sense (names, dates, events), they provide a remarkably coherent picture of an intricate legal and social system, one which saw little change over the three centuries of the commonwealth (960–1262). For this kind of history – dealing with matters such as the organization of a hierarchical society, the arranging of marriages and divorces, the obligations within the kin group with respect to feuds, and the handling of disputes (whether by the courts or by personal arrangement) – the sagas represent a large body of shared material so consistently that it cannot have been invented by any individual author. For details of the social setting see the Glossary, especially under 'Althing', 'Fifth Court', 'full outlawry', 'godi' and 'Lawspeaker'.

A fourth way in which the Sagas of Icelanders form a generic whole is their firm setting in historical time and their unified view of Iceland's evolving past. Many sagas – though not *Njal's Saga* – begin by mentioning the reign of Harald Fair-hair (r. 870–930), the first king to bring all of Norway under his control. *The Saga of Hrafnkel Frey's Godi*, for example, begins: 'It was in the days of King Harald Fair-hair ... that a man named Hallfred brought his ship to Breiddal in Iceland, below the district of Fljotsdal.' The common explanation in the sagas for the emigration of prominent families from the west coast of Norway is the desire to escape Harald's harsh rule, although in fact other reasons, such as over-population, were just as likely. Many of those who left Norway stopped first in Celtic territories in Britain and later brought women and slaves out to Iceland, so that the population was not pure Scandinavian. The flight from Norway led to the 'land-taking' or settlement of Iceland, an island previously uninhabited except for a few Irish monks, who soon left when they saw themselves deprived of the solitude that had drawn them there. It is reckoned that by the year 930 the population of the new land had reached at least 20,000.

In addition to this foundation story of flight and settlement, the historical awareness of the thirteenth-century Icelander would have included the importation of laws from Norway by a man named Ulfljot and the establishment of the Althing (general annual meeting), both around the year 930; a refinement of the laws by a division of the country into four quarters, around 965; the acceptance of Christianity at the Althing in 999 or 1000; and the establishment of the Fifth Court in the year 1004. All of these facts, from Harald Fair-hair to the Fifth Court and beyond, were set down around 1125 in a concise book by Ari Thorgilsson known as *The Book of the*

Icelanders. Not every Icelander in the thirteenth century had a copy of Ari's book, or knew the precise dates and details just outlined, but it is clear that the family sagas were written for an audience possessed of a lively knowledge of the historical development of their country and its institutions.

Njal's Saga does not mention the flight from Harald Fair-hair, but it embodies the historical legend by including two of the principal events – the Conversion (Chs. 100–105) and the establishment of the Fifth Court (Ch. 97) – and by incorporating, as do most of the family sagas, the detailed genealogies common to the genre of historical writings. Ari Thorgilsson mentions an earlier, expanded version of his short book, which contained 'Genealogies and Lives of the Kings', and there is other evidence that written genealogies were among the earliest secular writings in Iceland. Whether written or simply preserved in oral family tradition, a knowledge of one's ancestors and of the kinship relations of prominent figures was built into the consciousness of every Icelander. *Njála* begins by mentioning Mord Gigja and his father Sighvat the Red (his grandfather, according to *The Book of Settlements*). The next person introduced is Hoskuld Dala-Kolsson, and his line is traced back through his mother to a prominent female settler in the west of Iceland, Unn the Deep-minded. The text does not specify that Sighvat and Unn were settlers – this is not necessary, for the audience of the saga would have known this. Genealogies usually appear in the sagas when a character is introduced, often in combination with an insightful description.

Tracing of family lines goes forward as well as backward. The twelfth-century Icelandic historian, Saemund Sigfusson the Learned, is mentioned in *Njal's Saga* as a descendant of Ulf Aur-godi (Ch. 25) and also of Sigfus Ellida-Grimsson (Ch. 26). Gizur the White's son Isleif, mentioned in Ch. 46, became the first bishop of Iceland in 1056, and the audience would have known that Isleif's son was the influential Bishop Gizur who introduced the tithe to Iceland. In the fullest genealogy in the saga, that given for Gudmund the Powerful in Ch. 113, his line is traced not only to Bishop Ketil (d. 1145) but to the prominent thirteenth-century families of the Sturlungs and the people of Hvamm. The abundant genealogies, not to mention the abundance of characters, must have made *Njála* a rich shared experience for thirteenth-century Icelanders, most of whom could trace their ancestry back to at least one of the four hundred settlers and to other persons named in this and other sagas.

In this sense, the modern reader – unless he is an Icelander who can trace his lineage for a thousand years (as many can) – is an outsider, unable to share fully in the personal excitement of reading about one's family past and one's national past. There is no disadvantage, however, if the reader is prepared to understand sympathetically the historical background just described and what it must have meant to the men and women who wrote and read or listened to these sagas in the thirteenth and fourteenth centuries. It is well documented that the thirteenth century in Iceland was an ugly and troubled time, virtually a period of civil war, with large-scale battles, with power falling into fewer and fewer hands (instead of being distributed among the thirty-nine godis) and with interference from Norway in both secular and ecclesiastical affairs. The resolution of this turmoil was submission to Norwegian rule in the year 1262, and it was seven centuries before the Icelanders became an independent nation again, in 1944. Whether written before 1262 or after (like *Njal's Saga*), the sagas were written partly out of a need to affirm identity, both personal and national, with the past, a time when their ancestors fled Norwegian tyranny – rather than succumb to it – and built up a new society free of monarchical rule and governed by laws and institutions that functioned with dignity, if not without bloodshed.

THE SAGA

We have seen that the author of *Njal's Saga* worked with traditional materials, oral tales of historical (and non-historical) events and persons, combined with a strong consciousness of his country's history and social institutions. He apparently also worked with written sources, including genealogies, a book of laws, accounts of the Conversion (Chs. 100–105) and of the battle of Clontarf (Chs. 153–7) and works in Icelandic based on foreign sources such as the *Dialogues of*

Gregory the Great (see the note to Flosi's dream in Ch. 133). It is impossible to disentangle the four components in the saga – authentic history, the inventions of oral tradition, written sources and the contribution of the thirteenth-century author – but the saga shows so many signs of careful artistry that one is inclined to believe in a master craftsman at the final stage, perhaps even a writer who, as the Swedish poet and critic A. U. Bååth put it long ago, had the last line of his saga in mind when he wrote the first.

The last sentence of the saga in most manuscripts refers to it as *Brennu-Njáls saga*, which can be translated either 'the saga of the burning of Njal' (with an emphasis on the act of burning) or 'the saga of Njal of the burning' (i.e. of Njal who endured the burning). In either case this term (used as the title in most modern editions) points to the two things which are central, a man and a burning. The laws make it clear that burning a man's house was a heinous crime, punishable by full outlawry even if no persons were burned (*Laws of Early Iceland*, p. 169). The saga itself shows burning to be shameful as well as heinous. In the attack on Gunnar in Ch. 77, the option of burning was proposed by the malicious Mord Valgardsson, but firmly rejected. In the attack on Bergthorshvol, Flosi's own words before starting the blaze reveal his awareness of the shame attendant on such a deed (Ch. 128). The saga, like the tradition behind it, was fascinated by this horror. In one way or another all the events in the first part of the saga lead to the non-incendiary killing of Gunnar; all of the subsequent events, as well as many of the earlier events, lead to Njal's death by burning. After this climax there are still twenty-nine chapters in the saga (131–59); these are more than a coda, they are a necessary settling of scores and a hard-won return to equilibrium.

The man Njal is not the hero one expects from a work called 'saga'. His introductory description (Ch. 20) shows him to be an older man (or at least a man with grown children, as becomes clear in Ch. 25), known for his wisdom, his gift of prophecy, his skill at law, and – a surprising physical detail – his inability to grow a beard. Further, the beardless titular hero of this saga never kills, never fights, and is only once shown to carry a weapon, a rather useless short axe (Ch. 118). His neighbour and good friend Gunnar, on the other hand, is the very model of the blond, blue-eyed Viking, described chiefly in terms of his unmatched physical skills (Ch. 19). His two battles against Viking raiders abroad (Ch. 30) prove him to be the greatest of Icelandic fighters. His tragedy is that back in Iceland he is dragged into quarrels with men of inferior worth who envy his greatness and eventually bring him down. Njal and Gunnar form an ideal complementary pair, wisdom and strength, and Gunnar profits from Njal's advice and legal skills as long as he can – and then, in effect, gives up.

The presence of Njal at the centre of the saga is a sign that the emphasis is not on overt displays of masculine prowess, though of course there are a generous number of personal combats, carefully described with a connoisseur's eye to every movement, every swing of the sword and thrust of the spear, every gaping or severing wound. Many of these encounters, however, are not altogether heroic. Gunnar is on his own when he is attacked in his home by forty men, Hoskuld Thrainsson is killed in a cowardly attack by five men who lie in hiding until he comes out in the morning to sow grain, and Njal and his family are annihilated by men who take no risks and burn them inside their house. Much blood is shed in the saga, but much of it is shamefully shed – not exactly what seekers after Viking adventure want to read.

Rather than violent action, it is spiritual qualities that occupy the centre of interest in this saga – intelligence, wisdom, decisiveness, purposefulness, a shrewd business sense, the ability to give and follow advice, decency, a sense of honour. Njal says at one point, when he is calculating how to respond to the abusive language of the Sigfussons, 'they are stupid men' (Ch. 91). Those who plot evil, invent and pronounce gratuitous insults and envy the honest virtues of others are stupid. Between their stupidity and the clear-headedness of their antagonists lies the central conflict in the saga. It is emblematic that when Njal has a vision of some men about to attack Gunnar he reports that 'they seem in a frenzy but act without purpose' (Ch. 69).

In our age of self-doubt, identity crises and existential uncertainty, it is refreshing to read about firm decision-making and purposeful action by men and women with a sure sense of themselves. Hesitation is treated with scorn in *Njála*, as when Hallgerd whets Brynjolf in Ch. 38: he falls silent, and she insults him by saying that Thjostolf (now dead) would not have hesitated. When Sorli Brodd-Helgason gives a feeble response to Flosi's request for support, Flosi says 'I can see from your answer that your wife rules here' (Ch. 134). Some men of course are temporarily caught in a dilemma, like Flosi in Ch. 116, torn between blood vengeance and a peaceful settlement, or Ketil of Mork (Chs. 93 and 112) and Ingjald of Keldur (Chs. 116 and 124), torn between conflicting allegiances. Their decisions are not easy, and we sympathize with them. But we are thrilled by men who do not stop to weigh the odds, like Kari outside the hall of King Sigtrygg of Orkney in Ch. 155: when he overhears Gunnar Lambason's lying account of the burning, he dashes in and cuts off Gunnar's head in a single blow. We also admire Gunnar of Hlidarendi's change of mind: his decision to remain in Iceland rather than go abroad as an outlaw is taken quickly, resolutely and courageously (Ch. 75).

The good characters not only understand themselves and what is required of them, they also know what to expect of others, and often with remarkable precision. The fullest example of this is Njal's instructions to Gunnar in Ch. 22, where he is able to predict step by step exactly what will happen when Gunnar comes in disguise to Laxardal. A small example is Kari's ability to time the movement of Ketil and his men (beginning of Ch. 152). In between are many other cases where intelligent people show a keen ability to anticipate the actions and words of others.

A concentrated form of such intelligence is prophecy, a gift reserved for a special group, according to the statement in Ch. 114 that 'Snorri was called the wisest of the men in Iceland who could not foretell the future.' An unusual number of persons in *Njal's Saga* possess this gift. Njal is of course the main figure here. To mention just two examples: he knows that if Gunnar kills twice within the same bloodline and then does not keep the settlement for the second killing, he will be killed; he also knows, far in advance of the burning, what will be the cause of his death (Ch. 55). Hrut Herjolfsson is another man with prophetic power. In the opening chapter of the saga he is able to look at the young Hallgerd and predict both that many men will suffer because of her (and they do, not least Gunnar) and that she will steal (which she does). Hrut frequently makes wise predictions, as when he foresees that Gunnar will suffer for having taken Unn's dowry by force, and that he will later turn to Hoskuld and Hrut for friendship (Ch. 24).

Other characters too have their share of intelligent foresight: Glum knows in advance that Hallgerd will not have him killed (Ch. 13); Helgi Njalsson's second sight enables him to see trouble in Scotland for Earl Sigurd (Ch. 85); the old woman Saeunn curses the chickweed which she knows will be used to set a fire at Bergthorshvol (Ch. 124); Bjarni Brodd-Helgason knows that the man who undertakes Flosi's defence will die (Ch. 138). Many other examples will strike the reader's attention. Whether plain intelligence or a special gift of prophecy, there is an impressive amount of clear thinking in *Njála*.

Foresight and advice-giving go hand in hand, for the man who can predict the outcome of things is best equipped to give advice. Hrut and Njal are the two who most effectively and consistently combine these two skills. However, giving good advice is one thing, and following it is another. Gunnar, the chief beneficiary of Njal's advice, is a clear-headed man with a good and non-violent nature ('I want to get along well with everyone,' Ch. 32), but he fails all too often to heed good advice and warnings. He follows to the letter Njal's advice on how to reclaim Unn's dowry (Ch. 23), Kolskegg's advice to offer Otkel compensation for the theft (Ch. 49) and Njal's legal advice (Chs. 64–5). But he goes to the Althing against Njal's wishes (Ch. 32); he neglects to take the Njalssons along with him to Tunga, as he had promised (Ch. 60); he declines Asgrim's offer of company just before the ambush at Knafaholar (Ch. 61); he not only ignores Olaf Peacock's advice to travel in large numbers (Ch. 59), but declines Olaf's invitation to move west to Dalir when his life is in greatest danger (Ch. 75); in his final scene he refuses his mother's advice not to shoot one of the enemy's arrows back at them, and this contributes to his defeat (Ch. 77). Much of this may be regarded as part of the heroic code – the hero stands alone, he defies his enemies – but it is also imprudent.

Most crucially, after he has killed twice in the same bloodline,

Gunnar neglects to follow the second part of Njal's advice: not to break the settlement made for the killing (Ch. 55, repeated in Ch. 73). By deciding to remain in Iceland (Ch. 75), thus breaking the settlement, Gunnar seals his own fate.

There are a large number of proverbial sayings attributed to the characters in *Njal's Saga*, over fifty, and some are repeated twice or even three times. They emphasize the importance of intelligent wisdom, and in nearly every case they are uttered by good and wise characters; an exception is Sigmund in Ch. 41, but when he, after being told by Gunnar to avoid Hallgerd's advice, states that 'Whoever warns is free of fault', we can suspect insincerity, or even sarcasm, behind his words – he quickly ignores Gunnar's warning. Sometimes the proverbs have a resonance for the story as a whole, such as the twice-repeated statement that the effect of one's actions is often two-sided, or 'cold are the counsels of women', or 'the hand's joy in the blow is brief' (repeated three times). Akin to the proverb is the pithy saying, such as Rannveig's comment when she hears that Hallgerd is planning to have one of Njal's servants murdered: 'House-wives have been good here, even without plotting to kill men' (Ch. 36).

One final form of intellectual activity – telling the truth or lying – needs to be mentioned, for it contributes significantly to the unfolding of the saga. In addition to his wisdom and prophetic powers, Njal is known as a truth-teller. Hogni Gunnarsson says of him that 'he never lies' (Ch. 78), and similar statements are made on two other occasions. Hjalti Skeggjason and Runolf of Dal are also labelled as men who tell the truth, and many of the good characters, like Hrut and Hall of Sida, gain authority because they can be trusted. On the other hand there is some notable lying in the saga – Skammkel lies to Otkel (Ch. 50), Thrain lies to Earl Hakon (Ch. 88), Mord lies to Hoskuld and to the Njalssons (Chs. 109–10) – and their lies always have evil effects.

Telling the truth or its opposite forms an important part of the saga's large interest in reporting, telling news, spreading information. The saga as a whole claims at a number of places – with expressions such as 'It was said that' – to be a true report of what, according to tradition, really happened. The author scrupulously interrupts his account of the battle at the Althing to say that 'though a few of the things that happened are told here, there were many more for which no stories have come down' (Ch. 145). Within the saga there are constant references to what people are saying. 'The slaying of Gunnar was spoken badly of in all parts of the land' (Ch. 77). 'Here they ended their talk, but this became a topic of conversation among many' (Ch. 91). A person's honour depended on public opinion: when a settlement is made for Hallgerd's theft and Skammkel's lie, the narrator reports that 'Gunnar had much honour from this case. People then rode home from the Thing' (Ch. 51). We understand that the settlement was reported all over the country by those who had been at the Althing, and that Gunnar's reputation was enhanced in this way. The Iceland of *Njal's Saga* is alive with talk, and pregnant with proof of the power of words.

Unfortunately for the decent people in the saga, much of the talk is lies, and in particular slanderous lies about a man's effeminacy, which was inseparable from cowardice in the Old Norse way of thinking – together they indicated that a man was not fully a man. The worst defamation of all was to say that a man was not merely effeminate, but in fact played a woman's part in a homosexual relationship. Sexual slander against women consisted in a charge of lechery. Hallgerd's comment on Bergthora's deformed fingernails (Ch. 35) may be an instance of this; a clearer case is Skarphedin's calling Hallgerd 'either a cast-off hag or a whore' (Ch. 91).

It is regrettable that Mord Gigja made public the marital problems between Hrut and Unn, but at least no lie was told. Slander gets under way in Ch. 35, when Hallgerd calls attention to Njal's beardlessness, and it becomes deadly serious in Ch. 44 when Hallgerd invents the nicknames 'Old Beardless' for Njal and 'Dung-beardlings' for his sons, implying that their beards would not grow unless they put dung on their faces. Hallgerd gets Sigmund to compose verses on this theme, and of course these verses and Hallgerd's epithets circulate. In retribution the Njalssons (i.e. sons of Njal) slay Sigmund, their first act of violence. Later, in Ch. 91, Hallgerd revives the epithets when tension between the Njalssons and the Sigfussons is at its highest, and again the Njalssons are provoked to swift and appropriate revenge. Ancient Norwegian law, and presumably Icelandic law as well, sanctifies blood revenge for sexual defamation.

Since men are not supposed to weep in the world of the sagas, unlike the Homeric world, another form of sexual slander is to accuse a man of weeping. Skammkel spreads the word that Gunnar wept when Otkel's horse ran at him (Ch. 53), and at the burning Gunnar Lambason taunts Skarphedin with weeping (Ch. 130). Later, in Orkney, when Gunnar Lambason falsely states that Skarphedin wept at the burning, he is immediately slain by Kari (Ch. 155).

Two of the most highly charged scenes in this highly dramatic saga turn on sexual matters. When Hildigunn whets her uncle Flosi to take blood revenge for the slaying of her husband Hoskuld Thrainsson, she challenges him in the name of his 'courage and manliness', or else he will be 'an object of contempt to all men' (Ch. 116). The word translated as 'manliness' here could also be translated as 'masculinity' – Hildigunn's insinuation is that Flosi will be less than a man if he fails this duty. In the scene at the Althing where a settlement has been made for the slaying of Hoskuld (Ch. 123), Flosi questions the gifts which Njal placed on the pile of compensation money and revives Hallgerd's insulting epithet 'Old Beardless'. Skarphedin responds with the coarsest and bluntest sexual insult in the saga, alluding to a rumour (no doubt an invented one) that Flosi is used as a woman by the troll of Svinafell (Flosi's farm). This insult of course ends all hope of a peaceful settlement.

One effect of all the slander, even though based on lies and distortions, is to destabilize the opposition between masculine and feminine that is typical of the family sagas. The slander calls attention to some realities – a hero who cannot grow a beard, two heroes (Gunnar and Hrut) who in one way or another cannot satisfy their wives, and so on – which challenge traditional male and female roles. Added to this is the fact that the events of the saga are more shaped by women than appears at first glance. Women are sometimes married without being consulted, and they occasionally serve as passive counters in the game of power, but the first eighteen chapters are determined by the desires and needs of three women, Queen Gunnhild, Unn and Hallgerd (who avenges herself for being married against her will); Bergthora and Hallberd plot the reciprocal killings in Chs. 35–45, leaving their husbands to pick up the pieces; Hallgerd's derisive epithets, as we have seen, provoke two major killings; and the whetting of Flosi by Hildigunn sets the course towards the catastrophical burning, rather than the peaceful settlement Flosi would otherwise have accepted. It would be naïve to call *Njal's Saga* a man's saga.

If there is ambiguity in the treatment of sexuality, there is also ambiguity with regard to wisdom. The pessimistic tone of the saga derives largely from the fact that intelligent and good people (intelligence being a necessary part of goodness), making decisions of their own free will, cannot avert disaster. Worse, it appears that intelligence is uneven (as Hallgerd says of Njal in Ch. 44, derisively, but perhaps with a grain of truth). Time and again the actions of the wisest man in Iceland are the seeds of disaster. By helping Gunnar win back Unn's dowry, he makes her marriage with Valgard possible, and the fruit of this marriage is Mord Valgardsson. By advocating the Fifth Court and thus procuring a godord for Hoskuld Thrainsson (Ch. 97), he makes Hoskuld a likely target for slaying. The very procedure he proposes for the Fifth Court concerning the reduction of the number of judges from forty-eight to thirty-six (Ch. 97) becomes the technicality by which the suit for the burning is quashed (end of Ch. 144). We have already mentioned his misguided gift (of a robe and pair of boots) at the settlement for the slaying of Hoskuld Thrainsson (Ch. 123). His final piece of advice, that his sons come inside the house at Bergthorshvol rather than face the attackers outside, seems almost perverse in view of the fact that he has foreseen the coming conflagration. Like Gunnar when he changed his mind about leaving Iceland, Njal just seems to give up. One of Iceland's greatest saga scholars, Sigurður Nordal, found 'the complication of goodwill and ill-fate, wisdom and failure' so great in *Njála* that he called the saga 'a symbolic fable of the vanity of human wisdom'.

The ambiguities of sexuality and wisdom help to make *Njála* the richly complex saga that it is. A third kind of ambiguity has to do with character. None of the carefully sketched chief players – the list includes Hrut, Hallgerd, Gunnar, Njal, Mord, Thrain, Hildigunn,

Skarphedin, Flosi, Kari and Thorhall – is a simple type. They combine good and bad, weak and strong, with all the three-dimensionality of real life. We have seen that Gunnar and Njal do not run to type. Thrain Sigfusson is Gunnar's uncle and supporter, but compromises himself by agreeing to be present (though not participating) at the slaying of Njal's servant, Thord Freed-man's son (Ch. 41–2). In Norway he is at first a loyal supporter of Earl Hakon (Ch. 82), but then deceives the earl when he decides to aid Hrapp (Ch. 88). Back in Iceland he joins his brothers and Hrapp and Hallgerd in abusing the Njalssons, though at the same time he tries to prevent the others from using the epithets 'Old Beardless' and 'Dung-beardlings' (Ch. 91). He seems to be a man with the right instincts, but too easily persuaded to go against them. Flosi is another example of a 'mixed' character (the term is used of Hallgerd in Ch. 33). He is a godi, a forceful and highly respected man, but under great pressure he consents to lead others to the worst crime in the saga, the burning at Bergthorshvol. After the burning the saga very carefully builds up his character again.

The word 'fate' often comes up in discussions of *Njála*, and to some readers it may seem that the many accurate prophecies of the future and the many omens of disaster mean that the saga consists of a totally determined series of events. Frequent utterances like 'What is fated will have to be' (Ch. 13) and 'Things draw on as destiny wills' (Ch. 120) support this impression. Njal knows quite early what will be the cause of his death, 'Something that people would least expect' (Ch. 55), and after the slaying of Hoskuld he predicts the death of himself and his wife and all his sons, and good fortune for Kari (Ch. 111). Njal's advice, as well as his outright prophecies, often has the force of a prediction. When he advises Gunnar not to kill twice in the same bloodline, for example, the reader knows that of course he will, and when Njal tells him that he will live to old age if he keeps the settlement (Ch. 74), the reader knows that Gunnar will break it, despite his two disclaimers (in Chs. 73 and 74). Warnings and advice are often the equivalent of predictions of violence. So too are goading scenes and changes of complexion – it seldom happens that a goading, or suppressed anger, does not lead to violent action.

The fact that there is so little suspense for the reader, however, does not mean that on the story level, within the saga, the characters are constrained by fate. At the saga's most crucial and powerful moments the author stresses the element of free choice: Gunnar chooses to stay in Iceland at the same moment that his brother Kolskegg decides to continue on his way abroad (Ch. 75); Njal is given free exit from the flaming Bergthorshvol, but makes a reasoned decision to remain inside ('I'm an old man and hardly fit to avenge my sons, and I do not want to live in shame'), as does his wife ('I was young when I was given to Njal, and I promised him that one fate should await us both,' Ch. 129); his sons could stay outside where they have a good chance of repelling the attackers, but they go inside to their death because they choose to follow their father's wishes (Ch. 128). Even the strict requirements of the feud pattern and honour code allow free choice, as Hall of Sida illustrates so nobly.

LAW

More than any other family saga, *Njal's Saga* is about law. The first person mentioned – though he initiates only one case and is a minor figure in the saga – is described in terms of his ability at law. From Njal's famous statements that 'with law our land shall rise, but it will perish with lawlessness' (Ch. 70) and 'it will not do to be without law in the land' (Ch. 97), to the swift conversion to Christianity by means of an arbitrated settlement at the Law Rock (Ch. 105), to the lengthy trial in Chs. 141–4, the author shows a serious concern for law. This interest is also evident from his mastery of legal technicalities, whether he acquired it from lawbooks or from orally transmitted codes. The 'courtroom' scenes in Chs. 73 and 141–4 testify to a more than unusual delight in legal formulas and procedures, often to the reader's dismay. In some cases he seems to have copied down (or remembered) legal phrases without adapting them to the context in the saga. When Mord brings charges against Flosi Thordarson for having 'assaulted Helgi Njalsson and inflicted on him an internal wound or brain wound or marrow wound which proved to be a fatal wound' (Ch. 141), the author is slavishly repeating the entire 'textbook' phrase, without eliminating the two kinds of wounds that do not apply in this case. Mord's suit in Ch. 142 contains this statement: 'I declared all his property forfeit, half to me and half to the men in the quarter who have the legal right to his forfeited property. I gave notice of this to the Quarter Court in which this suit should be heard according to law.' Again, the formulation remains general, when it would have been proper to specify the East Quarter.

Although the author earnestly endeavours to give the impression of the full and proper procedure around the year 1000, the legal details reflect his own time rather than that of the saga age. Laws were first written down in Iceland in 1117, and some of the phraseology in the saga corresponds word-for-word with passages in the *Grágás* ('Grey-goose') legal texts, written down in the twelfth and thirteenth centuries – not as an official lawbook, but as private copies of the law. *Njála* also has borrowings from a later code, the *Járnsíða* ('Iron-side'), introduced from Norway in 1271.

Njála is not only a law saga, it is an Althing saga. Many of the most important scenes in the saga, and not only legal scenes, take place at the annual general assembly at Thingvellir. In the text, and in the translation, the simple form 'Thing' often appears, but we can assume, unless informed otherwise, that the reference is to the Althing at Thingvellir rather than to one of the local assemblies.

The Althing is often, but not always, the place where a feud could be regulated. The three ways in which this might be done are neatly summed up in a dialogue between Hildigunn and Flosi in the famous whetting scene in Ch. 116:

'What action can I expect from you for the slaying, and what support?' she asked.

Flosi said, 'I will prosecute the case to the full extent of the law, or else make a settlement that good men see as bringing honour to us in every way.'

She spoke: 'Hoskuld would have taken vengeance if it were his duty to take action for you.'

A legal case settled by the courts, arbitration (whether by a third party or directly between the two principals), or blood vengeance –

these are the three possibilities. In *Njal's Saga* there are many feuds and many killings, and a number of cases are brought to the Althing for trial, but not one legal case is ever concluded. Even though the percentage of adjudicated cases is low in the sagas in general, and even though arbitration and vengeance were socially acceptable elements of feud, one would hope that court trials would have a higher score than zero in a saga so obsessed with law.

That no conflict is settled in court in *Njála* is part of a larger irony, and no doubt a deliberate irony, since it is so obvious in the saga: law, even the elaborate law code of medieval Iceland, is incapable of controlling violence. As the saga progresses, there is increasing emphasis on blood vengeance, and after the burning at Bergthorshvol Kari refuses to consider any other form of settlement.

The third alternative, arbitration, is used with some effect in *Njála*, especially in the early part. The killings of Hallgerd's first two husbands are both settled peaceably by her father Hoskuld and her uncle Hrut, so satisfactorily that the offended parties (Osvif and Thorarin) are both said to be 'out of the saga' (end of Chs. 12 and 17). It is a relief to see a character leave the saga with dignity – and the assurance that no more trouble will come from him. Unfortunately this will not be the case in the remainder of the saga. There will be many arbitrated settlements (especially at Njal's suggestion) and many acts of blood vengeance, but none of them will put an end to violence. Even with the six reciprocal killings initiated by their wives, escalating dangerously but nonetheless settled amicably between Njal and Gunnar (Chs. 35–45), there is a false sense of security. For the fifth killing in this series, of Thord Freed-man's son by Sigmund and Skjold, Njal makes a settlement with Gunnar and asks Skarphedin to keep it. Skarphedin agrees – 'but if anything comes up between us, we shall have this old hostility in mind' (Ch. 43).

Old hostilities, lying under the surface but waiting to erupt in bloodshed, constitute the underlying narrative thread. The principal one goes straight from the slaying of Thord Freed-man's son (Ch. 42), to that of Thrain Sigfusson (Ch. 92), to that of Hoskuld Thrainsson (Ch. 111), to the burning at Bergthorshvol (Chs. 129–30). The direct links between these four acts, though sometimes overlooked by the reader, explain much of what is going on and illustrate the volatile nature of feud. When the Njalssons set out to kill Thrain in Ch. 92 they have a verbal exchange with their father that echoes the one they had in Ch. 44, when they set out to avenge Thord. After this conversation, when Kari asks Skarphedin why he killed Sigmund the White, Skarphedin's answer is straightforward: 'He had killed Thord Freed-man's son, my foster-father.' The killing of Thord – at which Thrain was a consenting presence – has led to the need to kill Thrain now (though Thrain has since given the Njalssons additional reason to kill him). The old hostility between the Njalssons and the Sigfussons, of whom Thrain was the most prominent, had been there all the time.

The slaying of Hoskuld Thrainsson is the next inevitable link in this chain, but it is not easy for the reader to comprehend the slaying of this innocent, non-violent man, Njal's beloved foster-son, especially since the killers are Njal's own sons. The overt reason is the slander spread by Mord Valgardsson, at the prompting of his father. If this were the only reason, the Njalssons would appear very gullible and foolish, but there are two underlying motivations. One has to do with power (and perhaps a touch of jealousy). Njal did not trouble to find a godord for Skarphedin, his oldest son, or even a prominent marriage. The much younger Hoskuld, on the other hand, is well married and on the way to becoming a powerful godi, as Valgard noticed. That might be tolerable in itself, but there is the additional fact that Hoskuld is the son of Thrain Sigfusson. Old hostilities do not die. (One might even question the wisdom of Njal's fostering the son of his own sons' bitter enemy.) The other motivation for the killing has to do with the rules of feud. Lyting's killing of Hoskuld Njalsson (Ch. 98) required vengeance by the Njalssons, and when Lyting is killed by Amundi in Ch. 106, the Njalssons direct their vengeance quite properly at the most prominent member of the offending family, who happens to be Hoskuld Thrainsson, their own foster-brother. It is a tragic clash of loyalties, and the Njalssons follow the course they think they must.

The two greatest crises in the saga, the death of Gunnar and the burning at Bergthorshvol, both occur when an arbitrated agreement has been broken. It was agreed that Gunnar should go abroad for three years after killing Thorgeir Otkelsson. When he breaks the agreement and decides to remain at home (Ch. 75) he invites the attack which will cause his death, as Njal has warned him. Later, the settlement which good men have carefully arbitrated for the slaying of Hoskuld is nullified by the unforgivable insults exchanged by Flosi and Skarphedin (Ch. 123).

The final legal scene in the saga (Chs. 141–4) is the longest, dramatizing finally and fully both the intricate complexity of the law and the futility of the law, even in face of the fact that the burning at Bergthorshvol was an unjustifiable act. After the lengthy formulaic presentation of the suit against the burners, Eyjolf Bolverksson (Flosi's lawyer) makes a number of attempts, using the fine points of the law, to quash the case. Thorhall Asgrimsson is able to meet each objection and save the case. It is a fine battle between the best lawyers in the land, told from the point of view of the spectators and creating the excitement of a good tennis game in which the advantage alternates between the two sides: 'Everyone. . . . agreed that the defence was stronger than the prosecution . . . they agreed that the prosecution was stronger than the defence.' Finally Eyjolf serves his final ace (end of Ch. 144), to which there is no answer. In a proper court this would have been the end of the procedure, but in *Njal's Saga* it is the occasion for violence. No scene better illustrates the failure of law and the failure of the Althing than when the lawyer Thorhall thrusts his spear into his infected leg, hobbles to the Fifth Court and kills the first kinsman of Flosi's that he meets, thus initiating the total disorder of the battle at the Althing (Ch. 145). 'With law our land shall rise, but it will perish with lawlessness.'

CHRISTIAN AND PAGAN

The pagan Germanic ethic of honour, courage and the blood feud is well illustrated in *Njála*. Men fight and die to enhance or at least preserve their good name. Hrut and Gunnar and Skarphedin and Kari and Flosi are noble men in the old mould, moved by a keen sense of personal honour. The saga has a pleasing abundance of epic situations – fights against overwhelming odds, heroes who set out on a journey despite warnings of danger, men caught in a difficult position because of divided allegiances. The narrative derives much of its impetus and interrelatedness from the rules of feud and the requirements of honour.

But there is another, softer strain in the saga. Njal, the central figure, never lifts a weapon, and he gains respect because of his jurisprudence, his prophetic wisdom and his good will. Gunnar, in many ways the perfect Germanic hero, fights (in Iceland at any rate) only when provoked to do so, and with great reluctance. Hoskuld Thrainsson never lifts a weapon, not even the one he is carrying on that fateful day when he is slain in his own field. Snorri the Godi is one of the most respected men in the land, but when Skarphedin taunts him for not having avenged his father, his answer is that of a mild man: 'Many have said that already, and I'm not angered by such words' (Ch. 119).

The person in the saga who illustrates this strain most steadily is Hall of Sida. His first action in the saga is to accept Christianity for himself and his household (Ch. 100). Repeatedly his voice is the voice of peace and conciliation: as spokesman for the Christian side, it is he who at great risk asks the pagan Thorgeir to decide which faith should prevail in Iceland (Ch. 105); after Flosi has been whetted to blood vengeance by Hildigunn, Hall tries to persuade him to make a peaceful settlement (Ch. 119); when the trial for the slaying of Hoskuld is thwarted, Hall persuades Flosi to accept arbitration (Ch. 122); when Flosi, after the burning, has paid an insulting visit to Asgrim, Hall tells him frankly that he went too far (Ch. 136); when Thorgeir and Kari have started on their course of revenge for the burning, it is Hall who performs the diplomatic task of persuading Flosi and Thorgeir to be reconciled (Chs. 146–7). Most impressive of all are his determined action to end the battle of the Althing, in which his son Ljot has been killed, and his plea to both sides to make a settlement: 'Hard things have happened here, both in loss of life and in lawsuits. I'll show now that I'm a man of no importance. I want to ask Asgrim and the other men who are behind these suits to grant us an even-handed settlement.' Shortly after, in order to facilitate the settlement, he adds:

All men know what sorrow the death of my son Ljot has brought me. Many will expect that payment for his life will be higher than for the others who have died here. But for the sake of a settlement I'm willing to let my son lie without compensation and, what's more, offer both pledges and peace to my adversaries. (Ch. 145)

When we read that one of the leading godis in Iceland calls himself 'a man of no importance' and renounces any form of redress for his dead son, we are witnessing the complete antithesis of the old code of honour, in fact a new kind of honour.

The two strains are neatly counterpointed in the feud between Hallgerd and Bergthora in Chs. 35–45. On the one hand the two women act systematically according to the code of feud, each killing giving the occasion for the next. On the other hand their husbands, who would normally carry out blood revenge, make generous offers of peace on each occasion.

How do these two strains relate to the Christian element in the saga? This element is especially strong during and after the account of the Conversion in Chs. 100–105, although as early as Ch. 81 Kolskegg (Gunnar's brother) is baptized in Denmark and becomes a Christian knight. Religious terms like 'baptism', 'preliminary baptism', 'Mass', 'the angel Michael', 'responsibility before God' and 'God is merciful' begin to appear after Ch. 100, and at least three memorable utterances catch the ear with their religious overtones: Hoskuld's dying words 'May God help me and forgive you' (Ch. 111); Njal's plangent cry over that same killing, 'when I heard that he had been slain I felt that the sweetest light of my eyes had been put out' (Ch. 122); and Njal's words of comfort at the burning, 'Have faith that God is merciful, and that he will not let us burn both in this world and in the next' (Ch. 129). The battle of Clontarf in the final chapters is pointedly fought between pagan and Christian forces, and the Christian side wins.

At times the two sets of values, Christian and pagan, intersect in a way that seems strange today. When Hildigunn goads Flosi by throwing Hoskuld's blood-stained cloak over his shoulders, her words combine Christian imprecation with an appeal to Flosi's sense of honour: 'In the name of God and all good men I charge you, by all the powers of your Christ and by your courage and manliness, to avenge all the wounds which he received in dying – or else be an object of contempt to all men' (Ch. 116). A few lines after Njal spoke the words of Christian comfort quoted above, he declines an offer of free exit from the burning house with these words: 'I will not leave, for I'm an old man and hardly fit to avenge my sons, and I do not want to live in shame.' It may be that in such conflations of Christian language and the code of honour we see best how Christianity functions in this saga – not as antithetical to pagan values but as complementary. Christianity did not at first condemn the blood feud, and the noblest pagan virtues were consonant with Christian values.

There is a clear Christian presence in the saga, but the question is, does it change anything? It has become common to regard the Conversion episode in Chapters 100–105 as marking a turning-point in the moral structure of the saga, whereby the older, pagan ethic of heroism and pride is replaced by a new Christian ethic of mildness and peace. Such a view is based on a false opposition between pagan and Christian; it overlooks the fact that there are other pagan virtues than heroism and pride, and that humility and a willingness to make peace are among them. Christianity does not affect the values already existing in the saga, in Gunnar's and Njal's moderation and love of peace, or in the young Hoskuld's willingness to be content with the compensation paid for his father (Ch. 94). Those values were there before the Conversion, and continue after it, though set in a changed historical context. A Christian reading would have to judge Flosi's burning of Bergthorshvol as a sin in the light of the martyr's death suffered by Njal. The saga, however, treats the burning as a necessary but regrettable deed, and Flosi emerges from it with honour. Nor does the coming of Christianity have any direct effect on the course of events. The Christian elements in the saga are part of its historical realism, of its rhetoric. After the Conversion in the year 1000 people are made to think and speak in religious terms, and there is a new spirit in the land, but the events of the saga follow their own course, quite unaffected by it.

The claim has also been made that it is their pilgrimages to Rome and the absolution they received there that enable Kari and Flosi to become reconciled at the end of the saga. The reconciliation comes *after* the pilgrimages, to be sure, but it does not come *because of* them. The reconciliation results from full and sufficient blood revenge, sheer exhaustion and the mutual respect these two good men have long had for each other. The feud, the longest and deadliest in any of the sagas, has simply run its course. What Kari demonstrates is not the value of Christian absolution, but that the only way to end a feud for once and for all is to carry out total vengeance.

The thirteenth-century author of *Njal's Saga* was a Christian, looking back with respect at his pagan forebears and the time when Christianity came to his country. He is not preaching a sermon, nor writing a theological treatise, for he knows that the two systems are in many ways compatible. His characters may convert, and acquire Christian rhetoric, but they do not change their nature. Njal is the same man after the Conversion as before, and Hall and Hoskuld would have been the same as they are had there been no Conversion. *Njal's Saga* is secular literature.

THE TWO PARTS

Finally, a consideration of parallels and contrasts between the two main parts of the saga, Gunnar's story and Njal's story, may help to clarify the shape of the saga. In both sections a series of events growing out of feuds lead to the hero's being attacked and killed at his own home, after which revenge is exacted. The attack comes when a settlement for a major offence committed by the hero's side is broken or rejected, leaving the way open for his enemies to attack in force. In both stories Mord Valgardsson plots to bring about the hero's downfall, which comes after two killings (of father and son) in the same family. The contrasts between the two sections are instructive: burning the besieged in his house, which was rejected as shameful in the attack on Gunnar, is the tactic used in the attack on Bergthorshvol, and Hallgerd's betrayal is counterpoised by

Bergthora's willingness to die with her husband. The chief contrasts between the Gunnar story and the Njal story, however, are in the nature of the narrative line and in dimension. Gunnar becomes entangled in a series of clashes with different opponents – Otkel and his allies, Starkad and Egil and their sons – who eventually join together to form an overwhelming force against him. In Njal's story there is a single, straight plot line, from the slaying of Thrain Sigfusson (and even before) to the burning. The other main contrast is the greatly increased scale, which creates, in addition to the rhythm of hopes raised and dashed, a sense of ever heavier seriousness. It may seem callous to speak of Gunnar's feuds as trivial, since enmities are aroused and men are killed, but in comparison to the immense gravity of the feud in the second part they come off as petty stuff. The killing of the promising Thorgeir Otkelsson is regrettable; the killing of the saintly Hoskuld Thrainsson is tragic. Forty men attack Hlidarendi; a hundred (meaning a hundred and twenty in the old sense of 'hundred') attack Bergthorshvol. After his death Gunnar sings in his mound like a bold pagan. The pathos of the deaths of Hoskuld and of Njal and his family, heightened by Christian overtones, is unmatched by anything in the first part of the saga. The vengeance for Gunnar occupies one chapter and falls on four men; for Njal it occupies twenty-seven chapters and some thirty men die. Gunnar's chief enemies were shallow men, though they dragged some prominent figures along with them. Njal's chief enemies include, with good reason, some of the best men in Iceland. *Njal's Saga* is a large and ponderous saga, and especially the second half shows how massive the effects of human folly – and how ineffective human intelligence – can be.

POSTSCRIPT

This introduction has been drafted in a rented cottage at Brekkuskógur in Biskupstunga in the south-west of Iceland, just short of the rim of the uninhabited central highland, about ten kilometres from the hot springs at Geysir. Two kilometres north of Geysir is Haukadal, where Thangbrand baptized Hall Thorarinsson (see Ch. 102), and where Ari Thorgilsson (author of *The Book of Icelanders*) spent his formative years in the late eleventh century. Two or three kilometres from where I sit, up the road towards Geysir, is the still-working farm Hlid (now called Uthlid), to which Geir the Godi 'retired' when he left our saga in Ch. 80.

Looking south-east from my veranda I see the steam rising from Reykir (the name means 'steams') five kilometres away, just as it rose a thousand years ago when the forces of Thorgeir Skorargeir and Mord Valgardsson met with Asgrim Ellida-Grimsson to ride together to the momentous Althing (Ch. 137). In that chapter it is reported that they first crossed the Bruara ('Bridge river'), and indeed the river at that point (width 25 metres, current swift) shows me that this was a detail worth mentioning, just as the impressive columns of steam would have made Reykir a natural meeting place. Looking beyond Reykir, twelve kilometres further on from where I sit rises the mountain of Mosfell, which gave its name to the farm at its southern foot where Gizur the White lived. And although an intervening rise prevents me from seeing it, I know that four kilometres south of Mosfell is Tunga, Asgrim Ellida-Grimsson's farm on the river Hvita. With such abundant, palpable evidence to hand it is not surprising that generations of Icelanders regarded the sagas as literally true. Is there any literature as firmly anchored to geographical reality, not to mention socio-historic reality, as the Icelandic sagas?

Fortunately, enjoying this saga to the full does not require having Icelandic blood or having trod the saga sites. In fact it can be misleading to know the sites, and an advantage not to know them. The alert reader will have noticed how, in my musings in the previous paragraph, I was beginning to think that Asgrim and Thorgeir really met at Reykir with their combined forces, and that Geir the Godi – though we can be fairly certain he lived at Hlid – in fact did the things the saga says he did. The reader should not be seduced by the dry, factual prose style and the convincing social and geographical setting into thinking that this is anything other than a masterful work of prose fiction.

Further Reading

Translations into English

The Story of Burnt Njal, translated by George Webbe Dasent (Edinburgh: Edmonston and Douglas, 1861); reprinted in Everyman's Library, 1911; reissued in 1957 with an introduction by E. O. G. Turville-Petre.

Njál's Saga, translated by Carl F. Bayerschmidt and Lee M. Hollander (New York: The American-Scandinavian Foundation, 1955); this translation has been reprinted, with an introduction by Thorsteinn Gylfason, by Wordsworth Editions Limited (1998).

Njal's Saga, translated by Magnus Magnusson and Hermann Pálsson (Harmondsworth: Penguin, 1960).

Njal's Saga, translated by Robert Cook, in Viðar Hreinsson *et al.* (eds.) *The Complete Sagas of Icelanders (Including 49 Tales)*, 5 volumes (Reykjavík; Leifur Eiríksson, 1997), III, 1–220; an earlier version of the present translation.

Other Primary Sources in Translation

Ari Thorgilsson, *The Book of the Icelanders*, translated in Gwyn Jones, *The Norse Atlantic Saga*, second edition (Oxford: Oxford University Press, 1986), pp. 143–55.

The Book of Settlements; some passages in the above; a translation of one version by Hermann Pálsson and Paul Edwards (Winnipeg: University of Manitoba Press, 1972).

Laws of Early Iceland. Grágás I-II, translated by Andrew Dennis, Peter Foote and Richard Perkins (Winnipeg: University of Manitoba Press, 1980 and 2000).

The Sagas of Icelanders, with an introduction by Robert Kellogg, includes the following: Egil's Saga; The saga of the People of Vatnsdal; The Saga of the People of Laxardal; The Saga of Hrafnkel Frey's Godi; The Saga of the Confederates; Gisli Sursson's Saga; The Saga of Gunnlaug Serpent-tongue; The Saga of Ref the Sly; The Vinland Sagas, (the Saga of the Greenlanders and Eirik the Red's Saga); and seven Tales (Harmondsworth, Penguin, 2000).

General Criticism of the Sagas of Icelanders

Andersson, Theodore M., *The Problem of Icelandic Saga Origins* (New Haven: Yale University Press, 1964).

——, 'The Textual Evidence for an Oral Family Saga', *Arkiv för nordisk filologi*, 81 (1966), 1–23.

——, 'The Displacement of the Heroic Ideal in the Family Sagas', *Speculum*, 45 (1970), 575–93.

Kellogg, Robert, and Scholes, Robert, *The Nature of Narrative* (New York: Oxford University Press, 1966).

Ker, W. P., *Epic and Romance* (London: Macmillan, 1897).

Miller, William Ian, *Bloodtaking and Peacemaking: Feud, Law, and Society in Saga Iceland* (Chicago: University of Chicago Press, 1990).

Nordal, Sigurdur, 'The Historical Element in the Icelandic Family Sagas', W. P. Ker Memorial Lectures, 15 (Glasgow, 1957).

Ólason, Vésteinn, *Dialogues with the Viking Age: Narration and Representation in the Sagas of the Icelanders*, translated by Andrew Wawn (Reykjavík: Mál og menning, 1998).

Schach, Paul, *Icelandic Sagas* (Boston: Twayne, 1984).

Studies of Njal's Saga

Allen, Richard F., *Fire and Iron: Critical Approaches to Njáls saga* (Pittsburgh: University of Pittsburgh Press, 1971).

Clover, Carol J., 'Hildigunnr's Lament', in John Lindow, Lars Lönnroth and Gerd Wolfgang Weber (eds.), *Structure and Meaning in Old Norse Literature* (Odense: Odense University Press, 1986), 141–83.

Dronke, Ursula, 'The Role of Sexual Themes in *Njáls Saga*', Dorothea Coke Memorial Lecture, University College London (London: Viking Society, 1981).

Fox, Denton, '*Njáls Saga* and the Western Literary Tradition', *Comparative Literature*, 15 (1963), 289–310.

Jesch, Judith, '"Good Men" and Peace in *Njáls saga*', in John Hines and Desmond Slay (eds.), *Introductory Essays on Egils saga and Njáls saga* (London: Viking Society for Northern Research, 1992), 64–82.

Lönnroth, Lars, *Njáls Saga: A Critical Introduction* (Berkeley: University of California Press, 1976).

Maxwell, Ian, 'Pattern in *Njáls saga*', *Saga-Book*, 15 (1957–61), 17–47.

Miller, William Ian, 'Justifying Skarpheðinn: Of Pretext and Politics in the Icelandic Bloodfeud', *Scandinavian Studies*, 55 (1983), 316–44.

Poole, Russell, 'Darraðarljóð: A Viking Victory over the Irish', in his *Viking Poems on War and Peace* (Toronto: University of Toronto Press, 1991), 116–56.

Sayers, William, 'Gunnar, his Irish Wolfhound Sámr, and the Passing of the Old Heroic Order in *Njáls saga*', *Arkiv för nordisk filologi*, 112 (1997), 43–66.

Sveinsson, Einar Ólafur, *Njáls Saga: A Literary Masterpiece*, edited and translated by Paul Schach (Lincoln: University of Nebraska Press, 1971).

A Note on the Translation

This translation is based on the edition of *Brennu-Njáls saga* by Einar Ólafur Sveinsson, Íslenzk Fornrit, 12 (Reykjavík, 1954). It differs from previous translations of *Njal's Saga*, except for Dasent's in 1861, in attempting to duplicate the sentence structure and spare vocabulary of the Icelandic text. Subordinate clauses, introduced by conjunctions like 'when', 'because', 'who', 'although' and so on, are relatively infrequent in the saga (indeed in all the Icelandic sagas), where there is a marked preference for independent clauses. The saga typically says: 'They had a short passage *and* the winds were good' (Ch. 9), not 'They had a short passage *because* the winds were good.' Often an independent clause stands alone, but at other times a group of independent clauses is joined by a series of 'ands' and 'buts', producing a sentence like this: 'Glum often raised this matter with Thorarin, *and* for a long time Thorarin avoided it, *but* finally they gathered men *and* rode off, twenty in all, westward to Dalir *and* they came to Hoskuldsstadir, *and* Hoskuld welcomed them *and* they stayed there overnight' (Ch. 13). This is an effective way of hastening the narrative when the author wants to cover a sequence of events quickly.

Another feature imitated in this translation is the absence of the present participle, a standard fixture in modern English and therefore natural in a passage like this (Ch. 145) from the translation by Magnus Magnusson and Hermann Pálsson:

Kari Solmundarson met Bjarni Brodd-Helgason. Kari seized a spear and lunged at him, *striking* his shield; and had Bjarni not wrenched the shield to one side, the spear would have gone right through him. He struck back at

Kari, *aiming* at the leg; Kari jerked his leg away and spun on his heel, *making* Bjarni miss. [italics added]

Here, by contrast, is the same passage as translated in this volume, in greater conformity with the original:

Kari Solmundarson came up to Bjarni Brodd-Helgason; he grabbed a spear and thrust it at him, and it hit his shield. Bjarni jerked his shield to the side – otherwise the spear would have gone through him. He swung his sword at Kari and aimed at the leg; Kari pulled his leg back and turned on his heel, so that Bjarni missed him.

This translation also tries to reproduce the limited vocabulary of the Icelandic text. In describing travel, for example, there is seldom much variation beyond 'go' and 'walk' and 'ride'. Direct speech (which, by the way, constitutes about forty per cent of this saga) is introduced by 'say' or 'speak' or 'ask' or 'answer'. This translation keeps to the principle of minimal variation and introduces no artificial additives like 'declare' (except in legal scenes), 'emphasize', 'assert', 'respond', 'retort', 'reply', 'question' and 'inquire'. The verb 'say' is often used with questions as well as with statements, and the result may seem to be an over-use of that verb, as in the following:

Njal *said*, 'I must tell you of the slaying of your foster-father Thord; Gunnar and I have just made a settlement on it, and he has paid double compensation.'

'Who killed him?' *said* Skarphedin.

'Sigmund and Skjold, but Thrain was close at hand,' *said* Njal.

'They thought they needed a lot of help,' *said* Skarphedin. 'But how far must this go before we can raise our hands?'

'Not far,' *said* Njal, 'and then nothing will stop you, but now it's important to me that you do not break this settlement.' (Ch. 43)

It is hoped that the reader of this translation will accept – and even learn to enjoy – these and other efforts at fidelity, though they may seem strange at first. The intent has been to create a translation with the stylistic 'feel' of the Icelandic original.

As is common in translations from Old Icelandic, the spelling of proper nouns has been simplified, both by the elimination of non-English letters and markings and by the reduction of inflections. Thus 'Hallgerðr' becomes 'Hallgerd', 'Höskuldr' becomes 'Hoskuld', and 'Sámr' (pronounced, roughly, 'Sowmer') turns dully into 'Sam'. Characters are frequently identified in terms of their fathers, and readers will soon grasp that '-dottir' means 'daughter of' and that '-son' means 'son of'. Place names have been rendered a trifle more conservatively than is usual, 'Laxárdalr' becoming 'Laxardal' rather than 'Lax River Valley'.

Chronology of Njal's Saga

The following table of some of the main events of the saga and of early Icelandic history is based on the research of Gudbrandur Vigfússon and Finnur Jónsson, as reviewed by Einar Ólafur Sveinsson in his 1954 edition of the saga. The dates are of course approximate, even for the events that actually took place (indicated in bold face). Of course, most events in the saga are fictional, and the dates estimated here are meant only to give an overview of the time span and sequence of events. It should be mentioned that the Establishment of the Fifth Court is out of historical sequence in the saga; the general view is that it took place in 1004.

Settlement of Iceland	870–930
Birth of Mord Gigja	900
Establishment of the Althing	935
Birth of Njal	935
Birth of Hallgerd	937–40
Birth of Gunnar	945
Hrut's journey abroad	961
Hrut's marriage to Unn	963
Division of Iceland into quarters	965
Death of Mord Gigja	968
Birth of Mord Valgardsson	970
Gunnar's marriage to Hallgerd	975
Slaying of Svart	976
Slaying of Kol	977
Slaying of Atli	978

NJAL'S SAGA

1 | There was a man named Mord whose nickname was Gigja. He was the son of Sighvat the Red, and he lived at Voll in the Rangarvellir district. He was a powerful chieftain and strong in pressing lawsuits. He was so learned in the law that no verdicts were considered valid unless he had been involved. He had an only daughter named Unn. She was beautiful, well mannered and gifted, and was thought to be the best match in the Rangarvellir.

Now the saga shifts west to the valleys of Breidafjord. A man named Hoskuld lived there, the son of Dala-Koll.[1] His mother was Thorgerd, the daughter of Thorstein the Red, who was the son of Olaf the White, the son of Ingjald, the son of Helgi. Ingjald's mother was Thora, the daughter of Sigurd Snake-in-the-eye, who was the son of Ragnar Shaggy-breeches. Thorstein the Red's mother was Unn the Deep-minded; she was the daughter of Ketil Flat-nose, the son of Bjorn Buna. Hoskuld lived at Hoskuldsstadir in the valley of Laxardal.

Hrut was Hoskuld's brother; he lived at Hrutsstadir. He had the same mother as Hoskuld, but his father was Herjolf. Hrut was a good-looking man, big and strong, a good fighter, and even-tempered, a very wise man, harsh towards his enemies but ready with good advice on important matters.

It happened once that Hoskuld held a feast for his friends, and his brother Hrut was there and sat next to him. Hoskuld had a daughter named Hallgerd; she was playing on the floor with some other girls. She was tall and beautiful, with hair as fine as silk and so abundant that it came down to her waist.

Hoskuld called to her, 'Come here to me.'

She went to him at once, and he took her by the chin and kissed her. Then she went back.

Hoskuld said to Hrut, 'How do you like this girl? Don't you find her beautiful?'

Hrut was silent. Hoskuld asked again.

Hrut then answered, 'The girl is quite beautiful, and many will pay for that, but what I don't know is how the eyes of a thief have come into our family.'

Hoskuld was angry at this, and for a time the brothers had little to do with each other.

Hallgerd's brothers were Thorleik, the father of Bolli; Olaf, the father of Kjartan; and Bard.

2 | It happened once that these brothers, Hoskuld and Hrut, rode together to the Althing. A great many people were there.

Hoskuld said to Hrut, 'I wish, brother, that you would improve your way of living and take a wife.'

Hrut said, 'I've thought long about that and been of two minds. But I'll do as you wish – where should we look?'

Hoskuld said, 'There are many chieftains here at the Thing, and a good selection of brides, but I have one in mind for you. There's a woman named Unn, the daughter of Mord Gigja, a very wise man. He's here at the Althing, and his daughter too, and you can see her now if you wish.'

The next day, when men were going to the Law Council, the brothers saw some well-dressed women outside the Rangarvellir booth. Hoskuld said to Hrut: 'There's Unn, the woman I told you about. How do you like her?'

'Well enough,' he said, 'but I don't know whether we're meant to be happy together.'

They continued on to the Law Council. Mord Gigja was explaining legal matters, as usual, and then went to his booth. Hoskuld and Hrut rose and went to Mord's booth and entered it. Mord was seated at the far end. They greeted him. He rose to receive them and gave Hoskuld his hand. Hoskuld sat down next to him, and Hrut sat down beside Hoskuld.

They discussed many things, and Hoskuld came around to saying, 'I want to propose an agreement between us: Hrut wants to make a marriage agreement for your daughter and to become your son-in-law, and I will not withhold my support.'

Mord answered, 'I know that you are a great chieftain, but I know nothing about your brother.'

Hoskuld said, 'He's a better man than I am.'

Mord said, 'You will have to come up with a large sum for him, since she will inherit everything I have.'

'You won't have to wait long for what I propose,' said Hoskuld: 'he shall have Kambsnes and Hrutsstadir and everything as far as Thrandargil. He also owns a trading ship, now at sea.'

Hrut then said to Mord, 'Keep in mind that it is out of affection that my brother makes so much of me. But if you're willing to consider this matter, I would like you to name the terms.'

Mord answered, 'I've already thought it over. She will get sixty hundreds,[1] to which you must add half, and if you have heirs you are to share the property equally.'

Hrut said, 'I agree to these terms. Let's find witnesses.'

They rose and shook hands, and Mord betrothed his daughter Unn to Hrut. The wedding was set for two weeks after midsummer, at Mord's farm.

Both parties then rode home from the Thing. Hoskuld and Hrut rode west by way of Hallbjarnarvordur (Hallbjorn's cairns). Thjostolf, the son of Bjorn Gold-bearer from Reykjadal, rode out to meet them and told them that Hrut's ship had come to the Hvita river and on it was Ozur, Hrut's father's brother, and he wanted Hrut to come to him as soon as possible. When Hrut heard this, he asked Hoskuld to go with him to the ship. Hoskuld did, and they both went, and when they came to the ship Hrut gave his uncle a warm and cheerful welcome, and Ozur offered them a drink in his booth. The gear was taken from their horses, and they went in and drank.

Hrut said to Ozur, 'Come west now, uncle, and spend the winter with me.'

'That is not to be,' he said, 'for I have to tell you of the death of your brother Eyvind; he willed his property to you at the Gula Thing, and your enemies will seize it if you don't come.'

'What am I to do now, brother?' said Hrut. 'Things are becoming difficult, for I have just made arrangements for my wedding.'

Hoskuld said, 'Ride south and visit Mord, and ask him to change the terms so that his daughter is pledged to you for three years. I will ride home and bring your wares to the ship.'

Hrut said, 'I want you first to take flour and timber and whatever else you want from this cargo.'

He gathered his horses and rode south, and Hoskuld rode west to his home.

Hrut went east to the Rangarvellir, to Mord, and had a good welcome there. He told Mord what had happened and asked for advice.

Mord said, 'How much wealth is at stake?'

Hrut said it was two hundred marks if he got it all.[2]

Mord said, 'That is a great deal, compared to what I will leave her. You must certainly go, if that's what you wish.'

Then they changed the terms of their agreement, and Unn was to stay pledged to him for three years.

Hrut rode to his ship and stayed with it during the summer until it was ready to sail. Hoskuld brought all of Hrut's wares to the ship. Hrut turned over to Hoskuld the care of his property in Iceland while he was abroad, and Hoskuld rode back to his farm.

Shortly after, a good wind came up and they sailed away. They were at sea for three weeks and then arrived at the Hern Islands,[3] and from there they sailed east to Vik (Oslo fjord).

3 | Harald Grey-cloak was then ruling over Norway. He was the son of Eirik Blood-axe, the son of Harald Fair-hair. His mother was Gunnhild, the daughter of Ozur Toti. Harald and his mother had their seat at Konungahella, in the east.[1]

A report came to Vik of the arrival of a ship from the west. As soon as Gunnhild heard it, she asked what Icelanders were on board; she was told that one of them was Hrut, the nephew of Ozur.

She said, 'I see it plainly: he's come to claim his inheritance – but a man named Soti has taken it into his keeping.'

Then she called for her servant, whose name was Ogmund: 'I'm sending you to Vik to meet Ozur and Hrut. Tell them that I invite them both to spend the winter with me and that I want to be their friend. If Hrut listens to my advice I will look after his property claim, as well as anything else he may undertake. I'll also put in a good word for him with the king.'

He then went and found them, and when they learned that he was Gunnhild's servant they welcomed him. He gave them the message in private. Then the two of them discussed between themselves what to do, and Ozur said to Hrut, 'It's clear to me, kinsman, that we have already taken our decision, for I know Gunnhild: if we don't go to her she will drive us from the land and grab all our possessions. But if we go to her she will show us the honour she has promised.'

Ogmund returned, and when he came to Gunnhild he gave his report and said that they would come.

Gunnhild said, 'I expected that, since Hrut is called a clever and capable man. Now watch for when they get here, and let me know.'

Hrut and Ozur travelled east to Konungahella, and when they arrived their kinsmen and friends came out and welcomed them warmly. They asked whether the king was in town, and were told that he was. Soon after that they met Ogmund; he gave them Gunnhild's greetings and added that for fear of gossip she would not invite them to come to her until they had met the king. 'It mustn't seem that I'm lavishing favours on them,' she had said, 'and yet I will help him as I see fit. Hrut is to speak boldly to the king and ask to be one of his followers.'

'And here are some noble robes,' Ogmund went on, 'which she has sent for you to wear when you come before the king.'

Then he returned.

The next day Hrut said, 'Let's go to the king.'

'Very well,' said Ozur.

They went twelve together, all kinsmen and friends, and entered the hall while the king was at drink. Hrut went ahead of the others and greeted the king. The king took a close look at this man, who was well dressed, and asked his name; Hrut gave it.

'Are you an Icelander?' the king said.

He said he was.

'What prompted you to come to us?'

'The wish to see your magnificence, my lord – and also because I have a large inheritance case in this realm, and I will need your help if I'm to have my just share.'

The king said, 'All men in this land have my promise of lawful procedure. Do you have any other purpose in visiting us?'

'My lord,' said Hrut, 'I beg to be taken into your bodyguard as one of your followers.'

The king made no answer.

Gunnhild spoke: 'It seems to me that this man is offering you great honour, for if there were many like him in your bodyguard it would be very well manned – so it seems to me.'

'Is he a clever man?' said the king.

'Both clever and ambitious,' she said.

'It seems that my mother wants you to have the position you are asking for. But out of respect for our royal dignity and the customs of this land, you must come again after half a month. Then you shall become my follower. In the meantime let my mother look after your needs – and then come back to me.'

Gunnhild spoke to Ogmund: 'Take them to my house and give them a good feast.'

Ogmund went out with them and led them to a hall built of stone. It was hung with beautiful tapestries, and there Gunnhild had her throne.

Ogmund spoke: 'Now you'll see that what I told you about Gunnhild is true. That's her throne – sit in it, and you'll be allowed to hold it even after she arrives.'

He then treated them to a feast. They had only been seated a short time before Gunnhild arrived. Hrut was all ready to jump up and greet her.

'Remain seated,' she said. 'You shall always have this seat, as long as you are my guest.'

She sat down beside him, and they drank together. That evening she said, 'You shall lie with me tonight in the upper room, just the two of us.'

'That's for you to decide,' he said.

Then they went to bed; she bolted the door and they slept there that night. In the morning they went down to drink together, and for a full two weeks they slept in the upper room, just the two of them.

Gunnhild spoke to the men she had there: 'You have nothing to lose but your lives if you tell anyone about me and Hrut.'

Hrut gave her a hundred ells of woven cloth and twelve homespun cloaks, and she thanked him for the gift. Hrut left, after he had kissed her and thanked her. She wished him well.

The next day he went before the king with thirty men and greeted him.

The king spoke: 'Now, Hrut, you will be wanting me to keep my promise to you.'

Hrut was then made his follower.

Hrut said, 'Where shall I sit?'

'My mother shall decide,' said the king.

She gave him a prominent seat, and he stayed with the king over the winter, well respected.

4 | In the spring Hrut heard a report about Soti, that he had gone south to Denmark with the inheritance. Hrut went to Gunnhild and told her of Soti's movements.

She spoke: 'I'll give you two longships, with crews, and also a very strong man, Ulf the Unwashed, the leader of our "guests".[1] But you must go and see the king before you leave.'

Hrut did so, and when he came before the king he told him of Soti's movements and said that he intended to pursue him.

The king spoke: 'What help has my mother given you?'

'Two longships and Ulf the Unwashed in charge of the men,' said Hrut.

'You've been well treated,' said the king. 'Now I want to give you another two ships – you'll surely need all this strength.'

Then he accompanied Hrut to his ship and said, 'May you fare well.'

Hrut sailed south with his men.

5 | There was a man named Atli, the son of Earl Arnvid of Gotland. He was a great warrior and had his base in Lake Malaren, with a fleet of eight ships. His father had withheld paying tribute to Hakon, foster-son of King Athelstan,[1] and then fled with his son from Jamtland to Gotland.

Atli sailed his fleet from Lake Malaren through Stokkssund and then south to Denmark, and there he lay in Oresund. He had been outlawed by both the Danish and the Swedish kings on account of the plunderings and killings he had committed in their two realms.

Hrut sailed south towards Oresund, and when he entered the sound he saw a number of ships there.

Ulf said, 'What's to be done now, Icelander?'

'Keep on course,' said Hrut. 'Nothing ventured, nothing gained. Ozur and I will lead with our ship, and you bring yours where you please.'

'Seldom have I used others as a shield for me,' said Ulf.

He positioned his ship alongside Hrut's, and in this way they advanced into the sound.

Those who were in the sound saw that ships were coming at them, and they told Atli. He answered, 'Then we have a good opportunity to earn some booty. Have the men take away the coverings and get all the ships ready for action, quickly. My ship will be in the centre of our fleet.'

The ships advanced, and when they were within call of each other Atli stood up and spoke: 'You're not very cautious. Didn't you notice there were warships here in the sound? What's the name of your leader?'

Hrut gave his name.

'Whose man are you?' said Atli.

'A follower of King Harald Grey-cloak,' said Hrut.

Atli said, 'It's been a long time since my father and I were in favour with your Norwegian kings.'

'That's your misfortune,' said Hrut.

'Our meeting will be such,' said Atli, 'that you won't live to tell about it,' and he gripped his spear and threw it towards Hrut's ship. The man in its way was killed.

The battle got under way, but boarding Hrut's ships proved difficult. Ulf fought boldly with sword and with spear. Asolf was the name of Atli's prow-man. He leaped onto Hrut's ship and killed four men before Hrut was aware of him, but then Hrut turned to face him. When they came together, Asolf thrust his spear through Hrut's shield, but Hrut struck back with his sword and that was a killing blow.

Ulf the Unwashed saw this and said, 'You strike a hard blow, Hrut – you owe a lot to Gunnhild.'

'I have the sense,' said Hrut, 'that you speak with a doomed mouth.'

Atli noticed an unprotected spot on Ulf and hurled his spear straight through him.

Then came some fierce fighting. Atli leaped on board the ship and cleared his way forward. Ozur turned and thrust at him with his spear, but fell backwards when another man thrust at him. Hrut then turned to meet Atli, who swung quickly at Hrut's shield and split it all the way down. Atli was then struck on his hand by a stone, and his sword fell. Hrut picked up the sword and cut off his leg; then he struck him his death wound.

Hrut and his men seized much booty and took the two best ships, and they stayed there for a short while.

Soti and his men sailed past them and back to Norway and came to land at Limgard. Soti went ashore and met Ogmund, Gunnhild's servant.

Ogmund recognized him at once and asked, 'How long are you planning to stay here?'

'Three nights,' said Soti.

'Where will you go then?' said Ogmund.

'West, to England,' said Soti, 'and I'll never return to Norway as long as this is Gunnhild's realm.'

Ogmund left him and went to Gunnhild – she was at a feast a little way off, with her son Gudrod. Ogmund told her of Soti's plans, and she told Gudrod to kill him. Gudrod set off at once and caught Soti by surprise and had him brought ashore and hanged. He took the money and brought it to his mother. She had men take it all to Konungahella, and then went there herself.

Hrut returned in the autumn with a great amount of booty and went at once to the king and had a good welcome. He offered the king and his mother as much as they wanted to take, and the king took a third. Gunnhild told Hrut that she had taken his inheritance and had Soti killed. He thanked her and gave her half of it.

6 | Hrut stayed with the king in high favour that winter. But when spring came he was very silent. Gunnhild noticed this and spoke to him when they were alone.

'Is something troubling you, Hrut?' she asked.

'There's a saying,' said Hrut, 'that "it's difficult to dwell in a distant land".'

'Do you want to go to Iceland?' she said.

'I do,' he said.

'Do you have a woman out there?' she said.

'No,' he said.

'I'm sure that you do, though,' she said. At this they stopped talking. Hrut went to the king and greeted him.

The king spoke: 'What do you wish to do now, Hrut?'

'I want to ask you, my lord,' he said, 'for permission to go to Iceland.'

'Will your prestige be greater there than here?' said the king.

'Probably not,' said Hrut, 'but a man must do what is set out for him.'

'You're pulling against a powerful man,'[1] said Gunnhild. 'Let him go as he sees fit.'

Supplies were low that year, but the king[2] gave him as much flour as he wanted. Then Hrut, together with Ozur, prepared to sail to Iceland. When they were ready, Hrut went to the king and Gunnhild.

She took him aside and spoke to him: 'Here is a gold bracelet which I want to give you,' and she put it around his arm.

'Many a good gift have I had from you,' said Hrut.

She put her arms around his neck and kissed him and spoke: 'If I have as much power over you as I think I have, then I cast this spell: you will not have sexual pleasure with the woman you plan to marry in Iceland, though you'll be able to have your will with other women. Neither of us comes out of this well, because you did not tell me the truth.'

Hrut grinned and went away. He then went before the king and thanked him. The king spoke kindly to him and wished him a good journey; he said that Hrut was a very brave man and well fit for the company of noble men. Hrut went at once to his ship and set sail, and with good winds he reached Borgarfjord. As soon as the ship was drawn up on land Hrut rode west to his home, and Ozur saw to the unloading.

Hrut rode to Hoskuldsstadir. Hoskuld welcomed him, and Hrut told him all about his travels. Then they sent a man east to Mord Gigja to tell him to prepare the feast, and then the brothers rode to the ship and Hoskuld told Hrut about his property, which had gained greatly in value while he was away.

Hrut said, 'Your reward is less than you deserve, but I will give you as much flour as you need for your household this winter.'

They drew the ship up on land and secured it, and transported all the cargo west to Dalir.

Hrut stayed at home at Hrutsstadir until six weeks before winter.[3] Then the brothers and Ozur made ready to ride east for the wedding, and they rode off with sixty men until they came to the Rangarvellir. Many guests from the neighbourhood had already arrived. The men took their places on the side benches, and the women occupied the cross-bench at the end. The bride had a sad look about her. The feasting and drinking went well. Mord paid out the dowry for his daughter, and she rode off west with Hrut's party. They rode until they reached home.

Hrut placed in her hands full authority over matters inside the house, and everyone was pleased at that. But there was little intimacy between her and Hrut, and so it went all through the winter.

When spring came Hrut had to travel to the West Fjords to get payment for his wares, and before he left his wife said to him, 'Will you be coming back before men ride to the Thing?'

'Why do you need to know that?' said Hrut.

'I want to ride to the Thing and see my father,' she said.

'So be it,' he said, 'and I'll ride to the Thing with you.'

'Good,' she said.

Then he rode away to the West Fjords and put the money he collected out to loan and rode back home. When he arrived from the west he prepared for the Althing and got all his neighbours to ride with him. His brother Hoskuld rode along too.

Hrut said to his wife, 'If you're as eager to go to the Thing as you said you were, get ready and ride along with me.'

She was soon ready, and they rode to the Thing. Unn went to her father's booth; he was happy to see her, but her spirits were rather heavy. When he noticed this he said to her, 'I've seen you look more happy. What's on your mind?'

She began to cry but gave no answer. Then he said to her, 'Why have you come to the Thing if you're not willing to take me into your confidence? Don't you find it good out there in the west?'

She answered, 'I would give everything I own never to have gone there.'

Mord said, 'I'll soon get to the bottom of this.'

He sent a man to fetch Hoskuld and Hrut, and they came at once. When they came into Mord's presence, he rose and greeted them warmly and asked them to sit down. They spoke at length and it went well.

Then Mord said to Hrut, 'Why does my daughter find it so bad out there in the west?'

Hrut said, 'Let her speak, if she has any charges to bring against me.'

But no charges were brought. Hrut then had his neighbours and his household questioned as to how he treated her. They gave him a good report and said that she had sole authority over as much as she wanted.

Mord said, 'Go home and be content with your lot, for all the evidence favours him rather than you.'

Then Hrut rode home from the Thing, together with his wife, and things went well between them that summer. But when winter came the difficulty returned, and it became worse as spring drew on. Hrut had to make another trip to the West Fjords and declared that he would not be riding to the Althing. His wife Unn had nothing to say about this. Hrut set off as soon as he was ready.

7 | The time for the Thing came near. Unn spoke with Sigmund Ozurarson[1] and asked if he would ride to the Thing with her. He said he would not, if it displeased his kinsman Hrut.

'I appealed to you because I thought that you, of all people, owed me a favour,' she said.

He answered, 'I'll make this condition, that you ride back again with me and have no hidden plot against Hrut or me.'

She promised this, and they rode to the Thing.

Mord, her father, was there. He welcomed her and asked her to stay in his booth during the Thing, and she did so.

Mord spoke: 'What have you to tell me about your partner Hrut?'

She answered, 'I can say only good things about him in the matters over which he has control.'

Mord took this silently.

'What's bothering you, daughter?' he said. 'I can see that you don't want anybody to know about this but me, and you can count on me as the best one to solve the problem.'

They went off to where no one could hear what they said.

Then Mord spoke to his daughter: 'Now tell me everything that's going on between you, however big it may seem in your eyes.'

'All right then,' she said. 'I want to divorce Hrut, and I can tell you what my main charge against him is – he is not able to have sexual intercourse in a way that gives me pleasure, though otherwise his nature is that of the manliest of men.'

'How can that be?' said Mord. 'Give me more details.'

She answered, 'When he comes close to me his penis is so large that he can't have any satisfaction from me, and yet we've both tried every possible way to enjoy each other, but nothing works. By the time we part, however, he shows that he's just like other men.'

Mord spoke: 'You've done well to tell me this. Now I have a plan which will serve you well, as long as you follow it carefully and don't deviate from it. First you must ride home from the Thing – your husband will have returned and will welcome you. Be pleasant and compliant, and he will think that there's been a change for the better. Don't show any sign of coldness. When spring comes you must pretend to be sick and stay in bed. Hrut will not try to get at the cause of your sickness and he will not find any fault with you – in fact he will ask everybody to do their best in caring for you. Then he will go to the West Fjords, together with Sigmund, to bring back all his holdings from there, and he will be away for much of the summer. When people ride to the Thing, and when all those from Dalir who plan to go have set off, get out of bed and summon men to travel with you. When you're ready, go to your bed with the men who are to travel with you, and at your husband's bedside name witnesses and declare yourself legally divorced from him, as is allowable according to the rules of the Althing and the law of the land. You must repeat the naming of witnesses at the men's door.[2] Then you must ride away, over Laxardal heath as far as Holtavarda heath, for you won't be pursued as far as Hrutafjord, and keep riding until you come to me. I'll take over the lawsuit then, and you will never come into his hands again.'

She rode home from the Thing; Hrut had already come home and he welcomed her warmly. She responded well to his words and was pleasant towards him. Their relations were good during the summer and winter. When spring came she took ill and lay in bed. Hrut went off to the West Fjords, but first asked that she be well taken care of. When it came time for the Thing she made ready to leave and did everything exactly as she had been told and then rode off. The men from the district looked for her, but did not find her. Mord welcomed his daughter and asked her how closely she had followed his plan.

'I didn't deviate from it at all,' she said.

He then went to the Law Rock and declared them legally divorced.[3] People thought this was a big event. Unn then went home with her father, and never again went west to Hrutsstadir.

8 | Hrut came home, and his brows shot up when he learned that his wife was gone. But he kept his temper and stayed at home all summer and winter and spoke to no one about it. The following summer he rode to the Althing with his brother Hoskuld and many others. When he came to the Thing he asked whether Mord Gigja was present. He was told that he was, and everyone expected that the two of them would discuss their case, but this did not happen.

One day when men went to the Law Rock, Mord named witnesses and gave notice of a claim against Hrut for his daughter's property, and he set the figure at ninety hundreds. He declared that this amount was to be paid and handed over, and he declared a fine of three marks.[1] He gave notice of this in the Quarter Court to which the suit legally belonged, and also gave legal notice in the hearing of all at the Law Rock.

When he had spoken this, Hrut answered, 'You are prosecuting your daughter's case more out of greed and aggressiveness than good will or decency, and since you do not yet have my money in your hands, my response is this: I hereby declare – and let all these listening here at the Law Rock be my witnesses – that I challenge you to a duel. The stakes shall be the amount of the marriage agreement, to which I will add an equal sum, and let the one who wins take it all. If you choose not to fight me, you lose all property claims.'

Mord was silent and sought advice from his friends about the duel. Jorund the Godi answered him: 'You have no need to talk over this matter with us, because you know that if you fight Hrut you will lose both your life and the money. He is well endowed, great by his own deeds and a very brave man.'

Mord then announced that he would not fight with Hrut. Great hooting and hissing went up at the Law Rock, and Mord was much disgraced.

After this men rode home from the Thing.

The brothers Hoskuld and Hrut rode west to Reykjadal and stayed overnight at Lund. Thjostolf the son of Bjorn Gold-bearer lived there. Rain had fallen heavily during the day and the men were wet, and long fires had been lit. Thjostolf sat between Hoskuld and Hrut, and two boys were playing on the floor, poor boys under Thjostolf's care. A girl was playing with them. The boys were very chatty, since they didn't know any better. One of them said, 'I'll be Mord and summon you to give up your wife for not screwing her.'

The other answered, 'I'll be Hrut, and I say that you must forfeit all property claims if you don't dare to fight with me.'

They repeated this a few times, and much laughter arose among the household. Hoskuld became angry and struck the boy who called himself Mord with a stick, and the stick hit him in the face and cut through the skin.

Hoskuld said to the boy, 'Out you go – and don't make fun of us!'

Hrut said, 'Come over here.'

The boy did. Hrut took a gold ring from his finger and gave it to him and said, 'Go away, and don't ever give offence again.'

The boy went away and said, 'I shall always remember your decency.'

Hrut was spoken well of for this. Afterwards the brothers went home, and here ends the episode² of Hrut and Mord.

9 | Now the story turns to Hallgerd, Hoskuld's daughter: she grew up to be a most beautiful woman, very tall, and therefore called Long-legs. She had lovely hair, so long that she could wrap herself in it. She was lavish and harsh-tempered.

Thjostolf was her foster-father,¹ a Hebridean by ancestry. He was strong and a good fighter and had killed many men and paid no compensation for them.² It was said that he did nothing to improve Hallgerd's character.

*

There was a man by the name of Thorvald, the son of Osvif. He lived out on Medalfellsstrond, at Fell. He was well off for property: he owned some islands in Breidafjord known as the Bjarneyjar; from them he got dried fish and flour. Thorvald was strong and well-mannered, but somewhat short-tempered.

One day he and his father were talking about where he might find himself a wife, and it was clear that Thorvald thought that none of the choices was good enough for him. Then Osvif said, 'Do you want to ask for the hand of Hallgerd Long-legs, Hoskuld's daughter?'

'She's the one I want,' he said.

'Things are not likely to be easy between you,' said Osvif. 'She's a strong-minded woman, and you're hard and unyielding.'

'I still want to give it a try,' he said, 'and there's no use trying to stop me.'

'The risk is all yours,' said Osvif.

They set off on a wooing trip to Hoskuldsstadir and were well received there. They told Hoskuld immediately the purpose of their visit and made the proposal of marriage.

Hoskuld answered, 'I know your standing, and I won't mislead you. My daughter is hard to get along with, but as for her looks and manners you can see for yourselves.'

Thorvald answered, 'Set the terms, for I will not let her temperament prevent our making a marriage agreement.'

Then they discussed the agreement – Hoskuld did not consult his daughter, because he had his mind set on marrying her off – and they came to full agreement on the terms. Hoskuld extended his hand, and Thorvald took it and betrothed himself to Hallgerd and rode home with the matter settled.

10 | Hoskuld told Hallgerd about the marriage agreement. She spoke: 'Now I have experienced what I have long suspected, that you do not love me as much as you have always said, since you didn't think it worth consulting me on this matter. Besides, this marriage is beneath what you promised me.'

It was perfectly plain that she considered herself ill-matched.

Hoskuld spoke: 'I don't rate your pride high enough to let it stand in the way of my plans, and it's my word that counts when we disagree, not yours.'

'You kinsmen have plenty of pride,' she said, 'and it's not surprising if I've inherited some of it' – and she walked away. She went to her foster-father Thjostolf and told him what had been arranged; she was upset.

Thjostolf said, 'Pick up your spirits. You will be married a second time, and then you will be consulted, for I'll carry out your every wish – unless it touches your father or Hrut.'

They said no more about this.

Hoskuld prepared for the feast and rode around to invite people and came to Hrutsstadir and called Hrut out for a talk. He came out, and they went to where they could talk and Hoskuld told him all about the terms of the marriage and invited him to the feast – 'and I hope that you don't take it amiss that I didn't send you word when the agreement was being decided.'

'I prefer having nothing at all to do with this,' said Hrut, 'because there will be no luck for either partner in this marriage, neither for him nor for her. But I'll come to the feast if you think that will bring honour.'

'I think it will, for certain,' said Hoskuld, and then rode home.

Osvif and Thorvald also invited guests, and no fewer than a hundred were invited.

There was a man named Svan who lived in Bjarnarfjord on a farm called Svanshol, to the north of Steingrimsfjord. Svan was skilled in magic; he was the brother of Hallgerd's mother, and he was overbearing and vicious to deal with. Hallgerd invited him to her wedding feast and sent Thjostolf to bring him. He went, and there was friendship between them at once.

The guests came to the feast, and Hallgerd sat on the cross-bench, a very cheerful bride. Thjostolf often went over to talk to her, and he also spoke with Svan now and then, and people wondered at all this talking. The feast went well, and Hoskuld paid over Hallgerd's dowry graciously.

Then he said to Hrut, 'Shall I also give some presents?'

Hrut answered, 'You'll have chance enough to throw away your money for Hallgerd's sake, so hold back for now.'

11 | Thorvald rode home from the feast, along with his wife and Thjostolf. Thjostolf rode close to Hallgerd's horse and they spoke constantly.

Osvif turned to his son and said, 'Are you pleased with the match? What was it like talking with her?'

'Fine,' he said. 'She shows me nothing but sweetness. You can tell by the way she laughs at everything I say.'

'Her laughter doesn't seem as good to me as it does to you,' said Osvif, 'and the proof of this will come later.'

They rode on until they reached home. That evening she sat next to her husband and placed Thjostolf at her other side. Thjostolf and Thorvald had little to do with each other and little to say, and it went that way all winter.

Hallgerd was bountiful and high-spirited and demanded to have whatever the neighbours had and squandered everything. When spring came there was a shortage of both flour and dried fish. Hallgerd went to talk to Thorvald and said, 'You can't afford to sit around – the household is in need of flour and dried fish.'

Thorvald said, 'I didn't lay in any less than before, and it always used to last well into the summer.'

Hallgerd said, 'It's none of my business if you and your father starved yourselves to get rich.'

Thorvald got angry and struck her in the face so hard that she bled and then went off and called together his servants and they launched a skiff, and eight of them jumped aboard and rowed out to the Bjarneyjar. There they took on dried fish and flour.

*

To return to Hallgerd: she was sitting outside and was upset. Thjostolf came to her and saw that she was cut on the face and said, 'Why have you been so badly treated?'

'My husband Thorvald did this,' she said, 'and if you cared for me you would not have been so far away.'

'I knew nothing about this,' he said, 'but still, I'll avenge it.'

He went down to the shore and launched a six-oared boat and held in his hand a large axe which he owned, with an iron-wrapped handle. He got on board and rowed out to the Bjarneyjar. When he got there everybody had rowed away except Thorvald and his companions. He was loading the skiff, and his men were carrying the provisions to him. Thjostolf came over, jumped up on the skiff and helped him with the loading and spoke: 'You're both a sluggish worker and a clumsy worker.'

Thorvald spoke: 'Do you think you can do better?'

'I can do better than you in whatever we try,' said Thjostolf. 'The wife you have is badly matched, and your dealings with her deserve to be brief.'

Thorvald grabbed a short sword which lay near him and made a lunge at Thjostolf. Thjostolf had already raised his axe shoulder-high and struck a return blow; it hit Thorvald on the arm and broke it, and his sword fell to the ground. Thjostolf then raised his axe a second time and brought it down on Thorvald's head, and he met his death at once.

12 | Thorvald's men were now coming down with their loads. Thjostolf acted quickly: with both hands on his axe he hacked at the side of the skiff and made an opening as wide as the space between three seats, and then he jumped into his boat. The coal-black sea poured into the skiff and it sank with all its cargo. Thorvald's body sank too, and his men could not see how he had been killed, but they knew one thing – that he was dead.

Thjostolf rowed away up the fjord, and they cursed him and wished him ill. He made no answer and rowed until he reached home and beached the boat and went up to the house with his axe on his shoulders; it was quite bloody.

Hallgerd was outside and spoke: 'Your axe is bloody. What have you done?'

'I've done something,' he said, 'which will permit you to marry a second time.'

'You're telling me,' she said, 'that Thorvald is dead.'

'That's right,' he said. 'Now you must come up with a plan for me.'

'I will,' she said. 'I'll send you north to Svanshol on Bjarnarfjord and Svan will welcome you with open arms; he is so daunting that no one will go after you there.'

He saddled his horse and mounted it and rode north to Svanshol on Bjarnarfjord. Svan welcomed him with open arms and asked for news, and Thjostolf told him about the slaying of Thorvald and how it had come about.

Svan said, 'That's what I call a man, someone who doesn't let little things seem large, and I promise you that if they follow you here they will be greatly humiliated.'

To return to Hallgerd: she asked Ljot the Black, her kinsman,[1] to saddle their horses for a trip together – 'for I want to ride home to my father.'

He made ready for their journey. She went to her chests, unlocked them and called together all her household and gave everybody gifts. They were all sorry at her leaving. She rode until she came to Hoskuldsstadir, and her father welcomed her, for he had not heard the news.

Hoskuld said to Hallgerd, 'Why hasn't Thorvald come with you?'

'He's dead,' she answered.

Hoskuld said, 'Thjostolf must have done it.'

She said that he had.

Hoskuld spoke: 'Whatever Hrut tells me can be trusted – he said that great misfortune would come from this marriage. But there's no use blaming oneself for what has already happened.'

To return to Thorvald's companions: they waited until a boat came out and then announced the slaying of Thorvald and asked for a boat to reach the mainland. They were lent one quickly and rowed to

Reykjanes,[2] found Osvif and told him the news. He said, 'Evil designs have evil results, and now I see how it has gone. Hallgerd has probably sent Thjostolf to Bjarnarfjord, and she herself has gone home to her father. Let's gather men and follow him north.'

They did this; they went around in search of support and put together a good number of men and rode to Steingrimsfjord and to Ljotardal, and from there to Selardal and on to Bassastadir and from there across the ridge to Bjarnarfjord.

Just then Svan had a yawning attack and declared, 'Osvif's personal spirits are coming this way.'[3]

Thjostolf leaped up and took his axe.

Svan said, 'Come outside with me. This won't take much doing.'

They both went outside. Svan took a goatskin and waved it over his head and spoke:

1.
Let there be fog,
And let there be monsters,
And fantastic sights to all
Who follow you.

To return to Osvif and his men: they rode up to the ridge and a great fog came towards them. Osvif said, 'This must be Svan's doing – we'll be well off if nothing worse follows.'

Soon there was such a thick blackness in front of their eyes that they could see nothing and fell off their horses and lost them and walked into the bog – some into the woods – so that they came close to harm. They also lost their weapons.

Then Osvif spoke: 'If I could find my horses and weapons, I would turn back.'

As soon as he had said this, they were able to see a little and found their horses and weapons. Many of the men urged that they give the pursuit another try, and so they did, but the same sights came to them as before. This happened three times.

Then Osvif spoke: 'Though our trip has brought us no honour, we must turn back. We'll try another plan, and what I have in mind now is to go to Hoskuld to ask for compensation for my son, for there's hope for honour where honour abounds.'

They rode from there to the valleys of Breidafjord, and there is nothing to tell of until they arrived at Hoskuldsstadir. Hrut had already come there from Hrutsstadir. Osvif called to Hoskuld and Hrut to come out. They both went out and greeted Osvif, and then they went off to talk. Hoskuld asked Osvif where he had come from. He said he had gone in search of Thjostolf, but had not found him.

Hoskuld said he had probably gone north to Svanshol – 'but it's not for everybody to catch him there.'

'That's why I've come here, to ask you for compensation for my son,' said Osvif.

Hoskuld answered, 'I didn't kill your son, and I didn't plan his death, but it's understandable that you should try somewhere.'

Hrut spoke: 'The nose is near to the eyes,[4] brother. We must forestall evil rumours and compensate him for his son and in this way restore your daughter's standing; our only choice is to have this case dropped, for it will be better if it's not much talked about.'

Hoskuld said, 'Will you arbitrate the case?'

'I will,' said Hrut, 'but I will not favour you in the settlement, for if the truth must be told, your daughter caused his death.'

Hoskuld turned blood red and said nothing for a while. Then he stood up and said to Osvif, 'Take my hand and give your consent to drop the case.'

Osvif stood up and spoke: 'It's not a fair settlement if your brother arbitrates, and yet you've been so helpful, Hrut, that I am quite willing to entrust the matter to you.'

He shook Hoskuld's hand, and they made an agreement to the effect that Hrut should arbitrate and reach a settlement before Osvif went away.

Hrut made his decision and spoke: 'For the slaying of Thorvald I award two hundred ounces of silver' – this was considered good compensation – 'and you are to pay this at once, brother, and do it readily.'

Hoskuld did.

Then Hrut said to Osvif, 'I want to give you a good cloak which I brought from abroad.'

Osvif thanked him for the gift and was well pleased with the way things had turned out and went home.

Hrut and Hoskuld went to Osvif to divide the property, and they made peace with him and went home with their share. Osvif is now out of the saga.

Hallgerd asked Hoskuld whether Thjostolf could move to Hoskuldsstadir. He agreed to this, and the slaying of Thorvald was long talked about. Hallgerd's property grew in value and became quite large.

13 | Three brothers are now brought into the saga. One was called Thorarin, the second Ragi, and the third Glum. They were the sons of Oleif Hjalti, and were men of high esteem and well off for property. Thorarin had the nickname Ragi's Brother. He held the office of lawspeaker after Hrafn Haengsson and was a very wise man. He lived at Varmalaek, and he and Glum owned that farm together.[1]

Glum had been making trips abroad for a long time. He was big and strong and handsome. Ragi, their brother, was a great fighting man. These brothers owned Engey and Laugarnes in the south.[2]

One day Glum and Thorarin were talking, and Thorarin asked Glum whether he was going abroad, as was his custom.

He answered, 'I'd been thinking rather of giving up these trading voyages.'

'What do you have in mind?' said Thorarin. 'Do you want to take a wife?'

'I'd like to,' he said, 'if I could make a good arrangement.'

Thorarin then listed the women in Borgarfjord who were unmarried, and asked if he wanted to marry any of these – 'and I'll ride along with you.'

He answered, 'I don't want to marry any of these.'

'Then name the one you want to marry,' said Thorarin.

Glum answered, 'If you want to know, her name is Hallgerd and she's the daughter of Hoskuld out west in Dalir.'

'Then you're not letting another man's woe be your warning, as the saying goes,' said Thorarin. 'She had a husband, and she had him killed.'

Glum spoke: 'Perhaps she won't have such bad luck a second time. I know for certain that she will not have me killed. If you want to do me honour, then ride with me to ask for her hand.'

Thorarin said, 'There's no stopping this. What is fated will have to be.'

Glum often raised this matter with Thorarin, and for a long time Thorarin avoided it, but finally they gathered men and rode off, twenty in all, westwards to Dalir and they came to Hoskuldsstadir, and Hoskuld welcomed them and they stayed there overnight. Early the next morning Hoskuld sent for Hrut, and he came at once. Hoskuld was outside when he rode up to the house. Hoskuld told Hrut who had come.

'What do they want?' asked Hrut.

'They haven't yet talked of any business,' said Hoskuld.

'But their business must be with you,' said Hrut. 'They will ask for the hand of your daughter Hallgerd, so how will you answer?'

'What would seem best to you?' asked Hoskuld.

'Answer them favourably, but tell them the good and bad sides of the woman,' said Hrut.

While the brothers were talking the guests came outside. Hoskuld and Hrut went towards them, and Hrut greeted Thorarin and his brother warmly. Then they all went off to talk, and Thorarin spoke: 'I have come here with my brother Glum for the purpose of asking, on his behalf, for the hand of your daughter Hallgerd. You must know that he is a worthy man.'

'I know that you are both men of great standing, but I must answer by saying that I arranged her first marriage, and it ended in great misfortune for us,' said Hoskuld.

Thorarin answered, 'We will not let that prevent our making a agreement, for one oath does not invalidate all oaths.[3] This marriage may turn out well, though the other ended badly, and in any case Thjostolf had most to do with ruining it.'

Then Hrut spoke: 'I'll give you some advice, if you are not going to let what happened before with Hallgerd stand in your way: Thjostolf must not move south with her if this marriage takes place, and he must not visit for more than three nights, unless Glum consents, and if he stays longer Glum may slay him as an outlaw. Glum is free to permit a longer stay, but I don't advise it. Also, this must not be done without Hallgerd's knowledge, as it was before. She is to learn all the terms of the agreement now and meet Glum and decide for herself whether or not she wishes to marry him, and then she will not be able to blame others if things do not turn out well. Everything must be free of deceit.'

Thorarin said, 'Now, as always, it's best that your advice be followed.'

Then Hallgerd was sent for, and she came there with two other women. She was wearing a woven black cloak and beneath it a scarlet tunic, with a silver belt around her waist. Her hair was hanging down on both sides of her breast and she had tucked it under her belt. She sat down between Hrut and her father; she greeted everyone with kind words and spoke well and boldly and asked for the news. Then she said no more.

Glum spoke: 'My brother Thorarin and I have had some words with your father about an agreement by which I would marry you, provided it is your wish as well as theirs. Now tell us, as a woman with a mind of your own, whether this match is to your liking. If you have no heart for an agreement with us, we will say no more about it.'

Hallgerd spoke: 'I know that you brothers are men of great standing, and I know that I will now be much better married than before, but I want to know what you have already discussed and how far you have come in deciding things. I like you well enough that I could come to love you, as long as our tempers match.'

Glum told her the terms himself, in full detail, and then asked Hoskuld and Hrut if he had put it correctly. Hoskuld said that he had.

Then Hallgerd spoke: 'You've treated me so well in this matter, father, and you, Hrut, that I'm willing to agree to your plan and let the marriage terms be as you have determined.'

Then Hrut spoke: 'I propose that Hoskuld and I name witnesses and that Hallgerd betroth herself – if this seems correct to the law expert here.'

'It is correct,' said Thorarin.

Hallgerd's property was then valued, and Glum was to add the same amount. They were to share equally in the property. After this Glum betrothed himself to Hallgerd, and the brothers rode south to their home. Hoskuld was to hold the wedding feast at his place.

Then things were quiet until it was time for men to ride to the feast.

14 | Glum and his brothers gathered a large band of people, and they rode west to Dalir and arrived at Hoskuldsstadir. Many guests had already arrived. Hoskuld and Hrut were seated on one bench, and the bridegroom on another. Hallgerd sat on the cross-bench and made a good impression. Thjostolf walked around with his axe at the ready and behaved loutishly, but no one took any notice of him. When the feast was over, Hallgerd went south with the brothers. When they got to Varmalaek, Thorarin asked Hallgerd if she would like to take charge of running the household.

'No, I don't want that,' she said.

Hallgerd controlled herself very well that winter, and people were not displeased with her.

In the spring the brothers discussed their property, and Thorarin said, 'I want to turn the farm at Varmalaek over to you, since that is handiest for you, and I will go south to Laugarnes and live there. We'll hold Engey in common.'

Glum was willing to do this. Thorarin moved south, and Glum and Hallgerd remained behind. Hallgerd took on more servants; she was lavish and bountiful. In the summer she gave birth to a girl. Glum asked her what her name should be.

'She shall be named after my father's mother, Thorgerd, because she was descended on her father's side from Sigurd Fafnisbani.'[1]

The girl was sprinkled with water[2] and given that name. She grew up there at Varmalaek and came to be like her mother in appearance.

Glum and Hallgerd got along well together, and things went this way for a while.

News came from up north in Bjarnarfjord that Svan had rowed out to fish in the spring and a great storm had come on them from the east. It drove them into Veidilausa bay and they were lost there. Fishermen who were at Kaldbak thought they saw Svan enter the mountain Kaldbakshorn and get a warm welcome there. Some denied this and said that there was nothing to it. Everyone was certain, however, that he was never found, alive or dead. When Hallgerd heard of this, she thought the loss of her mother's brother a big event.

Glum asked Thorarin to exchange farms, but he said he didn't want to – 'but if I outlive you, then I will take over Varmalaek.'

Glum told this to Hallgerd. 'Thorarin has a right to expect this from us,' she said.

15 | Thjostolf had beaten one of Hoskuld's servants, so Hoskuld sent him away. He took his horse and weapons and said to Hoskuld, 'Now I will go away and never come back.'

'Everyone will be pleased at that,' said Hoskuld.

Thjostolf rode until he came to Varmalaek. He received a warm welcome from Hallgerd, and a not unfriendly one from Glum. He told Hallgerd that her father had sent him away, and he asked her to look after him. She replied that she could not promise anything about his staying there until she had seen Glum.

'Are things going well between you?' asked Thjostolf.

'Yes, our love goes well,' she said.

Then she went to talk to Glum and put her arms around his neck and said, 'Will you grant me the favour I am about to ask of you?'

'I will, as long as it's honourable,' he said. 'What do you wish to ask?'

She said, 'Thjostolf has been sent away from Hoskuldsstadir, and I'd like you to let him stay here. But I won't take it badly if you're not keen to do so.'

Glum said, 'Since you're being so fair about it, I shall grant your request, but I tell you this – if he starts any trouble he must leave at once.'

She went to Thjostolf and told him. He answered, 'You have done well, as was to be expected.'

He stayed on there and controlled himself for a time, but soon he was thought to be harmful in every way. He showed no respect for anyone but Hallgerd, and yet she never spoke up for him when he clashed with others. Thorarin scolded his brother Glum for allowing him to stay there and said that something terrible would happen, and that things would go as they had before if Thjostolf remained. Glum answered politely but followed his own counsel.

16 | One autumn they had a bad time bringing in the sheep, and Glum was short many wethers. He spoke to Thjostolf, 'Go up to the mountain with my servants and see if you can find any of the sheep.'

'Searching for sheep does not suit me,' said Thjostolf, 'and besides, the simple fact is that I don't want to follow in the footsteps of your slaves.[1] You go yourself, and then I'll come along.'

This led to a strong exchange of words.

Hallgerd was seated outside; the weather was fine. Glum went to her and spoke: 'Thjostolf and I have had a bad clash, and we will not live together much longer.' He told her what had passed between them.

Hallgerd spoke up for Thjostolf, and they had a strong exchange of words. Glum struck her with his hand and said, 'I'm not quarrelling with you any longer' – and then he went away.

She loved him greatly and was not able to calm herself, and wept loudly. Thjostolf came to her and said, 'You've been badly treated, but this won't happen again.'

'You are not to take vengeance for this,' she said, 'or take any part in our affairs, no matter what happens.'

He went away grinning.

17 | Glum called his men to go out with him, and Thjostolf also got ready and went along. They went up South Reykjadal and then up along Baugagil as far as Thverfell and there they split up; some went to the Skorradal area, and others he sent south to the Sulur hills, and they all found many sheep.

Then it came about that the two of them, Glum and Thjostolf, were alone. They went south from Thverfell and found some nervous sheep and pursued them as far as the mountain, but the sheep got away up the mountain. Each blamed the other for this, and Thjostolf told Glum that he had no strength for anything except bouncing around on Hallgerd's belly.

Glum said, 'The only bad company comes from home.[1] Now I have to put up with insults from you, a fettered slave!'

Thjostolf said, 'You'll soon be saying whether I'm a slave or not, for I'm not about to yield to you.'

Glum was enraged and struck at him with his short sword, but Thjostolf put his axe in the way and the blow hit the axe blade and cut into it two fingers deep. Thjostolf quickly struck a return blow with the axe and hit Glum's shoulder and split the shoulder bone and the collar bone, and the wound bled internally. Glum seized Thjostolf with his other hand with such force that he fell, but Glum was not able to keep his hold because death was upon him. Thjostolf covered his body with stones and took a gold bracelet from him.

He walked back to Varmalaek. Hallgerd was outside and saw that his axe was bloody. He threw the gold bracelet to her.

She spoke: 'What news do you bring? Why is your axe bloody?'

He answered, 'I don't know how you'll take this, but I must tell you of the slaying of Glum.'

'You must have done it,' she said.

'That's true,' he said.

She laughed and said, 'You didn't sit this game out.'

'What advice do you have for me now?' he said.

'Go to my father's brother Hrut,' she said, 'and let him take care of you.'

'I don't know whether this is sound advice,' said Thjostolf, 'but I'll follow it anyway.'

He took his horse and rode away and did not stop until he came to Hrutsstadir that night. He tied up his horse behind the buildings, went around to the door and knocked with a loud blow. Then he went around to the north side. Hrut had been awake; he sprang to his feet and got into a tunic and pulled on his boots and took his sword; he wrapped a cloak around his left hand and arm. People woke up as he was going out.

He went around to the north side of the house and saw a big man and recognized him as Thjostolf. Hrut asked what news he had.

'I must tell you of the slaying of Glum,' said Thjostolf.

'Who did it?' said Hrut.

'I killed him,' said Thjostolf.

'Why did you ride here?' said Hrut.

'Hallgerd sent me to you,' said Thjostolf.

'Then she was not the cause of it,' said Hrut, and drew his sword.

Thjostolf saw this and did not want to be the second to strike, and quickly swung his axe at Hrut. Hrut slipped away from the blow and hit the side of the axe blade so sharply with his left hand that the axe flew out of Thjostolf's hand. With his right hand Hrut hacked Thjostolf's leg just above the knee and almost cut it through, and he rushed at him and knocked him down. Hrut then struck at Thjostolf's head and dealt him his death wound.

Hrut's servants came out and saw the signs of the slaughter. Hrut had Thjostolf's body carried away and covered. Then he went to Hoskuld and told him of the slaying of Glum and then of Thjostolf. Hoskuld thought the death of Glum a loss, but thanked Hrut for slaying Thjostolf.

A little while later, Thorarin Ragi's Brother learned of the slaying of his brother Glum. He rode with eleven men west to Dalir and came to Hoskuldsstadir. Hoskuld received him with open arms and he stayed there overnight. Hoskuld sent at once for Hrut to come there, and he came immediately.

The following day they talked at length about the death of Glum.

33

Thorarin said, 'Are you willing to pay me compensation for my brother, for I have had a great loss?'

Hoskuld answered, 'I didn't kill your brother, and my daughter didn't plan his death – and when Hrut found out about it, he killed Thjostolf.'

Thorarin became silent then and felt that the situation would be hard to solve.

Hrut spoke: 'Let's make his trip honourable. He has surely had a great loss and it will be well spoken of if we give him gifts and he becomes our friend for life.'

The outcome was that the brothers gave him gifts. Thorarin then rode back south.

He and Hallgerd exchanged farms in the spring: she went south to Laugarnes and he went to Varmalaek. Thorarin is now out of the saga.

18 | To tell now about Mord Gigja: he took ill and died, and that was thought a great loss. His daughter Unn inherited all his property. She had not been married a second time. She was very lavish and improvident with her property, and her wealth wasted away until she had nothing but land and personal items.

19 | There was a man named Gunnar. He was related to Unn. His mother was named Rannveig, and she was the daughter of Sigfus, the son of Sighvat the Red; he was slain at the ferry at Sandholar.[1] Gunnar's father was named Hamund; he was the son of Gunnar Baugsson, from whom Gunnarsholt gets its name. Hamund's mother was named Hrafnhild; she was the daughter of Storolf Haengsson. Storolf was the brother of Hrafn the Lawspeaker, and his son was Orm the Strong.

Gunnar Hamundarson lived at Hlidarendi in Fljotshlid. He was big and strong and an excellent fighter. He could swing a sword and throw a spear with either hand, if he wished, and he was so swift with a sword that there seemed to be three in the air at once. He shot with a bow better than anyone else, and he always hit what he aimed at. He could jump higher than his own height, in full fighting gear, and just as far backward as forward. He swam like a seal, and there was no sport in which there was any point in competing with him and it was said that no man was his match.

He was handsome and fair of skin and had a straight nose, turned up at its tip. He was blue-eyed and keen-eyed and ruddy-cheeked, with thick hair, blond and well-combed. He was very well-mannered, firm in all ways, generous and even-tempered, a true friend but a discriminating friend. He was very well off for property.

His brother was named Kolskegg; he was big and strong, a fine man and reliable in all ways. A second brother was named Hjort; he was then in his childhood. Orm Skogarnef was a bastard brother of Gunnar's, but he does not come into this saga.

Arngunn was the name of Gunnar's sister; she was married to Hroar the Godi of Tunga, who was the son of Uni the Unborn,[2] the son of Gardar who discovered Iceland. Arngunn's son was Hamund the Lame, who lived at Hamundarstadir.

20 | There was a man named Njal; he was the son of Thorgeir Gollnir, the son of Thorolf. Njal's mother was Asgerd, the daughter of the Norwegian hersir Askel the Silent; she had come out to Iceland and settled to the east of the Markarfljot river, between Oldustein and Seljalandsmuli. Her son was Holta-Thorir, the father of Thorleif Crow, from whom the people of Skogar are descended, of Thorgrim the Tall and of Thorgeir Skorargeir.

Njal lived at Bergthorshvol in the Landeyjar. He had a second farm at Thorolfsfell. He was well off for property and handsome to look at, but there was one thing about him: no beard grew on him. He was so well versed in the law that he had no equal, and he was wise and prophetic, sound of advice and well-intentioned, and whatever course he counselled turned out well. He was modest and noble-spirited, able to see far into the future and remember far into the past, and he solved the problems of whoever turned to him.

Bergthora was his wife's name. She was the daughter of Skarphedin, a woman with a mind of her own and a fine person, but a bit harsh-tempered. They had six children, three daughters and three sons, and the sons all play a part in this saga.

21 | To tell now about Unn, who had lost all her money: she travelled from her farm to Hlidarendi, and Gunnar welcomed his kinswoman and she stayed overnight. The next day they sat outside and talked and she came around to telling him how pressed she was for money.

'That's bad,' he said.

'What solution will you offer me?' she said.

He answered, 'Take as much as you need of the money I have out on loan.'

'I don't want to waste your property,' she said.

'Then what do you want?' he said.

'I want you to reclaim my property from Hrut,' she said.

'That doesn't seem likely,' he said, 'since your father wasn't able to reclaim the money, and he was a great lawyer – I know little about law.'

'It was through force rather than by law that Hrut pushed that through,' she said. 'My father was old, and that was why men thought it best for them not to fight. Besides, there's no one in my family to take up this matter if you don't have the backbone to do so.'

'I'm daring enough to try to get the money,' he said, 'but I don't know how to take up the case.'

She answered, 'Go to Njal at Bergthorshvol – he'll be able to come up with a plan, and besides, he's a great friend of yours.'

'I expect that he'll advise me as soundly as he does others,' he said.

Their talk ended with Gunnar taking up the case and giving her as much money as she needed for her household, and then she went home.

Gunnar rode to visit Njal, and he welcomed him and they went off to talk.

Gunnar said, 'I've come to ask you for good advice.'

Njal answered, 'I have many friends for whom it is fitting that I give good counsel, and yet I will take the greatest pains with you.'

Gunnar said, 'I want to tell you that I have taken on the reclaiming of Unn's property from Hrut.'

'That's a difficult matter,' said Njal, 'and a big risk however it goes. But I'll propose what seems to me the most promising plan, and it will work if you do not deviate from it. Your life will be in danger if you do.'

'I won't deviate from it at all,' said Gunnar.

Njal was silent for a while, and then said, 'I've thought the matter over, and this is what will work.'

22 | 'Ride from home with two men. Wear a hooded cloak on the outside and striped homespun underneath, and beneath this wear your good clothes and carry a short axe. Each of you should have two horses, one fat and the other lean. Take along some home-made articles from here. Start riding early tomorrow, and when you have crossed west over the Hvita river pull your hood way down. People will ask who the tall man is, and your companions should say that it is Peddler-Hedin the Mighty from Eyjafjord, travelling with his wares, and that he is a bad-tempered and loud-mouthed man, a know-it-all, that he often reneges on his deals and assaults people when things don't go the way he wants. Ride west to Borgarfjord and offer your wares everywhere but often renege on the deals. The word will get around that Peddler-Hedin is a terrible man to deal with and that whatever is said of him is no lie.

'Ride north then to Nordurardal and then to Hrutafjord and to Laxardal, until you come to Hoskuldsstadir. Stay there for the night, but sit near the door and keep your head down. Hoskuld will declare that no one should have dealings with Peddler-Hedin, that he is offensive. Leave in the morning and go to the farm closest to Hrutsstadir. Offer your wares, especially the worst ones, and conceal their flaws. The farmer will examine them and find the flaws. Snatch them away from him and say something foul. He will say that it was only to be expected that you would give him a hard time – "you give everybody

37

a hard time". Assault him – though you are not used to doing so – but don't use all your strength, lest you be recognized and arouse suspicion.

'A man will be sent then to Hrutsstadir to tell Hrut that it would be best to take you away. He will send for you at once, and you should go at once. You will be assigned to the lower bench, opposite Hrut's high seat. Greet him, and he will respond well. He will ask if you're from the north, and you should say that you're from Eyjafjord. He will ask whether there are many excellent men up there.

'"They do a lot of nasty things," you must say.

'"Are you familiar with Reykjadal?" he will say.

'"I am familiar with all of Iceland," you must say.

'"Are there any mighty heroes in Reykjadal?" he will say.

'"They're thieves and rogues," you must say.

'Hrut will laugh and find this great sport. He and you will then talk about the men in the East Fjords, and you should say something scornful about each of them. Your talk will then turn to the men in the Rangarvellir district. Say that there is a shortage of good men there since the death of Mord Gigja. Hrut will ask why you think that no man could fill his place, and you should answer that he was such a wise man and so strong in pressing lawsuits that his authority was never in doubt. He will ask whether you're aware of what went on between Mord and himself.

'"I've heard," you should say, "that he took your wife away from you and you did nothing about it."

'Then Hrut will answer, "Don't you think it was a mistake on his part when he didn't get the money, even after he brought a suit for it?"

'"I can easily answer that," you should say. "You challenged him to a duel, but he was an old man and his friends advised him not to fight with you, and this is how you quashed the suit."

'"I did challenge him," Hrut will say, "and foolish men took this to be the law, but he could have brought the suit up at another Thing, if he had the backbone."

'"I know that," you should say.

'He will then ask you whether you know anything about law.

'"Up north they thought I did," you should say, "but you will have to tell me how to bring up the suit."

'Hrut will ask what suit you are referring to.

'"A suit," you should say, "that's of no concern to me: how to go about reclaiming Unn's property."

'"A summons must be pronounced, either in my hearing or at my legal residence," Hrut will say.

'"Recite the summons," you should say, "and I'll repeat it after you."

'Hrut will then recite the summons – pay careful attention to every bit of his wording. Then he will ask you to repeat the summons; do so, but do it so badly that no more than every second word is correct. Hrut will laugh and have no suspicions, and he will say that not much was correct in your summons. Blame your companions and say that they distracted you. Then ask Hrut to recite it for you again and to let you recite it after him. He will grant this and recite the summons himself. Recite it after him and say it correctly, and then ask Hrut if the summoning was correct. He will say that no one could fault it. Then say softly, but so that your companions can hear, "I hereby make this summons in the suit turned over to me by Unn, the daughter of Mord."

'Later when people are asleep, get up quietly and take your saddles out to the pasture, to the fat horses, and ride away; leave the other horses behind. Ride up above the grazing fields and stay there for three nights – that's about how long they will look for you. Then ride south to your home – ride only at night, and lie quiet during the day. We ourselves will ride to the Thing and carry on with the suit.'

Gunnar thanked him and rode straight home.

23 | Gunnar rode from his home two days later, with two companions, and they rode until they came to Blaskogar heath. There some men came riding towards them and asked who the tall man was who showed so little of himself, and his companions said that it was Peddler-Hedin. The others said that with such a man out front it was not likely that a worse would follow. Hedin made as

if he were going to attack them, but then both parties went on their way.

Gunnar followed every detail of the plan that had been set forth: he spent a night at Hoskuldsstadir and from there went along the valley until he came to the farm closest to Hrutsstadir. There he offered his wares and sold three articles. The farmer saw that there was something wrong with them and called the deal a cheat; Hedin then assaulted him. This was told to Hrut, and he sent for Hedin; he went at once to Hrut and had a good welcome. Hrut assigned him a seat across from him. Their conversation went very much as Njal had expected: Hrut told him how the suit should be brought up and recited the summons; Hedin recited it after him and did it incorrectly; Hrut smiled and suspected nothing; then Hedin asked him to recite it once again, and Hrut did so; Hedin then recited the summons again, and did it correctly and called his companions as witnesses that he was making the summons in the suit turned over to him by Unn, the daughter of Mord.

That evening he went to bed along with the others, but when Hrut had fallen asleep he and his companions took their clothes and weapons and went out to their horses and rode across the river and then along it on the Hjardarholt side to the end of the valley and placed themselves between the mountains and Haukadal where they could not be found unless someone just happened to ride up there.

At Hoskuldsstadir Hoskuld woke up early in the night and woke all his household. 'I want to tell you what I dreamed,' he said. 'I saw a big bear go out of the house, and I was sure that there was none to equal it, and two cubs went along with it, and they were fond of the beast. It headed towards Hrutsstadir and went into the house there. Then I woke up. Now I want to know from you what you noticed about the tall man.'

One man answered, 'I saw, coming out from under his sleeve, gold lace and red cloth, and on his right hand he had a gold ring.'

Hoskuld said, 'This bear was the personal spirit of none other than Gunnar of Hlidarendi. Now, after the fact, I see it all. Let's ride to Hrutsstadir.'

They all went out and over to Hrutsstadir and knocked on the door, and a man came and unlocked it; they went in at once. Hrut was lying in his bed closet and asked who had come. Hoskuld told him and asked what guests were there.

He said, 'Peddler-Hedin is here.'

Hoskuld said, 'His back was broader than that; my guess is that it's Gunnar of Hlidarendi.'

'In that case there's been some outsmarting here,' said Hrut.

'What happened?' said Hoskuld.

'I told him how to take up Unn's suit. I summoned myself, and he recited the summons after me. He will use this as a first step in the suit, and it will be legitimate.'

'One of you has been much cleverer than the other,' said Hoskuld, 'but Gunnar did not come up with this by himself. Njal must have planned it all – no one is his match for cleverness.'

They searched for Hedin, but he was already gone. Then they gathered men and searched for three days, but could not find him.

Gunnar rode southwards from the mountain to Haukadal, east of the pass, and then north to Holtavarda heath and did not rest until he came home. He went to Njal and told him that the plan had worked well.

24 | Gunnar rode to the Althing. Hrut and Hoskuld also rode there, with many others. Gunnar began prosecuting the case and summoned neighbours as witnesses. Hrut and his men intended to attack him, but did not trust themselves to do so. Gunnar then went to the Breidafjord court and requested that Hrut listen to him swear his oath and to his presentation of the charges and the evidence. After that he swore his oath and presented the charges, and then brought forth his witnesses to the summons and to the taking over of the suit. Njal was not present at the court.

Gunnar continued the case to the point where he invited the other side to make its defence. Hrut named witnesses and declared that the suit was invalid because Gunnar had failed to present three witnessed statements that should have come before the court: the first at the bedpost, the second at the main door, and the third at the Law Rock.

Njal had now come to the court, and he said he would be able to revive the suit and the case if they wanted to go on with it.

'I don't want to,' said Gunnar, 'and I will give Hrut the same choice that he gave to my kinsman Mord. Are the brothers Hrut and Hoskuld close enough to hear what I'm saying?'

'We can hear you,' said Hrut. 'What do you want?'

Gunnar spoke: 'Let those listening here be witnesses that I challenge you, Hrut, to a duel, to be fought today on the island in the Oxara river. If you choose not to fight me you must pay over all the money today.'

Then Gunnar left the court, together with all his companions. Hoskuld and Hrut also went away, and from then on the case was neither prosecuted nor defended.

When Hrut came into the booth he said, 'It has never happened before that a man challenged me to a duel and I refused.'

'Then you must be planning to fight,' said Hoskuld, 'but not if I have any say, for you won't do any better against Gunnar than Mord would have done against you, so we'd better pay Gunnar the money, the two of us.'

The brothers then asked their followers what they would contribute, and they all said they would contribute whatever Hrut wanted.

'Let's go to Gunnar's booth then,' said Hoskuld, 'and pay out the money.'

They went to Gunnar's booth and called him out. He came to the door with some of his men.

Hoskuld said, 'Now the money is yours.'

Gunnar said, 'Give it to me then – I'm ready to take it.'

They paid the full amount readily.

Then Hoskuld spoke: 'May you enjoy it the same way you have earned it.'

'We'll enjoy it greatly, because the claim was a just one,' said Gunnar.

Hrut answered, 'Bad things will be your only reward for this.'

'Things will go as they must,' said Gunnar.

Hoskuld and his brother went back to their booth. He was very upset and said to Hrut, 'Will this threat of force never be avenged against Gunnar?'

'It will be avenged against him,' said Hrut, 'but the vengeance and the credit for it will not be ours. It's likely, in fact, that he will turn to our kin for friendship.'

With this they ended their conversation.

Gunnar showed the money to Njal.

'This has worked out well,' he said.

'And all because of you,' said Gunnar.

Everybody then rode home from the Thing, and Gunnar had gained much honour from the case. He turned over all the money to Unn and did not want to take any for himself, but said that he could now expect more support from her and her kinsmen than from other men. She said that this was true.

25 | There was a man named Valgard. He lived at Hof on the Ranga river. He was the son of Jorund the Godi, the son of Hrafn the Foolish, the son of Valgard, the son of Aevar, the son of Vemund the Eloquent, the son of Thorolf Pus-nose, the son of Thrand the Old, the son of Harald War-tooth, the son of Hraerek the Ring-scatterer. The mother of Harald War-tooth was Aud, the daughter of Ivar Vidfadmi, the son of Halfdan the Valiant. The brother of Valgard the Grey was Ulf Aur-Godi, from whom the people of Oddi are descended. Ulf Aur-Godi was the father of Svart, the father of Lodmund, the father of Sigfus, the father of Saemund the Learned. From Valgard is descended Kolbein the Young.

The two brothers, Valgard the Grey and Ulf Aur-Godi, went to seek the hand of Unn, and she married Valgard without the advice of her kinsmen. Gunnar and Njal and many others thought badly of this, because Valgard was a devious and unpopular man. They had a son, who was named Mord, and he will be in this saga for a long time. When he was fully grown he was bad to his kinsmen, and to Gunnar worst of all. He was cunning by nature and malicious in counsel.

The sons of Njal must now be named. Skarphedin was the eldest, a big and strong man and a good fighter. He swam like a seal and was swift of foot, quick to make up his mind and sure of himself; he spoke to the point and was quick to do so, though mostly he was even-tempered. His hair was reddish-brown and curled and he had fine eyes; his face was pale and sharp-featured, with a bent nose, a broad row of upper teeth and an ugly mouth, and yet he was very like a warrior.

Grim was the name of Njal's second son. He was dark-haired and more handsome than Skarphedin, big and strong.

Helgi was the name of Njal's third son. He was a handsome man with a good head of hair; he was strong and a good fighter, clever and even-tempered.

All these sons of Njal were unmarried.

Hoskuld was the name of Njal's fourth son. He was born out of wedlock: his mother was Hrodny, the daughter of Hoskuld and the sister of Ingjald at Keldur.

Njal asked Skarphedin whether he wanted to get married. He told his father to see to it. Njal then asked, on his behalf, for the hand of Thorhild, the daughter of Hrafn from Thorolfsfell, and that was how he came to own a second farm there. Skarphedin married Thorhild, but continued to live with his father. On behalf of Grim Njal asked for the hand of Astrid at Djuparbakki. She was a widow and quite rich. Grim married her, but continued to live with Njal.

26 | There was a man named Asgrim, the son of Ellida-Grim, the son of Asgrim, the son of Ondott Crow. Asgrim's mother was Jorunn, the daughter of Teit, the son of Ketilbjorn the Old from Mosfell. The mother of Teit was Helga, the daughter of Thord Beard, the son of Hrapp, the son of Bjorn Buna. Jorunn's mother was Olof, the daughter of the hersir Bodvar, the son of Viking-Kari. The brother of Asgrim Ellida-Grimsson was named Sigfus; his daughter was Thorgerd, the mother of Sigfus, the father of Saemund the Learned. Gauk Trandilsson, who was a most valiant and accomplished man, was foster-brother to Asgrim, but bad blood arose between them, with the result that Asgrim slew Gauk.[1]

Asgrim had two sons, both named Thorhall and both men of promise. Asgrim also had a son named Grim and a daughter Thorhalla. She was a very beautiful and well-mannered woman, and capable in every way.

Njal came to talk with his son Helgi. 'I have been thinking of a wife for you, my son, if you're willing to follow my advice.'

'I'm certainly willing,' he said, 'for I know that you're both wise and well-meaning. Who have you picked out?'

Njal answered, 'We'll ask for the hand of the daughter of Asgrim Ellida-Grimsson, for she's the best choice.'

27 | Shortly afterward they set out to ask for her hand and rode west across the Thjorsa river and kept on until they came to Tunga. Asgrim was at home and welcomed them, and they stayed overnight. The next day they began to talk, and then Njal brought up the proposal and asked for Thorhalla's hand on behalf of his son Helgi. Asgrim responded well to that and said there was nobody he would be more eager to make a marriage with than them. They talked about the terms, and the outcome was that Asgrim betrothed his daughter to Helgi and a wedding date was fixed.

Gunnar was present at this wedding feast, as well as many others of the best men.

After the feast Njal offered to be the foster-father to Thorhall Asgrimsson. Thorhall went to Njal's home and stayed with him for a long time. He loved Njal more than his own father. Njal taught him law so well that he became the greatest lawyer in Iceland.

28 | A ship came to the river mouth at Arnarbaeli; its skipper was Hallvard the White, a man from Vik. He went to Hlidarendi and spent the winter with Gunnar and kept telling him that he should go abroad. Gunnar did not speak much about it, but he did not rule it out. When spring came he went to Bergthorshvol and asked Njal whether he thought it wise for him to go abroad.

'I think it's wise,' said Njal. 'You will find favour wherever you go.'

'Will you look after my property while I am away?' said Gunnar. 'I want my brother Kolskegg to go with me, and I would like you and my mother to run the farm.'

'That should not stand in your way,' said Njal. 'I'll take care of whatever you want.'

'I wish you well,' said Gunnar. Then he rode home.

The Norwegian spoke to Gunnar again about going abroad. Gunnar asked if he had sailed to any other lands. He said he had been to all the lands which lie between Norway and Russia – 'and I have even sailed to Permia.'

'Will you sail with me to the Baltic?' said Gunnar.

'Certainly I will,' he said.

Gunnar then decided to go abroad with him. Njal looked after all of Gunnar's property.

29 | Gunnar went abroad, together with his brother Kolskegg. They sailed to Tunsberg and spent the winter there. There had been a change of rulers in Norway: Harald Grey-cloak and Gunnhild had died, and Earl Hakon Sigurdarson ruled the realm.[1] His father Sigurd was the son of Hakon, the son of Grjotgard. Hakon's mother was Bergljot, the daughter of Earl Thorir. Her mother, Olof Arbot, was Harald Fair-hair's daughter.

Hallvard asked Gunnar whether he wanted to take service with Earl Hakon.

'No, I don't,' he said. 'Do you have a longship?'

'I have two,' said Hallvard.

'Then I'd like us to go raiding,' said Gunnar. 'Let's find men to go with us.'

'I'd like that,' said Hallvard.

They went to Vik and took over the two ships and made ready to set out. They did well in finding men, for many good things were being said about Gunnar.

'Where do you want to go first?' said Gunnar.

'East to Hising,' said Hallvard, 'to meet my kinsman Olvir.'

'What do you want with him?' said Gunnar.

'He's a fine man,' he said, 'and he'll give us some help for our journey.'

'Let's go there, then,' said Gunnar.

When they were ready they headed east for Hising and had a good welcome. Gunnar had not been there very long before Olvir was greatly impressed by him. Olvir asked about Gunnar's intentions, and Hallvard said that he wanted to raid and gain wealth.

'That's not a good idea,' Olvir said. 'You don't have enough men.'

'You're free to add to our number,' said Hallvard.

'I think it's fine to support Gunnar in some way,' said Olvir – 'you may claim kinship with me, but I count him more of a man than you.'

'Then what are you willing to contribute?' said Hallvard.

'Two longships, one with seats for forty and the other with seats for sixty,' said Olvir.

'Who will man them?' said Hallvard.

'I'll man one of them with my own men, and the other with farmers. But I've heard news of trouble on the river, and I don't know whether you can get away from here.'

'Who's in the way?' said Hallvard.

'Two brothers,' said Olvir, 'one named Vandil and the other Karl, the sons of Snaeulf the Old from Gotland over in the east.'

Hallvard told Gunnar that Olvir had contributed more ships, and Gunnar was glad at that. They prepared to set out, and when they were ready they went to Olvir and thanked him, and he told them to watch out for the brothers.

30 | Gunnar made his way downriver; he and Kolskegg were on one ship and Hallvard on another. They saw the ships ahead of them.

Gunnar said, 'Let's make some preparations in case they attack us, but otherwise let's have nothing to do with them.'

They did as he said and made preparations. The Vikings divided their ships into two groups, with a passage between them. Gunnar sailed into it. Vandil picked up a grappling-hook and threw it into

Gunnar's ship and pulled it quickly alongside. Olvir had given Gunnar a good sword, and Gunnar drew it. He had not put on a helmet, but leaped at once into the prow of Vandil's ship and at once killed a man. Karl pulled up his ship on the other side of Gunnar's and threw a spear across it, aimed at Gunnar's waist. Gunnar saw the spear coming at him, and he turned around so quickly that no eye could follow and caught the spear in his left hand and threw it back at Karl's ship, and the man who was in its way was struck dead. Kolskegg picked up the anchor and threw it at Karl's ship and the fluke went all the way through the hull and the coal-black sea came pouring in, and all the men on board leaped onto other ships. Gunnar leaped back to his ship.

Then Hallvard drew near, and a fierce battle got under way. Gunnar's men saw that their leader was unflinching, and everyone did his utmost. Gunnar fought both with sword and with spear, and many a man fell dead at his hands. Kolskegg fought well at his side.

Karl leaped onto the ship of his brother Vandil, and the two of them fought from there all day. On Gunnar's ship Kolskegg stopped to rest, and Gunnar noticed this and said, 'You have served others better than yourself today – by taking away their thirst!'

Kolskegg took a goblet full of mead and drank it down, and then went back to fighting. After a time he and Gunnar leaped aboard Vandil and Karl's ship, and Kolskegg went down one side and Gunnar down the other. Vandil advanced towards Gunnar and quickly swung his sword at him, but it hit the shield. Gunnar twisted the shield with the sword stuck in it and the sword broke just under the hilt. Gunnar struck back, and it appeared to Vandil that there were three swords in the air at once and he could not see which side to protect. Gunnar cut both his legs from under him. Kolskegg thrust his spear through Karl. After that they took much booty.

From there they continued south to Denmark and then east to Smaland, and they were always victorious. They did not go back in the autumn.

The following summer they went on to Reval and ran into Vikings there and quickly fought and defeated them. Then they went east to the island of Osel and stayed for a while beside a headland. They saw a man coming down from the headland. Gunnar went ashore to meet him, and they talked together. Gunnar asked him his name, and he said it was Tofi. Gunnar asked what he wanted.

'I wanted to see you,' he said. 'There are warships here on the other side of the headland, and I'll tell you who commands them – two brothers, one named Hallgrim and the other Kolskegg. I know them to be mighty battlers, and also that they have good weapons that no one can match. Hallgrim has a halberd on which he has put a spell so that no weapon but this can kill him. Another thing about it is that you know at once when it is about to strike a death blow, for it first makes a loud singing noise – that's how much power it has. Kolskegg has a short sword and it too is a very good weapon. They have a third again as many men as you. They have a great treasure and have hidden it ashore, and I know exactly where it is. They sent a scouting ship around the headland and know all about you. They're now making full preparations and plan to attack you as soon as they're ready. You have two choices: either sail away at once, or prepare to meet them as quickly as you can. If you are victorious, I'll bring you to where all their treasure is.'

Gunnar gave him a ring and then went back to his men and told them that there were warships on the other side of the headland – 'and they know all about us. Let's take our weapons and get ready quickly – there's treasure to be won!'

They made their preparations, and when they were ready they saw ships coming at them. A fierce battle got under way; they fought long and the losses were great. Gunnar killed many men. Hallgrim and his brother leaped onto Gunnar's ship, and Gunnar turned to face him. Hallgrim thrust at him with his halberd. A boom lay across the ship, and Gunnar made a backwards leap over it; his shield was still in front of the boom and Hallgrim's halberd went through it and into the boom. Gunnar struck at Hallgrim's arm and the arm was crippled, but the sword did not bite. The halberd fell; Gunnar grabbed it and thrust it through Hallgrim. From then on he always had the halberd with him.

The two Kolskeggs fought, and it was hard to say who would prove the better. Then Gunnar came up and gave Kolskegg his death blow.

After that the Vikings begged for peace, and Gunnar granted it. He let his men search the slain and take whatever goods the dead men owned, but he let the survivors have their weapons and clothing and gave them peace and told them to return to their homelands. They went away, and Gunnar took everything they left behind.

Tofi came to Gunnar after the battle and offered to take him to where the Vikings had hidden their treasure and told him that it was both greater and better than what they had already taken. Gunnar said he was willing. He went ashore with Tofi. Tofi went into a wood, and Gunnar followed. They came to where a lot of timber had been gathered together. Tofi said the treasure was under the timber. They cleared it away and found gold and silver and garments and good weapons. They carried it all back to the ships.

Gunnar asked Tofi how he wanted to be rewarded. Tofi answered, 'I am a Dane by birth, and I'd like you to transport me to my kinsmen.'

Gunnar asked him how he had come to the Baltic.

'I was kidnapped by Vikings,' said Tofi, 'and put ashore here on Osel, and I've been here ever since.'

31 | Gunnar took him along and said to Kolskegg and Hallvard, 'Now let's return to the northern lands.'

They were pleased at this and told him to have his way. Gunnar sailed from the Baltic with a large amount of treasure. He had ten ships, and headed for Hedeby in Denmark. King Harald Gormsson was staying there.[1] He was told about Gunnar and that no one in Iceland was his equal. The king sent his men to invite Gunnar to visit him. Gunnar went at once to meet the king. The king welcomed him and gave him a seat next to his own.

Gunnar was there for half a month. For amusement the king had Gunnar contend with his own men in various sports, and there was not one sport in which they were a match for him.

The king spoke to Gunnar: 'It appears to me that your equal is not to be found far or near.'

The king offered to give him a wife and large holdings if he would settle down there. Gunnar thanked the king but said that first he wanted to return to Iceland to see his kinsmen and friends.

'Then you will never come back to us,' said the king.

'Fate must decide that, my lord,' said Gunnar.

Gunnar gave the king a good longship and many other valuables. The king gave him stately garments of his own, leather gloves embroidered with gold, a gold-studded headband, and a Russian hat.

From there Gunnar sailed north to Hising. Olvir welcomed him with open arms, and Gunnar gave him the ships he had taken and said that they were his share. Olvir accepted the booty and called him a fine man, and invited him to stay there for a while. Hallvard asked Gunnar if he wanted to go to Earl Hakon. Gunnar said this was near his heart – 'because now I've been tested somewhat – I was not tested at all the last time you asked me this.'

They made ready for the voyage and went north to Trondheim to meet Earl Hakon, and he received Gunnar well and invited him to spend the winter with him; Gunnar accepted. He had the respect of everybody there. At Yule the earl gave him a gold bracelet.

Gunnar fell in love with Bergljot, the earl's kinswoman, and it was often apparent that the earl would have married her off to Gunnar if he had asked for this.

32 | In the spring the earl asked Gunnar what his plans were. He said he wanted to return to Iceland. The earl said supplies were low that year – 'and there will not be much sailing abroad, but you may take on board as much flour and timber as you want.'

Gunnar thanked him and soon had his ship ready. Hallvard went along with him and Kolskegg.

They reached Iceland early in the summer, before the Althing, and came to land in the river mouth at Arnarbaeli. Gunnar rode home at once, together with Kolskegg, and got men to unload his ship. When they came home people were happy to see them. Gunnar and Kolskegg were cheerful towards their household, and they had not grown haughty.

Gunnar asked whether Njal was at home and he was told that he was. He had his horse fetched and rode to Bergthorshvol, together with Kolskegg. Njal was happy at their coming and asked them to stay the night. They did, and Gunnar told about his travels.

Njal said that he was a most valiant man – 'and though you have been much tried, you will be tried much more, because many men will envy you.'

'I want to get along well with everyone,' said Gunnar.

'Much will happen,' said Njal, 'and you will often have to defend yourself.'

'Then my grounds must be,' said Gunnar, 'that my cause is right.'

'It will be,' said Njal, 'as long as you do not have to pay for the doings of others.'

Njal asked Gunnar if he would be riding to the Thing. Gunnar said that he would and asked whether Njal would be riding. He said he would not – 'and I wish you would do the same.'

Gunnar gave Njal good gifts and thanked him for looking after his property. Then he rode home.

Kolskegg urged him to ride to the Thing – 'your honour will increase there, because many men will seek your company.'

'I haven't been very keen to puff myself up,' said Gunnar, 'but I think it's good to meet good men.'

Hallvard had also come to Hlidarendi and offered to ride to the Thing with them.

33 | Gunnar and all his company rode to the Thing. When they came there they were so well dressed that no others were dressed as well, and people came out of every booth to admire them. Gunnar rode to the booth of the people from the Rangarvellir district and stayed there with his kinsmen. Many men went to him to ask for his news. He was light-hearted and merry with everyone and told them whatever they wanted to hear.

It happened one day that Gunnar was walking from the Law Rock. He passed below the booth of the people from Mosfell. There he saw some women coming towards him, and they were well dressed. The woman in front was the best dressed. When they met, she greeted

Gunnar at once. He took pleasure at this and asked who she was. She gave her name as Hallgerd and said she was the daughter of Hoskuld Dala-Kollsson. She spoke boldly to him and asked him to tell her about his travels, and he said he would not refuse her. They sat down and talked.

She was dressed like this: she had on a red gown, much ornamented; over that she had a scarlet cloak trimmed with lace down to the hem. Her hair came down to her breasts and was both thick and fair. Gunnar was wearing the stately garments given him by King Harald Gormsson; on his arm he had the bracelet from Earl Hakon.

They talked aloud for a long time. Eventually he asked if she were unmarried.

She said that she was – 'and there aren't many who would take the risk.'

'Is there no one good enough for you?' he said.

'It's not that,' she said, 'but I'm very demanding when it comes to men.'[1]

'How would you answer if I were to propose to you?' said Gunnar.

'You can't have that on your mind,' she said.

'But I do,' he said.

'If it is on your mind,' she said, 'you must go to my father.'

With this they ended their talk.

Gunnar went straight to the booth of the people from Dalir and found men in front of the booth and asked them whether Hoskuld was inside, and they said that he was. Gunnar went in.

Hoskuld and Hrut welcomed him. He sat down between them, and there was no sign in their talk that there had been any clash between them. Gunnar came around to the point and asked how the brothers would answer if he asked to marry Hallgerd.

'Favourably,' said Hoskuld, 'if your mind is set on this.'

Gunnar said that he was serious – 'but our last parting was such that not many people would think a bond between us likely.'

'What do you think of this, brother Hrut?' said Hoskuld.

Hrut answered, 'This doesn't seem an even match to me.'

'What makes you say that?' said Gunnar.

Hrut said, 'I'll answer this with the truth: you are a valiant and accomplished man, but she has a mixed character, and I don't want to deceive you in any way.'

'I suppose you mean well,' said Gunnar, 'but I will take it that you are keeping up our old hostility if you're not willing to make this match.'

'It's not that,' said Hrut, 'but rather that I see you cannot restrain yourself. Even if we didn't make a marriage agreement, we would still want to be your friends.'

'I've been talking with her, and she's not against it,' said Gunnar.

'I see that you're both eager for this match, and you're the ones who take the greatest risk as to how it works out.'

Hrut told Gunnar, without being asked, everything about Hallgerd's character, and though it seemed to Gunnar at first that there were many faults, it finally came about that they made an agreement. Then Hallgerd was sent for, and it was talked about in her presence. As before, they let her betroth herself. The wedding feast was to take place at Hlidarendi, and at first it was to be a secret, but soon everybody knew about it.

Gunnar rode home from the Althing and then went to Bergthorshvol and told Njal about the agreement. Njal was upset over it. Gunnar asked him why he found it so ill-advised.

'Every kind of evil will come from her when she moves east,' said Njal.

'She shall never spoil our friendship,' said Gunnar.

'It will come close to that,' said Njal, 'but you will always make amends for her.'

Gunnar invited Njal to the wedding feast with as many of his household as he wanted to bring along. Njal promised to come. After that Gunnar rode home and then rode about the district to invite guests.

34 | There was a man named Thrain, the son of Sigfus, the son of Sighvat the Red. He lived at Grjota on Fljotshlid. He was Gunnar's uncle[1] and a man of great worth. His wife was Thorhild the Poetess; she was harsh with words and made up mocking verses.

Thrain had little love for her. He was invited to the feast at Hlidarendi, and his wife was to wait on the guests, along with Bergthora Skarphed-insdottir, Njal's wife.

Ketil was the second son of Sigfus. He lived at Mork, to the east of the Markarfljot river, and was married to Thorgerd Njalsdottir.

Thorkel was the third son of Sigfus, Mord the fourth, Lambi the fifth, Sigmund the sixth, and Sigurd the seventh. They were all uncles to Gunnar, and great fighters. Gunnar had invited them all to the feast.

He had also invited Valgard the Grey and Ulf Aur-Godi, and their sons Mord and Runolf.

Hoskuld and Hrut came to the wedding in a large company; Thorleik and Olaf, the sons of Hoskuld, were among them. The bride came with them, and her daughter Thorgerd, a very beautiful woman; she was then fourteen. Many other women came with her as well.

Also at the wedding were Thorhalla, the daughter of Asgrim Ellida-Grimsson, and two daughters of Njal, Thorgerd and Helga.[2]

Gunnar had invited many people from the neighbourhood, and he seated his guests in this way: he himself sat in the middle of the bench, and next to him, on the inside, sat Thrain Sigfusson, then Ulf Aur-Godi, Valgard the Grey, Mord, Runolf, and then the sons of Sigfus, with Lambi innermost. On the other side of Gunnar, towards the door, sat Njal, then Skarphedin, Helgi, Grim, Hoskuld,[3] Haf the Wise, Ingjald from Keldur, and then the sons of Thorir from Holt in the east. Thorir himself wanted to sit at the outer edge of the men of worth, for then everyone would think himself well seated.

Hoskuld Dala-Kollsson sat in the middle of the opposite bench, with his sons further in. Hrut sat on the other side of Hoskuld, towards the door. There is no report of how the others were seated.

The bride sat in the middle of the cross-bench. On one side of her sat her daughter Thorgerd, and on the other Thorhalla, the daughter of Asgrim Ellida-Grimsson.

Thorhild waited on the guests, and she and Bergthora carried the food to the tables. Thrain Sigfusson had his eyes fixed on Thorgerd.

His wife Thorhild noticed this; she became angry and made a couplet for him.

'Thrain,' she said,

2.

'This gaping is not good,
Your eyes are all agog.'

Thrain jumped at once across the table and named witnesses and declared himself divorced from her – 'I won't take any more of her mocking and malicious language.'

He was so vehement about this that he would not stay at the feast unless she were sent away. And so it was – she went away. After that, each man sat in his seat and they drank and were merry.

Then Thrain spoke up: 'I won't make a secret of what's on my mind. I want to ask you this, Hoskuld Dala-Kollsson: will you give your granddaughter Thorgerd to me as my wife?'

'I don't know about that,' said Hoskuld. 'It seems to me that you have barely parted from the one you had before. What kind of man is he, Gunnar?'

Gunnar answered, 'I don't want to say anything – the man is related to me. You say something, Njal, since everybody will believe you.'

Njal spoke: 'About this man it can be said that he is well off for property and skilled in every way and very powerful, and you may well make this match with him.'

Then Hoskuld said, 'What do you think, Hrut?'

Hrut answered, 'You may give your approval, since it's an even match for her.'

They talked about the agreement until they were agreed on all terms. Gunnar and Thrain then stood up and went to the cross-bench. Gunnar asked mother and daughter whether they would accept this agreement. They said they had nothing against it, and Hallgerd betrothed her daughter.

The women's places were shifted; now Thorhalla sat between the brides. The feast went on well. When it was over, Hoskuld and his people rode west, and the people from the Rangarvellir district returned to their homes. Gunnar gave gifts to many and this was much to his credit.

Hallgerd took over the running of the household and was bountiful and assertive. Thorgerd took over the household at Grjota and was a good housewife.

35 | It was the custom between Gunnar and Njal, because of their close friendship, that every winter one of them would invite the other to his home for a winter feast. It was now Gunnar's turn to be Njal's guest at the winter feast, and so he and Hallgerd went to Bergthorshvol. Helgi and his wife were not there. Njal welcomed them, and when they had been there a while Helgi and his wife Thorhalla returned.

Bergthora went up to the cross-bench, together with Thorhalla, and spoke to Hallgerd: 'You must move aside for this woman.'

Hallgerd spoke: 'I'll not move aside for anyone, and I won't sit in the corner like a cast-off hag.'

'I decide things here,' said Bergthora.

After that Thorhalla sat down.

Bergthora came to the table with water for washing hands. Hallgerd took her hand and said, 'There's not much to choose between you and Njal – you have gnarled nails on every finger,[1] and he's beardless.'

'That's true,' said Bergthora, 'and yet we don't hold it against each other. But your husband Thorvald was not beardless, and yet you had him killed.'

'There's little use to me in being married to the most manly man in Iceland,' said Hallgerd, 'if you don't avenge this, Gunnar.'

He sprang up and leaped across the table and spoke: 'I'm going home, and it would be best for you to pick quarrels with your servants, and not in the dwellings of others. I'm in debt to Njal for many honours, and I'm not going to be a cat's-paw for you.'

After that Gunnar and Hallgerd set off for home.

'Keep this in mind, Bergthora,' said Hallgerd, 'that we're not finished yet.'

Bergthora said that Hallgerd would not be better off for that. Gunnar said nothing more and went home to Hlidarendi and was there all through the winter. Summer came, and the time for the Thing.

36 | Gunnar got ready to ride to the Thing, and before he left he spoke to Hallgerd: 'Behave yourself while I'm away and don't show your bad temper where my friends are concerned.'

'The trolls take your friends,' she said.

Gunnar rode to the Thing, and saw that it was no good talking to her. Njal and all his sons also rode to the Thing.

Now to tell what was happening at home: Gunnar and Njal together owned some woodland at Raudaskrid. They had not divided it up, and each of them was in the habit of cutting what he needed, without blame from the other.

Kol was the name of Hallgerd's overseer. He had been with her a long time, and was the worst sort of person. A man named Svart was Njal and Bergthora's servant, and they were quite fond of him.

Bergthora spoke with Svart and told him to go to Raudaskrid and chop wood – 'and I will send men to haul it home.'

He said he would do as she wished. He went up to Raudaskrid and started chopping, and was to stay there for a week.

Some poor men came to Hlidarendi from east of the Markarfljot and reported that Svart had been at Raudaskrid chopping wood, and working hard at it.

'It seems that Bergthora is out to rob me in a big way,' said Hallgerd, 'but I'll see to it that he won't chop any more.'

Rannveig, Gunnar's mother, overheard this and spoke: 'Housewives have been good here, even without plotting to kill men.'

The night passed, and in the morning Hallgerd said to Kol, 'I have thought of a job for you,' and she handed him a weapon. 'Go up to Raudaskrid. You'll find Svart there.'

'What am I to do with him?' he said.

'Do you need to ask that?' she said. 'You – the worst sort of person? Kill him!'

'I can do that,' he said, 'and yet it's likely to cost me my life.'

'Everything grows big in your eyes,' she said, 'and this is bad of you after all the times I've spoken up for you. I'll find another man to do this if you don't dare.'

He took the axe and was very angry, and took a horse that Gunnar owned and rode until he came east to the Markarfljot. There he dismounted and waited in the woods until men had carried off the timber and Svart was left alone.

Kol charged towards him and said, 'More men than you know how to chop hard' – and he sank the axe into his head and struck him his death blow and then rode back and told Hallgerd of the slaying.

She said, 'I'll look after you so that no one will harm you.'

'That may be,' he said, 'but before I did the slaying I had a dream that pointed the other way.'

The men came back to the woods and found Svart dead and carried his body home.

Hallgerd sent a man to Gunnar at the Thing to tell him of the slaying. Gunnar did not find fault with Hallgerd in the presence of the messenger, and at first people did not know whether he thought well or ill of it. After a while he stood up and asked his men to come with him. They did, and went together to Njal's booth, and Gunnar sent a man to ask Njal to come outside. Njal came out at once, and he and Gunnar went apart to talk.

Gunnar spoke: 'I have a slaying to tell you of: my wife and my overseer Kol brought it about, and your servant Svart was the victim.'

Njal remained silent while Gunnar told him everything. Then he spoke: 'You must not let her have her way in everything.'

Gunnar said, 'You make the judgement yourself.'

Njal said, 'It's going to be hard for you to atone for all of Hallgerd's misdoings, and another time the effects will be greater than now, where just the two of us are involved – though this matter itself is far short of going well – and you and I will have to keep in mind the good things we've been saying to each other for a long time. I expect that you will do well, but you will be tested hard.'

Njal accepted self-judgement from Gunnar and said, 'I'm not going to push this too hard: pay me twelve ounces of silver. But I want to stipulate that if something happens from my side which you have to judge, you will not set harder terms than I have done.'

Gunnar paid the money readily and then rode home.

Njal and his sons returned from the Thing. Bergthora saw the money and said, 'This was moderately done – the same amount must be paid for Kol when the time comes.'

Gunnar returned from the Thing and reproached Hallgerd. She said that better men than Svart had died in many places without compensation.

Gunnar said she would decide her own actions – 'but I shall decide how the cases are settled.'

Hallgerd frequently boasted of the slaying of Svart, and Bergthora did not like that at all.

Njal and his sons went up to Thorolfsfell to look after their farm. The same day it happened that Bergthora was outside and saw a man riding up on a black horse. She remained where she was and did not go in. She did not recognize him. He had a spear in his hand and a short sword at his belt. She asked him his name.

'I'm called Atli,' he said.

She asked where he came from.

'I'm from the East Fjords,' he said.

'Where are you going?' she said.

'I have no place to work,' he said, 'and I was looking for Njal and Skarphedin, to see if they would take me on.'

'What work are you best at?' she asked.

'I do field work,' he said, 'and I'm good at many other things, but I won't hide the fact that I'm a harsh-tempered man and that many have had to bind up wounds on account of me.'

'I won't hold it against you,' she said, 'that you're not a coward.'

Atli said, 'Do you have any authority here?'

'I'm Njal's wife,' she said, 'and I have no less authority in hiring than he does.'

'Will you take me on?' he asked.

'I'll give you a chance,' she said, 'provided you do whatever I ask you to – even if I send you out to kill someone.'

'You surely have enough men,' he said, 'that you don't need me for such things.'

'I set the terms as I please,' she said.

'Let's agree on them, then,' he said, and she took him on.

Njal and his sons came home, and Njal asked Bergthora who this new man was.

'He's your servant,' she said. 'I hired him – he said he was good at working with his hands.'

'He'll be a hard worker, sure enough,' said Njal, 'but I don't know whether he'll be a good worker.'

Skarphedin took a liking to Atli.

The following summer Njal and his sons rode to the Thing. Gunnar was also there. One day Njal brought out a pouch of money.

Skarphedin asked, 'What money is that, father?'

'This is the money,' said Njal, 'that Gunnar paid to me for our servant last summer.'

'It may turn out to be useful,' said Skarphedin, and grinned.

37 | Now to what was happening at home: Atli asked Bergthora what work he should do that day.

'I've thought of a job for you,' she said. 'Go and look for Kol until you find him, for you must kill him today – if you want to do my will.'

'That's quite fitting,' he said, 'since both Kol and I are bad sorts. I'll go after him in such a way that one of us will die.'

'You'll do well,' she said, 'and you won't do this job for nothing.'

He went and got his weapons and horse and rode away. He rode up to Fljotshlid and met men there who were coming from Hlidarendi. They lived at Mork in the east. They asked where Atli was headed, and he said he was out riding to look for a work-horse. They said that that was a petty task for such a workman – 'but it would be best for you to ask those who were on the move last night.'

'And who are they?' he said.

'Killer-Kol, Hallgerd's servant, left the shieling just now,' they said, 'and he's been up all night.'

'I don't know if I dare to meet up with him,' said Atli. 'He's got a bad temper, and I'd best be warned by another man's woe.'

'From the look in your eyes,' they said, 'you seem anything but a coward' – and they directed him to where Kol was.

He spurred his horse and rode hard. When he came to Kol he said, 'Is your pack-horse work going well?'

'That's no business of yours, you scum,' said Kol, 'or of anybody from your place.'

Atli said, 'You still have the toughest task of all.'

Atli then thrust his spear and hit him in the waist. Kol swung his axe at him and missed and fell off his horse and died at once.

Atli rode until he met some of Hallgerd's workmen. 'Go up to the horse,' he said, 'and take care of it. Kol fell off its back, and he's dead.'

'Did you kill him?' they said.

He answered, 'It will occur to Hallgerd that he didn't die by his own hand.'

Then Atli rode home and told Bergthora. She thanked him, both for the deed and for the words which he had spoken.

'I don't know,' said Atli, 'what Njal will think of this.'

'He can handle it,' she said, 'and as a sign I can tell you that he took with him to the Thing the slave's price we received last summer, and this money will now pay for Kol. But even though there's a settlement, you must be on your guard, for Hallgerd will not honour any settlement.'

'Don't you want to send someone to Njal to tell him of the slaying?' he said.

'No, I don't,' she said. 'It would suit me better if Kol's death went uncompensated.'

Then they ended their talk.

Hallgerd was told of Kol's slaying and of Atli's comments. She said she would pay him back. She sent a man to the Thing to tell Gunnar of Kol's slaying. He had little to say about it and sent a man to Njal to let him know. Njal said nothing.

Skarphedin spoke: 'Slaves are much more active than they used to be: then they just got into brawls, and that seemed harmless enough, but now they're out to kill each other.'

He grinned.

Njal took down the money pouch which was hanging in the booth and went out; his sons went with him. They came to Gunnar's booth. Skarphedin said to the man who was standing in the doorway, 'Tell Gunnar that my father wants to see him.'

The man told Gunnar, and Gunnar came out at once and gave Njal a warm greeting. Then they went off to speak.

'Things have turned out badly,' said Njal; 'my wife has broken our settlement and had your servant killed.'

'She should not be blamed for this,' said Gunnar.

'You make the judgement,' said Njal.

'I will,' said Gunnar. 'I'll make Svart and Kol equal in value – pay me twelve ounces of silver.'

Njal took the money pouch and gave it to Gunnar. Gunnar recognized the money as the same that he had paid to Njal. Njal went back to his booth, and after that they got along as well as before.

When Njal arrived home he reproached Bergthora, but she said she would never give in to Hallgerd.

Hallgerd was very cross with Gunnar for having settled the slaying peacefully. Gunnar said that he would never turn against Njal or his sons, and she went on raging. Gunnar paid no attention.

Gunnar and Njal saw to it that nothing else happened that year.

38 | In the spring Njal said to Atli, 'I would like you to find work back in the East Fjords, so that Hallgerd cannot decide how long you shall live.'

'I'm not afraid of that,' said Atli, 'and I would like to stay at home here, if I have a choice.'

'That is less wise,' said Njal.

'I would rather die in your service than change masters,' said Atli. 'But I beg you that no slave's price be paid for me if I am slain.'

'You will be paid for like any other free man,' said Njal, 'and Bergthora will make you a promise, which she'll keep, that you will be paid for in blood.'

Atli then joined the household.

Now to return to Hallgerd: she sent a man west to Bjarnarfjord for her kinsman Brynjolf the Brawler, a very bad sort. Gunnar knew nothing about this. Hallgerd said he would make a good overseer. Brynjolf came east, and Gunnar asked what he was up to. Brynjolf said he would be staying there.

'You won't improve our household, from what I've heard,' said Gunnar. 'But I won't turn away any kinsman whom Hallgerd wants to have with her.'

Gunnar was short with him, but not unkind. So it went until the time for the Thing.

Gunnar rode to the Thing with Kolskegg, and when they came there they met with Njal; he was at the Thing with his sons. They were often together and it went well.

Bergthora spoke to Atli: 'Go up to Thorolfsfell and work there for a week.'

He went up and stayed there in secret, and burned charcoal in the woods.

Hallgerd spoke to Brynjolf: 'I have been told that Atli is not at home – he must be working at Thorolfsfell.'

'What do you think he's likely to be working at?' he said.

'Something in the woods,' she said.

'What am I to do with him?' he said.

'Kill him!' she said.

He became silent.

'This would not be so big in Thjostolf's eyes,' she said, 'if he were alive.'

'You won't have to taunt me this hard again,' said Brynjolf.

He took his weapons and horse and mounted and rode off to Thorolfsfell. To the east of the farm he saw thick smoke. He rode towards it and got off his horse and tethered it and walked to where the smoke was thickest. He saw the charcoal pit, and a man was next to it. He saw that the man had stuck his spear into the ground by his side. Brynjolf walked through the smoke right up to him; the man was working furiously and did not see him. Brynjolf hit him on the head with his axe. Atli moved so quickly that Brynjolf lost his grip on the axe, and Atli grabbed his spear and threw it at him. Brynjolf threw himself to the ground, and the spear passed over him.

'It's lucky for you that I wasn't ready,' said Atli. 'Hallgerd will now be pleased, for you will tell her of my death. But it's comforting to know that you will soon meet the same end. Now come here and take the axe.'

Brynjolf said nothing and did not take the axe until Atli was dead. He rode over to Thorolfsfell and announced the slaying, and after that rode home and told Hallgerd. She sent a man to Bergthorshvol to announce to Bergthora that the slaying of Kol had now been paid back.

Then Hallgerd sent a man to the Thing to tell Gunnar of Atli's slaying. Gunnar stood up, and so did Kolskegg.

Kolskegg said, 'The kinsmen of Hallgerd aren't much use to you.'

They went to see Njal.

Gunnar spoke: 'I have to tell you of the slaying of Atli' – and he told him who had done it. 'I want to offer you compensation, and I want you to fix the amount yourself.'

Njal said, 'We have tried to prevent disagreement between us, but I cannot value Atli as a slave.'

Gunnar said that was fair and gave him his hand. Njal took it and named witnesses, and they agreed to settle.

Skarphedin spoke: 'Hallgerd does not let our servants die of old age.'

Gunnar answered, 'Your mother will think that she too should take vengeance.'

'That is certainly so,' said Njal.

Njal then set the price at a hundred ounces of silver, and Gunnar paid it at once. Many of those standing around called this a high

price. Gunnar became angry and said that full compensation had
been paid for men who were no more worthy than Atli had been. At
this they rode home from the Thing.

Bergthora said to Njal, when she saw the money, 'You think you have
kept your promise, but mine has yet to be kept.'

'There's no need for you to keep it,' said Njal.

'But you've guessed that I will,' she said, 'and so it shall be.'

Hallgerd spoke to Gunnar: 'Did you really pay a hundred ounces of
silver for Atli's slaying and value him as a free man?'

'He was already a free man,' said Gunnar, 'and I'm not going to
treat Njal's servants as men who have no right to compensation.'

'You two are a real match for each other,' said Hallgerd. 'Both of
you are soft.'

'That remains to be seen,' he said.

Then Gunnar was cold with her for a long time, until she became
more yielding.

Things were quiet the rest of the year. In the spring Njal added no
more servants to his household. People rode to the Thing in the
summer.

39 | There was a man named Thord, and he was called Freed-man's
son. His father's name was Sigtrygg; he had been a slave freed
by Asgerd[1] and he drowned in the river Markarfljot; Thord was with
Njal after that. He was big and strong, and had fostered all of Njal's
sons. He was in love with Gudfinna Thorolfsdottir, Njal's kinswoman.
She was a housekeeper at Bergthorshvol and was then pregnant.

Bergthora went to speak with Thord Freed-man's son. 'You are to
go and kill Brynjolf,' she said.

'I'm no killer,' he said, 'but I'll do this if you wish it.'

'I wish it,' she said.

After that he took his horse and rode up to Hlidarendi and called
Hallgerd out and asked where Brynjolf was.

'What do you want with him?' she asked.

66

He said, 'I want him to tell me where he covered up Atli's body; I'm told he did a bad job of it.'

She pointed the way and said he was down at Akratunga.

'Take care,' said Thord, 'that what happened to Atli doesn't happen to him.'

'You're no killer,' she said, 'and nothing will happen if you two meet.'

'I've never seen man's blood,' he said, 'and I don't know how I'll take it' – and he dashed out of the hayfield and down to Akratunga.

Rannveig, Gunnar's mother, had heard their talk and spoke: 'You derided his courage, Hallgerd, but I think him a fearless man, and your kinsman will find that out.'

Brynjolf and Thord met on the beaten path.

Thord said, 'Defend yourself, Brynjolf – I don't want to act basely towards you.'

Brynjolf rode at Thord and swung at him. Thord swung back with his axe, and cut the handle of Brynjolf's axe in two, just above his hand, and quickly swung it a second time, and it hit him on his chest and went deep inside. Brynjolf fell off his horse and was dead at once.

Thord met one of Hallgerd's shepherds and announced that he had done the slaying and told him where Brynjolf was lying and asked him to tell Hallgerd of the slaying. Then he went back home to Bergthorshvol and told Bergthora and others about the slaying.

'Bless your hands!' she said.

The shepherd told Hallgerd of the slaying. She was bitter about it and said that much trouble would come from this, if she had her way.

40 | The news reached the Althing; Njal had it told to him three times and then said, 'More men than I expected have now become killers.'

Skarphedin said, 'That man who died at the hands of our foster-father – who had never seen man's blood before – was doomed to a quick death, and many must have expected that we brothers would be the ones to do this, given our temperament.'

'You have only a short time,' said Njal, 'before your turn will come, and then necessity will drive you.'

They went to find Gunnar and told him of the slaying. Gunnar said that it was no great loss – 'and yet he was a free man.'

Njal offered him a settlement at once. Gunnar agreed and was to judge the amount himself, and he fixed it at a hundred ounces of silver. Njal paid over the money at once, and with this they were at peace.

41 | There was a man named Sigmund; he was the son of Lambi, the son of Sighvat the Red. Sigmund was a great seafaring merchant, a well-mannered and handsome man, big and strong. He longed for fame and was a good poet and skilled in most sports; he was boisterous, sarcastic and overbearing.

He came to land at Hornafjord in the east. Skjold was the name of his companion, a Swede and a vicious man to deal with. They got themselves horses and rode west from Hornafjord and did not stop until they came to Hlidarendi on Fljotshlid. Gunnar welcomed them; there was close kinship between him and Sigmund.[1] Gunnar invited Sigmund to stay there for the winter; Sigmund said he would take the offer if his companion Skjold could stay there too.

'I've been told about him,' said Gunnar, 'that he does not improve your character – and what you certainly need is some improvement. Also, living here can lead to problems. My advice to you and all my kinsmen is that you don't spring into action at the prompting of my wife Hallgerd, for she undertakes many things that are far from my will.'

'Whoever warns is free of fault,' said Sigmund.

'Then remember my advice,' said Gunnar. 'You will often be tried, but stay close to me and follow my advice.'

After that they kept Gunnar's company. Hallgerd was good to Sigmund, and things became so intense that she turned over money to him and waited on him no less than she did her husband. Many talked about this and wondered what lay behind it.

Hallgerd said to Gunnar, 'There's no honour in being content with the hundred ounces of silver you accepted for my kinsman Brynjolf. I'm certainly going to avenge him if I can.'

Gunnar said he did not want to argue with her and walked away. He found Kolskegg and said to him, 'Go to Njal and tell him that Thord should be on his guard, in spite of our settlement, for I don't think it will last.'

Kolskegg rode off and told Njal, and Njal told Thord. Kolskegg rode back home, and Njal thanked him and Gunnar for their faithfulness.

One day it happened that Njal and Thord were sitting together outside. A he-goat had the habit of walking around the hayfield, and no one was allowed to chase it away.

Thord said, 'Now this is amazing.'

'What do you see that so amazes you?' said Njal

'I think I see the goat lying in the hollow over there, all covered with blood.'

Njal said there was no goat or anything else over there.

'What is it, then?' said Thord.

'You must be a doomed man,' said Njal, 'and you have seen your personal spirit, and now you must be on your guard.'

'That won't do me any good,' said Thord, 'if my fate is sealed.'

Hallgerd went to talk with Thrain Sigfusson and said, 'I would consider you a true son-in-law,' she said, 'if you killed Thord Freedman's son.'

'I will not do that,' he said, 'for then I would have to bear the anger of my nephew Gunnar. Besides, there is much at stake here, since this slaying will be swiftly avenged.'

'Who will avenge it?' she said. 'Not that old beardless fellow?'

'No, not him,' he said – 'his sons will take vengeance.'

Then they talked softly together for a long time, and no one knew what sort of plans they were making.

One day it happened that Gunnar was not at home, but Sigmund and Skjold were. Thrain had come from Grjota. They sat outside with Hallgerd and talked.

Hallgerd said, 'Sigmund and his companion Skjold have promised to kill Thord Freed-man's son, the foster-father of Njal's sons, and you, Thrain, have promised to be standing by.'

They all confirmed that they had made these promises.

'Now I'll give you the plan,' she said. 'You must ride east to Hornafjord for your goods, and then come back just at the beginning of the Thing – if you're home before then, Gunnar will want you to ride to the Thing with him. Njal will be at the Thing with his sons, and Gunnar too. That's when you must kill Thord.'

They agreed that this plan ought to be carried out. After that they set off for the East Fjords; Gunnar was not alert to their plans and rode to the Thing.

Njal sent Thord Freed-man's son east to the Eyjafjoll district and told him to stay away one night. He went east, but could not come back from there because the river was so high that for a long stretch it was unfordable. Njal waited one day for him, because he had planned that Thord would ride to the Thing with him. Then he told Bergthora to send Thord along to the Thing when he got home. Two nights later Thord came from the east. Bergthora told him that he was to ride to the Thing – 'but first ride up to Thorolfsfell and see to the farm there, and don't stay more than one or two nights.'

42 | Sigmund and his companions returned from the east. Hallgerd told them that Thord was at home, but that he was to ride to the Thing within a few days – 'Now you can catch him,' she said, 'but not if you let this chance slip by.'

Some people came to Hlidarendi from Thorolfsfell and told Hallgerd that Thord was up there. Hallgerd went to Thrain Sigfusson and the others and said, 'Thord is at Thorolfsfell now, and you'll have a chance to kill him when he goes home.'

'We'll do it,' said Sigmund.

They went out and took their weapons and horses and rode off to meet him.

Sigmund said to Thrain, 'You don't have to do anything – this won't need all of us.'

'I won't, then,' said Thrain.

After a little while Thord came riding towards them. Sigmund spoke to him: 'Give yourself up,' he said, 'for now you shall die.'

'Not at all,' said Thord. 'Come and fight me man-to-man.'

'Not at all,' said Sigmund – 'we'll make use of our numbers. But it's not strange that Skarphedin is so dauntless, for it's said that a man owes one-fourth of his character to his upbringing.'

'You'll learn the truth of that,' said Thord, 'for Skarphedin will avenge me.'

They began their attack, and Thord defended himself so well that he broke the shafts of both their spears. Then Skjold cut off his arm, and he defended himself with the other arm for some time, until Sigmund ran him through; then he fell dead to the ground. They covered his body with turf and stones.

Thrain spoke: 'We have done a bad deed, and Njal's sons will take the slaying badly when they hear of it.'

They rode home and told Hallgerd, and she was pleased with the slaying.

Rannveig, Gunnar's mother, spoke: 'There's a saying, Sigmund, that the hand's joy in the blow is brief, and so it will be here. Gunnar will resolve the matter for you, but if you rise to Hallgerd's bait again it will be your death.'

Hallgerd sent a man to Bergthorshvol to report the slaying, and she sent another man to the Thing to tell Gunnar. Bergthora said that she would not strike back at Hallgerd with harsh language: that, she said, would be no revenge for so great a matter.

43 | When the messenger arrived at the Thing to tell him of the slaying, Gunnar spoke: 'This has turned out badly, and no news could come to my ears which I could think worse. Still, let's go at once to Njal, and I expect he will persevere, even though he is being greatly provoked.'

They went to meet Njal and called him out for a talk. He went at once to Gunnar and they spoke together, and at first no one else was there except Kolskegg.

'I come bearing harsh tidings for you,' said Gunnar: 'the slaying of Thord Freed-man's son. I want to offer you the right of self-judgement for this slaying.'

Njal was silent for a while, and then spoke: 'That is well offered,' he said, 'and I will accept it. But it is not unlikely that I will be blamed for this by my wife and my sons, since they will take this very badly. And yet I will risk that, because I know I'm dealing with an honourable man, and I don't want any breach in our friendship to come from me.'

'Do you want your sons to be present?' said Gunnar.

'No, I don't,' said Njal, 'because they will not break the settlement that I make, but if they are present they will not make it easy.'

'So be it,' said Gunnar. 'Take care of it yourself.'

They shook hands and settled it well and quickly.

Njal said, 'I set the amount at two hundred ounces of silver, and this will seem high to you.'

'I don't think it's too high,' said Gunnar, and then went back to his booth.

Njal's sons came back to the booth, and Skarphedin asked where all the good money came from that Njal was holding in his hands.

Njal said, 'I must tell you of the slaying of your foster-father Thord; Gunnar and I have just made a settlement on it, and he has paid double compensation.'

'Who killed him?' said Skarphedin.

'Sigmund and Skjold, but Thrain was close at hand,' said Njal.

'They thought they needed a lot of help,' said Skarphedin. 'But how far must this go before we can raise our hands?'

'Not far,' said Njal, 'and then nothing will stop you, but now it's important to me that you do not break this settlement.'

'Then we won't,' said Skarphedin, 'but if anything comes up between us, we shall have this old hostility in mind.'

'At that time I will make no requests of you,' said Njal.

44 | People rode home from the Thing. When Gunnar came home he spoke to Sigmund: 'You're a man of more bad luck than I thought, and you make evil use of your abilities. But still I've made a settlement for you, and you must never rise to Hallgerd's bait again. You're not at all like me: you are given to mockery and sarcasm, while I am not. You get along well with Hallgerd, because you have more in common with her.'

Gunnar reproached him at length, and Sigmund took it well and said that from then on he would follow his advice more than he had in the past. Gunnar said that it would serve him well.

The settlement held firm for a while, and Gunnar and Njal and Njal's sons were on friendly terms, but the rest of their people had little to do with each other.

It happened one day that some itinerant women came to Hlidarendi from Bergthorshvol. They were talkative and rather malicious. Hallgerd had a women's room in which she often sat, and her daughter Thorgerd and Thrain were there, as well as Sigmund and a number of women. Gunnar was not there, nor was Kolskegg.

The itinerant women went into the room. Hallgerd greeted them and found seats for them and asked them for news, but they said they had none to report. Hallgerd asked where they had been that night, and they said they had been at Bergthorshvol.

'What was Njal up to?' she said.

'He was working hard – at sitting,' they said.

'What were Njal's sons doing?' she said. 'They think of themselves as real men.'

'They're pretty big to look at, but they are quite untested,' they said. 'Skarphedin was sharpening his axe, Grim was fixing a shaft to his spearhead, Helgi was riveting the hilt on his sword, and Hoskuld was fastening the handle on his shield.'

'They must be getting ready for something big,' said Hallgerd.

'We don't know about that,' they said.

'What were Njal's servants doing?' said Hallgerd.

'We don't know what all of them were doing,' they said, 'but one was carting shit to the hillocks.'

'What's the point of that?' said Hallgerd.

'He said this would make the hay there better than anywhere else,' they said.

'Njal's wisdom is uneven,' said Hallgerd, 'although he has advice on everything.'

'What do you mean?' they said.

'I'll point to what's true,' said Hallgerd – 'he didn't cart dung to his beard so that he would be like other men. Let's call him "Old Beardless", and his sons "Dung-beardlings", and you, Sigmund, make up a poem about this and give us the benefit of your being a poet.'

Sigmund said he was up to this and came up with three or four verses, all of them malicious.[1]

'You're a treasure,' said Hallgerd, 'the way you do just what I want.'

At that moment Gunnar came in. He had been standing outside the room and heard all the words that had passed. They were shocked when they saw him come in. They fell silent, but before there had been loud laughter.

Gunnar was very angry and said to Sigmund, 'You are foolish and unable to follow good advice if you are willing to slander Njal's sons, and even worse, Njal himself, on top of what you have already done to them, and this will lead to your death. And if any man here repeats these words he'll be sent away, and bear my anger besides.'

They were so terrified by him that no one dared repeat the words. After that he left.

The itinerant women talked among themselves about how they would get a reward from Bergthora if they told her what had been said. They went down to Bergthorshvol and told her, in private and without being asked.

Bergthora spoke to the men while they were at table: 'Gifts have been given to you all, father and sons, and you're not real men unless you repay them.'

'What gifts are these?' said Skarphedin.

'You, my sons, have all received the same gift: you have been called "Dung-beardlings", and my husband has been called "Old Beardless".'

'We're not made like women, that we become furious over everything,' said Skarphedin.

'But Gunnar became furious, on your behalf,' she said, 'and he is said to be gentle. If you don't avenge this, you'll never avenge any shame.'

'The old lady enjoys all this,' said Skarphedin and grinned, but sweat formed on his brow and red spots on his cheeks, and this was unusual for him.

Grim was silent and bit his lip. Helgi showed no change. Hoskuld went out with Bergthora.

She came in again and went on raging.

Njal spoke: 'Everything works itself out, woman, though it may take time. And it happens in many cases where men's tempers have been tried that the effect is two-sided, even after vengeance has been taken.'

That night, when Njal had gone to bed, he heard an axe strike the wall of his bed closet and make a loud ringing noise; there was another bed closet where the shields were hung up, and he saw that the shields were gone.

He said, 'Who's taken down our shields?'

'Your sons have gone out with them,' said Bergthora.

He pulled his shoes on his feet and went out at once and around to the other side of the house and saw that they were heading up the slope.

He said, 'Where are you going, Skarphedin?'

'To look for your sheep,' he said.

Njal said, 'You wouldn't be armed if you planned that, so it must be something else.'

'We're going salmon-fishing, father, if we don't find the sheep,' he said.

'If that's so, then it would be a good thing if the prey didn't slip away,' said Njal.

They went on their way, and Njal went in to bed.

He said to Bergthora, 'Your sons were outside, all of them, with weapons, and you must have egged them on to something.'

'I will give them all my thanks if they tell me of the slaying of Sigmund,' said Bergthora.

45 | To return to Njal's sons: they went up to Fljotshlid and stayed there that night, and when morning broke they went closer to Hlidarendi. That same morning Sigmund and Skjold got up and planned to go out to the breeding horses. They took bridles with them and caught horses in the hayfield and rode away. They looked for the stallion on the slope and found him between two brooks and brought the horses a good way down towards the road.

Skarphedin saw them, because Sigmund was in coloured clothing. He spoke: 'Do you see that red elf?'[1]

They looked and said they could see him.

Skarphedin said, 'You must have nothing to do with this, Hoskuld, for you will often be sent out alone and unprepared. I've marked Sigmund for myself – that's a man's job. And Grim and Helgi are to take on Skjold.'

Hoskuld sat down, and they went on until they met up with them.

Skarphedin spoke to Sigmund: 'Take your weapons and defend yourself; you need that more than you need to make lampoons about us.'

Sigmund took his weapons, and Skarphedin waited for him. Skjold turned to face Grim and Helgi, and they fought violently. Sigmund had a helmet on his head and a shield and a sword at his belt and a spear in his hand. He turned to face Skarphedin and thrust at him with his spear and it struck the shield. Skarphedin cut through the spearshaft with his axe and raised his axe again and swung at Sigmund, and it struck the shield and split it down to below the handle. Sigmund drew his sword with his right hand and struck at Skarphedin, but the sword hit the shield and stuck fast there. Skarphedin twisted the shield so quickly that Sigmund lost his grip on the sword. Then Skarphedin swung at Sigmund with his axe; Sigmund was wearing a corslet. The axe came down on his shoulder. Skarphedin cut through the shoulder blade and pulled the axe towards himself so that Sigmund fell forward on both his knees, but sprang up at once.

'You bowed to me just now,' said Skarphedin, 'and you'll be on your back² before we're through.'

'That's bad,' said Sigmund.

Skarphedin struck him on the helmet and then dealt the death blow.

Grim swung at Skjold's leg and took it off at the ankle, and Helgi pierced him with his sword, and then he met his death.

Skarphedin saw one of Hallgerd's shepherds. He had by this time cut off Sigmund's head; he placed it in the man's hands and told him to take it to Hallgerd and said that she would know whether this head had uttered slander about them. The shepherd threw the head down as soon as they left. He did not dare to do so while they were still there.

The brothers went on until they met some men at the Markarfljot and told them what had happened. Skarphedin announced that he had slain Sigmund, and Grim and Helgi that they had slain Skjold. Then they went home and told Njal what had happened.

He said, 'Bless your hands! This time there will be no self-judgement – not for the time being.'

To return to the shepherd: he came back to Hlidarendi and told Hallgerd the news.

'Skarphedin handed me Sigmund's head and told me to bring it to you, but I didn't dare,' he said, 'because I didn't know how you would take it.'

'It's too bad you didn't bring it,' she said. 'I would have brought it to Gunnar, and then he would have had to avenge his kinsman, or else be blamed by all men.'

After that she went to Gunnar and said, 'I must tell you of the slaying of your kinsman Sigmund. Skarphedin killed him and wanted his head brought to me.'

'Sigmund should have expected this,' said Gunnar, 'for evil designs have evil results, and you and Skarphedin have often behaved spitefully to each other.'

Gunnar then went away. He did not have any action brought for the slaying and in fact did nothing at all about it. Hallgerd often reminded him that no compensation had been paid for Sigmund, but Gunnar paid no attention to her prodding.

Three Things passed, at each of which people expected that he would prosecute the case. Then a problem arose which Gunnar did not know how to handle, and he rode over to see Njal. Njal received him warmly.

Gunnar said to him, 'I have come to seek your advice about a problem.'

'You deserve it,' said Njal and gave him advice on what to do. Gunnar then stood up and thanked him.

Njal took him by the arm and said to him, 'Your kinsman Sigmund has been without compensation for quite a long time.'

'He was compensated for long ago,'[3] said Gunnar, 'but I would not reject an honourable offer.'

Gunnar had never spoken ill of Njal's sons. Njal wanted nothing else but that Gunnar should set the amount. Gunnar set it at two hundred ounces of silver, and he allowed no compensation for Skjold. They paid the entire amount at once. Gunnar announced the settlement at the Thingskalar Assembly, at a time when it was most crowded, and he talked about how well Njal and his sons had acted, and about the malicious words which led Sigmund to his death. No one was ever to bring up these words again, and if anyone did he would be without right to compensation.[4]

The two of them, Gunnar and Njal, said that no matter would ever arise that they would not settle by themselves. They stood by this and always remained friends.

46 | There was a man named Gizur; he was the son of Teit, the son of Ketilbjorn the Old from Mosfell. Gizur's mother was Olof, the daughter of the hersir Bodvar, the son of Viking-Kari. Gizur's son was Isleif the bishop. Teit's mother was Helga, the daughter of Thord Beard, the son of Hrapp, the son of Bjorn Buna. Gizur the White lived at Mosfell and was a great chieftain.[1]

A man named Geir is now brought into the saga. He was called Geir the Godi. His mother was Thorkatla, the daughter of Ketilbjorn the Old from Mosfell.[2] Geir lived at Hlid. He and Gizur supported each other in all matters.

In those days Mord Valgardsson lived at Hof in the Rangarvellir. He was cunning and malicious. His father Valgard was abroad at the time, and his mother had died. He was very envious of Gunnar of Hlidarendi. He was well off for property but was not well liked.

47 | There was a man named Otkel, the son of Skarf, the son of Hallkel who fought with Grim of Grimsnes and killed him in a duel. Hallkel and Ketilbjorn the Old were brothers.[1] Otkel lived at Kirkjubaer. His wife was Thorgerd, the daughter of Mar, the son of Brondolf, the son of Naddod the Faroese.

Otkel was well off for property. He had a son named Thorgeir; he was still young but quite promising.

There was a man named Skammkel. He lived at the other farm called Hof and had a lot of property. He was malicious and untruthful, overbearing and vicious to deal with. He was a friend of Otkel's.

Hallkel was the name of Otkel's brother. He was big and strong and lived at Kirkjubaer with Otkel. They had another brother named Hallbjorn the White. He brought a slave named Melkolf out to Iceland; Melkolf was Irish and quite unlikeable. Hallbjorn went to stay with Otkel. Melkolf came along with him and often said that he would be happy if Otkel were his master. Otkel was kind to him and gave him a knife and a belt and a full set of clothes, and the slave did whatever he wanted him to. Otkel asked his brother to sell him the slave. Hallbjorn said he would give him to him, but also said that Melkolf was less of a prize than Otkel thought. Once Otkel owned the slave his work got worse and worse. Otkel often talked with Hallbjorn the White about how little work the slave seemed to be doing. Hallbjorn said that he had even worse qualities.

In those days there was a great famine, so that people lacked both hay and food, and this spread over all parts of Iceland. Gunnar shared hay and food with many people, and everybody who turned to him got supplies, as long as there were any.

At last Gunnar ran short of hay and food. He asked Kolskegg to go with him on a journey, along with Thrain Sigfusson and Lambi Sigurdarson.[2] They went to Kirkjubaer and called Otkel out. He greeted them. Gunnar responded politely.

'Things are such', said Gunnar, 'that I have come to buy hay and food from you, if there is any.'

'I have both,' said Otkel, 'but I'll sell you neither one.'

'Are you willing to give it to me then,' said Gunnar, 'and take your chances on my repaying you?'

'I won't do that either,' said Otkel.

Skammkel was advising him to act meanly.

Thrain Sigfusson said, 'It would be fitting if we just took it and left behind what it was worth.'

'The men of Mosfell[3] would all have to be dead,' said Skammkel, 'before you sons of Sigfus could rob them.'

'I will not do any robbing,' said Gunnar.

'Would you like to buy a slave from me?' said Otkel.

'I won't refuse that,' said Gunnar. He then bought Melkolf and went off, leaving things that way.

Njal found out about this and said, 'This was badly done, refusing to sell to Gunnar. There is no hope for others if men like him cannot get supplies.'

'Why do you need to say much about it?' said Bergthora. 'It would be much more noble to share our food and hay with him, since you're not short of either.'

Njal said, 'That's as true as day – I'll give him some supplies.'

He went up to the farm at Thorolfsfell with his sons and they loaded fifteen horses with hay, and another five with food. Njal came to Hlidarendi and called Gunnar out. Gunnar greeted them warmly.

Njal said, 'Here is hay and food which I want to give you. I don't want you ever to turn to anyone but me when you're in need.'

'Your gifts are good,' said Gunnar, 'but of greater worth to me is the friendship with you and your sons.'

Njal then went back home. The spring wore on.

48 | Gunnar rode to the Thing that summer. A great number of
men from Sida in the east had been staying at his farm, and he
invited them to stay again when they rode home from the Thing.
They said they would, and they rode off to the Thing. Njal was there
too, with his sons. The Thing was a quiet one.

Now to tell of Hallgerd, back at Hlidarendi: she spoke to the slave
Melkolf and said, 'I've thought of a task for you. You're to go to
Kirkjubaer.'

'What should I do there?' he said.

'You're to steal food from them, enough butter and cheese for two
horses to carry. Then set fire to the storage shed, and they'll all
think it was carelessness, and no one will suspect that anything was
stolen.'

The slave said, 'I've been bad, but I've never been a thief.'

'Listen to you!' she said. 'You make yourself out to be so good,
when you've been not only a thief but a murderer. Don't you dare
refuse this errand, or I'll have you killed.'

He was quite sure that she would do this if he did not go. That
night he took two horses and put pack-saddle pads on them and went
to Kirkjubaer. The dog knew him and did not bark, but instead ran
up to him and fawned on him. He went to the storage shed and
opened it and loaded the two horses with food, and then set fire to
the shed and killed the dog.

He returned along the Ranga river. There his shoe-string broke
and he took his knife and repaired it, but left his knife and belt lying
there. He went all the way to Hlidarendi and then noticed that the
knife was missing, but did not dare go back. He turned the food over
to Hallgerd. She was pleased.

Next morning, when the people at Kirkjubaer came outdoors, they
saw the great damage. A man was sent to the Thing to tell Otkel, for
that was where he was. He took it quite calmly and said that the cause
was that the storage shed was attached to the kitchen, and then
everybody thought that this was what happened.

*

People rode home from the Thing, and many rode to Hlidarendi. Hallgerd brought food to the table, including cheese and butter. Gunnar knew that such food was not to be had and asked Hallgerd where it came from.

'From such a place that you can well enjoy eating it,' she said. 'And besides, it's not for men to busy themselves with preparing food!'

Gunnar got angry and said, 'It's a bad thing if I'm partner to a thief' – and he slapped her on the face.

Hallgerd said she would remember this slap and pay it back if she could. She went out and he went with her, and everything was taken off the table and meat brought in instead, and they all guessed that this was because the meat had come in an honest way.

Then the travellers from the Thing went on their way.

49 | To turn now to Skammkel: he was riding along the Ranga river looking for sheep and saw something shiny on the path and got off his horse and picked it up. It was a knife and belt, and he thought he knew both of them and took them to Kirkjubaer. Otkel was outside and greeted him warmly.

Skammkel said, 'Do you perhaps recognize these things?'

'I certainly do,' said Otkel.

'Whose are they?' said Skammkel.

'The slave Melkolf's,' said Otkel.

'More than the two of us must see them,' said Skammkel – 'I'll give you trustworthy counsel.'

They showed them to many people, and everyone recognized them.

Then Skammkel said, 'What do you intend to do now?'

Otkel answered, 'We must go to Mord Valgardsson and bring it up with him.'

They went to Hof and showed Mord the things and asked if he recognized them. Mord said that he did – 'but what about it? Do you think anything of yours is to be found at Hlidarendi?'

'It's hard for us to deal with this,' said Skammkel, 'when such mighty men are involved.'

'That's true,' said Mord, 'but I know some things about Gunnar's household that neither of you knows.'[1]

'We'll give you money,' they said, 'if you'll take over this matter.'

Mord said, 'That money will be hard-earned, but it may be that I'll look into this.'

They gave him three marks of silver so that he would give them his help. He made this plan: that women should go travelling around with little items to give to housewives, and see what they were given in return – 'because people tend to get rid of stolen property first, if they have any, and that will be the case here if this was somebody's doing. The women must then show me what they were given at each place. And I'll have nothing more to do with the matter once the truth is known.'

They agreed on this, and Skammkel and Otkel went home.

Mord sent women around the district, and they were gone for half a month. Then they came back, with much to carry. Mord asked where they had been given the most. They said they had been given the most at Hlidarendi and that Hallgerd had been very generous with them. He asked what they had been given; they said they had been given cheese. He asked to see it. They showed it to him, and there were many slices; he took them and kept them.

Soon after this he went to see Otkel. He asked him to bring out Thorgerd's cheese mould, and he did so. Mord placed the slices into it and they matched the mould in every detail. They saw, too, that the women had been given a whole cheese.

Mord said, 'Now you see that Hallgerd must have stolen the cheese.'

They brought together all the evidence. Mord declared that he would have nothing more to do with the matter, and with that they parted.

Kolskegg had a talk with Gunnar and said, 'I have bad news: everybody is saying that Hallgerd stole the cheese and caused the great damage at Kirkjubaer.'

Gunnar said that this was probably true – 'but what shall we do about it?'

Kolskegg said, 'You're the one who has to make amends for your wife, and it seems best to me that you go to Otkel and make him a good offer.'

'That's well said,' said Gunnar. 'I'll do that.'

Soon after this Gunnar sent for Thrain Sigfusson and Lambi Sigurdarson, and they came at once. Gunnar told them where he was planning to go. They were pleased with that. They rode off to Kirkjubaer, twelve in all, and called to Otkel to come out.

Skammkel was there with Otkel and said, 'I'll go out with you – it's better to have our brains along. I want to be at your side when you most need help, as you will now. I think the best plan is for you to act with authority.'

They went out then, Otkel and Skammkel and Hallkel and Hallbjorn. They greeted Gunnar; he responded politely. Otkel asked where he was heading.

'No farther than here,' said Gunnar, 'and my purpose is to say, with regard to the great and terrible damage which took place here, that it was the work of my wife and the slave I bought from you.'

'This was to be expected,' said Hallbjorn.

Gunnar said, 'I want to make you a good offer, and I propose that the best men in this district decide on the amount.'

Skammkel said, 'The offer sounds good, but it's unfair: you have many friends among the farmers here, and Otkel does not have many friends.'

'Then I will offer,' said Gunnar, 'to fix the amount myself and announce it right away, and in addition promise you my friendship and pay it all at once: I will pay you double the amount of your loss.'

Skammkel said, 'Don't accept this. It would be naïve to grant him self-judgement when you should be the one to judge.'

Otkel said, 'I will not grant you self-judgement, Gunnar.'

Gunnar spoke: 'I sense here the advice of others, who will have their reward some day. But make the judgement yourself.'

Otkel leaned towards Skammkel and said, 'What shall I say now?'

Skammkel said, 'Say that this is a good offer and refer the matter to Gizur the White and Geir the Godi. Many people will then say that you are like your grandfather Hallkel, who was a great hero.'[2]

Otkel said, 'This is a good offer, Gunnar, but I want you to give me time to see Gizur the White and Geir the Godi.'

Gunnar said, 'Do as you wish. But some men will say that you cannot see where your honour lies if you turn down the choices I have offered.'

Gunnar then rode home.

When he was gone, Hallbjorn spoke: 'Here I see how different men can be: Gunnar made you good offers, and you were not willing to take any of them. What do you think you will gain by carrying on a quarrel with Gunnar, when no one is his equal? But still, he has such integrity that the offers will stand even if you accept them later. I think your best plan is to go and see Gizur the White and Geir the Godi at once.'

Otkel had his horse brought and made everything ready. He was not keen-sighted. Skammkel walked some of the way with Otkel. He said to him, 'I find it strange that your brother didn't want to do this for you. I'll offer to go in your place, because I know that you find it hard to travel.'

'I accept your offer,' said Otkel, 'but you must tell things exactly as they are.'

'I'll do that,' said Skammkel.

Then he took Otkel's horse and travelling-cloak, and Otkel went back home.

Hallbjorn was outside and spoke to Otkel: 'It's bad to have a scoundrel for a best friend, and we will always be sorry that you turned back – it's not a clever move to send the worst of liars on an errand on which, it may be said, men's lives depend.'

'You'd be terrified if Gunnar raised his halberd,' said Otkel, 'since you're this way now.'

'I don't know who would be most terrified then,' said Hallbjorn, 'but some day you will say that Gunnar is not slow to aim his halberd, once he is angry.'

Otkel said, 'All of you are running scared, except Skammkel.'

Both of them were angry.

50 | Skammkel came to Mosfell and reported all the offers to Gizur.
'It seems to me,' said Gizur, 'that these are very good offers.
Why didn't Otkel accept them?'

'His main reason,' said Skammkel, 'was that everybody wanted you
to have the honour, and so he waits for your decision – that will be
best for all.'

Skammkel stayed there overnight. Gizur sent a man to Geir the
Godi, and he came down from Hlid early the next morning. Gizur
told him the story – 'and now what do you think should be done?'

'Just what you must have already decided,' said Geir, 'to settle
things in the way that is best for all.[1] Let's have Skammkel tell the
story once more and see how he reports it this time.'

They did this.

Gizur said, 'You seem to have told the story correctly, and yet I
can see you are a most wicked man. Looks are no mark of character
if you turn out well.'

Skammkel went back, and rode first to Kirkjubaer and called Otkel
outside. Otkel welcomed him warmly. Skammkel gave him greetings
from Gizur and Geir – 'There is no need to talk quietly about this
case: it is the will of both Geir the Godi and Gizur that you make no
settlement in this matter. The advice they gave is to go and serve a
summons on Gunnar for receiving stolen goods, and on Hallgerd for
theft.'

Otkel said, 'Then we'll do exactly as they advise.'

'They thought it especially good,' said Skammkel, 'that you acted
with such authority, and I made you out to be a great man in every
way.'

Otkel told his brothers about this. Hallbjorn said, 'This must be a
huge lie.'

Time passed until the final Summons Days for the Althing.[2] Otkel
called on his brothers and Skammkel to ride along to Hlidarendi to
make the summons. Hallbjorn agreed to go along, but said that as
time went on they would regret this trip.

They rode, twelve in all, to Hlidarendi. When they rode into the hayfield Gunnar was outside, but he did not notice them until they had come all the way up to the house. He did not go inside. Otkel thundered out the summons at once.

When the summons had been served, Skammkel said, 'Was that done correctly, farmer?'

'You know the answer to that,' said Gunnar. 'But one day, Skammkel, I will remind you of this visit and the advice you've been giving.'

'That won't harm us,' said Skammkel, 'as long as your halberd isn't in the air.'

Gunnar was very angry and went inside and told Kolskegg. Kolskegg said, 'It's too bad we weren't all outside – their visit would have ended in full disgrace if we had been.'

'Everything in due course,' said Gunnar. 'This visit will not bring them any honour.'

Shortly after this Gunnar went to Njal and told him. Njal said, 'Don't let this trouble you, for it will bring you much honour before the Thing is over. All of us will be there to support you with advice and force.'

Gunnar thanked him and rode home.

Otkel rode to the Thing together with his brothers and Skammkel.

51 | Gunnar and all the Sigfussons rode to the Thing, as well as Njal and his sons. They all went along with Gunnar, and people were saying that no other group there was as vigorous as theirs.

One day Gunnar went to the booth of the men from Dalir. Hrut and Hoskuld were outside, and they gave Gunnar a warm greeting. Gunnar told them the whole story behind the lawsuit.

'What advice does Njal give?' said Hrut.

Gunnar answered, 'He asked me to come to you and say that he would be of one mind with you in this matter.'

'That must mean,' said Hrut, 'that he wants me, as your relative by marriage, to come up with a plan, and I'll do that. You must challenge

Gizur the White to a duel if they don't grant you self-judgement, and Kolskegg must challenge Geir the Godi. Men will be found to attack Otkel and his gang, and we already have a band of men so large that you'll be able to do as you wish.'

Gunnar went back to his booth and reported this to Njal.

Ulf Aur-Godi found out about these plans and told them to Gizur. Gizur then said to Otkel, 'Who gave you the idea of summoning Gunnar?'

'Skammkel told me that this was what you and Geir the Godi advised,' said Otkel.

'Where is that foul creature who told this lie?' said Gizur.

'He is lying sick in his booth,' said Otkel.

'May he never get up again,' said Gizur. 'And now we must all go to Gunnar and offer him self-judgement, though I don't know whether he'll be willing to accept it now.'

Many people spoke ill of Skammkel, and he lay sick for the rest of the Thing.

Gizur and his companions went to Gunnar's booth. Their coming was noticed and reported to Gunnar inside. He and his men came out and positioned themselves.

Gizur the White was out in front. He spoke: 'Our offer, Gunnar, is that you judge this case yourself.'

'It was not by your advice then that I was summoned,' said Gunnar.

'I didn't advise that,' said Gizur, 'and neither did Geir.'

'Then you will be willing to offer convincing proof of that,' said Gunnar.

'What do you require?' said Gizur.

'That you swear an oath,' said Gunnar.

'I'm willing to do that,' said Gizur, 'if you accept self-judgement.'

'I made that offer some time ago,' said Gunnar, 'but it seems to me there's more to judge now.'[1]

Njal spoke: 'The self-judgement is not to be turned down – the more at stake, the more honour to be earned.'

Gunnar said, 'I will do as my friends wish and judge the case. But I advise Otkel not to provoke me any more.'

Hoskuld and Hrut were sent for, and they came. Gizur swore an oath, and also Geir the Godi, and then Gunnar decided the award and consulted no one about it, and then he announced his terms.

'My terms are,' he said, 'that I should pay the value of the storage shed and the food that was in it. For the slave Melkolf's doings I will pay nothing, because you hid his faults from me, and I return him to you, since ears belong best in the place where they grew. I also find that you summoned me with intent to disgrace, and for that I award myself nothing less than the value of the shed and the contents that were burned. If you now think it better for us to be without a settlement, I still offer you that choice, but in that case I have one more plan, and it will be carried out.'

Gizur said, 'We are willing to have you pay nothing, but we ask that you be Otkel's friend.'

'That shall never be, as long as I live,' said Gunnar, 'but he can have Skammkel's friendship – it's what he's been leaning on for a long time.'

Gizur answered, 'We still want to settle the matter, even though you make all the terms yourself.'

All the terms of the settlement were then agreed on with hand-shakes.

Gunnar said to Otkel, 'It would be best for you to go and live with your kinsmen, but if you remain in this district, don't ever provoke me.'

Gizur said, 'That's sound advice, and he'll follow it.'

Gunnar had much honour from this case. People then rode home from the Thing. Gunnar stayed at home, and for a while everything was quiet.

52 | There was a man named Runolf, the son of Ulf Aur-Godi.[1] He lived at Dal, to the east of the Markarfljot. He stayed with Otkel on his way back from the Althing. Otkel gave him a black ox, nine years old. Runolf thanked him for the gift and invited him to his home, whenever he wished, but Otkel did not take him up on the invitation for some time. Runolf often sent men to him to remind him to come, and Otkel always promised to make the journey.

Otkel had two dun-coloured horses with a black stripe down the back. They were the best riding-horses in the district, and so fond of each other that they always ran together.

A Norwegian named Audolf was staying with Otkel. He was in love with Otkel's daughter Signy. Audolf was a big and strong man.

53 | In the spring Otkel announced that they would ride east to make the visit to Dal, and everyone expressed pleasure at that. Skammkel went along with Otkel, as did Otkel's two brothers, Audolf, and three other men. Otkel rode one of the dun-coloured horses, and the other ran loose at his side. They headed east towards the Markarfljot river, and Otkel galloped in front. Then the two horses got excited and ran away from the road, up towards Fljotshlid. Otkel was going faster than he wanted to.

Gunnar had walked away from his house all alone, with a basket of seed in one hand and his hand-axe in the other. He went to his field to sow grain and put his finely-woven cloak and the axe on the ground and sowed for a while.

To return to Otkel, who was going faster than he wanted to: he had spurs on his feet and came galloping up over the field, and neither he nor Gunnar saw each other. Just as Gunnar stood up straight, Otkel rode at him and his spur struck against Gunnar's ear and made a big gash, and blood flowed at once. Otkel's companions came riding up just then.

'You can all see,' said Gunnar, 'that you, Otkel, have made me shed blood, and this is indecent behaviour: first you summoned me, and now you knock me down and ride over me.'

Skammkel spoke: 'You're taking this well, but you were not at all calmer at the Althing when you were holding your halberd.'

Gunnar spoke: 'The next time we meet you'll see the halberd.'

At this they parted.

Skammkel shouted out, 'Brave riding, fellows!'

Gunnar went home and talked of this to no one, and nobody thought that the wound was a man's doing. One day, however, he told his brother Kolskegg.

Kolskegg said, 'You must report this to more people, so that it cannot be said that you bring charges against the dead[1] – the matter will be disputed if no witnesses know what happened between you and Otkel.'

Gunnar told his neighbours, and not much was said about it at first.

Otkel arrived at Dal over in the east, and they had a good welcome there and stayed for a week. Otkel told Runolf all about what happened between him and Gunnar. One of the men present asked how Gunnar had reacted.

Skammkel spoke: 'If he were just an ordinary man, it would be said that he cried.'

'That was an evil thing to say,' said Runolf, 'and the next time you and Gunnar meet you will have to admit that there is no trace of crying in his nature, and it would be a good thing if better men than you did not have to pay for your maliciousness. For now it seems best that I go along with you when you want to go home, for Gunnar will not harm me.'

'I don't want that,' said Otkel, 'but we'll cross the river further down.'

Runolf gave him good gifts and said that they would not meet again. Otkel asked him not to forget his son if that should prove true.

54 | Now to return to Hlidarendi: Gunnar was outside and saw his shepherd galloping towards the house. The shepherd rode into the hayfield. Gunnar asked, 'Why are you riding so fast?'

'I wanted to prove my loyalty,' he said. 'I saw some men riding down along the Markarfljot, eight of them altogether, and four were wearing coloured clothing.'

Gunnar said, 'It must be Otkel.'

'I have often heard much provocative language from them,' said the shepherd: 'Skammkel said over at Dal that you cried when they rode at you. I tell you this because I hate the things bad men say.'

'Let's not be overcome by their words,' said Gunnar, 'but from now on you must only do the work you want to do.'

'Shall I tell your brother Kolskegg about this?' said the shepherd.

'You go and sleep,' said Gunnar. 'I'll tell Kolskegg.'

The boy went to bed and fell asleep at once.

Gunnar took the shepherd's horse and put his saddle on it. He took his shield, girded himself with the sword he had received from Olvir, put on his helmet, and took his halberd; it rang loudly, and his mother Rannveig heard it.

She came to him and spoke: 'You look angry, my son. I never saw you like this before.'

Gunnar went out and thrust the halberd into the ground to vault into the saddle, and rode away. Rannveig went into the main room. There was a great din of voices there.

'You are talking loudly,' she said, 'but Gunnar's halberd was even louder when he went out.'

Kolskegg heard this and spoke: 'That means no small news.'

'Good,' said Hallgerd. 'Now they can find out whether Gunnar will go away from them crying.'

Kolskegg took his weapons and found himself a horse and rode after Gunnar as fast as he could.

Gunnar rode across Akratunga and then to Geilastofnar, and from there to the Ranga river and down to the ford at Hof. There were some women out at the milking-pen. Gunnar leaped from his horse and tied it.

Then Otkel and his party came riding up. There were slabs of hard clay on the paths to the ford.

Gunnar said to them, 'Now you must defend yourselves – my halberd is here. You'll find out now if I'll do any crying for you.'

They all leaped from their horses and charged at Gunnar. Hallbjorn was in the lead.

'Don't you attack me,' said Gunnar. 'You're the last one I would want to harm, but I won't spare anyone if I have to defend myself.'

'It cannot be helped,' said Hallbjorn. 'You're planning to kill my brother, and I would be shamed if I just stood by' – and with both hands he thrust a great spear at Gunnar.

Gunnar brought his shield to meet the spear, and Hallbjorn's thrust went through it. Gunnar brought the shield down so hard that it stuck in the ground, and then he grabbed his sword so swiftly that no eye could follow and swung it and hit Hallbjorn on the arm, above the wrist, and cut it off.

Skammkel ran up behind Gunnar and swung a great axe at him. Gunnar turned quickly to face him and struck the underside of the blade with his halberd, and the axe flew out of his hand and out into the Ranga river. Gunnar thrust with the halberd a second time, right through Skammkel, and lifted him up and threw him head first on the clay path.

Audolf seized his spear and threw it at Gunnar. Gunnar caught it in the air and threw it back and it went through both the shield and the Norwegian and into the ground.

Otkel swung his sword at Gunnar and tried to hit the leg below the knee. Gunnar leaped into the air, and Otkel missed him. Gunnar then thrust right through him with his halberd.

Kolskegg arrived then and rushed straight at Hallkel and dealt him a death blow with his short sword. Together they killed eight men.

A woman who saw this ran to the house and told Mord, and asked him to separate them.

'It's just men who, for all I care,' he said, 'can kill each other.'

'You don't mean that,' she said. 'Your kinsman Gunnar and your friend Otkel are there.'

'You're always babbling away, you foul wretch,' he said, and lay inside while they were fighting.

Gunnar and Kolskegg rode home after these deeds and rode swiftly along the river bank, and Gunnar sprang from his horse and landed on his feet.

Kolskegg said, 'Brave riding, brother!'

Gunnar said, 'Skammkel mocked me with those words when I said "You've ridden over me."'

'You've had your vengeance for that,' said Kolskegg.

'What I don't know,' said Gunnar, 'is whether I am less manly than other men because killing troubles me more than it does them.'

55 | The news spread far and wide, and many people said that it
had not happened any sooner than was likely. Gunnar rode to
Bergthorshvol and told Njal of these deeds.

Njal spoke: 'It's a big thing you've done, but you've been greatly
provoked.'

'What will come next?' said Gunnar.

'Do you want me to tell you of something which has not yet
happened?' said Njal. 'You will ride to the Thing and follow my
advice and earn great honour from this matter. This will be the
beginning of your career of killings.'

'Give me your sound advice,' said Gunnar.

'I will,' said Njal. 'Never kill more than once within the same
bloodline, and never break any settlement which good men make
between you and others, least of all if you have broken my first
warning.'

'I would have expected other men to do these things sooner than
me,' said Gunnar.

'That's so,' said Njal. 'And yet you must bear in mind that if these
two things happen, you will not have long to live – but otherwise you
will live to be an old man.'

Gunnar said, 'Do you know what will be the cause of your death?'

'I do,' said Njal.

'What?' said Gunnar.

'Something that people would least expect,' said Njal.

Then Gunnar rode home.

A messenger was sent to Gizur the White and Geir the Godi, since
it was up to them to bring a suit following the slaying of Otkel. They
met to talk about what to do. They agreed that the case should be
prosecuted by law. Then it was a question of who would undertake
this, and neither of them was willing.

'It seems to me,' said Gizur, 'that there are two possibilities: one of
us must bring the suit – and we decide this by lot – or else Otkel will
lie without compensation. We can expect that it will be hard to bring
this suit – Gunnar is well off for kinsmen and for friends. Whichever

of us does not draw the lot must ride along in support and not back out until the case has been concluded.'

Then they drew lots, and it was Geir the Godi who had to bring the suit.

Shortly after this they rode east over the rivers and came to where the encounter had taken place on the Ranga river. They dug up the bodies and named witnesses to the fatal wounds. Then they gave notice of their findings and summoned a panel of nine neighbours.

They were told that Gunnar was at home with thirty men. Geir the Godi asked Gizur whether he was willing to ride over there with a hundred men.

'I don't want to do that,' he said, 'even with such a great difference in numbers.'

They then rode back home. News of the starting of this suit spread to all districts of Iceland, and the talk was that this would be a stormy Thing.

56 | There was a man named Skafti, the son of Thorodd. Thorodd's mother was Thorvor; she was the daughter of Thormod Skafti, the son of Oleif the Broad, the son of Olvir Child-sparer. Skafti and his father were great chieftains and very expert in the law. Thorodd was considered devious and cunning. They both supported Gizur the White in all matters.[1]

The men from Fljotshlid and the men from the Ranga district assembled in great numbers for the Thing. Gunnar was so well liked that they all agreed to stand by him. They arrived at the Thing and put the coverings over their booths.

In alliance with Gizur the White were these chieftains: Skafti and Thorodd, Asgrim Ellida-Grimsson, Odd from Kidjaberg, and Halldor Ornolfsson.

One day men went to the Law Rock. Geir the Godi stood up and gave notice of a suit for homicide against Gunnar for the slaying of Otkel. He gave notice of a second suit for homicide against Gunnar for the slaying of Hallbjorn the White, then another for the slaying of Audolf and another for the slaying of Skammkel. Then he gave notice of a suit for homicide against Kolskegg for the slaying of Hallkel. When he had finished announcing all the suits, people said that he had spoken well. He asked about the district and the domicile of the defendants. Everybody then left the Law Rock.

The Thing went on until the day that the courts were to convene to hear the prosecution. Both sides gathered in large numbers. Geir the Godi and Gizur the White stood to the south of the Ranga court, Gunnar and Njal to the north. Geir the Godi requested that Gunnar listen to his oath, and then he swore it. After that he presented the charges. Then he produced witnesses that notice of the suit had been given; then he had the neighbours take their seats on the panel; then he invited his opponents to challenge the legitimacy of the panel; and then he asked the panel to announce its findings.

The neighbours who had been named went before the court and named witnesses and barred themselves from reaching a decision about Audolf, since the man who should prosecute was in Norway and it was not for them to deal with the case. After that they gave their decision in the case of Otkel and declared that Gunnar was truly guilty of the charge. After that Geir the Godi invited Gunnar to defend himself and named witnesses for each of the steps taken in the prosecution.

Gunnar in his turn requested that Geir the Godi listen to his oath and to the defence which he would present in the case. Then he swore his oath. He spoke: 'The defence which I present in this case is that I named witnesses and in the presence of neighbours declared Otkel an outlaw on account of the bloody wound which he inflicted on me with his spur. I forbid you by law, Geir the Godi, to prosecute this case, and the judges to judge it, and I hereby declare the initiation of your suit invalid. I forbid you according to a lawful, incontestable, absolute and binding right of prohibition, as I am entitled by the rules of the Althing and common law. I also want to tell you of another procedure I have in mind.'

'Are you,' said Geir, 'going to challenge me to a duel, as is your custom, and disregard the laws?'

'Not that,' said Gunnar, 'but I will charge you at the Law Rock for calling a panel to sit on the case of Audolf, when it was not for them to deal with that case, and for this I hold you deserving of outlawry for three years.'

Njal spoke: 'You can't go on like this, for it will only lead to a hard-fought dispute. There are strong arguments, it seems to me, on both sides of the case. There are some slayings, Gunnar, for which you cannot ward off being found guilty.[2] At the same time you have brought a suit against Geir by which he will be found guilty. And you, Geir the Godi, must understand that there is a charge of full outlawry against you which has not yet been brought, and it will be brought if you don't do as I say.'[3]

Thorodd the Godi spoke: 'It seems to Skafti and me that the peaceful thing to do is make a settlement between yourselves. But why do you have so little to say, Gizur the White?'

'It seems to me,' said Gizur, 'that some mighty obstacles block our suit, for it's clear that Gunnar's friends are standing by him, and the best thing for our side would be for good men to arbitrate a settlement – if Gunnar so wills.'

'I have always been glad to settle peacefully,' said Gunnar. 'You have much to seek redress for, but I still think I have been pushed hard.'

By the advice of the wisest men it was concluded that the case should be settled by arbitration; six men were to arbitrate the case. It was to be done at once, at the Thing.

The decision was that Skammkel should lie without compensation, that the amounts for Otkel's death and for the spur-wound were to cancel each other out and that the other slayings were to be paid for according to each man's worth. Gunnar's kinsmen contributed enough money so that all the slayings were paid for at once, at the Thing. Geir the Godi and Gizur the White then made pledges of peace to Gunnar.

Gunnar rode home from the Thing. He thanked men for their support and gave gifts to many and earned much honour from all this. Then he remained honourably at home.

57 | There was a man named Starkad. He was the son of Bork
Black-tooth-beard, the son of Thorkel Bound-leg, who settled
the area around the mountain Thrihyrning. Starkad was a married
man, and his wife's name was Hallbera. She was the daughter of
Hroald the Red and of Hildigunn, the daughter of Thorstein Sparrow.
Hildigunn's mother was Unn, the daughter of Eyvind Karfi and
the sister of Modolf the Wise, from whom the Modylfing clan are
descended. The sons of Starkad and Hallbera were Thorgeir, Bork
and Thorkel. Their sister was Hildigunn the Healer. The brothers
were very prone to violence, mean-spirited and overbearing; they
had no respect for the rights of others.

58 | There was a man named Egil. He was the son of Kol, the son
of Ottar Boll, who settled the area between Stotalaek and
Reydarvatn. Egil's brother was Onund of Trollaskog, the father of
Halli the Strong, who was at the slaying of Holta-Thorir together
with the sons of Ketil the Smooth-talker. Egil lived at Sandgil. His
sons were Kol and Ottar and Hauk. Their mother was Steinvor,
Starkad's sister. Egil's sons were big and aggressive men and the worst
trouble-makers. They always took sides with the sons of Starkad.
Their sister was Gudrun Night-sun, a very well-mannered woman.

Egil had taken in two Norwegians, one named Thorir and the
other Thorgrim. They were on their first trip out to Iceland and were
well liked and wealthy. They were good fighters and brave in every
way.

Starkad had a good stallion, reddish in colour, and he and his sons
thought that no other horse could match it in a fight. One day it
happened that the brothers from Sandgil were over near Thrihyrning.
They had a great chat about all the farmers in Fljotshlid and eventually discussed whether any of them would fight his horse against
theirs. Some men, to praise and flatter them, said that no one dared
to fight his horse against theirs, and in fact that no one even owned
such a horse.

Then Hildigunn answered, 'I know a man who would dare to fight his horse against yours.'

'Name him!' they said.

She said, 'Gunnar of Hlidarendi has a brown stallion and he will dare to fight it against your horse or anybody else's.'

'You women always think that no one is a match for Gunnar,' said the men, 'but just because Geir the Godi and Gizur the White came off so poorly against him, it doesn't mean that we will too.'

'It will be much worse for you,' she said, and they got into a great quarrel over this.

Starkad said, 'Gunnar is the last man I'd want you to go after, because it will be hard for you to counter his good luck.'

'But you will let us challenge him to a horse-fight,' they said.

'I will,' he said, 'as long as you don't play any tricks on him.'

They said they would not.

Then they rode to Hlidarendi. Gunnar was at home and came outside. Kolskegg came out too, along with their brother Hjort, and they greeted them warmly and asked where they were headed.

'No farther than here,' they said. 'We've been told that you have a good stallion, and we'd like to offer you a horse-fight.'

Gunnar answered, 'There can't be many stories told about my stallion; he's young and totally untested.'

'But you will give him a chance to fight, won't you?' they said. 'Hildigunn mentioned that you were quite proud of your horse.'

'How did you happen to be speaking about that?' said Gunnar.

'There were men,' they said, 'who were saying that no one would dare fight his horse against ours.'

'I would dare,' said Gunnar, 'but that seems to me a mean-spirited thing to say.'

'Can we count on the fight, then?' they said.

'You'll think your trip was worth making,' said Gunnar, 'if you have your way, but I want to request this – that we fight our horses to provide pleasure for others and not trouble for ourselves, and that you don't try to shame me. If you do to me as you do to others, my only course will be to turn against you in a way that you'll find hard to take. I'll do the same to you as you do to me.'

They rode back home, and Starkad asked them how it had gone. They said that Gunnar had made their trip a good one – 'he promised to let his horse fight, and we decided when the fight was to take place. But it was clear from everything that he felt inferior to us and that he was trying to get out of it.'

'It's often the case with Gunnar,' said Hildigunn, 'that he's slow to be drawn into quarrels but hard to tame if he can't get out of them.'

Gunnar rode over to see Njal and told him about the horse-fight and the words that had passed between them – 'and how do you think the horse-fight will turn out?'

'You will have the upper hand,' said Njal, 'but the death of many men will come from it.'

'Will my death perhaps come from this?' said Gunnar.

'Not from this,' said Njal, 'but they will remember their old hostility with you and add a new one, and you will have no choice but to fight back.'

Then Gunnar rode home.

59 | There Gunnar learned of the death of his father-in-law Hoskuld. A few days later Thorgerd at Grjota, the wife of Thrain, gave birth to a boy. She sent a man to her mother and asked her to choose whether the boy should be named Glum or Hoskuld. Hallgerd asked that he be named Hoskuld, and that was the name given to the boy.[1]

Gunnar and Hallgerd had two sons. One was called Hogni and the other Grani. Hogni was an able man, quiet, not easily persuaded and truthful.

Men rode to the horse-fight and came in great numbers: Gunnar was there, and his brothers and the Sigfussons and Njal and his sons. Starkad and his sons and Egil and his sons also came. They told Gunnar that they should bring on the horses. Gunnar said that they should.

Skarphedin said, 'Do you want me to prod your horse, Gunnar my friend?'

'No, I don't,' said Gunnar.

'But it would be better if I did,' said Skarphedin. 'I'm the violent sort, like them.'

'You wouldn't have to say or do much,' said Gunnar, 'before trouble arose, but this way it will come more slowly, even though it turns out the same.'

The horses were then brought on. Gunnar prepared for the prodding, and Skarphedin brought up his horse. Gunnar was wearing a red tunic and a wide silver belt; he was holding a stick in his hand. The horses went to it and bit at each other for a long time so that there was no need to touch them, and it was great sport.

Then Thorgeir and Kol made a plan that the next time the horses went at each other they would give their horse a push and see if this would knock Gunnar down. The horses went to it, and Thorgeir and Kol shoved their horse from behind. Gunnar pushed back with his, and in no time at all Thorgeir and Kol were flat on the ground, with their horse on top of them. They sprang up and rushed at Gunnar. Gunnar jumped to the side and grabbed Kol and threw him on the ground so hard that he lay senseless. Thorgeir Starkadarson struck such a blow at Gunnar's horse that its eye fell out. Gunnar hit Thorgeir with his stick. He too fell senseless.

Gunnar went over to his horse and said to Kolskegg, 'Kill this horse – he must not live maimed.'

Kolskegg killed the horse.

Then Thorgeir got to his feet and took his weapons and wanted to rush at Gunnar, but a great crowd came up and he was stopped.

Skarphedin spoke: 'I'm getting tired of this jostling – it's much more manly when men fight with weapons.'

Gunnar stood so calmly that one man was enough to hold him, and he said nothing that was improper. Njal tried to make a settlement or a truce, but Thorgeir said he would neither give nor receive any pledges of peace and that he would prefer to see Gunnar dead because of the blow he struck.

Kolskegg spoke: 'Gunnar has always stood too firm to be felled by mere words, and so it is now.'

Men rode away from the horse-fight then, each to his home.

Nobody made an attack on Gunnar, and things stayed this way during the winter.

At the Thing the following summer Gunnar met his brother-in-law Olaf Peacock,[2] and Olaf invited him home, but warned him to be on his guard – 'because they will do us whatever harm they can, so always travel in large numbers.'

Olaf gave him much sound advice, and they declared great friendship for each other.

60 | Asgrim Ellida-Grimsson had a case to prosecute at the Althing; it was an inheritance case. The defendant was Ulf Uggason. Asgrim was doing well until – and this was unusual – there was a flaw in his case: the flaw was that he had named five neighbours to the panel when he should have named nine, and the other side made this their defence.

Gunnar spoke: 'I challenge you to a duel, Ulf Uggason, if people can not get their rights from you. Njal and my friend Helgi[1] would expect me to take part in your defence, Asgrim, if they could not be here themselves.'

'This is not a quarrel between you and me,' said Ulf.

'It comes to the same thing,' said Gunnar.

The outcome was that Ulf had to pay over the full amount.

Asgrim then said to Gunnar, 'I invite you to my home this summer, and I shall always take your side in lawsuits, and never be against you.'

Gunnar rode home from the Thing.

Shortly after, he met with Njal. Njal asked him to be on his guard and said that he had been told that the men up at Thrihyrning were planning to attack him and he asked Gunnar never to travel in small numbers and always to have his weapons handy. Gunnar said he would do so. He said that Asgrim had invited him for a visit – 'and I plan to go there in the autumn.'

'Let no one know beforehand that you're going,' said Njal, 'or how long you will be away. In any case, I'll have my sons ride with you, and then you won't be attacked.'

They came to an understanding on this.

The summer went on until it was eight weeks before winter. Gunnar said to Kolskegg, 'Get ready for a trip – we're going to ride to Tunga for a visit.'

'Shouldn't you send word to Njal's sons?' said Kolskegg.

'No,' said Gunnar. 'They must not get into trouble because of me.'

61 | The three of them, Gunnar, Kolskegg and Hjort, rode together. Gunnar had his halberd and the sword that Olvir had given him, and Kolskegg had his short sword. Hjort was also fully armed. They rode to Tunga. Asgrim welcomed them, and they stayed there for some time. After that they made it known that they planned to go home. Asgrim gave them good gifts and offered to ride east with them. Gunnar said that this was not needed, and so Asgrim did not go along.

There was a man named Sigurd Swine-head. His home was at Thjorsa, and he had promised to spy on Gunnar's movements. Now he came to Thrihyrning and told them about Gunnar's return and said that there would be no better time than this, since Gunnar was with only two others.

'How many will we need for an ambush?' said Starkad.

'Ordinary men will be weak facing him,' he said. 'It's not wise to have fewer than thirty men.'

Starkad said, 'Where shall we ambush him?'

'At Knafaholar,' said Sigurd. 'There he won't see us until he arrives.'

'Go to Sandgil,' said Starkad, 'and tell Egil to get fifteen men ready from there, and we'll head for Knafaholar with another fifteen.'

Thorgeir spoke to Hildigunn: 'Tonight this hand will bring you evidence of Gunnar's death.'

'My guess,' she said, 'is that you will be carrying both head and hand low when you come from this encounter.'

Starkad and his three sons left Thrihyrning along with eleven others. They went to Knafaholar and waited there.

Sigurd came to Sandgil and said, 'I've been sent here by Starkad and his sons to say that you, Egil, and your sons should go to Knafaholar to lie in wait for Gunnar.'

'How many of us should go?' asked Egil.

'Fifteen, counting me,' he said.

Kol spoke: 'Today I'll try myself against Kolskegg.'

'I would say you're taking on a lot,' said Sigurd.

Egil asked his Norwegian guests to come along. They said they had no quarrel with Gunnar – 'and you must need a lot of help,' said Thorir, 'if it takes such a horde to attack three men.'

Egil left them in anger. His wife said to Thorir, 'My daughter Gudrun was wrong to put aside her pride and sleep with you, if you don't dare to go along with your father-in-law. You're just a coward.'

'I'll go with your husband,' he said, 'but neither of us will come back.'

He went to his companion Thorgrim and said, 'Take the keys to my chests since I won't be unlocking them any more. I want you to take as much of our property as you wish and leave Iceland, and don't think of avenging me. If you don't leave, it will be your death.'

Thorir gathered his weapons and took his place in their band.

62 | Now to return to Gunnar: he rode east across the Thjorsa river, and when he was only a short way beyond the river he became very sleepy. He asked his companions to stop, and they did so. He fell into a deep sleep but slept restlessly.

Kolskegg said, 'Gunnar is having a dream.'

Hjort said, 'I'd like to wake him.'

'Don't do that,' said Kolskegg. 'Let him finish his dream.'

Gunnar lay there for a long time and then threw off his cloak, and he was very warm.

Kolskegg said, 'What were you dreaming, brother?'

'I dreamed something,' said Gunnar, 'that would have kept me from leaving Tunga with so few men, if I had dreamed it there.'

Kolskegg said, 'Tell us the dream.'

'I dreamed,' said Gunnar, 'that I was riding past Knafaholar. There I saw many wolves, and they attacked me, but I got away and down to the Ranga river. There they attacked again, from all sides, and we defended ourselves. I shot all those who were in front, until they came too close for me to use my bow. So I drew my sword and swung it with one hand, and with the other hand I thrust with my halberd. I didn't shield myself, and I didn't know what was shielding me. I killed many wolves, and you were by my side, Kolskegg, but they trampled Hjort down and tore open his chest, and one wolf had his heart in his mouth. I was so angry that I sliced the wolf in two, just behind the shoulder, and after that the wolves fled. Now, brother Hjort, it's my advice that you ride back west to Tunga.'

'That I won't do,' said Hjort. 'Though I know my death to be certain, I will stay with you.'

They rode on east and came to Knafaholar. Kolskegg said, 'Do you see all those spears coming up behind the hills, Gunnar, and men with weapons?'

'It's no surprise to me,' said Gunnar, 'that my dream is coming true.'

'What are we to do now?' asked Kolskegg. 'I guess you don't want to run away from them.'

'They won't be able to taunt us with that,' said Gunnar. 'Let's ride down to that point of land by the Ranga river. That's a place to defend ourselves.'

They rode down to the point and prepared to fight. When they rode past, Kol said, 'Are you going to run away, Gunnar?'

Kolskegg answered, 'Ask that when this day is done.'

63 | Starkad then urged his men on; they headed toward those who were on the point of land. Sigurd Swine-head was out in front and was holding a small round shield, and a hunting-spear in the other hand. Gunnar saw him and shot at him with his bow. Sigurd

raised his shield when he saw the arrow flying high, but it went through the shield and into his eye and out at the back of his neck. That was the first slaying.

Gunnar shot another arrow at Ulfhedin, Starkad's overseer, and it struck him in the waist and he fell at the feet of a farmer, and the farmer tripped over him. Kolskegg threw a stone and it hit the head of the farmer, and that was his death.

Then Starkad said, 'We won't get anywhere as long as Gunnar has the use of his bow, so let's make a good and swift charge.'

They all urged each other on. Gunnar defended himself with bow and arrows as long as he could; then he threw them down, took his halberd and sword and fought with both hands. The battle was fierce for a long time. Gunnar and Kolskegg killed many men.

Then Thorgeir Starkadarson said, 'I vowed to bring Hildigunn your head, Gunnar.'

'She can't have set much store by that,' said Gunnar, 'but still, you'll have to come closer.'

Thorgeir said to his brothers, 'Let's all charge him together – he has no shield, and we'll have his life in our hands.'

Bork and Thorkel ran forward and were quicker than Thorgeir. Bork took a swing at Gunnar. Gunnar struck back so hard with his halberd that the sword flew out of Bork's hand. Then he saw Thorkel on his other side, within striking distance. Gunnar had pulled back a little; he made a sweep with his sword and hit Thorkel on the neck, and the head flew off.

Kol Egilsson said, 'Let me have a go at Kolskegg. I've been saying for a long time that we two would be a fair match.'

'Now's our chance to find out,' said Kolskegg.

Kol thrust his spear at him. Kolskegg had just slain a man and had his hands full and so could not get his shield up, and the spear hit him on the outside of the thigh and went through it. Kolskegg moved quickly and stepped towards him and struck him on the thigh with his short sword and cut off his leg and spoke: 'Did that hit you or not?'

'This is what I get,' said Kol, 'for not shielding myself' – and he stood for a while on his other leg and looked at the stump.

Kolskegg spoke: 'You don't need to look: it's just as you think, the leg is gone.'

Then Kol fell down dead. When Egil saw that he rushed at Gunnar and swung at him. Gunnar lunged with his halberd and it went into his waist. He lifted him up on the halberd and flung him out into the Ranga.

Then Starkad said, 'You're quite useless, Thorir the Norwegian, if you don't take part. Egil, your host and father-in-law, has been slain.'

Thorir sprang to his feet and was very angry. Hjort had caused the death of two men. The Norwegian charged at him and hacked at his chest. Hjort fell down dead at once.

Gunnar saw this and threw himself at the Norwegian with a hacking blow and cut him in two at the waist. Shortly after that he lunged at Bork with his halberd; it went into his waist and through him and into the ground. Kolskegg then cut off the head of Hauk Egilsson, and Gunnar cut off the arm of Ottar Egilsson at the elbow.

Then Starkad said, 'Let's flee – these aren't men we're dealing with.'

Gunnar spoke: 'Telling stories about this won't be easy unless there's something on you to show that you've been in battle.'

Then he charged at Starkad and his son Thorgeir and gave them both bloody wounds. After that they parted, and Gunnar and his brothers had wounded many of those who got away.

In this battle fourteen men died, and Hjort was the fifteenth.

Gunnar rode home with Hjort laid out on his shield, and he was buried in a mound there. Many people mourned his loss, for he had been well liked.

Starkad and Thorgeir came home, and Hildigunn treated their wounds and said, 'You would give a great deal now not to have got on Gunnar's bad side.'

'We certainly would,' said Starkad.

64 | Steinvor[1] at Sandgil asked Thorgrim the Norwegian to take care of her property and not leave Iceland, but rather to stay and remember the death of his comrade and kinsman.

He answered, 'My comrade Thorir predicted that I would die at the hands of Gunnar if I stayed here, and he must have foreseen that, just as he foresaw his own death.'

She said, 'I will give you my daughter Gudrun and all the property.'

'I didn't know that you would pay that much,' he said.

They made an agreement that he would marry Gudrun, and the wedding took place that summer.

Gunnar rode to Bergthorshvol, and Kolskegg went with him. Njal was outside with his sons, and they went forward to receive them and welcomed them warmly. Then they went apart for a talk.

Gunnar said, 'I have come to ask for your support and sound advice.'

Njal said it was his due.

'I have fallen into deep trouble and killed many men,' said Gunnar, 'and I want to know what you think I should do.'

'Many would say,' said Njal, 'that you have been pushed hard. Now give me time to come up with a plan.'

Njal walked off alone and thought the matter over and then came back and said, 'I've thought of something, but I expect it will take boldness and daring. Thorgeir has made my kinswoman Thorfinna pregnant, and I'll turn over to you the lawsuit for seduction, and I'll also let you take over a second full outlawry case, against Starkad for cutting trees in my woods on Thrihyrning ridge, and you will prosecute both these cases. Go to the place where you fought and dig up the bodies and name witnesses to the fatal wounds and then declare all the dead men outlaws because they attacked you with the intent to give you and your brothers wounds and a swift death. If this is tried at the Thing and it is objected that you had previously struck Thorgeir and are thus barred from prosecuting your own suit or those of others, I will answer and say that at the Thingskalar Assembly I restored your right to prosecute both your own case and those of others, and that will quash the objection. You must also go and see Tyrfing at Berjanes, and he will turn over to you a suit against Onund at Trollaskog, who is the one to take action for the slaying of his brother Egil.'

Gunnar then rode home.

A few days later he and the sons of Njal rode to where the bodies were and dug up all those that had been buried. Gunnar demanded a sentence of outlawry against them on charges of assault and conspiracy to kill and then rode home.

65 | That same autumn Valgard the Grey came from abroad to his home at Hof. Thorgeir Starkadarson went to visit him and Mord and told them how preposterous it was for Gunnar to declare that all the men he had killed were outlaws. Valgard said it must have been at Njal's advice and that this would not be the end of the advice Njal had given him. Thorgeir asked Valgard and Mord for help and backing, but they held out for a long time and asked for a high sum. Finally they agreed on a plan: Mord was to ask for the hand of Thorkatla, the daughter of Gizur the White, and Thorgeir was to ride west over the rivers with Valgard and Mord at once.

The next day they rode off, twelve in all, and came to Mosfell. They were given a warm reception, and stayed there overnight. Then they brought up the marriage offer with Gizur; the outcome was that they made an agreement and that the wedding would take place at Mosfell two weeks later. Then they rode home.

Later they rode to the wedding. Many guests from the neighbourhood had already arrived, and the feast went well. Afterwards, Thorkatla went home with Mord and took over the household, and Valgard went abroad that summer.

Mord urged Thorgeir to start a lawsuit against Gunnar. Thorgeir went to see Onund and asked him to start a suit for the slaying of his brother Egil and Egil's sons — 'and I will start a suit for the slaying of my brothers and for the bloody wounds to myself and my father.'

Onund said he was ready to do this. They went and announced

the slayings and summoned to the scene of the fight a panel of nine men who were neighbours.

News of the starting of the lawsuit reached Hlidarendi. Gunnar rode to see Njal and told him and asked what he thought should be done.

'You must now,' said Njal, 'summon your own neighbours to the scene of the fight and name witnesses and choose Kol as the slayer of your brother Hjort, for this is lawful.[1] Then you must give notice of a suit for homicide against Kol, even though he's dead. Then you must name witnesses and summon neighbours to ride to the Althing to testify whether Kol and his companions were on the spot and in the attack when Hjort was slain. You must also summon Thorgeir for seduction, and likewise Onund of Trollaskog in the case which Tyrfing will turn over to you.'

Gunnar went ahead with all the matters in which he had been advised by Njal. People thought this an odd way to start proceedings. These cases came to the Thing.

Gunnar rode to the Thing, as did Njal and his sons and the Sigfussons. Gunnar had also sent a man to his brothers-in-law[2] to tell them to ride to the Thing with a large number of men, for this was going to be a hard-fought case. A large force gathered from the west.

Mord Valgardsson rode to the Thing, and also Runolf of Dal, the men from Thrihyrning, and Onund of Trollaskog.

66 | When they came to the Thing they joined company with Gizur the White and Geir the Godi. Gunnar and the Sigfussons and the Njalssons all went in one group and moved along so briskly that people had to get out of their way to keep from being knocked down. And nothing was talked about all over the Thing as much as this great lawsuit.

Gunnar went to meet his brothers-in-law, and they greeted him warmly. They asked him about the battle, and he told them about it in detail and with fairness and then told them what he had done since then.

Olaf said, 'It's worth a lot to have Njal standing by you with good advice.'

Gunnar said he would never be able to pay that back and asked them for their help and backing, and they said it was his due.

The suits from both sides then came before the court, and each side presented its case. Mord asked how it was that a man like Gunnar, who should be outlawed for what he did to Thorgeir, could be bringing a suit.

Njal answered, 'Were you at the Thingskalar Assembly last autumn?'

'Certainly I was,' said Mord.

'Did you hear,' said Njal, 'that Gunnar made them an offer of full compensation?'

'Certainly I heard it,' said Mord.

'At that time,' said Njal, 'I restored Gunnar's rights to carry on all legal matters.'

'That's lawful,' said Mord, 'but what reason was there for Gunnar to charge Kol with the slaying of Hjort, when the Norwegian killed him?'

'That was lawful too, since he chose him as the slayer before witnesses,' said Njal.

'I suppose that's correct,' said Mord, 'but by what right did Gunnar proclaim them all outlaws?'

'You don't have to ask that,' said Njal, 'since they set out to give bloody wounds and cause death.'

'But this did not happen to Gunnar,' said Mord.

'Gunnar had two brothers, Kolskegg and Hjort,' said Njal. 'One of them was killed and the other wounded.'

'What you say is according to the law,' said Mord, 'but it's hard to accept.'

Then Hjalti Skeggjason of Thjorsardal[1] came forward and spoke: 'I have taken no part in these lawsuits of yours, but now I want to ask you, Gunnar, how much you will do at my request and for my friendship.'

'What do you ask?' said Gunnar.

'This,' he said: 'that you submit the whole matter to arbitration and let good men reach a settlement.'

Gunnar said, 'Only if you promise never to be against me, no matter who I'm dealing with.'

'I promise you that,' said Hjalti. Then he talked things over with Gunnar's opponents and brought it about that everyone agreed to make peace, and then each side gave pledges to the other. Thorgeir's bloody wound was offset by the seduction charge against him, and Starkad's wound was offset by the wood which he had cut illegally. Thorgeir's brothers were to get half compensation, with the other half cancelled because of their attack on Gunnar. Tyrfing's suit and the slaying of Egil of Sandgil offset each other, and the slaying of Hjort was offset by the slaying of Kol and of the Norwegian. All the others were to be given half compensation.

Njal took part in this settlement, along with Asgrim Ellida-Grimsson and Hjalti Skeggjason.

Njal had a large amount of money on loan to Starkad and to the people at Sandgil, and he turned all of this over to Gunnar to pay these fines. Gunnar had so many friends at the Thing that he paid up at once for all the slayings and gave gifts to the chieftains who had helped him, and he earned great honour from all this and everyone agreed that he had no equal in the South Quarter.

Gunnar rode home from the Thing and stayed there in peace, but his enemies were very envious of the honour he had earned.

67 | To return now to Thorgeir Otkelsson: he grew up to be a worthy man, big and strong, honest and straightforward, but somewhat pliable. He was well liked by the best people and loved by his kinsmen.

One day Thorgeir Starkadarson went to see his kinsman Mord. 'I am ill-pleased,' he said, 'with the outcome of the lawsuit we had with Gunnar. I paid you to help us as long as we both lived, and now I want you to come up with a good plan, so think hard on it. I speak plainly because I know that you are Gunnar's greatest enemy, just as he is yours. I will add greatly to your honour if you manage this well.'

'It has always turned out that I am greedy for money,' said Mord, 'and it's still so. It will be difficult to manage things so that you don't become a truce-violator or peace-breaker, and yet get what you're after. I've been told, however, that Kolskegg is going to bring a suit to regain one-fourth of the farm at Moeidarhvol, which was paid to your father in compensation for his son. He has taken over this case from his mother, and it is Gunnar's plan to pay cash and not let the land go. Let's wait until this has been done, and then charge Gunnar with breaking the settlement with you. He has also taken a grainfield from Thorgeir Otkelsson and thus broken the settlement with him. You must go to see Thorgeir Otkelsson and bring him into this, and then attack Gunnar. If something goes wrong and you fail to get Gunnar, attack him again and again.

'I can tell you something else: Njal made a prophecy to Gunnar about the course of his life and told him that if he killed more than once within the same bloodline, his death would follow swiftly – if it also happened that he broke a settlement made for that killing. This is the reason you must get Thorgeir involved, since Gunnar has already killed his father, and if the two of you are together in a fight, you must protect yourself and let him go ahead, and Gunnar will slay him. Then he will have killed twice within the same bloodline, and you must flee the fight. If this is to lead to his death, he will break the settlement made for this slaying. Until then there's nothing to be done.'

After this Thorgeir went home and told his father this in private. They agreed between themselves that they should go ahead with the plan secretly.

68 | Soon after this Thorgeir Starkadarson from Kirkjubaer went to call on the other Thorgeir and they went aside for a talk and spent the whole day talking quietly. When they finished, Thorgeir Starkadarson gave Thorgeir Otkelsson a spear inlaid with gold and then rode home. They had made a very friendly alliance.

At the Thingskalar Assembly that autumn Kolskegg laid claim to the land at Moeidarhvol and Gunnar named witnesses and offered to pay to the people at Thrihyrning either money or another piece of land, at a legally determined value. Thorgeir then named witnesses to the charge that Gunnar had broken the settlement with them. After that the Assembly was over.

A year passed. The two Thorgeirs met often, and there was great warmth between them.

Kolskegg spoke to Gunnar: 'I've been told that Thorgeir Otkelsson and Thorgeir Starkadarson have become great friends, and many people are saying that they are not to be trusted, and I'd like you to be on your guard.'

'Death will come to me no matter where I am,' said Gunnar, 'if that is my fate.'

With this they stopped talking.

In the autumn Gunnar gave orders that his people should work one week at home at Hlidarendi and the next week down at Eyjar and finish the haymaking this way. He also said that everybody should leave the farm except himself and the women.

Thorgeir at Thrihyrning went to see the other Thorgeir, and as soon as they met the two of them started talking, as they usually did. Thorgeir Starkadarson said, 'I'd like us to gather our courage and attack Gunnar.'

'Clashes with Gunnar have always ended the same way,' said Thorgeir Otkelsson: 'few have gained from them – and besides, I would not like to be known as a truce-violator.'

'They broke the settlement, not we,' said Thorgeir Starkadarson. 'Gunnar took your grainfield from you, and he took Moeidarhvol from my father and me.'

Then they made an agreement between themselves to attack Gunnar. Thorgeir said that Gunnar would be at home alone in a few days – 'and then you must bring eleven men to meet me, and I'll have the same number.'

Then he rode home.

69 | When Kolskegg and the servants had been at Eyjar for three
     | days, Thorgeir Starkadarson found out about it and sent word
to the other Thorgeir to meet him at Thrihyrning ridge. Then he
made ready to leave the farm at Thrihyrning with eleven men. He
rode up to the ridge and waited for his namesake.

Gunnar was now alone at his farm. The two Thorgeirs rode into a
wood; heaviness came over them and they could do nothing but
sleep.[1] They fastened their shields to the branches, tied their horses
and placed their weapons by their sides.

Njal was over at Thorolfsfell for the night and was unable to sleep
and kept walking in and out of the house. Thorhild asked Njal why
he couldn't sleep.

'Many things are passing before my eyes,' he said. 'I see the fierce
personal spirits of many of Gunnar's enemies, but there is something
strange about them – they seem in a frenzy but act without purpose.'

Shortly after this a man rode to the door and dismounted and went
in; it was the shepherd of Skarphedin and Thorhild.

Thorhild said, 'Did you find the sheep?'

'I found something of greater importance,' he said.

'What was that?' said Njal.

'I found twenty-four men up in the woods,' he said. 'They had tied
their horses and were sleeping. They had fastened their shields to
the branches.'

He had studied them so closely that he was able to describe all
their weapons and clothing.

Then Njal knew exactly who each of them was, and he said to him,
'What good hiring, if there were many like you! You will always
benefit from this, but now I want to send you on an errand.'

The shepherd agreed to go.

'Go to Hlidarendi,' said Njal, 'and tell Gunnar to go to Grjota and
send for men, and I will go to those men in the woods and frighten
them away. This is moving nicely along – they'll gain nothing in this
venture and lose much.'

The shepherd went off and told Gunnar all that had happened. Gunnar then rode to Grjota and they sent for men to come there.

To return to Njal: he rode off to where the two Thorgeirs were.

'It's careless to be lying around here,' he said. 'What's this expedition all about? Gunnar is not a man to be pushed around, and if the truth be told, this is the lowest sort of plot to kill. You'd better know that Gunnar is gathering forces and will soon come here and kill you, unless you get away and ride home.'

This struck terror into them and they acted quickly and took their weapons and mounted their horses and galloped back to Thrihyrning.

Njal went to Gunnar and asked him not to break up his band. 'I will act as go-between and try to make a settlement. They are properly frightened now. Since all of them are implicated, the payment for this plot against your life must be no less than a payment for the slaying of either of the Thorgeirs, should that occur. I'll hold on to the money and see to it that it's ready for you if you need it.'

70 | Gunnar thanked him for his help. Njal rode to Thrihyrning and told the two Thorgeirs that Gunnar would not break up his band of men until matters between them had been concluded. They made offers and were very frightened and asked Njal to go back with offers of settlement. Njal said he would only go back with offers that had no deceit behind them. They asked Njal to take part in the arbitration and promised to stand by whatever settlement he made. Njal said he would only do so at the Thing, and only if the best men were there. They agreed to this.

Njal then acted as go-between, until each side pledged peace and reconciliation to the other. Njal was to arbitrate and to choose those he wanted to help him.

Shortly after this the two Thorgeirs went to Mord Valgardsson. Mord rebuked them strongly for having turned over the matter to Njal, since he was Gunnar's great friend; he said that this would not turn out well.

*

People rode to the Althing as usual. Both sides were there. Njal called for silence and asked all the best men who had come there what claim they thought Gunnar had against the two Thorgeirs for the plot on his life. They answered that such a man had great right on his side. Njal asked whether he should charge all of them or whether only the leaders would have to answer. They said that it would fall mostly on the leaders, but that all of them were much to blame.

'Many people will say,' said Mord, 'that they didn't act without cause, since Gunnar broke a settlement with the Thorgeirs.'

'It's not breaking a settlement,' said Njal, 'if a man deals lawfully with another – with law our land shall rise, but it will perish with lawlessness.'

Then Njal told them that Gunnar had offered land or other payment for Moeidarhvol. The Thorgeirs then felt deceived by Mord and rebuked him strongly and said that the fine would be his fault.

Njal chose twelve men to judge the case. Every man who had gone along with the Thorgeirs was made to pay a hundred in silver, and the Thorgeirs had to pay two hundreds each. Njal took the money and kept it, and each side made pledges of peace and loyalty to the other, saying the words after Njal.

From the Althing Gunnar rode west to Hjardarholt in Dalir. Olaf Peacock welcomed him; he stayed there for half a month. He travelled widely around Dalir, and everybody welcomed him gladly.

At their parting Olaf said, 'I want to give you three gifts – a gold ring, a cloak which King Myrkjartan of Ireland once owned, and a dog which was given to me in Ireland. He is large and no worse as a companion than a strong man. He also has the intelligence of a man – he will bark at anyone he knows to be your enemy, but never at your friends. He can also see in any man whether he means you well or ill, and he will lay down his life out of loyalty to you. The dog's name is Sam.'

Then he said to the dog, 'Go with Gunnar now and serve him the best you can.'

The dog went at once to Gunnar and lay down at his feet.

Olaf asked Gunnar to be on his guard, and told him that he had many who envied him – 'since you are thought to be the most outstanding man in the whole land.'

Gunnar thanked him for his gifts and sound advice and rode home. He stayed at home for a while, and all was quiet.

71 | Shortly after this the two Thorgeirs met with Mord. The three of them were not in harmony. The Thorgeirs thought they had lost a lot of money because of Mord and had nothing in return, and they asked him to come up with another plan for doing harm to Gunnar.

Mord said that he would – 'and now my advice is that you, Thorgeir Otkelsson, seduce Ormhild, Gunnar's kinswoman,[1] and Gunnar's hatred for you will be even greater. I will then spread a rumour that Gunnar won't put up with these doings of yours. Soon after this the two of you must attack Gunnar, but not at his home, because no one will risk that as long as his dog is alive.'

They agreed among themselves that this plan should be carried out.

The summer continued to its end. Thorgeir made a habit of visiting Ormhild. Gunnar was not at all pleased at this, and great antipathy arose between them. This went on all winter long. Summer returned, and the secret meetings became even more frequent.

Thorgeir Starkadarson from Thrihyrning often met with Mord and they planned an attack against Gunnar at the time when he would ride down to Eyjar to oversee the work of his farmhands. One day Mord found out that Gunnar was riding down there, and he sent a man to Thrihyrning to tell Thorgeir that this was the right moment to go after him. Thorgeir and his men acted quickly and went down, twelve men in all. When they came to Kirkjubaer there were thirteen men waiting. They discussed where they should ambush Gunnar and agreed to go to the Ranga river and wait for him there.

When Gunnar rode up from Eyjar, Kolskegg rode with him. Gunnar had his bow and arrows and his halberd. Kolskegg had his short sword and was fully armed.

72 | Now it happened, as they were riding up to the Ranga, that a great deal of blood appeared on the halberd. Kolskegg asked what this meant, and Gunnar said that when such a thing happened in other lands it was called 'wound rain' – 'Olvir told me that it was a sign of great battles.'[1]

They went on riding until they saw men beside the river; they had tied their horses and were waiting.

Gunnar said, 'It's an ambush!'

Kolskegg answered, 'They've been untrustworthy for a long time. What are we going to do now?'

'Let's ride past them to the ford,' said Gunnar, 'and make our stand there.'

The others saw this and turned after them. Gunnar put a string to his bow, took out his arrows and threw them before him on the ground, and started shooting as soon as they were within range. He wounded many men this way, and killed a few.

Thorgeir Otkelsson said, 'This isn't doing us any good. Let's attack as hard as we can.'

They did this. In the forefront was Onund the Fair, a kinsman of Thorgeir Otkelsson. Gunnar thrust at him with his halberd; it struck his shield and split it in two and passed through him. Ogmund Floki rushed at Gunnar from behind, but Kolskegg saw this and cut off both his legs and pushed him out into the river, and he drowned at once. The fight then became fierce. Gunnar slashed with one hand and thrust with the other. Kolskegg killed a good number of men and wounded many others.

Thorgeir Starkadarson spoke to the other Thorgeir: 'There's not much sign that you have a father to avenge.'

He answered, 'It's true that I haven't made much progress, but you haven't exactly been close on my heels – and now I won't take any more of your taunts.'

He ran at Gunnar in great anger and thrust his spear through the shield and through Gunnar's arm. Gunnar twisted the shield so hard that the spear broke apart at the socket. Gunnar saw another man come within reach of his sword and struck him his death blow and then seized the halberd in both hands. Thorgeir Otkelsson had meanwhile moved in close, with his sword at the ready. Gunnar turned towards him quickly in great anger and thrust his halberd through him and lifted him up and threw him out into the river, and the body drifted down to the ford and was stopped there by a boulder. That place has since been known as Thorgeir's ford.

Thorgeir Starkadarson said, 'Let's get away from here! We've no hope of winning at this rate.'

They all turned away.

'Let's go after them,' said Kolskegg. 'Bring your bow and arrows and get within shooting distance of Thorgeir.'

Gunnar said, 'Our purses will be empty enough by the time compensation has been paid for the ones already lying dead.'

'You won't be short of money,' said Kolskegg. 'But Thorgeir won't stop until he has caused your death.'

'There will have to be a few more like him in my path before I take fright,' said Gunnar.

They rode home and told what had happened. Hallgerd was pleased at the news and praised them for what they did.

Rannveig spoke: 'It may be that what they did was good, but I expect that bad rather than good will come of it.'

73 | The news travelled widely, and Thorgeir's death was lamented by many. Gizur the White and Geir the Godi rode to the place and gave notice of the slayings and summoned neighbours to appear at the Thing. Then they rode back west.

Njal and Gunnar met and talked about the fight. Njal spoke to him: 'Be careful from now on. You have killed twice within the same bloodline and you must consider, for your own sake, that your life is in danger if you don't keep the settlement that will be made.'

'In no way do I intend to break it,' said Gunnar, 'but I'll need your support at the Thing.'

Njal answered, 'I'll stand by you loyally as long as I live.'

Then Gunnar rode home.

*

The time came for the Thing, and both sides came in large numbers. There was much talk about how this case would turn out. Gizur and Geir the Godi discussed which of them should bring the charge for the slaying of Thorgeir, and finally Gizur took over the case and gave notice of the suit at the Law Rock and spoke in these words: 'I give notice of a suit against Gunnar Hamundarson for a punishable assault, in which he ran at Thorgeir Otkelsson in a punishable assault and inflicted an internal wound which proved to be a fatal wound, and Thorgeir died from it. I declare that he deserves the sentence of full outlawry and that he should not be fed, nor helped on his way, nor given any kind of assistance. I declare that his property should be forfeit, half to me and half to the men in the quarter who have the legal right to forfeited property. I give notice to the Quarter Court in which this case should be heard according to law. I give this legal notice in the hearing of all at the Law Rock; I give notice of the prosecution of Gunnar Hamundarson for full outlawry.'

Gizur named witnesses a second time[1] and gave notice of a suit against Gunnar Hamundarson for having wounded Thorgeir Otkelsson with an internal wound which proved to be a fatal wound, and Thorgeir died from it at the place where Gunnar had made a punishable assault against Thorgeir. Then he gave notice as he had done with the first one. Then he asked Gunnar for his district and domicile. After that people left the Law Rock, and everybody said that Gizur had spoken well.

Gunnar was even-tempered and said little.

The Thing went on until the time for the courts to meet. Gunnar and his men stood to the north of the Ranga Court; Gizur the White and his men stood to the south and he named witnesses and requested that Gunnar listen to his oath-swearing and his presentation of the suit and the evidence he intended to bring forth. Then he swore his oath; then he presented the charges as previously formulated to the court. He had witnesses testify to the notice he had given. Then he asked the neighbours on the panel to be seated and invited the opposition to challenge the legitimacy of the panel members.

74 | Then Njal spoke: 'There's no use in sitting still. Let's go over
to where the panel is sitting.'

They went there and removed four members of the panel and
asked the remaining five to constitute a panel for the defence in
Gunnar's case and declare whether Thorgeir Starkadarson and Thorgeir Otkelsson had set out with the intention of meeting up with
Gunnar and killing him, if they could. They all declared at once that
this was so.[1] Njal called this a legitimate defence in the case and he
said he would present it unless they agreed to arbitration. Many
chieftains then joined in asking for arbitration, and it was agreed that
twelve men would decide the case. Both sides then came forward and
shook hands on this settlement.

After that the case was arbitrated and the amount of payment was
set, all of it to be paid at once at the Thing, and Gunnar and Kolskegg
were to go abroad and stay there for three years. If Gunnar had a
chance to leave and did not take it, he could be killed with impunity
by the kinsmen of the slain Thorgeir.[2]

Gunnar gave no indication that he thought this settlement unfair.[3]
He asked Njal for the money which he had turned over to him for
safekeeping. Njal had earned interest on it and paid it all out; it matched
the amount that Gunnar had to pay out. People then rode home.

Njal and Gunnar rode together from the Thing.

Njal spoke to Gunnar: 'Please see to it, my friend, that you abide
by this settlement, and remember what we have talked about before,'
he said. 'Just as your first trip abroad brought you great honour, you
will gain even more honour this time. Then you will return home
with great respect, and live to be an old man, and no one here will
be your equal. But if you break this settlement and don't go abroad,
you will be killed in this land, and that will be a terrible thing for
your friends to bear.'

Gunnar said he did not intend to break the settlement.

He rode home and reported on the settlement. Rannveig said it
would be good if he went abroad and if his enemies took on someone
else for the time being.

75 | Thrain Sigfusson told his wife that he was planning to go abroad that summer; she said that would be good. He took passage on Hogni the White's ship. Gunnar and Kolskegg took passage with Arnfinn from Vik.

Two of Njal's sons, Grim and Helgi, asked their father for permission to go abroad. Njal answered, 'Your travels will be troublesome, and it is not clear that you will hold on to your lives, though you will earn honour and respect. It is also likely that your travels will lead to problems here when you return.'

They still asked to go, and finally he told them to go if they wished. They took passage on the ship of Bard the Black and Olaf, the son of Ketil of Elda. There was much talk then about how the district was being drained of its best men.

Gunnar's sons, Hogni and Grani, were now young men. They were quite different from each other: Grani had much of his mother's character, but Hogni was a fine person.

Gunnar had his and Kolskegg's things brought to the ship. When everything was there and the ship was nearly ready, he rode to Bergthorshvol and other farms to thank everybody who had given him support.

Early the next day he made ready to go to the ship and told all his people that he was leaving for good, and they took it hard but hoped for his return later. Gunnar embraced every one of them when he was ready to leave, and they all came outside with him. He thrust his halberd into the ground and leaped into his saddle, and he and Kolskegg rode off.

They rode towards the Markarfljot river, and then Gunnar's horse slipped, and he sprang from the saddle. He happened to be facing the hillside and the farm at Hlidarendi, and spoke: 'Lovely is the hillside – never has it seemed so lovely to me as now, with its pale fields and mown meadows, and I will ride back home and not leave.'[1]

'Don't give your enemies the pleasure of breaking your agreement,' said Kolskegg, 'for no one would expect this from you. And you can be sure that everything will turn out just as Njal said.'

'I will not leave,' said Gunnar, 'and I wish you wouldn't either.'

'That won't be,' said Kolskegg. 'I will not be false to this agreement or to any other in which I am counted on, and this is the only thing that will separate us. Tell my kinsmen and my mother that I don't expect to see Iceland again, for I will hear the report of your death, and then nothing will draw me back.'

With this they parted, and Gunnar rode home to Hlidarendi, and Kolskegg rode to the ship and sailed abroad.

Hallgerd was pleased that Gunnar returned home, but his mother had little to say. Gunnar remained at home that autumn and winter, and did not have many men around him. The winter came to an end.

Olaf Peacock sent a man to Gunnar to ask him and Hallgerd to move west and turn over the farm to his mother and his son Hogni. Gunnar found this attractive at first and accepted, but when the time came he was not willing to go.

At the Thing that summer Gizur and Geir the Godi declared Gunnar a full outlaw at the Law Rock. Before the Thing broke up, Gizur called all of Gunnar's enemies together in the Almannagja gorge: Starkad from Thrihyrning and his son Thorgeir, Mord and Valgard the Grey, Geir the Godi and Hjalti Skeggjason, Thorbrand and Asbrand the sons of Thorleik, Eilif and his son Onund, Onund of Trollaskog, and Thorgrim of Sandgil.

Gizur spoke: 'I want to propose to you that we attack Gunnar this summer and kill him.'

Hjalti said, 'I made a promise to Gunnar here at the Thing, when he did just as I wished, that I would never take part in an attack against him – and I shall keep this promise.'[2]

Hjalti then left, and those who remained decided to attack Gunnar. They shook hands on it and fixed a penalty for anyone who withdrew. Mord was to spy out when they might best get at Gunnar. There were forty men in this band, and they thought it an easy matter to catch Gunnar while Kolskegg and Thrain and many other friends of his were abroad.

People rode home from the Thing.

*

Njal went to see Gunnar and told him of his outlawry and the planned attack on him.

'You have done well,' said Gunnar, 'to put me on my guard.'

'What I want now,' said Njal, 'is for Skarphedin and my son Hoskuld to come to you and wage their lives with yours.'

'No,' said Gunnar. 'I don't want your sons slain for my sake – you don't deserve this from me.'

'It won't matter,' said Njal. 'Once you're dead the trouble will be directed towards my sons.'

'That's not unlikely,' said Gunnar, 'but I would not like it to come from me. I want to ask you one thing, though – that you keep an eye on my son Hogni. About Grani I have nothing to say, for he does many things that are not to my liking.'

Njal promised this and rode home.

It is told that Gunnar rode to all gatherings and assemblies, and that his enemies never dared to attack him. And thus for a while things were as if he were not an outlaw.

76 | That autumn Mord Valgardsson sent word that Gunnar was at home alone, while all his people were down at Eyjar to finish the haymaking. Gizur the White and Geir the Godi rode east across the rivers when they heard this, and then across the sands to Hof. Then they sent word to Starkad at Thrihyrning, and all those who were to attack Gunnar met at Hof and planned how to go about it. Mord said that they would not take Gunnar by surprise unless they seized a farmer named Thorkel from the neighbouring farm, and forced him to come along with them and go up to Gunnar's farm, alone, to take the dog Sam.

They went off east to Hlidarendi and sent men after Thorkel, seized him and gave him two choices: either they would kill him or he would take the dog, and he chose to preserve his life and went with them.

There was an enclosure above the yard at Hlidarendi, and the party of attackers made a halt there. The farmer Thorkel went down to the house; the dog was lying on the roof, and Thorkel lured him away up the lane. But as soon as the dog saw that there were men up there, he jumped at Thorkel and bit him in the groin. Onund of Trollaskog hit the dog in the head with his axe, and it went right into the brain. The dog gave out a loud howl that was like none they had heard before, and then he fell down dead.

77 | Inside the hall, Gunnar woke up and said, 'You've been cruelly used, my foster-child Sam, and it is to be expected that our deaths are meant to be close together.'

Gunnar's hall was built entirely of wood, with overlapping boards on the outside and windows along the roof beams, fitted with shutters. Gunnar slept in a loft above the hall, together with Hallgerd and his mother.

When the attackers came near they did not know whether Gunnar was at home, and they asked for someone to go first and find out. Thorgrim the Norwegian went to the hall while the others sat down on the ground. Gunnar saw a red tunic at the window and he made a thrust with his halberd and hit Thorgrim in the waist. The Norwegian lost his grip on his shield, his feet slipped and he fell off the roof and then walked to where Gizur and the others were sitting on the ground.

Gizur looked at him and spoke: 'Well, is Gunnar at home?'

Thorgrim answered, 'Find that out for yourselves, but I've found out one thing – that his halberd's at home.'

Then he fell down dead.

The others then made for the buildings. Gunnar shot arrows at them and defended himself, and they could do nothing. Some men then climbed up on the buildings and planned to attack from there. Gunnar could still reach them with his arrows and they could do nothing, and it went on like this for a while. They took a rest and made a second attack. Gunnar kept shooting arrows at them, and again they could do nothing and fell back a second time.

Gizur the White said, 'We must attack harder – we're not getting anywhere.'

They made a third charge and were at it for a long time. Then they pulled back.

Gunnar spoke: 'There's an arrow out there on the edge of the roof, one of theirs, and I'll try to shoot it at them – it will shame them to be hurt by their own weapons.'

His mother spoke: 'Don't do that – don't stir them up now that they have turned away.'

Gunnar reached for the arrow and shot it at them. It struck Eilif Onundarson and gave him a great wound. He had been standing off by himself, and the others did not notice that he was wounded.

'An arm reached out over there,' said Gizur, 'with a gold bracelet around it, and it grabbed an arrow that was lying on the roof; he would not be looking out here if he had enough inside. Now is the time to attack.'

Mord spoke: 'Let's burn him to death inside.'

'That shall never be,' said Gizur, 'even if I knew that my life depended on it. But a man as cunning as you're said to be should be able to come up with a plan that works.'

There were ropes lying on the ground, used for securing the buildings.

Mord said, 'Let's tie these ropes around the ends of the roof beams and tie the other ends to boulders, and then twist the ropes with poles and pull the whole roof frame off the hall.'

They took the ropes and rigged them in this way, and Gunnar was not aware of it until they had pulled off the whole roof. He kept on shooting with his bow, so they could not get at him. Then Mord said once more that they should burn Gunnar to death inside.

Gizur answered, 'I don't know why you want to keep talking of something that nobody else wants – that shall never be!'

At that moment Thorbrand Thorleiksson leaped up on the roof and cut through Gunnar's bow string. Gunnar grasped his halberd with both hands and turned quickly towards him and drove the halberd through him and flung him off the roof. Then Asbrand, Thorbrand's brother, leaped up; Gunnar thrust at him with the halberd, and Asbrand brought his shield to meet it. The halberd went through the shield and between the upper arm and forearm. Gunnar twisted the halberd so that the shield split and both his arm-bones broke, and Asbrand fell off the roof.

By this time Gunnar had wounded eight men and killed two. Then he received two wounds, and everybody said that he flinched at neither wounds nor death.

He spoke to Hallgerd: 'Give me two locks of your hair, and you and my mother twist them into a bowstring for me.'

'Does anything depend on it?' she said.

'My life depends on it,' he said, 'for they'll never be able to get me as long as I can use my bow.'

'Then I'll recall,' she said, 'the slap you gave me, and I don't care whether you hold out for a long or a short time.'[1]

'Everyone has some mark of distinction,' said Gunnar, 'and I won't ask you again.'

Rannveig spoke: 'You do evil, and your infamy will long be remembered.'

Gunnar defended himself well and courageously and wounded eight more men so badly that many were close to death. He defended himself until he fell from weariness. They dealt him many bad wounds, but he still evaded them and went on for a long time defending himself, until at last they killed him.

Thorkel Elfaraskald wrote about his defence in this verse:

3.
We have heard how, in the south,
the skipper of the sea-steed   *sea-steed*: ship
Gunnar, greedy for gore,
guarded himself with his halberd.
Wielding weapons against attack,
he gave wounds to sixteen
of the battle-bearers,   *battle-bearers*: warriors
and brought death to two.

Gizur spoke: 'We have now laid low a great warrior, and it has been hard for us, and his defence will be remembered as long as this land is lived in.'

Then he went to Rannveig and said, 'Will you give us land for our two dead men to be buried in?'

'Gladly for these two, but even more gladly if it were for all of you,' she said.

'You have good reason for saying that,' he said, 'for your loss has been great' – and he gave orders that they should not steal or destroy anything. Then they went away.

Thorgeir Starkadarson said, 'We won't be safe from the Sigfussons at home on our farms, unless you, Gizur, or Geir stay here in the south for a while.'

'That's probably true,' said Gizur, and he and Geir drew lots, and it fell to Geir to stay behind. He went to Oddi and settled in there. He had a son named Hroald; he was born out of wedlock and his mother was Bjartey, the sister of Thorvald the Sickly, who was slain at Hestlaek in Grimsnes.[2] Hroald boasted that he had given Gunnar his death blow. He went to Oddi with his father. Thorgeir Starkadarson boasted of the wound that he had dealt to Gunnar.

Gizur stayed at home at Mosfell.

The slaying of Gunnar was spoken badly of in all parts of the land, and his death brought great sorrow to many.

78 | Njal was distressed over the death of Gunnar, and so were the Sigfussons. They asked Njal whether he thought they should give notice of the slaying and start a case. He said that that was not possible for a man who had been outlawed and that it would be better to kill some men in revenge and whittle down their honour this way.

They raised a burial mound for Gunnar and placed him in it sitting up. Rannveig did not want the halberd to go into the mound and said that only a man who was willing to avenge Gunnar should have it. So no one took the halberd. She was so fierce towards Hallgerd that she was on the verge of killing her, and she said that Hallgerd had brought about the slaying of her son. Hallgerd fled to Grjota, along with her son Grani. They made a division of the property: Hogni was to have the land and the farm at Hlidarendi, and Grani was to have the land which was rented out.

One day at Hlidarendi it happened that a shepherd and a servant woman were driving cattle past Gunnar's mound. Gunnar seemed to them to be in high spirits and reciting verses in the mound. They went home and told this to Gunnar's mother Rannveig, and she asked them to tell Njal. They went off to Bergthorshvol and told him, and he had them repeat it three times. Then he talked privately with Skarphedin for a long time.

Skarphedin took his axe and went with the servants to Hlidarendi. Hogni and Rannveig welcomed him and were happy to see him. Rannveig asked him to stay for a long time, and he promised to do so. He and Hogni were always going in and out together. Hogni was a courageous and capable man, but not easily persuaded, and for this reason they did not dare to tell him about the apparition.

One evening Skarphedin and Hogni were outside, to the south of Gunnar's mound. The moon was shining brightly, though occasionally dimmed by clouds. It appeared to them that the mound was open, and that Gunnar had turned around and was looking at the moon. They thought they saw four lights burning in the mound, and there were no shadows. They saw that Gunnar was happy and had a very cheerful look. He recited a verse so loudly that they could hear it clearly, even at a distance:

4.
The bright bestower of rings,
the man bold in deeds, who
fought with full courage, the
father of Hogni, spoke:
the shield-holding ghost would sooner
wear his helmet high
than falter in the fray,
rather die for battle-Freyja   *battle-Freyja*: valkyrie
– and die for battle-Freyja.

Then the mound closed again.

'Would you have believed this,' said Skarphedin, 'if others told it to you?'

'I would believe it if Njal told me,' said Hogni, 'for it's said that he never lies.'

'Such an apparition is full of meaning,' said Skarphedin, 'when Gunnar comes forth and tells us that he preferred to die rather than falter before his enemies. He has taught us what to do.'

'I won't get anywhere,' said Hogni, 'unless you help me.'

Skarphedin spoke: 'I remember how Gunnar behaved after the slaying of your kinsman Sigmund.[1] I will now give you whatever help I can. My father promised this to Gunnar, whenever you and his mother should need it.'

Then they walked back to Hlidarendi.

79 | Skarphedin spoke: 'Let's start out at once, tonight, for if word gets around that I'm here, they'll be much more on their guard.'

'I'll do whatever you say,' said Hogni.

When everyone else was in bed, they took their weapons. Hogni took down the halberd, and it rang. Rannveig jumped up in a rage and asked, 'Who's taking the halberd, after I gave orders that no one should touch it?'

'I'm bringing it to my father,' said Hogni, 'so that he may have it with him in Valhalla and use it in battle.'

'First you must carry it yourself and avenge your father,' she said, 'because the halberd is announcing death, for one man or more.'

Hogni then went out and told Skarphedin of his words with his grandmother.

After this they went to Oddi. Two ravens flew with them all the way. They came to Oddi during the night and drove the sheep up to the house. Hroald and Tjorvi rushed out and chased the sheep into the lanes, and had their weapons with them.

Skarphedin jumped out and said, 'You don't have to look further – it's just what you think.'

Then he dealt Tjorvi his death blow.

Hroald had a spear in his hand, and Hogni sprang at him. Hroald made a thrust at him. Hogni severed his spear shaft with the halberd and then drove it through him.

They left the dead men and went up to Thrihyrning. Skarphedin leaped up on the roof and began pulling out the grass, and the people inside thought that it was sheep. Starkad and Thorgeir took their weapons and clothing and ran outside and along the wall, and when Starkad saw Skarphedin he was frightened and wanted to turn back.

Skarphedin struck him dead by the side of the wall. Then Hogni faced Thorgeir and killed him with the halberd.

From there they went to Hof. Mord was out in the field and asked for peace and offered full reconciliation. Skarphedin told him about the slaying of the four men and said that he would be going the same way unless he offered Hogni self-judgement – if Hogni were willing to accept it. Hogni said he had not intended to make peace with the slayers of his father, but finally he accepted self-judgement.

80 | Njal worked at getting those who had to take action for the slayings of Starkad and Thorgeir to agree to a settlement, and a district assembly was called and men were appointed to arbitrate. All the facts were weighed, even the attack on Gunnar, although he had been in a state of outlawry. Mord paid what payments there were, for they did not finish fixing the amount against him until they had fixed the amount in the other case, and they balanced the one side against the other. Then they were fully reconciled.[1]

But at the Thing there was much talk about the case between Geir the Godi and Hogni,[2] and the outcome was that they agreed to a settlement, and they kept to this settlement from then on. Geir the Godi lived at Hlid until his death, and he is now out of the saga.

Njal asked, on behalf of Hogni, for the hand of Alfeid, the daughter of Veturlidi the Poet, and she was married to him. Their son was Ari, who sailed to Shetland and married there. Einar the Shetlander, a very brave man, is descended from him.

Hogni kept up his friendship with Njal, and is now out of this saga.[3]

81 | To turn now to Kolskegg: he went to Norway and stayed at Vik that winter, and the next summer he went east to Denmark and entered the service of King Svein Fork-beard[1] and received great honour there.

One night he dreamed that a man came to him. This man was gleaming with light. Kolskegg dreamed that the man woke him up.

The man spoke to him: 'Rise and come with me.'

'What do you want with me?' asked Kolskegg.

'I shall find you a wife, and you shall be my knight.'

Kolskegg dreamed that he agreed to this, and then he woke up. He went to a wise man and told him the dream, and he interpreted it to mean that he should travel to southern lands and become God's knight.

Kolskegg was baptized in Denmark but found no contentment there and went east to Russia and spent one winter there. From there he went to Constantinople and became a mercenary. The last that was reported of him was that he married in Constantinople and became a leader in the Varangian guard[2] and stayed there until his death; he is now out of the saga.

82 | To tell now about Thrain Sigfusson's coming to Norway: they reached Halogaland in the north and then continued south to Trondheim and to Lade. When Earl Hakon heard about this, he sent men to find out what men were on the ship, and they came back and told Hakon who they were. The earl then sent for Thrain Sigfusson, and Thrain came to him. The earl asked who his kin were, and he said that he was closely related to Gunnar of Hlidarendi.

The earl spoke: 'You will benefit from that, for I've met many Icelanders, but none to match him.'

Thrain spoke: 'My lord, are you willing to have me here with you over the winter?'

The earl took him on. Thrain stayed there that winter and was well treated.

There was a man named Kol, a Viking. He was the son of Asmund Ash-side of Smaland. Kol lay waiting out east in the Gota river, with five ships and a large band of men. From there he made his way to Vestfold in Norway and made a surprise attack on Hallvard Soti. They found Hallvard in a loft, and he defended himself well until they set the place on fire. Then he surrendered, but they killed him and seized much booty and sailed back to Lodose.

News of this reached Earl Hakon, and he had Kol declared an outlaw throughout his realm and set a price on his head.

One day the earl spoke these words: 'Gunnar of Hlidarendi is too far away from us now; he would kill this outlaw of mine if he were here, but now he will be killed by Icelanders, and it's a bad thing he didn't come back to us.'

Thrain Sigfusson answered, 'I'm not Gunnar, but I'm kin to him, and I'm ready to take on this venture.'

The earl said, 'I accept this eagerly. I'll fit you out well for your mission.'

Then Eirik, the earl's son, spoke up: 'You've made fine promises to many men, father, but you've been uneven in carrying them out. This is a most difficult mission, for this Viking is tough and a vicious one to deal with. You must choose your men and ships with great care.'

Thrain said, 'I will go, even though the venture is not promising.'

The earl gave him five ships, all well manned.

With Thrain were Gunnar Lambason and Lambi Sigurdarson. Gunnar was a son of one of Thrain's brothers and had come to him as a young man, and they were very fond of each other. Earl Hakon's son Eirik helped them: he looked over the crew and the supply of weapons and made changes when he thought it necessary. Finally, when they were ready, Eirik gave them a pilot.

They sailed south along the coast, and wherever they put in to land the earl allowed them to have what they needed. They headed east towards Lodose, and then found out that Kol had gone to Denmark, so they headed south after him. When they reached Helsingborg they met some men in a boat, and these men told them that Kol was in the area and planning to stay there for a while.

The weather was good that day. Kol saw the ships which came towards them, and said that he had dreamed of Earl Hakon during the night and that these must be Hakon's men, and so he ordered all his men to take their weapons. They made themselves ready, and the clash began. They fought for a long time without either side getting anywhere. Then Kol jumped aboard Thrain's ship and cleared a space around himself and killed many men. He was wearing a golden helmet.

Thrain saw that things were not going well, and he urged his men to go along with him, and he himself went in the lead and met up with Kol. Kol swung at him and his sword landed on Thrain's shield and split it from top to bottom. Then Kol was struck on the hand by a stone and his sword fell down. Thrain swung at Kol, and the blow hit his leg and cut it off. After that they killed him. Thrain cut off Kol's head and kept it, and threw the body overboard.

They took much booty there, and then sailed north to Trondheim to meet the earl; he welcomed Thrain. Thrain showed him Kol's head, and the earl thanked him for the deed. Eirik said it was worth more than just words. The earl answered that this was so, and asked them to walk along with him. They walked to where the earl was having some good ships built. He had had one ship built which was not like a longship; it had a griffin's head, much ornamented.

The earl said, 'You're a great one for show, Thrain – you and your kinsman Gunnar have that in common. I want to give you this ship – it's called *Griffin*. My friendship goes along with it. I want you to stay with me as long as you wish.'

Thrain thanked the earl for his kindness and said he was not eager to return to Iceland just then.

The earl had to make a trip east to meet the Swedish king at the border. Thrain travelled with him that summer as skipper and steered the *Griffin* and sailed so fast that few could keep up with him, and he was much envied. It was plain that the earl valued Gunnar highly, for he sternly curbed all those who tried to bother Thrain.

Thrain stayed with the earl all that winter. In the spring the earl asked him whether he wanted to stay on or go to Iceland. Thrain said he had not yet decided and added that he would first like to have some news from Iceland. The earl said he should do whatever suited him. Thrain stayed with him.

Then news came from Iceland that seemed weighty to many: the death of Gunnar of Hlidarendi. The earl did not want Thrain to go to Iceland then, and so he stayed on.

83 | To turn now to Grim and Helgi, the sons of Njal: they left Iceland the same summer that Thrain sailed abroad and were on a ship with Bard and Olaf Elda, the son of Ketil. They ran into such fierce north winds that they were carried south, and such a thick fog came over them that they could not tell where they were going, and their passage was long. Then they came to a great area of shallow water and knew that they must be near land. The Njalssons asked Bard whether he had any idea what land they were coming to.

'After the driving winds we've had,' he said, 'there are many possibilities – Orkney, or Scotland, or Ireland.'

Two days later they saw land on both sides and heavy surf running into the fjord. They cast anchor outside the surf. In the evening the weather began to subside, and by morning it was calm. Then they saw thirteen ships sailing out toward them.

Bard said, 'What shall we do now? It looks as if these men are going to attack us.'

They discussed whether they should defend themselves or surrender, but the Vikings reached them before they made up their minds. Each side asked the other for the names of its leaders. The leaders of the merchants gave their names and asked who was in charge of the other force. One man gave his name as Grjotgard, and another as Snaekolf, sons of Moldan of Duncansby in Scotland and kinsmen of the Scottish king Melkolf.[1]

'You have two choices,' said Grjotgard: 'you can go ashore, and we'll take your property, or we'll attack you and kill every man we catch.'

Helgi answered, 'The merchants choose to defend themselves.'

The merchants said, 'Damn you for saying that! What defence can we offer? Money means less than life.'

Grim made it a point to shout at the Vikings so that they would not hear the wretched grumbling of the merchants.

Bard and Olaf said to the merchants, 'Don't you see that the Icelanders will pour scorn on your behaviour? Grab your weapons and defend yourselves.'

They all took up their weapons and made a pact with each other that they would never give up as long as they were able to defend themselves.

84 | The Vikings started shooting at them and the fight began. The merchants put up a good defence. Snaekolf ran at Olaf and thrust his spear right through him. Grim thrust his spear at Snaekolf so hard that he fell overboard. Then Helgi joined with Grim and they pushed back the Vikings, and the Njalssons were always there where the need was greatest. The Vikings called to the merchants and asked them to give up; they answered that they would never give up.

Just then they happened to look out to sea. They saw ships coming from the south around a headland, no fewer than ten. They were rowing hard and heading straight towards them, with shield after shield along the sides. On the leading ship a man stood by the mast; he was wearing a silk tunic and had a gilded helmet on his head, and his hair was thick and fair. This man was holding a gold-inlaid spear in his hand.

He asked, 'Who are the players in this uneven match?'

Helgi gave his name and said that Grjotgard and Snaekolf were on the other side.

'And who are your skippers?' he said.

Helgi answered, 'One of them, Bard the Black, is still alive, but the other, whose name was Olaf, is dead, and the man with me here is my brother Grim.'

'Are you Icelanders?' he said.

'That's right,' said Helgi.

He asked whose sons they were, and they told him. He recognized the names and said, 'You and your father are well known.'

'Who are you?' said Helgi.

'Kari is my name, and I am the son of Solmund.'

'Where are you coming from?' said Helgi.

'From the Hebrides,' said Kari.

'Your coming will be welcome,' said Helgi, 'if you're willing to give us some help.'

'I'll help as much as you need,' said Kari. 'What are you asking?'

'That you attack them,' said Helgi.

Kari said he would. They pulled up to the Vikings, and the fight started up again. After they had fought for a while, Kari jumped aboard Snaekolf's ship; Snaekolf turned to meet him and quickly swung his sword at him. Kari made a backward leap over a boom which lay across the ship. Snaekolf struck so hard at the boom that both edges of his sword were buried in it. Kari swung at him and the sword hit his shoulder; the blow was so hard that it cut off the arm, and Snaekolf died at once. Grjotgard threw his spear at Kari, but Kari saw it coming and leaped into the air, and the spear missed him.

By this time Helgi and Grim had joined Kari. Helgi dashed at Grjotgard and ran his sword through him, and that was his death. They made their way through the rest of the ships, and the men begged for peace. They spared them all, but took all their goods. Then they sailed the ships out into the shelter of the islands.

85 | Sigurd was the name of the earl who ruled over Orkney. He was the son of Hlodver, the son of Thorfinn Skull-splitter, the son of Turf-Einar, the son of Earl Rognvald of More, the son of Eystein the Noisy.

Kari was one of Earl Sigurd's followers and had been collecting tribute for him from Earl Gilli in the Hebrides. Kari asked Grim and Helgi to go along to Mainland[1] and said that Earl Sigurd would welcome them. They agreed to this and went with Kari and came to Mainland. Kari brought them to meet the earl and told him who these men were.

'How did they happen to meet you?' said the earl.

Kari answered, 'I found them in the Scottish firths, fighting with the sons of Moldan. They were putting up a good defence – they moved swiftly from one position to another, and were always there where the need was greatest. I wish now to ask a place for them among your followers.'

'You shall have your way,' said the earl; 'you've already taken much responsibility for them.'

They stayed with the earl that winter and were well respected.

Helgi became silent as the winter passed. The earl had no idea what caused this and asked him why he was silent and whether he liked it there.

'I like it here,' said Helgi.

'Then what's on your mind?' said the earl.

'Do you have any land to protect in Scotland?' said Helgi.

'So we think,' said the carl, 'but what of it?'

Helgi answered, 'The Scots have taken the life of your man in charge there and blocked all messages from crossing the Pentland Firth.'

The earl spoke: 'Do you have second sight?'

Helgi answered, 'There's been little experience of that.'

'I shall add to your honour,' said the earl, 'if this proves true. Otherwise you will pay.'

'He's not that sort of man,' said Kari. 'His words will come true, for his father has second sight.'

The earl then sent men south to Arnljot at Stroma, his man in charge there. Then Arnljot sent men south across the Pentland Firth, and they found out that Earl Hundi and Earl Melsnati had taken the life of Havard, Earl Sigurd's brother-in-law, at Freswick. Arnljot sent word to Earl Sigurd to come south with a large band of men and drive these earls from the land, and when the earl heard this he gathered an army from all the islands.

86 | The earl then went south with his army, and Kari and the Njalssons went with him. They came to Caithness. The earl owned these lands in Scotland: Ross, Moray, Sutherland and Argyll. Scotsmen from these lands joined them and said that the earls were a short distance away with a large army. Earl Sigurd led his army towards them, and they met above a place called Duncansby Head and a great battle broke out. The Scots had detached some of their men from the main army, and these now attacked the earl's men from the rear, and the losses were heavy until the Njalssons went at them and fought them and put them to flight. But then the battle became even fiercer. Helgi and Grim charged forward close to the earl's banner and fought well.

Kari came face to face with Earl Melsnati. Melsnati threw his spear at Kari, and Kari shot it back, right through the earl. Earl Hundi then fled, and they chased the fugitives until they learned that Melkolf was gathering an army at Duncansby. Earl Sigurd took counsel with his men, and they all thought it best to turn back rather than fight with such a large army. So they turned back.

When Earl Sigurd came to Stroma he divided the booty. Then he went north to Mainland. The Njalssons and Kari went with him. The earl held a great feast, and there he gave a good sword and gold-inlaid spear to Kari, a gold bracelet and cloak to Helgi, and a shield and sword to Grim. Then he made Grim and Helgi his followers and thanked them for their good effort.

They were with the earl that winter and the next summer, until Kari went off raiding; they went with him. They raided far and wide that summer and were victorious everywhere. They fought and defeated King Gudrod of the Isle of Man and returned with much booty. That winter they stayed with the earl in high favour.

In the spring the Njalssons asked leave to go to Norway. The earl said that they should go if they wished, and he gave them a good ship and brave men. Kari said that he would go to Norway that summer with the tribute money for Earl Hakon and that they should meet there, and they agreed on this. The Njalssons set out and sailed to Norway and came to land in the north at Trondheim.

87 | There was a man named Kolbein Arnljotarson, from Trond-
heim. He sailed to Iceland the same summer that Kolskegg and the Njalssons sailed away from there. He spent the winter in Breiddal, in the east. The next summer he made his ship ready to sail in Gautavik. When they were nearly finished, a man came rowing up in a boat and tied it to the trading vessel, and then went up on the ship to meet Kolbein. Kolbein asked him his name.

'My name is Hrapp,' he said.

'What do you want with me?' said Kolbein.

'I want to ask you,' said Hrapp, 'to take me overseas.'

'Whose son are you?' said Kolbein.

He answered, 'I am the son of Orgumleidi, the son of Geirolf the Warrior.'

Kolbein asked, 'What need are you in?'

'I have killed a man,' said Hrapp.

'What man,' said Kolbein, 'and who will take action over him?'

He said, 'I have killed Orlyg the son of Olvir, the son of Hrodgeir the White, and the men of Vopnafjord are the ones who will take action.'

'My guess,' said Kolbein, 'is that whoever takes you will land in trouble.'

Hrapp spoke: 'I am a friend to my friends, but when something bad is done to me, I pay it back. Anyway, I will spare no expense for my passage, since I have plenty of money for that.'

Then Kolbein took him on board.

Soon afterward a good breeze came and they sailed out to sea. Once at sea, Hrapp ran out of food. He helped himself from those who were sitting next to him. They leaped up with curses on their lips, and this led to blows, and Hrapp quickly had two men down. This was reported to Kolbein, and he offered his food to Hrapp, and Hrapp accepted.

They came to land and dropped anchor off Agdenes.

Kolbein asked, 'Where's the money you offered for your passage?'

Hrapp answered, 'It's back in Iceland.'

Kolbein spoke: 'You will cheat more men than me, but I'll let you off for the passage.'

Hrapp thanked him for this – 'and what advice do you have for me now?'

'First of all,' said Kolbein, 'that you leave the ship as soon as you can, for all the Norwegians are going to give you a bad word, and I have a second piece of sound advice – never betray your lord.'

Hrapp then went ashore with his weapons; in his hand he had a large axe with a handle bound in iron. He travelled until he came to Gudbrand of Dalarna. Gudbrand was a very close friend to Earl Hakon; together they owned a temple, which was never opened unless the earl went there. It was the second largest temple in Norway; the largest was at Lade. Gudbrand had a son, Thrand, and a daughter, Gudrun.

Hrapp went to Gudbrand and greeted him well. Gudbrand asked who he was. Hrapp gave his name and said that he came from Iceland. Then he asked Gudbrand to take him into his service.

Gudbrand spoke: 'You don't look to me like a man of good luck.'

'I see that a lot of lies have also been told about you,' said Hrapp, 'for it was said that you took in all those who asked, and that no man was as noble as you. I'll tell a different story if you don't take me in.'

Gudbrand said, 'I suppose you'll have to stay here, then.'

'Where do you want me to sit?' said Hrapp.

'On the lower bench,' said Gudbrand, 'facing my high seat.'

Hrapp went to his seat. He had a lot of stories to tell, and at first Gudbrand and many others found him amusing, but as time went on they found his jesting overdone.

After a while he started conversing with Gudrun, so that many said he was out to seduce her. When Gudbrand found out about this, he rebuked her sternly for talking to him and told her to avoid speaking with him altogether unless everybody could hear them. At first she promised to obey, but after a while they were talking as before. Then Gudbrand told Asvard, his overseer, to go with her wherever she went.

One day she asked to go to a nut grove to amuse herself, and Asvard went with her. Hrapp went looking for them and found them in the grove and took her by the hand and led her off alone. Asvard went looking for her and found the two of them lying together in some bushes. He ran at them with his axe raised and hacked at Hrapp's leg, but Hrapp moved quickly and Asvard missed him. Hrapp sprang to his feet as fast as he could and seized his axe. Asvard tried to get away; Hrapp hacked his backbone in two.

Then Gudrun spoke: 'The deed you've just done means that you may no longer stay with my father. But there is another thing which will displease him even more – I'm going to have a child.'

Hrapp answered, 'He won't learn this from others. I'll go back and tell him both these things.'

'You won't get away from there with your life then,' she said.

'I'll take that chance,' he said.

After that he took her to the other women, and he went to the hall.

Gudbrand was sitting in his high seat, and only a few men were in the room. Hrapp walked up to him holding his axe high.

Gudbrand asked, 'Why is your axe bloody?'

'I have been taking care of Asvard's backache,' he said.

'Not out of good will, I suppose,' said Gudbrand. 'You must have killed him.'

'That's true,' said Hrapp.

'What was the reason?' said Gudbrand.

'It will seem petty to you,' said Hrapp, 'but he was trying to cut off my leg.'

'What had you done before that?' asked Gudbrand.

'Something that was none of his business,' said Hrapp.

'All the same, tell me what it was,' said Gudbrand.

Hrapp spoke: 'If you really must know, I was lying with your daughter, and he didn't like that.'

Gudbrand spoke: 'On your feet, men, and seize him and put him to death!'

'Small benefit I get from being your son-in-law,' said Hrapp. 'Anyway, you don't have the manpower for that to happen soon.'

The men rose to their feet, but he backed out of the hall. They chased him, but he got away into the forest and they did not catch him. Gudbrand gathered men and had them search the forest, but they did not find him, for the forest was large and thick.

Hrapp went through the forest until he saw ahead of him a clearing and a house and a man outside chopping wood. Hrapp asked his name, and he gave it as Tofi. Tofi asked his name, and Hrapp gave it. Hrapp asked why he lived so far away from other men.

'Because,' he said, 'here I don't have to bother with other men.'

'We're not being straight with each other,' said Hrapp, 'so I'll tell you first who I am. I've been staying with Gudbrand of Dalarna, and I ran away because I killed his overseer. I know that both of us are bad types, because you wouldn't be here, far away from other men, unless you were outlawed by someone. I'll give you a choice: either we go halves on whatever is here, or I'll give you away.'

The farmer said, 'It's just as you say. I made off with this woman who's here with me, and many a man has been looking for me.'

Then he brought Hrapp inside. The house was small but well made. The farmer told his wife that he had arranged to have Hrapp stay with them.

'Most people will have misfortune from this man,' she said, 'but I guess you'll have it your way.'

So Hrapp stayed there. He was often on the move and was never at home. He managed to see Gudrun frequently. Gudbrand and his son Thrand laid ambushes for him but were never able to get their hands on him, and it went on this way for a whole year.

Gudbrand sent word to Earl Hakon about the problem he was having because of Hrapp. The earl had Hrapp declared an outlaw and set a price on his head, and also promised to come himself to try to find him, but never did, and yet he thought it an easy matter for someone to catch Hrapp, since he was so careless.

88 | To return to the Njalssons: they travelled that same summer from Orkney to Norway and traded there.

Thrain Sigfusson made his ship ready to sail to Iceland and was nearly set to leave.

Earl Hakon went to a feast at Gudbrand's. That night Killer-Hrapp went to the temple owned by the earl and Gudbrand and entered it. He saw Thorgerd Holda-bride[1] in her seat; she was as tall as a grown man. She had a large gold bracelet on her arm and a linen hood on her head. He snatched off her hood and took the gold bracelet from her. Then he saw Thor's chariot and took a bracelet from him. He took a third one from Irpa, and dragged the three idols outside the temple and took off all their garments. Then he set fire to the temple and burned it to the ground. After that he went away. The dawn was coming. He crossed a cultivated field; six armed men sprang up and attacked him there, but he put up a good defence. The outcome was that he killed three men and mortally wounded Thrand, and chased the other two into the forest so that they could not bring word to the earl.

Then he returned to Thrand and spoke: 'I could kill you now, but I won't. I'll show more respect for my in-laws than you and your father have shown me.'

Hrapp was about to return to the forest, but he saw men between him and the forest and dared not risk that, so he lay down in some bushes and stayed there for a while.

Early that morning Earl Hakon and Gudbrand went to the temple and found it burned to the ground and the three idols outside, stripped of their belongings.

Gudbrand declared: 'Much might has been given our gods: they walked away from the fire by themselves.'

'This was not done by the gods,' said the earl. 'A man must have burned the temple and carried the gods out. The gods are in no hurry to avenge themselves, but the man who did this will be banished from Valhalla and never enter there.'

At that moment four of the earl's men came running up and told them the bad news, that they had found three men slain in the field and Thrand mortally wounded.

'Who did this?' said the earl.

'Killer-Hrapp,' they said.

'Then it was he who burned down the temple,' said the earl.

They thought that he was indeed likely to have done this.

'Where can he be now?' said the earl.

They said that Thrand told them that he had hidden in some bushes. The earl went looking for him there, but Hrapp had taken off. The earl then ordered them to search for him, but they could not find him. The earl himself joined the search and began by telling the men to rest. He went apart from the others and gave orders that no one should follow him and stayed away for some time. He fell to his knees and held his hands over his eyes. Then he went back to the others.

He spoke to them: 'Come with me.'

They went with him, and he turned sharply from the path they had been taking and came to a dell. Hrapp turned up there, right in front of them, for that was where he had hidden himself. The earl urged his men to chase him, but Hrapp was so swift that they came nowhere near him.

Hrapp headed for Lade. Both Thrain Sigfusson and the Njalssons were there and about to sail.

Hrapp rushed to where the Njalssons were, still on shore. He spoke: 'Save me, my good fellows, for the earl is out to kill me.'

Helgi looked at him and spoke: 'You look to me like bad luck, and things will go better for the man who does not take up with you.'

'Then it's my wish,' said Hrapp, 'that you two have bad trouble because of me.'

'I'm man enough to pay you back for that,' said Helgi – 'when the time comes.'

Then Hrapp turned to Thrain Sigfusson and asked him for help.

'What trouble are you in?' said Thrain.

Hrapp said, 'I have burned down the earl's temple and killed some of his men, and he'll be here soon, for he's hunting me himself.'

'It would not be right for me to help you,' said Thrain, 'after the earl has done me so much good.'

Hrapp then showed him the treasures he had taken from the temple and offered them to him. Thrain said he would not accept them without paying for them.

Hrapp said, 'I'm going to stay here and be killed in front of your eyes, and for that you will receive blame from all men.'

They could see the earl and his men coming. Thrain then took Hrapp into his care and had a boat cast off to carry them out to the ship.

Thrain said, 'The best way to hide you is to break out the bottoms of two barrels and let you get inside.'

This was done, and Hrapp crawled into the barrels and they were tied together and lowered over the side of the ship.

Then the earl arrived with his men. He approached the Njalssons and asked them whether Hrapp had come there. They said that he had. The earl asked where he had gone, and they said they had not noticed.

The earl spoke: 'Whoever tells me where Hrapp is will receive great honour from me.'

Grim spoke softly to Helgi: 'Why shouldn't we tell? I doubt that Thrain will treat us well in any case.'

'But still, we shouldn't tell,' said Helgi, 'since his life is at stake.'

Grim said, 'It may be that the earl will turn his vengeance against us, since he's so furious now that his wrath will have to be felt somewhere.'

'We'll not guide ourselves by that,' said Helgi. Now we must cast off and put out to sea when the right wind comes.'

They brought the ship out to an island and waited there for the wind.

The earl went to the ships' crews and asked them all, but everybody denied knowing about Hrapp.

Then the earl said, 'Now we must ask my friend Thrain, and he will turn the man over if he knows where he is.'

They took one of the longships and sailed out to the trading vessel. Thrain saw the earl approaching and rose and greeted him warmly.

The earl took the greeting well and spoke: 'We're looking for a man named Hrapp, an Icelander. He's done us every kind of evil. We ask you to turn him over or tell us where he is.'

Thrain spoke: 'You recall, my lord, that I killed a man whom you had outlawed and risked my life in doing so, and I received great honour from you in return.'

'You shall now have even greater honour,' said the earl.

Thrain thought things over and was not certain what the earl would place highest.[2] Finally, he denied that Hrapp was there and asked the earl to search the ship. The earl spent only a short time doing so and went back to land. He walked away from the other men and was so angry that no one dared to speak with him.

Then the earl said, 'Bring me to the Njalssons. I'll force them to tell me the truth.'

He was told that they had already launched their ship.

'That's out, then,' he said. 'But there were two water casks beside Thrain's ship, and a man could easily have hidden in them. If Thrain was hiding Hrapp, he must be there, so let's go and visit Thrain once more.'

Thrain saw that the earl was setting out again and said, 'The earl was angry before, but now he'll be twice as angry, and the lives of all of us on board are at risk.'

They all promised to keep quiet, for every man feared for his life. They took some sacks out of the cargo and put Hrapp in their place, and then other, lighter sacks were placed on top of him. The earl arrived just when they had finished with him. Thrain greeted the earl, and the earl took his time returning the greeting, and they could see that he was very angry.

The earl spoke to Thrain: 'Hand over Hrapp, since I know for a fact that you've hidden him.'

'Where would I have hidden him, my lord?' said Thrain.

'That's for you to know,' said the earl, 'but if I am to make a guess, I would say that you hid him in the water casks the last time.'

'I wish you wouldn't charge me with lying, my lord,' said Thrain, 'and I would rather have you search the ship.'

The earl boarded the ship and searched it, but found nothing.

'Will you clear me now?' said Thrain.

'Far from it,' said the earl, 'but we can't find him, and I don't know why not. I seem to see through everything when I come ashore, but not when I come here.'

He had himself rowed ashore. He was so angry that no one could speak with him.

His son Svein was with him. He spoke: 'This is strange behaviour, letting innocent men feel one's wrath.'

The earl walked away from the other men again. Then he returned to them and said, 'Let's row out to them once more.'

They did.

'Where do you suppose he was hiding?' asked Svein.

'It doesn't matter,' said the earl, 'because he will have left that place by now, but there were two sacks lying to the side of the cargo. He probably took their place in the pile.'

Thrain spoke: 'The earl and his men are putting their ship out again and will come to us. Let's take Hrapp out of the cargo and put something else in his place, but leave those two sacks where they are.'

They did this.

Then Thrain said, 'Let's put Hrapp into the sail where it is rolled up on the yard.'

They did this. Then the earl arrived. He was very angry and said, 'Will you hand the man over now, Thrain? This is getting worse and worse.'

Thrain said, 'I would have handed him over long ago if he'd been in my care. Where might he have been?'

'Among the cargo,' said the earl.

'Why didn't you look for him there?' said Thrain.

'It didn't occur to us,' said the earl.

Then they searched all over the ship and did not find him.

Thrain said, 'Will you clear me now, my lord?'

'Certainly not,' said the earl, 'for I know you've hidden him, even though I can't find him. But I would rather that you were false to me than I to you.'

He returned to land.

'Now I see it,' said the earl: 'he hid Hrapp in the sail.'

The wind came up then, and Thrain sailed away into the sea. He spoke this couplet, which has been repeated ever since:

5.
Let *Griffin* fly forward,
Thrain does not flinch.

When the earl learned what Thrain had spoken, he said, 'This was not due to my lack of insight, but to the friendship between Thrain and Hrapp, which will drag them both to their deaths.'

Thrain had a swift sea journey to Iceland and went home to his farm. Hrapp went with him and stayed with him for a year, and the following summer Thrain gave him a farm at Hrappsstadir. Hrapp lived there, but spent most of his time at Grjota. There he was thought to be harmful in every way. Some said that he and Hallgerd were on friendly terms and that he had seduced her, but others denied this. Thrain gave his ship to his kinsman Mord the Careless. This Mord killed Odd Halldorsson out east at Gautavik in Berufjord.

All of Thrain's kinfolk looked on him as a chieftain.

89 | To return to the point where Earl Hakon let Thrain slip away: the earl said to his son Svein, 'Let's take four longships and row out after the Njalssons and kill them, since they must have been in on this with Thrain.'

'It's not well advised,' said Svein, 'to take action against innocent men and let the one who is guilty escape.'

'I'll decide this matter,' said the earl.

The earl then went looking for the Njalssons and found them next to an island. Grim was the first to see the earl's ship.

'Warships are heading here,' he said. 'I can make out the earl, and he's not coming to offer us peace.'

'It is said,' said Helgi, 'that the fearless man fights whomever he must. We too shall defend ourselves.'

They all asked him to take charge. They took up their weapons.

The earl came near and called to them and asked them to surrender. Helgi answered that they would defend themselves as long as they were able. The earl offered safe conduct to those who chose not to fight for Helgi, but Helgi was so well liked that they all preferred to die with him.

The earl and his men attacked, but they defended themselves well and the Njalssons were always where the fighting was hardest. The earl made repeated offers of safe conduct, but they answered as before and said they would never give in. Then Aslak of Langey attacked hard and boarded their ship three times.

Grim spoke: 'You're attacking hard, and it would be good for you to get what you're after.'

He grabbed his spear and threw it at his throat, and Aslak died instantly. Soon after this Helgi killed Egil, the earl's standard-bearer. Then Svein Hakonarson attacked and had his men pen them in with shields, and the Njalssons were captured.

The earl wanted to have them killed at once, but Svein said that must not be, and said too that it was night.

The earl said, 'Let them be killed tomorrow then, but tie them securely for the night.'

'So will it be,' said Svein, 'but I have never met braver men than these, and it is a great pity to take their lives.'

The earl said, 'They have killed two of our bravest men, and for that we must kill them.'

'That makes them all the braver,' said Svein, 'and yet it must be as you wish.'

Helgi and Grim were then tied up and fettered. After that the earl went to sleep.

When he was asleep, Grim said to Helgi, 'I'd like to get out of here if I could.'

'Let's try to find out how,' said Helgi.

Grim said that an axe was lying there with its edge pointing up. He crawled over to it and used it to cut the bowstring with which he was bound, but cut his arms badly. Then he freed Helgi. After that they crept overboard and came ashore, without the earl and his men knowing. They broke the fetters and walked to the other side of the island.

Dawn was coming. They saw a ship and realized that Kari Solmundarson had arrived there; they went straight to him and told him of their shameful treatment and showed him their wounds and said that the earl and his men were asleep.

Kari spoke: 'It's wrong that you should be treated shamefully because of bad men. What do you want most now?'

'To attack the earl and kill him,' they said.

'Fate will not allow that,' said Kari, 'but you don't lack courage. Anyway, let's find out if he's still there.'

They went there, but the earl was gone. Kari then sailed into Lade to see the earl and turn over the tribute money.[1]

The earl said, 'Have you taken the Njalssons into your keeping?'

'Yes, I have,' said Kari.

'Are you willing to turn them over to me?' said the earl.

'I am not,' said Kari.

'Will you swear,' said the earl, 'that you did not plan to attack me?'

The earl's son Eirik spoke up: 'It's not fair to ask that. Kari has always been our friend, and these things wouldn't have happened if I'd been there – the Njalssons would have been left alone and the ones who made the trouble would have been punished. I think it more fitting to give the Njalssons good gifts to make up for the shameful treatment they suffered, and their wounds.'

The earl said, 'Yes, it would be, but I don't know whether they're willing to come to terms.'

He said that Kari should see whether the Njalssons would be willing. Kari then asked Helgi whether he would accept an honourable settlement from the earl.

Helgi answered, 'I will accept it from his son Eirik, but I want nothing to do with the earl.'

Kari reported their answer to Eirik.

'So be it,' said Eirik. He shall receive an honourable settlement from me, if he prefers it that way, and tell them that I invite them to stay with me, and that my father will not harm them.'

They accepted this and went to Eirik and stayed with him until Kari was ready to sail west. Eirik then made a feast for Kari and gave good gifts to him and also to the Njalssons.

Kari and the Njalssons then sailed west across the sea to Earl Sigurd. He gave them a warm reception, and they stayed with him that winter.

In the spring Kari asked the Njalssons to go raiding with him, and Grim said they would, if Kari would then come with him to Iceland. Kari gave his promise.

They went raiding with him and raided in the south around Anglesey and all the Hebrides. Then they made for Kintyre and went ashore and fought with the people there and took much booty and returned to their ships. Then they went south to Wales and raided there; from there they went to the Isle of Man. There they met King Gudrod of Man and fought with him. They were victorious and killed Dungal, the king's son, and took much booty. From there they went north to Coll and met up with Earl Gilli and he welcomed them, and they stayed with him for a while. The earl went with them to Orkney to meet Earl Sigurd. In the spring Earl Sigurd gave his sister Nereid to Earl Gilli in marriage. Then he returned to the Hebrides.

90 | That summer Kari and the Njalssons prepared to sail to Iceland, and when they were ready they went to the earl. He gave them good gifts, and they parted in great friendship. Then they put out to sea. They had a short passage, and the winds were good, and they came ashore at Eyrar. There they took horses and rode from the ship to Bergthorshvol, and when they arrived home everybody was happy to see them. They brought their goods home and drew the ship up on land. Kari spent that winter with Njal.

In the spring Kari asked for the hand of Helga, Njal's daughter, and Grim and Helgi spoke up for him, with the result that she was betrothed to Kari and a wedding date was set and the feast took place two weeks before midsummer, and the couple spent the next winter with Njal. Then Kari bought land at Dyrholmar, over to the east in Myrdal, and set up a farm there. He and Helga put men in charge of it and went on living with Njal.

91 | Hrapp had a farm at Hrappsstadir, but he was always at Grjota, and he was thought to be harmful in every way. Thrain was good to him.

One time when Ketil of Mork was at Bergthorshvol the Njalssons told of their shameful treatment in Norway and said that they had much to settle with Thrain Sigfusson, should they ever bring it up. Njal said it would be best if Ketil spoke to his brother Thrain. Ketil promised to do so. They gave him time to talk with Thrain.

Some time later they raised this matter with Ketil, and he said he would not like to repeat many of the words that passed between him and Thrain – 'for it was clear that Thrain thought I set great store on being your brother-in-law.'

After this they stopped talking and realized that things were not going to be easy and asked their father for advice about what to do. They said that they were not willing to let things stand as they were.

Njal answered, 'This is not an easy matter. It would seem unjustified if they were killed now, and my advice is that you send as many people as possible to talk to them, so that if they make ugly remarks, many will hear them. Then Kari is to bring it up with them, for he is an even-tempered man. The hostility between you will grow, because they will pile up their abusive language as others join them – they are stupid men. It may also happen that people will say that my sons are slow to take action, and you must put up with that for a while, for the effect of every action is two-sided.[1] Only speak out if you are pushed hard and intend to act. If you had sought my advice at the outset, you would never have spoken out at all, and there would have been no disgrace in that, but now you face a very hard test. Your disgrace will grow to the point where you have no other choice than to deal with the difficulty and wield weapons to kill – and that is why we must put out such a wide net.'[2]

Here they ended their talk, but this became a topic of conversation among many.

One day the brothers told Kari that he should go to Grjota. He said that any other journey would seem better, but agreed to go if that was Njal's advice. Kari then went to see Thrain. They talked the matter over, but they did not see things the same way. Kari returned and the Njalssons asked him how he and Thrain had got along. Kari said he would not repeat the words that had passed between them – 'but it's likely that they will be said in your hearing.'

Thrain had fifteen men fit for fighting at his farm, and eight of them rode with him wherever he went. He was a great one for show and always rode out in a black cloak and a gilded helmet and carried the spear given to him by the earl and a beautiful shield, and wore a sword at his belt. Always with him as he travelled were Gunnar Lambason and Lambi Sigurdarson and Grani Gunnarsson of Hlidarendi. Killer-Hrapp was his closest companion, however. Thrain had a servant named Lodin; he too was always with Thrain when he travelled. So was Lodin's brother, whose name was Tjorvi.

Killer-Hrapp and Grani were the ones who spoke most abusively about the Njalssons and they saw to it that there was no offer of compensation.

The Njalssons often spoke to Kari about going with them to Grjota, and finally he did, and said that it would be good for them to hear Thrain's words for themselves. The four Njalssons, with Kari as a fifth, prepared themselves. They went to Grjota.

The porch at Grjota was wide, and many men could stand there side by side. There was a woman outdoors, and she saw the approach of the Njalssons and told Thrain. He ordered his men to take their weapons and go to the porch, and they did. Thrain stood in the middle, and on either side of him stood Killer-Hrapp and Grani Gunnarsson. Next came Gunnar Lambason, then Lodin and Tjorvi, then Lambi Sigurdarson, and then the others one by one, for all the men were at home.

Skarphedin and the others walked up to them, with Skarphedin in the lead, then Kari, then Hoskuld and Grim and Helgi. When they came up, there were no greetings at all from those who were waiting.

Skarphedin said, 'Welcome to all of us!'

Hallgerd was standing on the porch and had whispered something to Hrapp.

She spoke: 'No one standing here will say that you are welcome.'

Skarphedin spoke: 'Your words don't count, for you're either a cast-off hag³ or a whore.'

'You'll be paid for those words,' she said, 'before you go home.'

Helgi spoke: 'I've come, Thrain, to see if you will make me some compensation for the shameful treatment I suffered in Norway because of you.'

Thrain spoke: 'I never thought that you brothers would try to get money out of your manhood; how long do you intend to carry on this begging?'

'Many would say,' said Helgi, 'that you should have offered compensation, since your life was at stake.'

Then Hrapp spoke: 'It shows a difference in our luck that you were treated shamefully and we slipped away – the blow fell where it should have.'

'There's very little luck,' said Helgi, 'in breaking faith with the earl and taking up with you.'

'Aren't I the one you should be asking for redress?' said Hrapp. 'I'll pay you – as I think fitting.'

'The only exchange between us,' said Helgi, 'won't do you any good.'

Skarphedin spoke: 'Let's not exchange words with Hrapp, but just pay him a red skin for his grey one.'⁴

Hrapp spoke: 'Be quiet, Skarphedin. I won't be stingy about driving my axe into your head.'

'It remains to be seen,' said Skarphedin, 'which of us will be placing stones over the other's head.'

'Go home, Dung-beardlings,' said Hallgerd. 'We're going to call you that from now on, and we'll call your father Old Beardless.'

They did not leave until all those who faced them, except Thrain, had made themselves guilty of using those words. Thrain tried to restrain them from using those words.

The Njalssons left and went home. They told their father what had happened.

'Did you name any witnesses to their words?' said Njal.

'None,' said Skarphedin. 'We're going to prosecute this case in an assembly of weapons.'

'No one thinks any longer,' said Bergthora, 'that you have the nerve to use your weapons.'

'Go easy on goading your sons,' said Kari – 'they're already eager enough.'

After that Njal and his sons and Kari had a long hushed talk.

92 | There was much talk about this conflict of theirs, and everybody realized that as things were it would not calm down.

Runolf, the son of Ulf Aur-Godi from out east at Dal, was a friend of Thrain's and had invited Thrain to visit him. It was decided that he should come east in the third or fourth week of winter. Thrain asked Killer-Hrapp, Grani Gunnarsson, Gunnar Lambason, Lambi Sigurdarson, Lodin and Tjorvi to travel with him. There were eight men in all, and Thorgerd and Hallgerd were to go, too. Thrain let it be known that he planned to visit his brother Ketil at Mork, and he made clear how many days he planned to be away. They were all fully armed.

They rode east over the Markarfljot river and met some poor women, and they asked to be helped across to the west side of the river. They helped them.

They then rode on to Dal and had a good reception. Ketil of Mork was there ahead of them. They stayed for two days. Runolf and Ketil asked Thrain to make peace with the Njalssons, but he answered sharply and said he would never pay them a thing and that he would never be unprepared to take on the Njalssons, no matter where they met.

'Perhaps that is so,' said Runolf, 'but my understanding is quite different, that no one, since Gunnar of Hlidarendi died, is a match for them, and it is more likely that this will lead to death on one side or the other.'

Thrain said he was not afraid of that.

Thrain went up to Mork and stayed there for two days. Then he rode back down to Dal, and at both places he was sent away with fitting gifts.

The Markarfljot was flowing between ledges of ice, with frozen arches spanning the stream here and there. Thrain said that he planned to ride home that evening. Runolf asked him not to and said that it would be more prudent not to leave at the time he had given.

Thrain answered, 'That would be showing fear, and I don't want that.'

The women whom they had helped across the river came to Berg-thorshvol, and Bergthora asked where they had come from, and they said from over east in the Eyjafjoll district.

'Who helped you across the Markarfljot?' said Bergthora.

'The biggest show-offs around,' they said.

'And who were they?' said Bergthora.

'Thrain Sigfusson and his companions,' they said, 'and we didn't like the way they were so loud-mouthed and foul-mouthed in talking about your husband and his sons.'

'Many are unable to choose the words directed at them,' said Bergthora.

Then the women went away, and Bergthora gave them good gifts and asked them how long Thrain would be away, and they said that he would be away four or five days. Bergthora then told this to her sons and her son-in-law Kari, and they talked at length in secret.

The same morning that Thrain and his men were riding from the east, Njal woke up early and heard Skarphedin's axe strike the wall of his bed closet. Njal rose and went outside. He saw all his sons with their weapons, and also Kari, his son-in-law. Skarphedin was in front, in a black jacket, holding a small round shield with his axe ready on his shoulder. Next came Kari. He had on a silk jacket and a gilded helmet, and a shield with a lion drawn on it. After him came Helgi. He wore a red tunic and a helmet and was carrying a red shield marked with a hart. They were all in dyed clothing.

Njal called to Skarphedin, 'Where are you going, son?'

'To look for sheep,' he said.

'That's what you said the other time,' said Njal, 'but then you were hunting men.'[1]

Skarphedin laughed and said, 'Do you hear what the old man said? He's not naïve.'

'When was the other time you said this?' said Kari.

'When I killed Sigmund the White, Gunnar's kinsman,' said Skarphedin.

'Why?' said Kari.

'He had killed Thord Freed-man's son, my foster-father,' said Skarphedin.

Njal went inside, and they went up to Raudaskrid and waited. From there they could see the others when they rode west from Dal. The sun was shining and the skies were clear that day.

Thrain now came riding down from Dal along the gravel plain.

Lambi Sigurdarson spoke: 'Shields are shining over there at Rauda-skrid when the sun hits them – some men must be lying in ambush.'

'Then let's turn and ride down along the river,' said Thrain, 'and they'll come to meet us if they have any business with us.'

They turned and went downstream along the river.

Skarphedin spoke: 'They've seen us now, because they're changing their course, and now the only thing is to run down there ahead of them.'

Kari spoke: 'Many men lay ambushes with better odds than this – there are eight of them and five of us.'

They headed down along the river and saw where a frozen arch spanned it downstream, and they decided to cross over there.

Thrain and his men made their stand on the ice on the upriver side of the arch.

Thrain said, 'What can these men want? There are five of them, and eight of us.'

Lambi Sigurdarson said, 'My guess is that they would risk it even if one more were waiting for them.'

Thrain took off his cloak and his helmet.

It happened to Skarphedin, while they were running down along the river, that his shoe-string snapped, and he fell behind.

'Why are you holding back, Skarphedin?' said Grim.

'I'm tying my shoe,' said Skarphedin.

'Let's go on ahead,' said Kari; 'I doubt that he'll be any slower than we are.'

They moved down towards the frozen arch at great speed. Skarphedin jumped up as soon as he tied his shoe and had his axe raised. He ran to the river, but it was so deep that for a long stretch it was unfordable. A broad slab of ice, smooth as glass, had formed on the other side of the river, and Thrain and his men were standing in the middle of it. Skarphedin took off into the air and leaped across the river from one ice ledge to the other and made a steady landing and shot on in a glide. The ice slab was very smooth, and Skarphedin went along as fast as a bird in flight.

Thrain was about to put on his helmet, but Skarphedin came at him first and swung his axe at him and hit him on his head and split it down to the jaw, so that the molars fell out on the ice. This happened in such rapid sequence that no one could land a blow on Skarphedin; he went gliding away at a furious speed. Tjorvi threw a shield in his way, but he hopped over it and kept his balance and glided to the end of the ice slab. Then Kari and the others came up to him.

'A manly attack, that!' said Kari.

'Your part is yet to come,' said Skarphedin.

Then they went at them. Grim and Helgi saw where Hrapp was and headed for him. Hrapp swung his axe at Grim. Helgi saw this and swung at Hrapp's arm and cut it off, and the axe fell down.

Hrapp spoke: 'You've done what needed doing – that arm brought wounds and death to many a man.'

'This will put an end to it,' said Grim and thrust his spear through him. Hrapp fell down dead.

Tjorvi went against Kari and threw his spear at him. Kari leaped into the air and the spear flew under his feet. Then Kari rushed at him and swung at him with his sword, and it hit the chest and went deep inside, and Tjorvi died at once.

Skarphedin grabbed hold of both Gunnar Lambason and Grani Gunnarsson and spoke: 'I've caught two puppies. Now what should I do with them?'

'You could choose to kill them both,' said Helgi, 'if you wanted to seal their fate.'

'I don't have the heart,' said Skarphedin, 'to help Hogni[2] and at the same time kill his brother Grani.'

'Some day it will come about,' said Helgi, 'that you will wish you had killed him, for he will never keep faith with you, nor will any of these who are here now.'

Skarphedin spoke: 'I will not fear them.'

So they spared Grani Gunnarsson and Gunnar Lambason and Lambi Sigurdarson and Lodin.

After that they went back home, and Njal asked what had happened. They told him everything.

Njal spoke: 'These are serious events, and it is likely that the death of one of my sons will result from this, if nothing worse.'

Gunnar Lambason returned home and brought Thrain's body to Grjota, and there a mound was raised over him.

93 | Ketil of Mork was married to Njal's daughter Thorgerd, but he was also Thrain's brother and he felt himself to be in a difficult position. He rode to Njal and asked if he were willing to pay compensation for the slaying of Thrain.

Njal answered, 'I will pay such compensation that all will be well. But I want you to persuade your brothers, who have the right to the payment, to accept a settlement.'

Ketil said he would be glad to do that. They decided that Ketil should visit all those who were entitled to payment and get them to agree to peace.[1] Then Ketil rode home.

Later he went to his brothers and summoned them all to Hlidarendi and discussed the matter with them there, and Hogni took his side on every point, with the result that men were selected as arbitrators. A meeting was called and payment was awarded for the slaying of Thrain, and they all accepted compensation, according to law. After that a state of peace was declared and secured as well as possible. Njal paid the full amount readily. Things were then quiet for a while.

One day Njal rode up to Mork, and he and Ketil met and talked the whole day long. In the evening Njal rode back home, and no one knew what plans had been made.

Ketil went to Grjota. He spoke to Thorgerd: 'I was always very fond of my brother Thrain – now I want to show it by offering to foster his son Hoskuld.'

'I'll grant you this,' she said, 'provided you do everything you can for him when he is grown, and avenge him if he is killed with weapons, and contribute to his morning gift when he marries – and you are to swear to this.'

Ketil agreed to all this. Hoskuld then went back home with him. Some time passed, during which Hoskuld was with Ketil.

94 | One day Njal rode up to Mork and was given a good reception; he stayed there for the night. That evening Njal called to the boy, and he came to him. Njal had a gold ring on his finger and showed it to the boy. The boy took it and looked at it and put it on his finger.

Njal spoke: 'Will you accept this ring as a gift?'

'I will,' said the boy.

'Do you know,' said Njal, 'what caused the death of your father?'

The boy answered, 'I know that Skarphedin killed him, but we don't have to mention that, since the matter was settled and full compensation was paid.'

'Your answer is better than my question,' said Njal, 'and you will be a good man.'

'I am glad for the good you foretell for me,' said the boy, 'for I know that you see the future and never lie.'

Njal spoke: 'Now I want to offer to make you my foster-son, if you are willing.'

He said he would accept both this kindness and any other that Njal should do. It was settled that Hoskuld went home with Njal, and Njal raised him as his foster-son. He did everything he could for him and loved him very much. The sons of Njal took him along everywhere and did all they could to favour him.

Time passed, until Hoskuld was fully grown. He was big and strong, a very handsome man with beautiful hair, fair of speech, generous, even-tempered, and skilled in fighting, with a kind word for everybody. He was well liked. The sons of Njal and he never disagreed about anything.

95 | There was a man named Flosi. He was the son of Thord Frey's Godi, the son of Ozur, the son of Asbjorn, the son of Heyjang-Bjorn, the son of Helgi, the son of Bjorn Buna. Flosi's mother was Ingunn, the daughter of Thorir of Espihol, the son of Hamund Dark-skin, the son of Hjor, the son of Half who led Half's Warriors,

the son of Hjorleif the Womanizer. Thorir of Espihol's mother was Ingunn, the daughter of Helgi the Lean who settled Eyjafjord. Flosi was married to Steinvor, the daughter of Hall of Sida. She was born out of wedlock, and her mother was Solvor, the daughter of Herjolf the White.[1]

Flosi lived at Svinafell and was a great chieftain. He was big and strong and very forceful.

He had a brother named Starkad; they shared the same father, but Starkad's mother was Thraslaug, the daughter of Thorstein Sparrow, the son of Geirleif. Thraslaug's mother was Unn, the daughter of Eyvind Karfi the settler and the sister of Modolf the Wise.

Flosi's other brothers were Thorgeir, Stein, Kolbein and Egil.

Hildigunn was the daughter of Flosi's brother Starkad. She was a woman with a mind of her own and very beautiful. Few women could match her skill at handiwork. She was an unusually tough and harsh-tempered woman, but a fine woman when she had to be.

96 | There was a man named Hall, known as Hall of Sida. He was the son of Thorstein Bodvarsson. Hall's mother was Thordis, the daughter of Ozur, the son of Hrodlaug, the son of Earl Rognvald of More, the son of Eystein the Noisy. Hall was married to Joreid, the daughter of Thidrandi the Wise, the son of Ketil Thrym, the son of Thorir Thidrandi of Veradal. Joreid's brothers were Ketil Thrym of Njardvik and Thorvald, the father of Helgi Droplaugarson. Hallkatla was the sister of Joreid and the mother of Thorkel and Thidrandi Geitisson.[1]

Thorstein, known as Broad-belly, was Hall's brother. He had a son Kol, whom Kari was to slay in Wales.[2]

The sons of Hall of Sida were Thorstein, Egil, Thorvard, Ljot and Thidrandi, whom, it is said, the *dísir* killed.[3]

There was a man named Thorir, known as Holta-Thorir. His son was Skorargeir, and Skorargeir's brothers were Thorleif Crow, from whom the people of Skogar are descended, and Thorgrim the Tall.[4]

97 | To tell now about Njal, who had these words with Hoskuld: 'I
would like to arrange a marriage, my foster-son, and find a
woman for you.'

Hoskuld said that Njal should decide and asked where he thought
best to look.

Njal answered, 'There's a woman named Hildigunn, the daughter
of Starkad, the son of Thord Frey's Godi. She's the best choice I know
of.'

Hoskuld said, 'You take care of it, my foster-father. I'll go along
with whatever you arrange.'

'We'll ask for her, then,' said Njal.

After this Njal gathered men for the journey. The Sigfussons and
all of Njal's sons and Kari Solmundarson went with him. They rode
east to Svinafell and were given a good reception there.

The next day Njal and Flosi had a talk together. Njal eventually
came around to saying, 'The reason for our journey here is to propose
a link with your family, Flosi, by asking for the hand of Hildigunn,
your brother's daughter.'

'On behalf of whom?' said Flosi.

'On behalf of Hoskuld Thrainsson, my foster-son,' said Njal.

'That's a good proposal,' said Flosi, 'but the relationship between
you and Hoskuld is very precarious.[1] What can you say about Hoskuld?'

'Only good things can be said about him,' said Njal, 'and I shall
put up as much money as you think fitting, if you're willing to give
this your consideration.'

'We'll call her,' said Flosi, 'and find out how she likes the man.'

They called her and she came. Flosi told her of the proposal.

She said she was a proud woman – 'and I don't know how it would
suit me to be involved with such people, especially since the man has
no godord. You told me once that you would not marry me to a man
who was not a godi.'

'It's reason enough for me to turn down the offer,' said Flosi, 'if you
don't want the marriage.'

'I'm not saying,' she said, 'that I wouldn't marry Hoskuld if they
found a godord for him. But otherwise I won't consider it.'

'In that case,' said Njal, 'I'd like you to let this matter wait for three years.'

Flosi agreed to this.

'I will make one condition,' said Hildigunn, 'that if this marriage goes ahead, we live here in the east.'

Njal said he would leave that up to Hoskuld, and Hoskuld said that he trusted many men, but none as much as his foster-father. Then they rode back west.

Njal tried to find a godord for Hoskuld, but no one was willing to sell his.

The summer moved on until time for the Althing. That year there were many lawsuits. As usual, many people came to consult Njal, but he gave advice which, unlikely as it seemed, ruined both prosecution and defence and led to much wrangling when cases could not be settled, and men rode home from the Thing unreconciled.

Time passed until the next Thing. Njal went to it. Everything was calm at first, until Njal declared that it was time for men to give notice of their lawsuits. Many said that this was hardly worth it, for even cases brought to the Thing were getting nowhere – 'and we would rather,' they said, 'press our claims with point and blade.'

'That you must not do,' said Njal, 'for it will not do to be without law in the land. But there is much truth in what you say, and those of us who know the law should shape it. The best step, it seems to me, is for us to call a meeting of all the chieftains to talk about it.'

Then the Law Council convened. Njal spoke: 'I appeal to you, Skafti Thoroddsson,[2] and all you other chieftains – I think we have come to an impasse when we prosecute cases in the Quarter Courts and they become so entangled that they can not be settled or even moved along. The wisest course, in my opinion, would be to have a Fifth Court and prosecute cases there that can't be settled in the Quarter Courts.'

'How can you set up a Fifth Court,' said Skafti, 'when the Quarter Courts were set up on the basis of the traditional number of godis, thirty-six from each Quarter?'

'I see a way around this,' said Njal, 'by creating new godords and appointing the best qualified men from each Quarter, and whoever wants to can declare allegiance to these new godis.'

'We will accept this plan,' said Skafti, 'but what sort of cases should be prosecuted in this court or referred to it?'

'All violations of Thing procedure should be referred to it,' said Njal, 'as well as cases of perjury or false verdict. Also, cases in which no agreement was reached in the Quarter Court shall be referred to the Fifth Court, as well as cases involving the offer or acceptance of payment for assistance in legal suits[3] and giving shelter to slaves or debtors.

'The firmest kind of oaths shall be sworn in this court, with two men backing each oath by swearing on their honour to what the others swear.

'If one party prosecutes its case correctly, and the other incorrectly, the judgement shall be awarded to the one who followed correct procedure.

'Every case is to be prosecuted here just as in the Quarter Courts, with the difference that since forty-eight men will be appointed to the Fifth Court, the prosecution is to remove six and the defence another six. If the defence chooses not to do so, the prosecution is to remove those that the defence should have removed, and if the prosecution fails to do this the case is invalidated, for the number of judges must be thirty-six.

'We should also set up the Law Council so that those sitting on the middle benches are empowered to decide on laws and exemptions, and the most wise and capable men should be chosen for this. The Fifth Court shall also sit there. If the members of the Law Council cannot agree on granting exemptions or making laws, a majority vote shall decide. If someone is unable to gain access to the Council or has had his suit repelled by force, he shall present a veto within the hearing of the Council and thereby invalidate all exemptions and legal decisions the Council has made.'

After this, Skafti Thoroddsson put the Fifth Court into law, along with everything that had been proposed. Then people went to the Law Rock; they set up the new godords. In the North Quarter they were given to the people of Mel in Midfjord and the people of Laufas in Eyjafjord.

Then Njal called for silence and spoke: 'What happened between my sons and the men of Grjota is well known, that they killed Thrain Sigfusson, and yet we settled the matter peaceably, and I took Hoskuld into my home, and now I have arranged a marriage for him, provided that he becomes a godi. But no godi is willing to sell his office. I therefore ask your permission to set up a new godord at Hvitanes for Hoskuld.'

Everyone approved this; then he set up a new godord for Hoskuld, who was called the Godi of Hvitanes from then on. After that people rode home from the Thing.

Njal was home only a short time before he and his sons rode east to Svinafell and brought up the marriage proposal with Flosi, and Flosi said he would keep his word. Hildigunn was then betrothed to Hoskuld and a date for the wedding feast was fixed and the matter was settled. Then they rode home.

They rode to Svinafell again for the wedding. Flosi paid out the agreed dowry for Hildigunn and did so readily. The couple went to Bergthorshvol and lived there for a year, and Hildigunn and Bergthora got along well.

The next summer Njal bought land at Ossabaer and gave it to Hoskuld, and he went and settled there.[4] Njal hired all the servants for him. They were on such warm terms that no one took a decision unless all the others agreed to it.

Hoskuld lived for a long time at Ossabaer, and he and the Njalssons added to each other's prestige, and they went with him on his journeys. So fervent was their friendship that they invited each other to a feast every autumn and exchanged generous gifts. This went on for a long time.

98 | There was a man called Lyting, who lived at Samsstadir. He was married to a woman named Steinvor Sigfussdottir, Thrain's sister. Lyting was a big, strong man, prosperous but vicious to deal with.

One day it happened that Lyting had a feast at Samsstadir. He had invited Hoskuld and the Sigfussons, and they all came. Grani Gunnarsson and Gunnar Lambason and Lambi Sigurdarson were also there.

Hoskuld Njalsson[1] and his mother Hrodny had a farm at Holt, and Hoskuld often rode there from Bergthorshvol and passed by the farm at Samsstadir. Hoskuld had a son called Amundi, who had been born blind. He was none the less big and powerful.

Lyting had two brothers, one named Hallstein and the other Hallgrim. They were the worst troublemakers and always lived with their brother because no one else could stand them.

Lyting was mostly outdoors on the day of the feast, but went inside now and then. When he took his seat, a woman who had been outdoors came in.

She spoke: 'It's too bad you were not outside when the show-off rode past the farm.'

'Who's this show-off you're talking about?' asked Lyting.

'Hoskuld Njalsson,' she said, 'has just ridden past the farm.'

Lyting spoke: 'He often rides past, and not without annoyance to me, and I'll offer to go with you, Hoskuld, if you want to avenge your father and kill Hoskuld Njalsson.'

'I don't want that,' said Hoskuld, 'for then I would be repaying my foster-father far worse than he deserves. May no luck come to you and your feast!' – and he jumped up from the table and called for his horses and rode home.

Then Lyting spoke to Grani Gunnarsson: 'You were there when Thrain was slain, and it must be fresh in your mind, and you too, Gunnar Lambason and Lambi Sigurdarson. I want us to ride out to meet him and kill him this evening when he rides home.'

'No,' said Grani, 'I will not attack the Njalssons and break a settlement which good men have made.'

Gunnar and Lambi spoke similar words, and so did the Sigfussons, and they all decided to ride away. When they were gone, Lyting said, 'Everyone knows that I have not received compensation for my brother-in-law Thrain,[2] and I'll never be content until there is blood revenge.'

Then he called together his two brothers and three servants for the trip. They went to where Hoskuld would be coming and lay in ambush in a hollow north of the farm and waited there until six in the evening. Then Hoskuld came riding towards them. They all sprang up with their weapons and attacked him. Hoskuld defended himself so bravely that for a long time they made no headway. As time went on he wounded Lyting on the arm and killed two of his servants and then was slain. They had given him sixteen wounds, but did not cut off his head. They went into the woods east of the Ranga river and hid there.

That evening Hrodny's shepherd found Hoskuld's body and went home and told her of the slaying of her son.

She spoke: 'He isn't really dead – was his head off?'

'No, it wasn't,' he said.

'I'll know when I see him,' she said. 'Get my horse and sled.'

He did and made everything ready, and then they went to where Hoskuld lay. She looked at his wounds and spoke: 'It's as I thought – he's not quite dead, and Njal can heal worse wounds than these.'

They took the body and laid it on the sled and drove to Bergthorshvol and dragged the body into the sheep shed and placed it sitting upright against the wall. Then they went to the house and knocked on the door, and a servant came. Hrodny rushed past him and made her way to Njal's bed. She asked him whether he was awake.

He said he had been sleeping until now but was awake – 'but why have you come here so early?'

Hrodny spoke: 'Get up from those cushions and away from that other woman,[3] and come outside with me – she too, and your sons.'

They all got up and went outside.

Skarphedin said, 'Let's take our weapons with us.'

Njal had nothing to say to this, and they ran back inside and came out again with their weapons. She went ahead, until they came to the sheep shed. She went in first and asked them to follow.

Then she raised her lantern and spoke: 'Here, Njal, is your son Hoskuld – he's had many wounds and now he needs healing.'

Njal spoke: 'I see signs of death on him, and no signs of life. Why didn't you do the closing rite for him? His nostrils are still open.'[4]

'I was saving that for Skarphedin,' she said.

Skarphedin came forward and did the closing rite for him. Then he spoke to his father: 'Who do you say killed him?'

Njal answered, 'Lyting of Samsstadir and his brothers must have killed him.'

Hrodny spoke: 'Skarphedin, I place in your hands the vengeance for your brother, and even though he was not born in wedlock I expect you to do well and pursue this with the greatest zeal.'

Bergthora spoke: 'You men act strangely – you kill when the cause is small, but in matters like this you swallow and chew until nothing comes of it. When word of this comes to Hoskuld the Godi of Hvitanes, he'll come and ask you to make a settlement, and you'll grant him that – but now's the time to take action, if you have the will.'

Skarphedin said, 'Our mother's goading is well founded.'

Then they rushed out. Hrodny went into the house with Njal and was there that night.

99 | To turn to Skarphedin and his brothers: they were on their way up towards the Ranga river. Skarphedin said, 'Let's stop here and listen.'

Then he said, 'Let's move softly, because I hear men's voices upriver. Now which do you prefer, to deal with Lyting or with his two brothers?'

They said they would rather deal with Lyting.

'He's the bigger catch,' said Skarphedin, 'and I wouldn't like it if he got away – I trust myself best to see that he doesn't.'

'If we get close to him,' said Helgi, 'we'll fix it so he doesn't get away.'

They went to where Skarphedin had heard voices and saw Lyting and his brothers by the side of a stream. Skarphedin at once jumped over the stream and onto the gravel slope on the other side. Hallgrim and his brothers were standing up above. Skarphedin swung at Hallgrim's thigh so hard that he took the leg off at once, and with his other hand he grabbed Hallkel. Lyting thrust at Skarphedin; Helgi came up then and caught the blow on his shield. Lyting picked up a stone with his other hand and hit Skarphedin with it, and Hallkel got free. He ran up the slope but could not manage except by crawling on his knees. Skarphedin smashed his axe at him and hacked through his backbone.

Lyting turned to flee, but Grim and Helgi went after him and they each inflicted a wound on him. He fled across the river to the horses and galloped off, all the way to Ossabaer.

Hoskuld was at home, and Lyting went to him at once. He told him what had happened.

'This was to be expected of you,' said Hoskuld. 'You acted very rashly. Here is the proof of the saying that the hand's joy in the blow is brief, and now it seems to me that you must be in some doubt as to whether you'll be able to save your life.'

'It's true,' said Lyting, 'that I barely escaped, but now I'd like you to arrange a settlement between me and Njal and his sons, one by which I could keep my farm.'

'I'll do that,' said Hoskuld.

Hoskuld then had his horse saddled and rode with five others to Bergthorshvol. Njal's sons had come back by then and gone to bed. Hoskuld went to Njal at once, and they went off for a talk.

Hoskuld spoke to Njal: 'I have come here to plead for Lyting, my aunt's husband. He has done you great harm: he has broken the settlement and killed your son.'

Njal spoke: 'Lyting must think he has paid dearly with the death of his brothers. If I give him a chance, I do so for your sake, but first I set these conditions – that Lyting's brothers be treated as outlaws and that Lyting receive nothing for his wounds and also pay full compensation for Hoskuld.'

Hoskuld said, 'I want you to decide the terms yourself.'

Njal said, 'I'll do as you wish.'

'Do you want your sons to be present?' said Hoskuld.

Njal said, 'In that case we would not get close to a settlement, but they'll keep to whatever I decide.'[1]

Then Hoskuld spoke: 'Let's settle the matter now, and you must offer peace to Lyting on behalf of your sons.'

'So be it,' said Njal. 'I want him to pay two hundreds in silver for the slaying of Hoskuld, and he may continue to live at Samsstadir, but it would seem to me wiser for him to sell that land and move away – not because I or my sons will break peace with him, but because someone may turn up there whom he had best avoid. So that it doesn't seem that I am outlawing him from the district, I'll allow him to stay here, but then he's responsible for himself.'

Then Hoskuld went home.

The Njalssons woke up and asked their father what had happened, and he told them that his foster-son Hoskuld had been there.

'He must have made a plea on behalf of Lyting,' said Skarphedin.

'Yes,' said Njal.

'That's bad,' said Grim.

'Hoskuld wouldn't have been able to shield Lyting,' said Njal, 'if you had killed him, as you were meant to.'

'Let's not blame our father,' said Skarphedin.

It has to be said that this settlement between them was kept.

100 | There was a change of rulers in Norway. Earl Hakon had passed away, and in his place came Olaf Tryggvason.[1] The end of Earl Hakon's life came when the slave Kark cut his throat at Rimul in Gaulardal.

Along with this came news of a change of religion in Norway: they had given up their old faith, and the king had also converted the western lands – the Shetlands, Orkney, and the Faroe Islands – to Christianity.

Many people were saying, and Njal heard them, that it was absurd to reject the old faith. Then Njal said, 'It seems to me that this new faith is much better, and that he who accepts it will be happy. If the men who preach this religion come out here, I will speak in favour of it.'

He said this often. He often went apart and murmured to himself.

That autumn a ship came into Berufjord in the east and landed at a place called Gautavik. Thangbrand was the name of the skipper; he was the son of Count Vilbaldus of Saxony. Thangbrand had been sent out here to Iceland by King Olaf Tryggvason to preach the faith. With him was an Icelander called Gudleif, who was the son of Ari, the son of Mar, the son of Atli, the son of Ulf the Squinter, the son of Hogni the White, the son of Otrygg, the son of Oblaud, the son of King Hjorleif the Womanizer of Hordaland. Gudleif was a great warrior and very brave, tough in every way.

Two brothers lived at Berunes. One was called Thorleif and the other Ketil. They were the sons of Holmstein, the son of Ozur from Breiddal. The brothers called men to a meeting and forbade them to trade with Thangbrand and Gudleif.

Hall of Sida learned of this; he lived at Thvotta in Alftafjord. He rode to the ship with thirty men and went straight to Thangbrand and said, 'There's not much trading, is there?'

Thangbrand said that this was true.

'Then I want to tell you why I have come,' said Hall. 'I want to invite all of you to stay with me, and I will see if I can find a market for your goods.'

Thangbrand thanked him and went to Thvotta.

That same autumn Thangbrand went out early one morning and had a tent set up and sang mass in the tent and made a great show of it, for it was a major feast-day.

Hall said to Thangbrand, 'In whose memory are you celebrating this day?'

'The angel Michael's,' he said.

'What features does this angel have?' said Hall.

'Many,' said Thangbrand. 'He weighs everything that you do, both good and evil, and he is so merciful that he gives more weight to what is well done.'

Hall said, 'I would like to have him for my friend.'

'That you may,' said Thangbrand; 'give yourself to him today, in the name of God.'

'I'll do it on this condition,' said Hall: 'that you promise, on his behalf, that he shall be my guardian angel.'

'I promise,' said Thangbrand.

Hall and all his household were then baptized.

101 | The following spring Thangbrand travelled around preaching the faith, and Hall went with him. When they came west across Lon heath to Stafafell a man called Thorkel was living there. He spoke strongest of all against the faith and challenged Thangbrand to a duel. Thangbrand carried a crucifix rather than a shield, and yet the outcome was that he won the duel and killed Thorkel.

From there they went to Hornafjord and were guests at Borgarhofn, west of Heinabergssand. Hildir the Old lived there; his son was Glum, who later went to the burning with Flosi. Hildir and all his household took the faith.

From there they went to the Fell District and were given hospitality at Kalfafell. Kol Thorsteinsson, Hall's nephew, lived there, and he and all his household took the faith.

From there they went to Breida. Ozur Hroaldsson, another kinsman of Hall's, lived there and took the sign of the cross.[1]

From there they went to Svinafell, where Flosi took the sign of the cross and promised to support them at the Althing.

From there they went west to the Skogar district and were given hospitality at Kirkjubaer. Surt lived there, the son of Asbjorn, the son of Thorstein, the son of Ketil the Foolish. All these men, fathers and sons, had already become Christians.

After this they left the Skogar district and went to Hofdabrekka. Word of their travels had come there before them.

There was a man called Hedin the Sorcerer, who lived at Kerlingardal. The heathens there paid him to put Thangbrand and his companions to death, and he went up to Arnarstakk heath and performed a great sacrifice there. Then, when Thangbrand was riding from the east, the earth split open under his horse; he leaped off the horse and climbed up to the rim of the chasm, but the earth swallowed up his horse with all its gear, and they never saw it again. Then Thangbrand gave praise to God.

102 | Gudleif went looking for Hedin the Sorcerer and found him on the heath and chased him down to the river Kerlingardalsa. He came within range of him and threw his spear at him and through him.

From there they went to Dyrholmar and held a meeting there, and Thangbrand preached the faith, and Ingjald, the son of Thorkel Haeyjar-Tyrdil, became a Christian.

From there they went to Fljotshlid and preached the faith there. Veturlidi the Poet and his son Ari spoke strongest of all against them, and for this reason they killed Veturlidi. This verse was composed about it:

6.

The tester of shields	*tester of shields*: warrior (Thangbrand)
took his victory-tools south	*victory-tools*: weapons
to smite the Balder of weapons	*Balder of weapons*: warrior (Veturlidi)
in his smithy of prayers.	*smithy of prayers*: breast
The brave battler for faith	
brought down with a clang	
his axe of awful death	
on the anvil of Veturlidi's head.	*anvil*: crown

From there Thangbrand went to Bergthorshvol, and Njal accepted the faith, together with his household. Mord and Valgard fought hard against the faith.

They went west from there across the rivers and came to Haukadal and baptized Hall, who was then three years old.[1]

From there they went to Grimsnes. Thorvald the Sickly mobilized a band of men against them and sent word to Ulf Uggason to attack Thangbrand and kill him. Thorvald sent him this verse:

7.

I, Ygg of armour   *Ygg of armour*: warrior
send this order to Ulf –
I'm fond of the son of Uggi,
the steerer of steel –   *steerer of steel*: warrior
that he crush the cowardly
blaspheming cur
against the loud lodge of Geitir,   *Geitir*: a giant; *his lodge*: cliffs
and I'll look after another.

Ulf Uggason replied with another verse:

8.

Though the dear friend
of the drink of Odin's hall   its *friend*: poet (Thorvald)
orders me, I am not   *drink of Odin's hall* poetry;
accepting the offered bait;
I won't fall for the fly
from the seafaring fellow;
bad things are brewing –
I'd better watch out.

'I don't intend to be his puppet,' he said, 'and he'd better take care that his tongue doesn't twist itself around his neck.'

After this the messenger returned to Thorvald the Sickly and repeated Ulf's words. Thorvald had many men with him and announced that he would lay an ambush for them on Blaskogar heath.

Thangbrand and Gudleif rode out of Haukadal and met a man who rode up to them. He asked for Gudleif, and when he met him he said, 'You can thank your brother Thorgils in Reykjaholar that I'm letting you know that they have laid many ambushes for you, and also that Thorvald the Sickly is with his men at the brook Hestlaek in Grimsnes.'

'That won't keep us from riding to meet them,' said Gudleif.

They turned down towards Hestlaek. Thorvald had already crossed the brook.

Gudleif said to Thangbrand, 'There's Thorvald. Let's get him!'

Thangbrand sent his spear right through Thorvald and Gudleif cut off his arm at the shoulder, and that was his death.

After that they rode to the Thing, and the kinsmen of Thorvald were about to attack them, but Njal and the men from the East Fjords gave them their support.

Hjalti Skeggjason spoke this verse:

9.
In barking at gods I am rich:
Freyja strikes me as a bitch;
one or the other must be:
Odin's a dog – or else she.

Hjalti and Gizur the White went abroad that summer. Thangbrand's ship, the *Bison*, was wrecked off Bulandsnes in the east.

Thangbrand travelled through all the western part of the land. Steinunn, the mother of Ref the Poet, came to meet him. She preached heathenism and lectured at great length to Thangbrand. Thangbrand was silent while she spoke, but then spoke at length and showed everything she said to be wrong.

'Have you heard,' she said, 'that Thor challenged Christ to a duel and that Christ didn't dare to fight with him?'

'What I have heard,' said Thangbrand, 'is that Thor would be mere dust and ashes if God didn't want him to live.'

'Do you know,' she said, 'who wrecked your ship?'

'What can you say about it?' he said.

'I'll tell you,' she said:

10.
The shaping gods drove ashore
the ship of the keeper of bells;   *keeper of bells*: priest (Thangbrand)
the slayer of the son of the giantess   *slayer of the son of the giantess*: Thor
smashed *Bison* on the sea-gull's rest;   *sea-gull's rest*: sea
no help came from Christ
when the sea's horse was crushed;   *sea's horse*: ship
I don't think God was guarding
Gylfi's reindeer at all.   *Gylfi*: a sea-king; his *reindeer*: ship

She spoke another verse:

11.

Thor drove Thangbrand's beast
of Thvinnil far from its place;   *Thvinnil*: a sea-king; his *beast*: ship
he shook and shattered
the ship and slammed it ashore;
never will that oak of Atal's field   *Atal*: a sea-king; *oak* of his *field*: ship
be up to seafaring again;
the storm, sent by him,   *him*: Thor
smashed it so hard into bits.

After that, Steinunn and Thangbrand parted, and Thangbrand and
his men went west to Bardastrond.

103 | Gest Oddleifsson lived at Hagi on Bardastrond; he was so very
wise a man that he foretold people's fates. He held a feast to
welcome Thangbrand and his men, and they went to Hagi, sixty in
all. It was said that two hundred heathens were already there and
that a berserk named Otrygg was expected, and everybody feared
him. Many stories were told of him, such as that he feared neither
fire nor sword, and the heathens feared him greatly.

Thangbrand asked whether the people were willing to accept the
faith, and all the heathens spoke strongly against it.

'I will give you a chance,' said Thangbrand, 'to prove which is the
better faith. We will build three fires – you heathens bless one, I'll
bless another, and the third will be unblessed. If the berserk fears the
one which I blessed but walks through your fire, then you must accept
the faith.'

'That's well spoken,' said Gest, 'and I'll agree to this for myself and
my household.'

When Gest had said this, many others agreed, and there was loud
approval.

Then word came that the berserk was nearing the house, and the
fires were built and kindled; men took their weapons and jumped up
on the benches and waited. The berserk came charging through the

door with his weapons. He advanced into the room and walked at once through the fire which the heathens had blessed and came up to the fire which Thangbrand had blessed, but did not dare to walk through it and said that he was burning all over. He swung his sword towards the benches, but on the upswing it stuck fast in the crossbeam. Thangbrand struck him on the arm with his crucifix and a great miracle happened: the sword fell from the berserk's hand. Then Thangbrand drove his sword into the berserk's chest, and Gudleif hacked at his arm and cut it off. Many men then came up and finished off the berserk.

After this Thangbrand asked whether they were willing to accept the faith. Gest said that he intended to keep what he had promised. Thangbrand then baptized him and all his household and many others.

Thangbrand asked Gest's advice about whether he should go to the fjords further west, but Gest discouraged him and said that people there were rough and vicious to deal with – 'but if this faith is destined to take hold it will take hold at the Althing. All the chieftains from the whole land will be there.'

'I have already spoken at the Thing,' said Thangbrand, 'and there I had the most trouble of all.'

'But still, you've done most of the work,' said Gest, 'even though others may be destined to make the faith law. As they say, a tree doesn't fall at the first blow.'

Gest gave Thangbrand good gifts, and then Thangbrand went south again.

He went first to the South Quarter and from there to the East Fjords. He was a guest at Bergthorshvol, and Njal gave him good gifts. Then he rode east to Alftafjord, to Hall of Sida. He had his ship repaired, and the heathens called it *Iron Basket*. Thangbrand sailed abroad on this ship, with Gudleif.

104 | That summer at the Thing Hjalti Skeggjason was outlawed for mocking the gods.[1]

*

Thangbrand told King Olaf about the hostile acts of the Icelanders against him and said they were such sorcerers that the earth broke open under his horse and swallowed it up. King Olaf was so angry at this that he ordered all men from Iceland to be seized and put in a dungeon, and he planned to put them to death. But then Gizur the White and Hjalti came forth and offered to stand as pledges for these men and to go to Iceland and preach the faith. The king was pleased with this and all the Icelanders were released.

Gizur and Hjalti then prepared their ship for the journey to Iceland and were soon ready. They came to land at Eyrar when ten weeks of the summer had passed. They found horses at once, and men to unload the ship. They rode to the Thing, thirty in all, and sent word to the Christians to be ready for them.

Hjalti stayed behind at Reydarmuli, because he learned that he had been outlawed for mocking the gods, but when the others came to Vellandkatla, below Gjabakki, he came after them and said he did not want to let the heathens think that he feared them.

Many Christians rode out to meet them, and they rode to the Thing in a large company. The heathens had also assembled a company, and the whole assembly came close to breaking out in a fight, but that did not happen.

105 | There was a man called Thorgeir who lived at Ljosavatn; he was the son of Tjorvi, the son of Thorkel the Long.[1] His mother was called Thorunn, and she was the daughter of Thorstein, the son of Sigmund, the son of Gnupa-Bard. Gudrid was his wife; she was the daughter of Thorkel the Black of Hleidrargard: his brother was Orm Box-back, the father of Hlenni the Old from Saurbaer. Thorkel and Orm were sons of Thorir Snepil, the son of Ketil Brimil, the son of Ornolf, the son of Bjornolf, the son of Grim Hairy-cheeks, the son of Ketil Haeng, the son of Hallbjorn Half-troll from Hrafnista.

The Christians covered their booths, and Gizur and Hjalti were in the booth of the men from Mosfell. The next day both sides went to the Law Rock and both Christians and heathens named witnesses and declared themselves no longer bound by law to the other, and there was such an uproar at the Law Rock that no one could hear anyone else.

After this men went away, and everyone thought things looked most precarious. The Christians chose Hall of Sida as their lawspeaker, but he went to Thorgeir the Godi of Ljosavatn and gave him three marks of silver to proclaim the law, though this was a risky step, since Thorgeir was a heathen.

Thorgeir spread a cloak over his head and lay this way for a whole day, and no one spoke to him.[2] The next day people went to the Law Rock.

Thorgeir asked for silence and spoke: 'It appears to me that our affairs will reach an impasse if we don't all have the same law, for if the law is split asunder, so also will peace be split asunder, and we cannot live with that. Now I want to ask the heathens and the Christians whether they are willing to accept the law that I proclaim.'

They all assented to this. Thorgeir said that he wanted oaths from them and pledges that they would stick by them. They assented to this, and he took pledges from them.

'This will be the foundation of our law,' he said, 'that all men in this land are to be Christians and believe in one God – Father, Son and Holy Spirit – and give up all worship of false idols, the exposure of children, and the eating of horse meat. Three years' outlawry will be the penalty for open violations, but if these things are practised in secret there shall be no punishment.'[3]

A few years later all of these heathen practices were prohibited, so that they could be practised neither openly nor in secret.

Thorgeir then talked about the keeping of the Lord's day and fast days, Christmas and Easter and all major feasts. The heathens considered that they had been greatly deceived, but the new law took effect and everybody became Christian in this land.

After this people went home from the Thing.

106 | It happened three years later that Amundi the Blind, the son
of Hoskuld Njalsson, was present at the Thingskalar Assembly.
He had himself led from one booth to another. He came to the one
where Lyting from Samsstadir was; he had himself led into the booth
and up to where Lyting was sitting.

He spoke: 'Is Lyting of Samsstadir here?'

'What do you want of me?' said Lyting.

'I want to know,' said Amundi, 'what compensation you will pay
me for my father. I was born to him out of wedlock and I have
received no compensation.'[1]

'I have paid full compensation for the slaying of your father,' said
Lyting, 'and your father's father and brothers took the money, while
my brothers went without compensation. I committed an evil deed,
but I paid heavily for it.'

'I'm not asking,' said Amundi, 'whether you paid them compensation – I know that you made a settlement with them. I'm asking
what compensation you will pay to me.'

'None whatsoever,' said Lyting.

'I don't find that to be just before God,' said Amundi, 'seeing that
you struck so close to my heart. I can say this – if I were sound in
both my eyes, I would either have compensation for my father or take
blood revenge, and may God now settle between us.'

After that he went out, but as he reached the door he turned and
faced back into the booth; at that moment his eyes were opened.

He spoke: 'Praise be to God, my Lord. Now it can be seen what
He wants.'

After that he rushed back into the booth until he came up to
Lyting, and hit him in the head with his axe so that it sank all the
way to the back edge, and then he pulled it towards him. Lyting fell
forward, dead on the spot. Amundi went to the door and when he
reached the very place at which his eyes had opened, they closed
again, and he was blind all the rest of his life.

After that he had someone bring him to Njal and his sons. He told
them of the slaying of Lyting.

'You are not to be blamed for that,' said Njal, 'for such things are preordained, and when they occur they are a warning not to decline the claims of close kin.'

Njal then offered to make an agreement with Lyting's kinsmen. Hoskuld the Godi of Hvitanes worked on them to accept compensation, and the case was turned over to arbitration. Half of the normal compensation was disallowed on account of the just cause which Amundi was thought to have. After that they made pledges of good faith, and Lyting's kinsmen pledged good faith to Amundi.

People then rode home from the Thing, and for a long time it was peaceful.

107 | Valgard the Grey returned to Iceland; he was still a heathen. He went to his son Mord at Hof and spent the winter there.

He spoke to Mord: 'I've been riding far and wide in this district, and I can hardly recognize it as the same. I went to Hvitanes and saw many new booths and great changes. I went also to the place of the Thingskalar Assembly, and there I saw all our booths falling apart. What's the reason for this scandal?'

Mord said, 'New godords and a fifth court have been created, and people have stopped being my thingmen and gone over to Hoskuld.'[1]

Valgard spoke: 'You've repaid me poorly, with your unmanly handling of the godord I turned over to you. Now I want you to repay them in a way that will drag them all to their deaths. The way to do this is to turn them against each other with slander, so that the Njalssons kill Hoskuld. Many men will take action for this slaying, and the Njalssons will be killed because of it.'

'I won't be able to bring that off,' said Mord.

'I'll give you a plan,' said Valgard. 'You must invite the Njalssons home and send them away with gifts. You must begin spreading slander only when the friendship between you is strong and they trust you no less than they do each other. You will be able to take vengeance against Skarphedin for the money they took from you after Gunnar's death. You will regain your authority only when these men are all dead.'

They agreed with each other that this plan should be carried out.

'I wish, father, that you would accept the faith,' said Mord. 'You're an old man.'

'I don't want to,' said Valgard, 'and in fact, I would like you to renounce the faith and then see what happens.'

Mord said he would not do that. Valgard broke Mord's crosses and all his holy objects. Then Valgard fell sick and died and was buried in a mound.

108 | Some time later Mord rode to Bergthorshvol and met Skarphedin and his brothers. He spoke to them in flattering tones and talked all day and said he wanted to see much more of them. Skarphedin took all this well, but said that Mord had never made this effort before. Eventually, Mord entered into such great friendship with them that neither side took a decision unless the other agreed.[1] Njal was always displeased when Mord came there, and he always let his dislike be known.

One day when Mord came to Bergthorshvol, he spoke to the Njalssons: 'I've arranged a memorial feast for my father, and I want to invite you Njalssons and Kari, and I promise that you will not go away without gifts.'

They promised to come. He went home and prepared the feast. He invited many farmers, and the feast was well attended. The Njalssons and Kari also came there. Mord gave a large gold belt buckle to Skarphedin and a silver belt to Kari, as well as good gifts to Grim and Helgi.

They came home and praised these gifts and showed them to Njal. He said that they would end up paying the full price for them – 'and see to it that you don't pay him what he wants.'

109 | A short time later Hoskuld and the Njalssons exchanged visits, and the Njalssons invited Hoskuld first.

Skarphedin had a dark-brown horse, four years old, big and handsome. It was a stallion and had not yet fought another horse. Skarphedin gave this horse to Hoskuld, along with two mares. The others gave Hoskuld gifts, too, and affirmed their friendship with him.

Then Hoskuld invited the Njalssons to visit him at Ossabaer. He had many guests from the neighbourhood, and there was a large crowd. He had torn down his hall, but had three storehouses, and they were arranged for sleeping in.

Everyone whom he had invited came to the feast; it went very well. When people were ready to go home, Hoskuld chose good gifts for them and went along with the Njalssons on their way. The Sigfussons and all the others accompanied him. Both sides said that no one would ever come between them.

Some time later Mord came to Ossabaer and asked Hoskuld to talk with him. They went apart for a talk.

Mord spoke: 'There's a big difference between you and the Njalssons: you gave them good gifts, but they gave you gifts in great mockery.'

'What proof do you have of that?' said Hoskuld.

'They gave you a dark-brown horse, which they called an untested colt, and they did that in mockery because they consider you untested, too. I can also tell you that they envy your godord. Skarphedin took it over at the Thing when you failed to come to a meeting of the Fifth Court. He doesn't ever intend to part with the godord.'

'That's not true,' said Hoskuld. 'I took it back at the autumn assembly.'

'That was Njal's doing, then,' said Mord. 'But they also broke the agreement with Lyting.'

'I don't think they can be blamed for that,' said Hoskuld.[1]

'You won't deny,' said Mord, 'that when you and Skarphedin went east to the Markarfljot an axe fell from under his belt and that he had planned to kill you with it.'

'That was his wood-axe,' said Hoskuld, 'and I saw him put it under his belt. And for my part let it be said here and now that no matter what evil you speak of the Njalssons I will never believe it. And even if you happen to be telling the truth and it came down to their killing me or my killing them, I would much rather suffer death from them than do them any harm. You are the worse a man for having spoken these things.'

Mord then went home.

Some time later Mord went to see the Njalssons and said many things to the brothers and Kari.

'I've been told,' said Mord, 'that Hoskuld said that you, Skarphedin, broke the agreement with Lyting, and I've also found out that he thought you were plotting to murder him when the two of you rode east to the Markarfljot. And I don't consider it less of a murder plot when he invited you to a feast and put you in the storehouse which was farthest from the house and had wood carried to it all night long and was planning to burn you inside. As it turned out, Hogni arrived during the night and nothing came of the plan because they were afraid of him. Then Hoskuld and a large band of men went along with you on your way – he was going to make another attempt on your life and had put Grani Gunnarsson and Gunnar Lambason up to it, but they lost heart and didn't dare to attack.'

When he said these things they objected at first. But eventually they believed him, and great coldness grew up on their part towards Hoskuld, and they barely spoke to him when they met. Hoskuld made no reaction to this, and so it went on for a time.

Hoskuld went east to Svinafell for a feast that autumn, and Flosi welcomed him. Hildigunn was also there.

Flosi said to Hoskuld, 'Hildigunn tells me that there is great coldness between you and the Njalssons, and I don't like that at all, and so I propose that you don't ride back west, and I'll give you the farm at Skaftafell and send my brother Thorgeir to live at Ossabaer.'

'Then some would say,' said Hoskuld, 'that I was fleeing out of fear, and I don't want that.'[2]

'Then it is very likely', said Flosi, 'that this will lead to great trouble.'

'That's too bad,' said Hoskuld, 'for I would rather die without the right to compensation than that many should come to harm because of me.'

Hoskuld made ready to go home a few days later, and Flosi gave him a scarlet cloak trimmed with lace down to the hem. Hoskuld rode home to Ossabaer. There was peace for a time. Hoskuld was so well liked that he had hardly any enemies, but the same unpleasantness between him and the Njalssons continued all that winter.

Njal had taken Kari's son, called Thord, as his foster-son. He had also fostered Thorhall, the son of Asgrim Ellida-Grimsson. Thorhall was a vigorous man and resolute in everything. He had learned the law from Njal so well that he was one of the three greatest lawyers in Iceland.[3]

Spring came early that year, and men sowed their grain early.

110 | It happened one day that Mord came to Bergthorshvol. He and the Njalssons and Kari went apart to talk. Mord slandered Hoskuld as usual and added many new tales and kept provoking Skarphedin and the others to kill Hoskuld and said that Hoskuld would beat them to it if they did not act at once.

'You shall have what you want,' said Skarphedin, 'provided that you go along with us and take part.'

'I'm ready to do that,' said Mord.

They made a firm pact and agreed that Mord should come there that evening.

Bergthora asked Njal, 'What are they discussing out there?'

'I'm not in on their planning,' said Njal, 'but I was seldom left out when their plans were good.'

Skarphedin did not go to bed that evening, nor did his brothers or Kari. That night Mord Valgardsson came to them, and the Njalssons and Kari took their weapons and they all rode away. They rode until they came to Ossabaer and waited there by a wall. The weather was good and the sun had risen.

III | About that time Hoskuld the Godi of Hvitanes awoke; he put
on his clothes and covered himself with his cloak, Flosi's gift.
He took his seed-basket in one hand and his sword in the other and
went to his field and started sowing.

Skarphedin and the others had agreed that they would all inflict
blows. Skarphedin sprang up from behind the wall. When Hoskuld saw
him he wanted to turn away, but Skarphedin ran up to him and spoke:
'Don't bother taking to your heels, Hvitanes-Godi' – and he struck
with his axe and hit him in the head, and Hoskuld fell to his knees.

He spoke this: 'May God help me and forgive you.'

They all ran at him and finished him off.

When it was over Mord said, 'I've just had an idea.'

'What is it?' said Skarphedin.

'That I first go home, and then up to Grjota to tell them what
happened and express my disapproval of the deed. I know that
Thorgerd will ask me to give notice of the slaying, and I will do so,
because that will cause serious damage to their case.[1] I'll also send a
man to Ossabaer to find out how quickly Hildigunn and the men
there plan to act – he will hear about the slaying from them, and then
I'll pretend that this is how I first heard about it.'

'Go and do this, by all means,' said Skarphedin.

The Njalssons and Kari went home, and when they came they told
Njal what had happened.

'Tragic news,' said Njal, 'and terrible to hear, for it is fair to say
that I am so deeply touched with grief that I would rather have lost
two of my sons, as long as Hoskuld were still alive.'

'You may be excused for saying that,' said Skarphedin. 'You are an
old man and it's to be expected that this should touch you deeply.'

'It's not my old age,' said Njal, 'as much as the fact that I know
more clearly than you what will follow.'

'What will follow?' asked Skarphedin.

'My death,' said Njal, 'and that of my wife and all my sons.'

'What do you foresee for me?' asked Kari.

'It will prove hard for them to contend with your good fortune,'
said Njal, 'for you will outmatch them all.'

This was the only thing that ever touched Njal so deeply that he could never speak of it without being moved.

112 | Hildigunn woke up and saw that Hoskuld had left the bed. She said, 'My dreams have been harsh, not good – go and search for Hoskuld.'

They searched for him around the farm and did not find him. By then she had dressed. She went with two men to the field; there they found Hoskuld slain.

Mord's shepherd came up just then and told her that Skarphedin and his party had been riding away from there – 'and Skarphedin called out to me and announced that he had done the slaying.'

'A manly deed this would have been,' she said, 'if one man had done it.'

She picked up the cloak and wiped up all the blood with it and wrapped the clotted blood into the cloak and folded it and placed it in her chest.

Next she sent a man up to Grjota to carry the news there. Mord had already come and told them. Ketil of Mork had also come there.

Thorgerd spoke to Ketil: 'Hoskuld is dead, as we know. Now keep in mind what you promised when you took him as your foster-son.'

'It may well be,' he said, 'that I made many promises then, because I never expected that days like these would come. In fact, I'm in a difficult position, since I'm married to Njal's daughter – the nose is near to the eyes.'[1]

'Do you want Mord to give notice of the slaying, then?' said Thorgerd.

'I'm not sure,' said Ketil, 'for it seems to me that evil comes from him more often than good.'

But when Mord spoke to him, Ketil was the same as other men – he believed that Mord could be trusted – and they agreed that Mord should give notice of the slaying and prepare the case for action at the Althing.

*

Mord then went down to Ossabaer. Nine neighbours who lived closest to the scene of the slaying came there. Mord had ten men with him. He showed the neighbours Hoskuld's wounds and named witnesses to the fatal ones and named a man for every wound but one. He pretended not to know who had caused that one, but it was the one he had inflicted himself. He charged Skarphedin with the slaying, and his brothers and Kari with the wounds; next he summoned the nine neighbours to the Althing. After that he rode home.

He hardly ever met the Njalssons, and when they met they were cool towards each other, and this was according to their plan.

The slaying of Hoskuld spread to all parts of the land and was spoken badly of.

The Njalssons went to see Asgrim Ellida-Grimsson and asked for his support.

'You can count on my helping you in all large matters,' he said, 'but this one troubles me, because there are so many to prosecute the case, and the slaying is being spoken badly of all over the land.'

Then the Njalssons went home.

113 | There was a man called Gudmund the Powerful, who lived at Modruvellir in Eyjafjord. He was the son of Eyjolf, the son of Einar, the son of Audun the Rotten, the son of Thorolf Butter, the son of Thorstein Skrofi, the son of Grim Kamban. Gudmund's mother was Hallbera, the daughter of Thorodd Helmet, and Hallbera's mother was Reginleif, the daughter of Saemund the Hebridean; Saemundarhlid in Skagafjord is named for him. The mother of Eyjolf, Gudmund's father, was Valgerd Runolfsdottir, and Valgerd's mother was called Valborg; her mother was Jorunn the Unborn, the daughter of King Oswald the Saint. Jorunn's mother was Bera, the daughter of King Edmund the Saint. The mother of Einar, Eyjolf's father, was Helga, the daughter of Helgi the Lean who settled Eyjafjord. Helgi was the son of Eyvind the Norwegian; Helgi's mother was Rafarta, the daughter of the Irish king Kjarval. Helga's mother was Thorunn Hyrna, the daughter of Ketil Flat-nose, the son of Bjorn Buna, the

son of Grim the hersir; Grim's mother was Hervor, and her mother was Thorgerd, the daughter of King Haleyg of Halogaland.

Thorlaug was the name of Gudmund the Powerful's wife. She was the daughter of Atli the Mighty, the son of Eilif Eagle, the son of Bard of Al, the son of Ketil the Sly, the son of Skidi the Old. Thorlaug's mother was Herdis, the daughter of Thord at Hofdi, the son of Bjorn Byrdusmjor, the son of Hroald Hrygg, the son of Bjorn Iron-side, the son of Ragnar Shaggy-breeches, the son of Sigurd Ring, the son of Randver, the son of Radbard. The mother of Herdis was Thorgerd Skidadottir; her mother was Fridgerd, the daughter of the Irish king Kjarval.

Gudmund was a great and wealthy chieftain; he had a hundred servants. He oppressed the other chieftains north of Oxnadal heath so much that some had to leave their farms, others lost their lives to him, and others gave up their godords because of him. From him are descended all the best people of Iceland: the people of Oddi, the Sturlung family, the people of Hvamm and of Fljot, Bishop Ketil and many eminent men.

Gudmund was a friend of Asgrim Ellida-Grimsson, and Asgrim planned to ask him for support.

114 | There was a man called Snorri, who went by the name of Snorri the Godi. He lived at Helgafell until Gudrun Osvifsdottir bought that land from him, and she lived there from then on, and Snorri moved to Hvammsfjord and lived at Saelingsdalstunga. Snorri's father was Thorgrim, the son of Thorstein Cod-biter, the son of Thorolf Moster-beard, the son of Ornolf Fish-driver. Ari the Learned, however, says that Thorolf was the son of Thorgils Whale-side. Thorolf Moster-beard was married to Osk, the daughter of Thorstein the Red. Thorgrim's mother was Thora, the daughter of Olaf Feilan, the son of Thorstein the Red, the son of Olaf the White, the son of Ingjald, the son of Helgi. Ingjald's mother was Thora, the daughter of Sigurd Snake-in-the-eye, the son of Ragnar Shaggy-breeches. Snorri the Godi's mother was Thordis Sursdottir, the sister of Gisli.

Snorri was a great friend of Asgrim Ellida-Grimsson, and Asgrim planned to ask him for support.

Snorri was called the wisest of the men in Iceland who could not foretell the future. He was good to his friends, but fierce to his enemies.

That summer people rode to the Thing in large numbers from all quarters of the country, and many lawsuits had been prepared .

115 | Flosi learned of the slaying of Hoskuld and it caused him much grief and anger, but he remained even-tempered. He was told of the lawsuit that had been started over the slaying, but he made no comment.

He sent word to his father-in-law Hall of Sida and to Hall's son Ljot that they should come to the Thing with a large following. Ljot was thought to be the most promising chieftain-to-be in the east. It had been foretold that if he rode to the Thing for three summers and came home safe and sound, he would become the greatest chieftain in his family, and the oldest. He had already ridden one summer to the Thing and now he was going for the second time.

Flosi sent word to Kol Thorsteinsson; to Glum, the son of Hildir the Old; to Geirleif, the son of Onund Box-back; and to Modolf Ketilsson, and they all rode to join him. Hall also promised to come with a large following.

Flosi rode to Surt Asbjarnarson at Kirkjubaer; then he sent for Kolbein Egilsson, his brother's son, and he came there.

From there he rode to Hofdabrekka, where Thorgrim the Showy lived, the son of Thorkel the Fair. Flosi asked him to ride to the Althing with him, and he agreed to go along and said to Flosi, 'You have often been merrier than now, but you have a right to be as you are.'

Flosi spoke: 'It's true that I would give everything I own if this matter had never arisen. But when evil seed has been sown, evil will grow.'

From there he rode across Arnarstakk heath and came to Solheimar in the evening. Lodmund Ulfsson, a close friend of Flosi's, lived there, and he stayed overnight. In the morning Lodmund rode with him to Dal, and they spent the night there. Runolf, the son of Ulf Aur-Godi, lived there.

Flosi spoke to Runolf: 'Here we can hear the true story of the slaying of Hoskuld Hvitanes-Godi. You are a truthful man and live close to where it took place, and I will believe everything you tell me about how these men fell out with each other.'

Runolf said, 'There's no point in using pretty words. He was slain, though more than innocent, and his death is mourned by everybody – but by no one as much as his foster-father Njal.'

'Then it will be hard for them to find supporters,' said Flosi.

'That's right,' said Runolf, 'as long as things don't change.'

'What's been done so far?' said Flosi.

'The panel of neighbours has been summoned,' said Runolf, 'and notice of the slaying has been given.'

'Who gave the notice?' said Flosi.

'Mord Valgardsson,' said Runolf.

'Can he be trusted?' said Flosi.

'He's my kinsman,' said Runolf, 'but I must say, in truth, that more evil than good comes from him. Now I want to ask you to give your wrath a rest and take the course which will lead to the least trouble, for Njal and others of the best men will make good offers.'

Flosi said, 'Ride to the Thing, Runolf; your words will carry much weight with me, unless there's a change for the worse.'

With this they stopped talking, and Runolf promised to go. Runolf sent for Haf the Wise, his kinsman; he rode to him at once.

Flosi rode from there to Ossabaer.

116 | Hildigunn was outside and said, 'All my men are to be outside when Flosi rides up to the farm, and the women are to clean the house and put up the hangings and make the high seat ready for Flosi.'

Soon Flosi rode into the hayfield.

Hildigunn came to meet him and spoke: 'Greetings and salutations, kinsman – my heart rejoices at your coming.'

Flosi said, 'We shall eat our day-meal[1] here and then ride on.'

Then their horses were tethered. Flosi went into the main room and sat down and pushed aside the cushioned high seat and spoke: 'I'm neither a king nor an earl, and there's no need to fix up the high seat for me, and no need to make fun of me.'

Hildigunn was close by and said, 'It's too bad that this offends you, for we meant well.'

Flosi spoke: 'If you mean well, your deeds will praise themselves, but they will condemn themselves if you mean evil.'

Hildigunn laughed a cold laugh and spoke: 'This is nothing yet – we'll come to closer grips before we're through.'

She sat down next to Flosi and they talked quietly for a long time.

Then the tables were brought out and Flosi and his men washed their hands. Flosi took a good look at the towel: it was all in tatters and torn off at one end. He threw it on the bench and refused to dry his hands on it, but tore a piece off the table-cloth and dried his hands on it and threw it to his men. Then he sat down at the table and told his men to eat.

Hildigunn entered the room and went before Flosi and wiped the hair away from her eyes and wept.

Flosi spoke: 'Your spirits are heavy, kinswoman, and so you weep, but it is well that you weep for a good man.'

'What action can I expect from you for the slaying, and what support?' she asked.

Flosi said, 'I will prosecute the case to the full extent of the law, or else make a settlement that good men see as bringing honour to us in every way.'

She spoke: 'Hoskuld would have exacted blood-vengeance if it were his duty to take action for you.'

Flosi answered, 'You don't lack fierceness, and it's clear what you want.'

Hildigunn spoke: 'Arnor Ornolfsson from Fossarskogar did less to Thord Frey's Godi, your father, and yet your brothers Kolbein and Egil killed him at the Skaftafell Assembly.'[2]

Hildigunn then went out and opened up her chest. She took from it the cloak which Flosi had given Hoskuld and in which Hoskuld was slain, and which she had kept there with all its blood. She went back into the main room with the cloak. She walked silently up to Flosi. Flosi had finished eating and the table had been cleared. Hildigunn placed the cloak on Flosi's shoulders; the dried blood poured down all over him.

Then she spoke: 'This cloak, Flosi, was your gift to Hoskuld, and now I give it back to you. He was slain in it. In the name of God and all good men I charge you, by all the powers of your Christ and by your courage and manliness, to avenge all the wounds which he received in dying – or else be an object of contempt to all men.'

Flosi flung off the cloak and threw it into her arms and said, 'You are the worst monster and want us to take the course which will be worst for us all. Cold are the counsels of women.'[3]

Flosi was so stirred that his face was, in turn, as red as blood, as pale as grass, and as black as Hel itself.[4]

He and his men went to the horses and rode away. He rode to Holtsvad and waited there for the Sigfussons and other friends of his.

Ingjald lived at Keldur; he was the brother of Hrodny, the mother of Hoskuld Njalsson. He and Hrodny were the children of Hoskuld the White, the son of Ingjald the Strong, the son of Geirfinn the Red, the son of Solvi, the son of Gunnstein the Berserk-slayer. Ingjald was married to Thraslaug Egilsdottir; her father was the son of Thord Frey's Godi. Egil's mother was Thraslaug, the daughter of Thorstein Sparrow and Unn, who was the daughter of Eyvind Karfi and the sister of Modolf the Wise.

Flosi sent word to Ingjald that he should join him. Ingjald went at once with fourteen men, all from his household. Ingjald was a big and strong man. He never spoke much at home, but was very brave and a generous man to his friends.

Flosi welcomed Ingjald warmly and spoke to him: 'We have a great problem on our hands, kinsman, and it will be hard to find a way out. I ask you not to abandon my cause before this problem is settled.'

Ingjald said, 'I'm in a difficult position on account of my relationship to Njal and his sons, and other large matters that stand in the way.'

Flosi said, 'I thought, when I married you to my brother's daughter, that you promised to support me in all things.'[5]

'It's very likely,' said Ingjald, 'that I will do so, but first I want to ride home, and go from there to the Thing.'

117 | The Sigfussons – Ketil of Mork, Lambi, Thorkel, Mord and Sigmund – learned that Flosi was at Holtsvad and rode there to join him. Lambi Sigurdarson, Gunnar Lambason, Grani Gunnarsson and Vebrand Hamundarson also came along. Flosi rose and welcomed them gladly.

They walked down along the river. Flosi had them give a true report, and it did not differ from Runolf's.

Flosi spoke to Ketil of Mork: 'I have to ask you something: how determined are you and the other Sigfussons in this matter?'

Ketil spoke: 'I would prefer to have a peaceful settlement between us. And yet I've sworn not to quit until it's settled one way or the other, and I'll stake my life on this.'

Flosi said, 'You're a real man, and such men are good to have around.'

Grani Gunnarsson and Gunnar Lambason both spoke at once: 'We want outlawry and death.'

Flosi said, 'It's not certain that we can have everything the way we want it.'

Grani said, 'It's been in my mind ever since they killed Thrain at the Markarfljot river, and then his son Hoskuld, that I would never make full peace with them – I want to be there when they're all slain.'

Flosi spoke: 'You've been close enough to take vengeance, if you only had the courage and the manliness. It occurs to me that you and many others are asking for something which, as time goes by, you would pay much money not to have taken part in. I can see clearly that even if we kill Njal and his sons, they are such prominent and well-born men that the action taken on their behalf will be immense, and we will have to beg at the knees of many men before we're out of the predicament. You can also expect that many who have great wealth now will be poor, and some will lose both wealth and life.'

*

Mord Valgardsson rode to meet Flosi and said that he and all his followers wanted to ride to the Thing with him. Flosi accepted and then made the proposal that Mord should marry off his daughter Rannveig to Starkad, Flosi's nephew, who lived at Stafafell. Flosi did this because he thought this a way to secure Mord's loyalty and that of his many followers. Mord reacted favourably and requested that Flosi talk about it with Gizur the White at the Thing. Mord was married to Thorkatla, Gizur the White's daughter.

Mord and Flosi rode to the Thing together and spoke together every day.

118 | Njal spoke to Skarphedin: 'What plans do you have now, you brothers and your brother-in-law Kari?'

Skarphedin answered, 'We don't follow dreams in most of the things we do. I can tell you that we're going to ride to Asgrim Ellida-Grimsson at Tunga, and from there to the Thing. Are you thinking of going, father?'

Njal said, 'I will ride to the Thing, because it is a point of honour not to quit your cause while I am still alive. I expect that there will be many there who will have a good word for me, and you will be helped rather than hurt by my presence.'

Thorhall Asgrimsson, Njal's foster-son, was standing there. The Njalssons laughed at him because he was wearing a coarse brown-striped cloak, and they asked him how long he intended to have it on.

Thorhall replied, 'I will have thrown it away by the time I have to take action for the slaying of my foster-father.'

Njal spoke: 'When you're most needed you will prove your full worth.'

Then they all made ready to leave home, nearly thirty in number, and they rode to the Thjorsa river. There they were joined by Njal's kinsmen Thorleif Crow and Thorgrim the Tall. They were the sons of Holta-Thorir and offered the Njalssons their men and their support, and the Njalssons accepted. They all rode across the Thjorsa together and then on to Laxarbakki, and stopped there for a rest.

Hjalti Skeggjason joined them there, and he and Njal had a long talk together in private.

Afterwards, Hjalti spoke: 'I always want my thoughts out in the open. Njal has asked me for help; I have agreed and promised him my support. He has already paid me, and many others, with his sound advice.'

Hjalti told Njal all about Flosi's movements. They sent Thorhall ahead to Tunga to say that they planned to come there that evening. Asgrim made preparations at once and was outside when Njal rode into the hayfield. Njal was wearing a black cape and a felt hood and carried a short axe in his hand. Asgrim helped Njal off his horse and carried him in and placed him on the high seat. Then all the Njalssons and Kari went in. Asgrim went back out. Hjalti was about to leave – he thought there were too many there. Asgrim seized the reins and said that Hjalti was not going to slip away, and he had the saddles taken off the horses and led him inside and placed him next to Njal. Thorleif and Thorgrim sat on the other bench with their men.

Asgrim sat down on a stool facing Njal and asked, 'What are your thoughts on the case?'

Njal answered, 'Rather heavy ones, for I fear that the men involved are not blessed with good fortune.'

He went on, 'Send for all your thingmen and ride to the Thing with me.'

'I've been planning that,' said Asgrim, 'and I promise you here and now never to give up your cause as long as I have any men left.'

Everybody in the room thanked him and said that he had spoken nobly. They stayed there overnight, and the next morning all Asgrim's followers arrived. Then they all rode to the Thing, where their booths had already been covered.

119 | Flosi had already arrived at the Thing and took charge of his booth. Runolf took charge of the booth of the men from Dal, and Mord the booth of the men from the Rangarvellir district. Hall of Sida had come the longest distance from the east and was almost the only man from there. He had, however, brought a large number of men from

his district and at once joined forces with Flosi and asked him to accept a peaceful settlement. Hall was a wise and good-hearted man. Flosi answered him well but did not commit himself.

Hall asked who had promised him support. Flosi named Mord Valgardsson and said that he had asked for the hand of Mord's daughter for his nephew Starkad. Hall said that the woman was good, but that it was bad to have dealings with Mord – 'and you'll have proof of this before the Thing is over.'

At this they stopped talking.

One day Njal and his sons talked privately for a long time with Asgrim. Then Asgrim jumped up and spoke to the Njalssons: 'Let's go and find ourselves some friends, so that we're not overcome by force of numbers, for this is going to be a hard-fought case.'

Asgrim went out, followed by Helgi Njalsson, then Kari Solmundarson, then Grim Njalsson, then Skarphedin, then Thorhall Asgrimsson, then Thorgrim the Tall and Thorleif Crow. They went to Gizur the White's booth and entered. Gizur stood up to receive them and asked them to sit and drink.

Asgrim said, 'That's not how things are, and let me be blunt – what support can I expect from you, as my kinsman?'

Gizur answered, 'My sister Jorunn will not expect me to avoid helping you[1] – one fate awaits us both, now and always.'

Asgrim thanked him and then went out.

Skarphedin asked, 'Where shall we go now?'

Asgrim answered, 'To the booth of the men from Olfus.'

They went there. Asgrim asked whether Skafti Thoroddsson was in the booth. He was told that he was, and they went in. Skafti was sitting on the cross-bench and welcomed Asgrim, and he responded politely. Skafti asked him to sit beside him. Asgrim said he would stay only a short time – 'but I've come to you for a reason.'

'Let's hear it,' said Skafti.

'I want to ask your support,' said Asgrim, 'for me and my kinsmen.'

'I'd been hoping for something different,' said Skafti – 'to keep your troubles out of my house.'

Asgrim answered, 'Those are ugly words, and you're of least use when the need is greatest.'

'Who's that man,' said Skafti, 'who goes fifth in line, a big man with a pale and luckless look about him, but fierce and troll-like?'

He answered, 'My name is Skarphedin, and you have often seen me here at the Thing, but I must be smarter than you because I don't need to ask your name. You're Skafti Thoroddsson, but you called yourself Brush-head after you killed Ketil of Elda; you shaved your head and smeared tar on it. Then you paid slaves to cut some turf and prop it up so you could crawl under it for the night. Later you went to Thorolf Loftsson at Eyrar, and he took you in and smuggled you abroad in his flour sacks.'[2]

Then Asgrim and his party left.

Skarphedin spoke: 'Where shall we go now?'

'To Snorri the Godi's booth,' said Asgrim.

They went to Snorri's booth. A man was standing out in front. Asgrim asked whether Snorri was in the booth; he said that he was. Asgrim and all the others went inside. Snorri was sitting on the cross-bench. Asgrim went up to him and greeted him warmly. Snorri received him cordially and invited him to sit down. Asgrim said he would stay only a short time – 'but I've come to you for a reason.'

Snorri asked him to state it.

Asgrim said, 'I would like you to go to court with me and give me your support, for you are a clever and accomplished man.'

'Our legal matters are going badly now,' said Snorri, 'and many men are pressing us hard, and so we're not eager to take on the troubles of men from other quarters.'

'That's reason enough,' said Asgrim, 'since you have no debt to us.'

'I know you to be a fine man,' said Snorri, 'and I promise not to take sides against you or give help to your enemies.'

Asgrim thanked him.

Snorri spoke: 'Who is that man, who goes fifth in line, pale-looking, sharp-featured, with a toothy sneer and an axe on his shoulder?'

'Hedin's my name,' he said, 'but some call me by my full name Skarphedin. Is there any more you wish to say to me?'

Snorri spoke: 'I see that you are fierce and daunting, and yet my guess is that your good luck is at an end and that you have only a short time to live.'

'Good,' said Skarphedin, 'because that's a debt we all have to pay. But you need to be avenging your father rather than predicting my fate.'[3]

'Many have said that already,' said Snorri, 'and I'm not angered by such words.'

After that they left the booth, and had no support from him.

From there they went to the booth of the men from Skagafjord. Haf the Wealthy owned the booth. He was the son of Thorkel, the son of Eirik of Goddalir, the son of Geirmund, the son of Hroald, the son of Eirik Stiff-beard who killed Grjotgard in Sokndal in Norway. Haf's mother was Thorunn, the daughter of Asbjorn the Bald of Myrka, the son of Hrossbjorn.

Asgrim and the others entered the booth. Haf was sitting in the middle and was talking to a man. Asgrim went up to him and greeted him. Haf welcomed him and asked him to sit down.

Asgrim spoke: 'I prefer to ask you to support me and my kinsmen.'

Haf responded quickly that he did not want to take on their troubles – 'but I want to ask who that pale-looking one is who goes fifth in line, and is as foul-looking as if he had come out of a sea-cliff.'

Skarphedin spoke: 'Don't fuss about that, milksop. I would dare to go where you were waiting in ambush for me, and I wouldn't be afraid at all if there were boys like you in my path. It would be more fitting for you to rescue your sister Svanlaug, whom Eydis Iron-sword and Anvil-head took from your home.'[4]

Asgrim said, 'Let's go – there's no hope of support here.'

Then they went to the booth of the men from Modruvellir and asked whether Gudmund the Powerful was inside, and they were told that he was. Asgrim entered the booth. There was a high seat in the middle and Gudmund was sitting in it. Asgrim went up to him and greeted him. Gudmund welcomed him and invited him to sit down.

Asgrim spoke: 'I don't want to sit – I want to ask you for help, since you are a forceful and great chieftain.'

Gudmund said, 'I will not be against you. But if I'm inclined to support you, we can talk about that later' – and he was kind to them in every way. Asgrim thanked him for his words.

Gudmund spoke: 'There's a man in your group whom I've been looking at for a while and who seems to me unlike other men I have seen.'

'Which one is he?' said Asgrim.

'He's fifth in line,' said Gudmund, 'chestnut-haired and pale in complexion, of great size and powerful-looking, and so clearly fit for manly deeds that I would rather have him on my side than any ten others. And yet he's a luckless man.'

Skarphedin spoke: 'I know that you're talking about me, and that we're both men with bad luck, though in different ways. I deserve the blame for the slaying of Hoskuld the Godi of Hvitanes, as is to be expected. But Thorkel Bully and Thorir Helgason have been spreading slander about you and you deserve blame for that.'[5]

Then they went out.

Skarphedin said, 'Where shall we go now?'

'To the booth of the men from Ljosavatn,' said Asgrim.

Thorkel Bully had set up that booth. He was the son of Thorgeir the Godi, the son of Tjorvi, the son of Thorkel the Long, and his mother was Thorunn, the daughter of Thorstein, the son of Sigmund, the son of Gnupa-Bard. Thorkel Bully's mother was Gudrid; she was the daughter of Thorkel the Black from Hleidrargard, the son of Thorir Snepil, the son of Ketil Brimil, the son of Ornolf, the son of Bjornolf, the son of Grim Hairy-cheeks, the son of Ketil Haeng, the son of Hallbjorn Half-troll.[6]

Thorkel Bully had travelled abroad and earned fame in other lands. He had killed a trouble-maker out east in Jamtskog, and then he went to Sweden and became the companion of Old Sorkvir and they went raiding in the Baltic. One evening, east of Balagardssida,[7] Thorkel had to fetch their water. He met with a creature half-man, half-beast,[8] and fought it off for a long time, and the fight ended with Thorkel killing the creature. Then he went south to Estonia; there he killed a flying dragon. After that he went back to Sweden and from there to

Norway and to Iceland, and he had these mighty feats of his carved above his bed closet and on a stool in front of his high seat.

He and his brothers fought against Gudmund the Powerful at the Ljosavatn Assembly, and the men of Ljosavatn were victorious. It was then that Thorir Helgason and Thorkel Bully spread slander about Gudmund.

Thorkel claimed that there was no one in Iceland he would refuse to fight with in single combat, or give way to. He was called Thorkel Bully because neither in word nor in deed would he spare any man whom he faced.

120 | Asgrim Ellida-Grimsson and his companions went to Thorkel's booth. Asgrim spoke to the others: 'This booth belongs to Thorkel Bully, a great champion, and it would mean a lot if we could have his help. We must watch our every step, for he is headstrong and obstinate. I must ask you, Skarphedin, not to take part in our conversation.'

Skarphedin grinned. He was dressed in a black tunic and blue-striped trousers and high black boots; he had a silver belt around his waist and in his hand the axe with which he had killed Thrain – he called it Battle-hag – and a small shield, and around his head he had a silk band, with his hair combed back over his ears. He looked the complete warrior, and everybody recognized him without having seen him before. He walked in his assigned place, neither ahead nor behind.

They went into the booth and all the way to the end. Thorkel was sitting in the middle of the bench, with his men on both sides of him. Asgrim greeted him; Thorkel responded politely.

Asgrim spoke: 'We've come here to ask you to support us by going to court with us.'

Thorkel said, 'What need do you have of my support, since you have already gone to Gudmund? He must have promised to help you.'

Asgrim answered, 'We did not get his support.'

Thorkel spoke: 'Then Gudmund thought your case to be unpopular, and he must be right, for the worst sort of deed has been committed. I see now what has brought you here: you thought I would be less scrupulous than Gudmund and that I would back an unjust cause.'

Asgrim remained silent and thought that things were looking difficult.

Thorkel spoke: 'Who is that big and frightening man who goes fifth in line, pale-looking and sharp-featured, with a wicked and luckless look about him?'

Skarphedin spoke: 'My name is Skarphedin and there's no need for you pick out insulting words for me, an innocent man. It's never happened that I threatened my own father or fought him, as you did with your father. Also, you haven't come to the Althing often or taken part in lawsuits, and you're probably handier at dairy work amidst your little household at Oxara. You really ought to pick from your teeth the pieces from the mare's arse you ate before riding to the Thing – your shepherd watched you and was shocked that you could do such a filthy thing.'[1]

Thorkel sprang up in great anger and seized his short sword and spoke: 'I got this sword in Sweden, where I killed a mighty champion for it, and I've since killed many others with it. As soon as I'm close enough I'll run you through with it, and that's what you'll get for your foul language.'

Skarphedin stood with his axe at the ready and grinned and spoke: 'I had this axe in my hand when I leaped twelve ells across the Markarfljot river and killed Thrain Sigfusson; eight men were standing around him and they didn't manage to catch me.[2] And I've never lifted a weapon against any man without hitting my mark.'

With that he broke away from his brothers and Kari and rushed towards Thorkel.

Then he spoke: 'You have two choices, Thorkel Bully: sheathe your sword and sit down, or I'll smash this axe into your head and split it down to your shoulders.'

Thorkel sheathed his sword at once and sat down; such a thing never happened to him before or after.

Asgrim and the others went out.

Skarphedin said, 'Where shall we go now?'

Asgrim answered, 'Back to our booth.'

'Off to our booth, bored with begging,' said Skarphedin.

Asgrim turned towards him and said, 'At many of our visits you were rather sharp-tongued, but I think you gave Thorkel just what he deserved.'

They went back to their booth and told Njal everything in detail. He spoke: 'Things draw on as destiny wills.'

Gudmund the Powerful learned what had happened between Skarphedin and Thorkel and had this to say: 'You are all aware how things have gone between us and the people at Ljosavatn, but I've never had as much humiliation from them as Thorkel had just now from Skarphedin, and it's good that it happened.'

Then Gudmund spoke to his brother Einar of Thvera: 'Go along with all my men and help the Njalssons when the court convenes, and if they need help next summer, I'll give it myself.'

Einar agreed to this and sent word to Asgrim. Asgrim said, 'There are few chieftains like Gudmund.'

Then he told Njal.

121 | The next day Asgrim, Gizur the White, Hjalti Skeggjason and Einar of Thvera came together. Mord Valgardsson was also there. He had by then given up the prosecution and turned it over to the Sigfussons.

Asgrim spoke: 'I turn first to you, Gizur the White and Hjalti and Einar, to tell you how the suit stands. You're aware that Mord started the proceedings, but the fact is that Mord was present at the slaying of Hoskuld and delivered the wound for which no one was named. In my opinion the suit is invalid according to the law.'

'Then we must present this at once,' said Hjalti.

Thorhall Asgrimsson spoke up and said it would be unwise not to keep this hidden until the court convened.

'What difference does it make?' said Hjalti.

Thorhall spoke: 'If they find out now that the suit was improperly initiated, they will be able to save it by quickly sending someone home from the Thing to make the charge from there and summon neighbours to the Thing, and then the prosecution will be valid.'

'You're a clever man, Thorhall,' they said, 'and we'll take your advice.'

After that each of them went back to his booth.

The Sigfussons gave notice of the suit at the Law Rock and asked the defendants to declare their district and domicile, and the court was to convene on Friday evening to hear the prosecution. Until then it was quiet at the Thing. Many tried to reconcile the two sides, but Flosi was firm, though less vocal than others, and the outlook was not promising.

Friday evening came, and time for the court to convene. The whole Thing went to the court. Flosi and his men stood to the south of the Rangarvellir court; with him were Hall of Sida and Runolf Ulfsson and the others who had promised him help. To the north of the Rangarvellir court stood Asgrim, Gizur the White, Hjalti, and Einar of Thvera, while the Njalssons were back at their booth with Kari and Thorleif Crow and Thorgrim the Tall. They sat there with their weapons ready, a hard band to attack.

Njal had requested the judges to start proceedings, and now the Sigfussons prosecuted the case. They named witnesses and asked the Njalssons to listen to their oath-swearing; then they swore their oaths; then they presented the charges; then they produced witnesses to the notification of the slaying; then they asked the panel of neighbours to take their seats; then they invited the defendants to challenge the panel.

Thorhall Asgrimsson named witnesses and prohibited the panel from announcing its findings and objected that the person who had given notice of the suit had violated the law and deserved to be outlawed himself.

'To whom are you referring?' said Flosi.

Thorhall answered, 'Mord Valgardsson went with the Njalssons to the slaying of Hoskuld and gave him the wound for which no one was named when witnesses to the wounds were named. You cannot contest the fact that the case is invalid.'

122 | Njal stood up and spoke: 'I request Hall of Sida and Flosi and all the Sigfussons, as well as all our men, not to leave but to listen to my words.'

They did as he asked.

He spoke: 'It appears that this case has reached an impasse, which is to be expected since it sprang from evil roots. I want you to know that I loved Hoskuld more than my own sons, and when I heard that he had been slain I felt that the sweetest light of my eyes had been put out,[1] and I would rather have lost all my sons to have him live. Now I ask Hall of Sida, Runolf of Dal, Gizur the White, Einar of Thvera and Haf the Wise to allow me to make a settlement for the slaying, on behalf of my sons, and I would like those who are best suited to serve as arbitrators.'

Gizur and Einar and Haf each spoke at length about this and begged Flosi to accept a settlement and promised him their friendship in return. Flosi made polite answers but no promises.

Hall of Sida spoke to Flosi: 'Will you now keep your word and grant me the favour you promised when I helped your kinsman Thorgrim Stout-Ketilsson leave the country after he killed Hall the Red?'[2]

Flosi spoke: 'I will grant you this, father-in-law, for you are only asking what will make my honour greater than before.'

Hall said, 'Then I want you to be reconciled quickly and let good men arbitrate, and thereby win the friendship of the best men.'

Flosi said, 'I want you all to know that I am willing to follow the wishes of my father-in-law Hall and others of the best men and have six men from each side, lawfully chosen, arbitrate this matter. It seems to me that Njal deserves that I grant him this.'

Njal thanked them all, and the others who were there said that Flosi had done well.

Flosi said, 'Now I shall choose my arbitrators. I choose first Hall, and then Ozur of Breida, Surt Asbjarnarson of Kirkjubaer, Modolf Ketilsson' – he was then living at Asar – 'Haf and Runolf of Dal, and everyone will agree that these are the most suited of my men for this duty.'

He then asked Njal to choose his arbitrators.

Njal rose and said, 'I choose Asgrim Ellida-Grimsson first, and then Hjalti Skeggjason, Gizur the White, Einar of Thvera, Snorri the Godi, and Gudmund the Powerful.'

Then Njal and Flosi and the Sigfussons shook hands, and Njal did so on behalf of all his sons and Kari. These twelve men were now to decide, and it could be said that the whole Thing was pleased with this.

Men were then sent to bring Snorri and Gudmund, since they were in their booths. It was agreed that the arbitrators should sit in the Law Council and that everyone else should leave.

123 | Snorri the Godi spoke: 'Here we are now, the twelve arbitrators to whom this case has been referred. I beg all of you not to raise any objections that might keep these men from being well reconciled.'

Gudmund said, 'Are you in favour of district banishment or exile?'

'Neither one,' said Snorri, 'for these penalties have often worked out badly, and men have been killed and become enemies. I prefer to set a fine so huge that no man in Iceland will ever have been more costly than Hoskuld.'

His words were well received. Then they discussed it but could not agree on who should be the first to declare how high the fine should be, and in the end they cast lots and the lot fell on Snorri.

Snorri spoke: 'I won't sit on this matter any longer – I'll tell you now what my decision is: I want triple compensation to be paid for Hoskuld, six hundred ounces of silver. You must now change this, if you think it too much or too little.'

They answered that they would not change it.

'And on top of this,' said Snorri, 'the total amount must be paid out here at the Thing.'

Then Gizur said, 'I don't think this can work, for they won't have enough money with them to pay the fine.'

Gudmund said, 'I know what Snorri wants. He wants all of us arbitrators to contribute as much as our generosity allows, and then many others will do the same.'

Hall of Sida thanked him and said that he would be willing to give as much as the highest giver. All the arbitrators then approved Snorri's proposal.

After that they went away and agreed among themselves that Hall should announce their decision at the Law Rock.

After that the bell was rung and everybody went to the Law Rock.

Hall stood up and spoke: 'We have reached an agreement on the case which we have been arbitrating, and we fix an amount of six hundred ounces of silver. We arbitrators will pay half of it ourselves, and all of it must be paid out here at the Thing. It is my entreaty to all you people that you give something, in the name of God.'

Everyone responded favourably. Hall named witnesses to the settlement, so that no one would break it. Njal thanked them for the settlement.

Skarphedin was standing nearby and kept silent and grinned.

People then went from the Law Rock to their booths.

The arbitrators brought to the farmers' churchyard[1] the money they had promised to give. Njal's sons turned over the money which they had, and so did Kari, and it came to one hundred ounces of silver. Njal added all the money he had, and that made a second hundred. All this money was then taken to the Law Council, and others gave so much that not a penny was lacking.

Njal took a silk robe and a pair of boots and placed them on top of the pile.[2]

Then Hall told Njal to go and bring his sons – 'and I will bring Flosi, and they can pledge peace to each other.'

Njal went back to the booth and spoke to his sons: 'Now our case has turned out well. We have been reconciled and all the payment money has been brought to one place. Both sides are to meet and give each other promises of faith and peace. I beg you not to spoil this in any way.'

Skarphedin stroked his forehead and grinned. Then they all went to the Law Council.

Hall came to Flosi and said, 'Come now to the Law Council. All the money has been paid readily and brought together in one place.'

Flosi asked the Sigfussons to go with him. They all came out and walked from the east towards the Law Council. Njal and his sons came walking from the west. Skarphedin went to the middle bench and stood there.

Flosi went into the Law Council to examine the money and said, 'This is a large amount of good money and readily paid out, as was to be expected.'

Then he picked up the robe and asked who had given it, and no one answered him. He waved the robe a second time and asked who had given it, and laughed, and no one answered.

Flosi said, 'Which is it, that none of you knows whose garment this is or that you don't dare to tell me?'

Skarphedin said, 'Who do you think might have given it?'

Flosi spoke: 'If you want to know, then I'll tell you what I think – it's my guess that your father gave it, Old Beardless, for there are many who can't tell by looking at him whether he's a man or a woman.'

Skarphedin spoke: 'That's a wicked thing to do, making slurs about him in his old age, and no man worthy of the name has ever done this before. You can tell he's a man because he has had sons with his wife. And few of our kinsmen have been buried uncompensated by our wall, without our taking vengeance for them.'

Then Skarphedin picked up the robe and threw a pair of black trousers at Flosi, and said that he had more need of these.[3]

Flosi said, 'Why do I need them more?'

Skarphedin spoke: 'Because if you are the sweetheart of the troll at Svinafell, as is said, he uses you as a woman every ninth night.'[4]

Flosi pushed the money away and said he would not take a penny of it, and that it would now be one of two things: either there would be no redress at all for Hoskuld, or they would take blood-vengeance for him. Flosi would neither offer nor accept peace, and he spoke to the Sigfussons: 'Let's go back to our booth. One fate awaits us all.'

Then they went back to their booth.

Hall said, 'The men carrying on this quarrel are men of great bad luck.'

*

Njal and his sons went back to their booth.

Njal spoke: 'What I have long feared is now coming true, that this case will bring us terrible harm.'

'That's not so,' said Skarphedin. 'They can never prosecute us, according to the laws of the land.'[5]

'Then what will come,' said Njal, 'will be worse for everybody.'

The men who had contributed the money talked about taking it back.

Gudmund spoke: 'I do not choose to bring shame on myself by taking back what I have given, neither here nor anywhere.'

'That is well spoken,' they said. No one wanted to take back his money then.

Snorri the Godi said, 'It's my advice that Gizur the White and Hjalti Skeggjason hold on to this money until the next Althing. I have a sense that it won't be long until it will be needed.'

Hjalti took and held half of the money, and Gizur the rest. Then people went back to their booths.

124 | Flosi told all his men to go up to the Almannagja gorge and went there himself. By that time his men had arrived, a hundred in all.

Flosi said to the Sigfussons, 'What can I do for you in this affair that would please you the most?'

Gunnar Lambason said, 'Nothing will please us until all the brothers – the Njalssons – are slain.'

Flosi spoke: 'I will promise you Sigfussons not to give up until one side or the other perishes. I also want to know if there's anyone here who doesn't want to see this through with us.'

They all said that they would see it through.

Flosi said, 'Come to me, all of you, and swear an oath not to abandon the cause.'

They all went to Flosi and swore oaths to him.

Flosi said, 'Let's also shake hands on it that whoever drops out forfeits both life and property.'

These were the chieftains with Flosi: Kol, the son of Thorstein

Broad-belly and the nephew of Hall of Sida; Hroald Ozurarson from Breida; Ozur the son of Onund Box-back; Thorstein the Fair, son of Geirleif; Glum Hildisson; Modolf Ketilsson; Thorir the son of Thord Illugi of Mortunga; Flosi's kinsmen Kolbein and Egil; Ketil Sigfusson and his brother Mord; Thorkel and Lambi; Grani Gunnarsson, Gunnar Lambason and his brother Sigurd; Ingjald of Keldur; and Hroar Hamundarson.

Flosi said to the Sigfussons, 'Choose the man you think best suited to be our leader, since someone will have to be in charge.'

Ketil answered, 'If the choice is up to us brothers, we would all choose you to lead us. Many things argue for that – you are well born, a great chieftain, unbending and clever. We think you're the best one to look after our interests in this matter.'

Flosi spoke: 'It's fitting that I go along with your request. Now I'll lay out the course we will take. It's my advice that everyone ride home from the Thing and look after his farm this summer as long as the haymaking is in process. I too will ride home and stay there this summer. On the Lord's Day which falls eight weeks before winter[1] I will have mass sung for me at home and then ride west across Lomagnupssand. Each of us will take two horses. I won't add more men to those who have just now sworn oaths, because we have quite enough as long as everyone lives up to his oath. I'll ride that Lord's Day, and the night too, and by early evening of the second day of the week I'll be at Thrihyrning ridge. All of you who are bound by oath should have come there by then, and if anyone who has joined our cause has not come, he will lose nothing but his life – if we have our way.'

Ketil said, 'How will you be able to leave home on the Lord's Day and arrive at Thrihyrning ridge on the second day of the week?'

Flosi spoke: 'I will ride up from Skaftartunga and keep to the north of Eyjafjallajokul glacier, and then go down into Godaland, and this can be done if I ride hard. And now I'll tell you the rest of my plan – when we're all together we'll ride to Bergthorshvol in full force and attack the Njalssons with fire and iron, and not leave until they're all dead. You must keep this plan a secret, for the lives of all of us are at stake. Now let's take our horses and ride home.'

They went back to their booths. Flosi had their horses saddled and then they rode home and did not wait for anyone. Flosi did not want to meet his father-in-law Hall, for he was quite certain that Hall would oppose strong measures.

Njal and his sons rode home from the Thing, and they all stayed there that summer. Njal asked Kari whether he was thinking of riding east to his farm at Dyrholmar.

Kari answered, 'I won't be riding east, because one fate awaits your sons and me.'

Njal thanked him and said that he had expected as much from him.

There were close to twenty-five men in fighting form at Berg-thorshvol, including the servants.

One day Hrodny Hoskuldsdottir came to Keldur. Her brother Ingjald welcomed her warmly. She did not respond to the greeting, and asked him to step out with her. He did as she asked and went out. They walked together away from the farm. Then she grabbed at him and they sat down.

She spoke: 'Is it true that you've sworn an oath to attack Njal and his sons and kill them?'

He answered, 'It's true.'

'You're a real back-stabber,' she said, 'considering that Njal has saved you three times from outlawry.'

'But the way it is now,' he said, 'my life's at risk if I don't do this.'

'That's not so,' she said. 'You'll live on, and you'll be called a good man as long as you don't betray the one to whom you owe the most.'

Then she took a linen cap out of her pouch, covered with blood and full of holes, and she spoke: 'Hoskuld Njalsson was wearing this cap when they killed him. It doesn't seem at all right to me that you should help those who brought that about.'

He answered, 'Then I will not take any action against Njal, no matter what that may lead to. But I know that they're going to make things difficult for me.'

She said, 'You could do Njal a great service now by telling him their plans.'

'That I will not do,' said Ingjald, 'because I would deserve the scorn of all men if I told what they confided to me. But it's a manly thing to break away from their cause when I know that they'll take vengeance. Tell Njal and his sons to be on their guard all summer and keep many men at hand – this sound advice will serve him well.'

Then Hrodny went to Bergthorshvol and told Njal this whole conversation. Njal thanked her and said she had done well – 'for if he, of all men, opposed me it would be the worst sort of wrong.'

She went home then, and Njal told this to his sons.

There was an old woman at Bergthorshvol called Saeunn. She was wise in many ways and could foretell the future, but she was very old and the Njalssons called her doddering because she talked so much, and yet much of it came true. One day she grabbed a stick and went around the house to a pile of chickweed. She hit the pile and cursed it for being so contemptible.

Skarphedin laughed at this and asked why she was carrying on so over the pile of chickweed.

The old woman spoke: 'This chickweed will be taken and set afire when Njal is burned in his house, along with my foster-daughter Bergthora – put it in water,' she said, 'or burn it, as fast as you can.'

'We won't do that,' said Skarphedin, 'for if this is not here something else will be found to start the fire, if that is what's fated.'

The old woman kept nagging about the chickweed pile all summer, that it should be taken inside, but it never was.

125 | At Reykir in Skeid lived a man named Runolf Thorsteinsson. His son was named Hildiglum. On the night of the Lord's Day twelve weeks before the beginning of winter, Hildiglum went outside. He heard a great crash, and it seemed as if both earth and sky were quaking. Then he looked toward the west and thought he saw a fiery ring and a man on a grey horse inside the ring. The man passed quickly by, and was moving fast; he was carrying a flaming torch in his hand. He rode so close that Hildiglum saw him clearly. He was black as pitch and Hildiglum heard him speak this verse in a loud voice:

12.

I ride a horse
with hoarfrost mane
and dripping forelocks,
bringing evil;
the torch ends burn,
the middle brings bane;
Flosi's plans
are like a flung torch;
Flosi's plans
are like a flung torch.

Then Hildiglum saw the man throw the torch at the mountains in the east, and such a great flame sprang up that he could no longer see the mountains. He saw the man ride east and disappear in the flames.

Hildiglum went back inside and lay down in his bed and was in a swoon for a long time and then came out of it. He remembered everything that had passed before him and told it to his father, and he asked him to tell it to Hjalti Skeggjason. Hildiglum went and told him.

Hjalti spoke: 'You have seen a witch-ride; it always occurs before great events.'

126 | Flosi prepared to leave the east when it was two months before winter, and he sent for all the men who had promised to go with him. Each of them had two horses and good weapons. They all came to Svinafell and were there for the night. Flosi had mass sung early on the Lord's Day; then he went to table. He told the members of his household what work each of them should do while he was away; then he went to his horses.

Flosi and his men rode west to Sand.[1] He told his men not to ride too hard at first – they would do that at the end of the journey – and he said that they should all wait if anyone had to fall behind. They rode west to the Skogar district and arrived at Kirkjubaer, and Flosi asked all his men to go with him to church and pray; they did so.

Then they mounted their horses and rode up into the mountains and on to Fiskivotn lakes and on to the west of these, and then headed due west for Sand, with the glacier Eyjafjallajokul to their left, and then down to Godaland and from there to the Markarfljot river. At mid-afternoon on the second day they came to Thrihyrning ridge and waited there until early evening. By that time everybody had arrived except Ingjald of Keldur, and the Sigfussons condemned him strongly, but Flosi told them not to blame Ingjald while he was not there – 'we'll settle with him later.'

127 | Now to tell about Bergthorshvol: Grim and Helgi had left there and gone to Holar – their children were being fostered there – and had told their father that they would not be back that night. They were at Holar all day. Some poor women came there and said they had come a long way. Grim and Helgi asked them for news. They said there was none to speak of, but that they could tell of something unusual. The brothers asked what unusual thing they had to tell and told them not to hide it. They said they would tell.

'We were coming down from Fljotshlid and saw all the Sigfussons riding, fully armed and heading up towards Thrihyrning ridge, in a group of fifteen. We also saw Grani Gunnarsson and Gunnar Lambason, five men altogether, and they all rode in the same direction. You might say that everything's hurrying and scurrying.'

Helgi Njalsson said, 'Then Flosi must have come from the east, and all the others are joining up with him. Grim and I should be where Skarphedin is.'

Grim said this was so, and they set out for home.

Back at Bergthorshvol, Bergthora spoke to her household: 'Choose your food for tonight. Each of you is to have what he likes best, for this evening is the last time that I will serve food to my household.'

'That cannot be,' said those who were there.

'Yet it will be so,' she said, 'and I could tell of much more, if I wanted, and this will be a sign – Grim and Helgi will come back this evening, before people are finished eating. If this proves true, then the rest will be as I say.'

Then she brought food to the table.

Njal spoke: 'Strange things are happening to me. I look around the room and imagine that I see both gable-walls gone, and the table and food all covered with blood.'

This seemed a big thing to everyone except Skarphedin. He asked them not to grieve or behave in an unseemly way that people could comment on – 'from us more than from others it's expected that we bear up well, and that's as it should be.'

Grim and Helgi came home before the tables were taken away, and everyone was much alarmed at that. Njal asked why they had returned in such a hurry, and they told what they had heard.

Njal said that no one should go to bed that night.

128 | To return to Flosi: he said, 'Now let's ride to Bergthorshvol and be there by nightfall.'

They did this. There was a depression in the knoll at Bergthorshvol, and they rode into it and tethered their horses and stayed there until late at night.

Flosi said, 'Now let's go up to the house and keep close together and walk slowly, and see what they do.'

Njal was standing outside with his sons and Kari and all their servants; they had arranged themselves in the yard in front of the house, almost thirty in all.

Flosi came to a halt and said, 'Let's see what they decide to do, for I don't think that we'll ever be able to overcome them if they stay out here.'

'Our trip will be wasted,' said Grani, 'if we don't dare attack them.'

'It won't come to that,' said Flosi; 'we'll attack them even if they stay outside, but then we'll pay dearly, and not many will live to say which side won.'

Njal said to his men, 'What do you say about the size of their force?'

'They have a tough force,' said Skarphedin, 'and large too, but they have halted there because they think they will have a hard time defeating us.'

'That's not so,' said Njal, 'and I want everyone to go inside, for they had a hard time against Gunnar of Hlidarendi, and yet he faced them all alone. This house is solid, just as his was, and they won't be able to overcome us.'

'That's not the way to look at it,' said Skarphedin. 'The men who attacked Gunnar were chieftains of such integrity that they would rather have turned back than burn him in his house. But these men will attack us with fire if they can't do it in any other way, for they'll do anything to finish us off. They must realize, and it's not unlikely, that if we get away it will be their death. Besides, I'm not eager to let myself be suffocated like a fox in his hole.'

Njal spoke: 'Now it will be as often before, my sons, that you'll over-rule me and show me no respect. When you were younger you did otherwise, and you were better off.'

Helgi spoke: 'Let's do as our father wishes – that will be best for us.'

'I'm not so sure about that,' said Skarphedin, 'for he is now a doomed man. But still, I'm ready to please him by burning in the house with him, for I'm not afraid to face my death.'

He spoke to Kari: 'Let's all stay close together, brother-in-law, so that nobody is separated from the rest.'

'That's been my plan,' said Kari, 'but if it's fated to be otherwise, then that's the way it will be, and there's nothing we can do about it.'

'Avenge us,' said Skarphedin, 'and we shall avenge you if we live through this.'

Kari said that he would. They all went inside then and took positions at the doors.

Flosi spoke: 'Now they are doomed, for they've gone inside. Let's move quickly up to the house and form up tightly at the doors and see to it that no one gets away, neither Kari nor the Njalssons – otherwise it's death for us.'

They went up to the house and took positions all around it, in case there was a secret exit. Flosi went to the front of the house with his own men. Hroald Ozurarson ran to where Skarphedin was standing and thrust at him with his spear. Skarphedin hacked the point off his shaft and ran at him and swung his axe at him, and it came down on the shield and pushed it against him, and the forward point of the blade hit him in the face, and he fell back dead at once.

Kari said, 'There's no getting away from you, Skarphedin; you're the boldest of us all.'

'I don't know about that,' said Skarphedin and stretched his lips into a grin.

Kari and Grim and Helgi made many spear-thrusts and wounded many men, and Flosi and his men could do nothing.

Flosi spoke: 'Our men have been hurt badly; many are wounded, and one is slain, the one whom we least wanted to lose. It's clear now that we cannot defeat them with weapons – there are many here who are not attacking as sharply as they intended. Now we'll have to try something else. There are two choices, and neither of them is good. One is to turn back, but that would lead to our death – the other is to bring fire and burn them inside, and that's a great responsibility before God, for we're Christian men. Still, that is the course we must take.'

129 | Then they came with fire and started a great blaze in front of the doors.

Skarphedin said, 'Building a fire, boys? Are you going to cook something?'

Grani answered, 'That's right, and it'll be as hot as you need for baking.'

Skarphedin spoke: 'This is how you reward me for avenging your father – you're the kind of man who places greater value on a lesser duty.'

The women then poured whey on the flames and put them out.

Kol Thorsteinsson said to Flosi, 'I have a plan. I saw a loft above the crossbeams in the hall. Let's build a fire there and start it with the pile of chickweed at the back of the house.'

They took the chickweed and set fire to it, and the people inside did not notice it until flames started coming down all over the hall. Then Flosi and his men started big fires in front of all the doors. The women inside started to suffer badly.

Njal spoke to them: 'Bear this bravely and don't express any fear, for it's only a brief storm, and it will be a long time before we have another like it. Have faith that God is merciful, and that he will not let us burn both in this world and in the next.'

Such were the words he had for them, and others even more reassuring.

Now the whole house began to burn.

Njal went to the door and said, 'Is Flosi near enough to hear me?'

Flosi said he could hear.

Njal said, 'Are you at all willing to make a settlement with my sons, or let some people leave the house?'

Flosi answered, 'I will not make any settlement with your sons – our dealings with them will soon be over, and we won't leave here until they're all dead. But I'm willing to allow the women and children and servants to come out.'

Njal went back in and said to his people, 'All those who've been allowed must now go. And you go, too, Thorhalla Asgrimsdottir, along with everybody else who has permission.'

Thorhalla said, 'My parting from Helgi will be different from what I had long expected, but I shall incite my father and my brothers to take vengeance for the killings which are done here.'

Njal said, 'You will do well, for you're a good woman.'

Then she left, and many others went with her.

Astrid of Djuparbakki said to Helgi, 'Come out with me – I'll throw a woman's cloak over you and wrap a kerchief around your head.'

Helgi declined at first, but then went along with their request. Astrid wrapped a kerchief around his head, and Thorhild put the cloak on him, and he walked out between the two of them. Then his sisters Thorgerd and Helga and many others went out.

When Helgi came out, Flosi said, 'That woman there is big and broad-shouldered – grab her and hold on to her!'

When Helgi heard this he threw off the cloak. He had been carrying a sword under his arm, and swung it at one of the men and hit his shield, and it cut off the lower part of the shield and the man's leg as well. Then Flosi came up and struck at Helgi's neck, and the head came off at once.

Flosi went to the door and said that Njal and Bergthora should come and talk with him. They did so.

Flosi spoke: 'I want to offer you free exit, for you do not deserve to be burned.'

Njal spoke: 'I will not leave, for I'm an old man and hardly fit to avenge my sons, and I do not want to live in shame.'

Flosi spoke to Bergthora: 'Then you come out, Bergthora, for by no means do I want to burn you in your house.'

Bergthora spoke: 'I was young when I was given to Njal, and I promised him that one fate should await us both.'[1]

Then the two of them went back in.

Bergthora said, 'What are we to do now?'

Njal answered, 'We will go to our bed and lie down.'

Then she said to the boy Thord, Kari's son, 'Someone will carry you out – you must not be burned here.'

'You promised me, grandmother,' said the boy, 'that we would never be parted, and so it must be, for I think it much better to die with you.'

Then she carried the boy to the bed.

Njal said to his foreman, 'Now you must see where we lie down and how I lay us out, for I don't intend to budge from this spot, no matter how much the smoke and the fire bother me – then you will know where our remains can be found.'

He said he would. An ox had been slaughtered, and its hide was lying there. Njal told the foreman to spread the hide over them, and he promised to do so. They lay down in the bed and placed the boy between them. Then they crossed themselves and the boy and put their souls in God's hands, and this was the last that people heard them speak. The foreman took the hide and spread it over them and then went out of the house. Ketil of Mork met him and hurried him out and asked carefully about his father-in-law Njal. The foreman told exactly what had happened.

Ketil spoke: 'A great ordeal has been dealt us, that we should share so much bad luck.'

Skarphedin had seen his father lie down and how he arranged things, and he spoke: 'Our father has gone to bed early, which is to be expected – he's an old man.'

Then Skarphedin and Kari and Grim seized the burning pieces as fast as they fell and threw them at those outside, and this went on for a while. Then the attackers threw spears at them, and they caught them all in the air and hurled them back.

Flosi told them to stop – 'for every exchange of blows with them goes badly for us. Just wait until the fire overcomes them.'

They did as he said. Then large timbers from the roof began falling down.

Skarphedin spoke: 'Now my father must be dead, and not a groan or a cough has been heard from him.'

Then they went to the end of the hall, where the crossbeam had fallen down, much burned in the middle.

Kari said to Skarphedin, 'Run outside on this – I'll help you start and run right behind you, and we'll both get away if we do this, because the smoke is all lying this way.'

Skarphedin said, 'You run out first, and I'll be right behind.'

'There's no need for that,' said Kari, 'because I'll get out somewhere else if I don't make it here.'

'I don't want that,' said Skarphedin. 'You run out first, and I'll be right on your heels.'

Kari spoke: 'Every man is obliged to save his own life, and so shall I. But our parting now will mean that we'll never meet again. If I run out of the fire, I won't have the courage to run back into it to join you, and then each of us will have to go his own way.'

Skarphedin said, 'It cheers me, brother-in-law, to think that if you escape you will avenge us.'

Then Kari took hold of a flaming piece of wood and ran up the crossbeam and threw the piece down from the roof, and it fell on the men outside; they ran away. By then all of Kari's clothing and even his hair were aflame. He jumped down from the roof and scurried along under cover of the smoke.

One of the men outside said, 'Did someone jump off the roof over there?'

'Far from it,' said another – 'that was Skarphedin throwing another burning piece at us.'

After that they suspected nothing. Kari ran until he came to a stream, and he threw himself into it and put out the flames. From there he ran under cover of the smoke to a hollow and rested there, and that place has since been called Kari's hollow.

130 | To return to Skarphedin: he ran up the crossbeam right after Kari, but when he reached the point where it was most burned, it gave way under him. He landed on his feet and quickly tried again, this time up the wall, but then the roof beam started towards him and he stumbled back.

Skarphedin spoke: 'It's clear now how it will be.'

Then he went along the side wall.

Gunnar Lambason leaped up on the wall and saw Skarphedin and said, 'What's this? Are you crying now, Skarphedin?'

'Not at all,' he said, 'though it's true that my eyes are smarting. But it seems to me that you're laughing – or am I wrong?'

'You're right,' said Gunnar, 'and this is the first time I have laughed since you killed Thrain.'

Skarphedin said, 'Then here's something to remember him by.'

He took from his purse one of the molars he had hacked out of Thrain and threw it at Gunnar's eye and knocked it out onto his cheek. Gunnar then fell off the roof.

Skarphedin went to his brother Grim; they joined hands and stamped out the fire. When they reached the middle of the hall Grim fell down dead. Skarphedin went on to the end of the house, and then there was a loud crash, and the whole roof fell down. He was caught between it and the gable wall and could not budge.

*

Flosi and his men stayed at the fire all night, until well after dawn. Then a man came riding towards them. Flosi asked his name. He said he was Geirmund, a kinsman of the Sigfussons, and he said, 'You have done a mighty deed here.'

Flosi answered, 'Men will call this both a mighty and an evil deed. But that can't be helped now.'

Geirmund said, 'How many notable people have died here?'

Flosi answered, 'Those who have died here are Njal and Bergthora, Njal's sons Helgi and Grim and Skarphedin, Thord Karason, Kari Solmundarson, and Thord Freed-man.[1] And there are others, less familiar to us, about whom we don't know for sure.'

Geirmund spoke: 'You listed one man as dead whom we know to have escaped – I spoke with him this morning.'

'Who is that?' said Flosi.

'Kari Solmundarson – my neighbour Bard and I came across him,' said Geirmund, 'and Bard gave him a horse, and his hair and his clothes were burned off him.'

'Did he have any weapons?' said Flosi.

'He had the sword Life-taker,' said Geirmund, 'and one of its edges had turned blue, and we said that it must have lost its temper, but he said he would harden it with the blood of the Sigfussons and the other burners.'

Flosi said, 'What did he say about Skarphedin and Grim?'

'He said that they were both alive when he left,' said Geirmund, 'but he expected them to be dead by now.'

Flosi spoke: 'You have told us things which bode no peace for us, for the man who has escaped comes closest to Gunnar of Hlidarendi in all respects. You must now think of this, you Sigfussons and the rest of our men, that the actions taken in response to this burning will be so great that they will cost many men their heads, and others will lose all their property. I suspect that none of you Sigfussons will dare to stay at home now, and with good reason. I want to invite all of you to come east with me, and let one fate await us all.'

They thanked him.

Modolf Ketilsson spoke this verse:

13.

From Njal's house one lived   *one*: Kari
when fire burned the rest;
the sons of Sigfus,
stalwart men, set it.
Now the kin of Gollnir is paid   *kin of Gollnir*: Njal
for the killing of brave Hoskuld;
the blaze burned through the house,
bright flames in the hall.

'We must find other things to boast of,' said Flosi, 'than the burning
of Njal, for there's no distinction in that.'

Flosi went up on the gable wall, with Glum Hildisson and some
others.

Glum said, 'Is Skarphedin dead yet?'

The others said he had been dead for a long time. The fire flared
up one moment and died down the next. Then they heard, from
down in the embers, this verse being spoken:

14.

Gunn of gold will not hold back   *Gunn* (valkyrie) *of gold*: woman
the gushing tears from her brow
over the sparring of spears   *sparring of spears*: fight
of the spirited shield-warrior,
when the allies of the edge   *allies of the edge*: warriors
exulted in the slaughter –
I boldly sing this song –
and spears tried in wounds cried out.[2]

Grani Gunnarsson said, 'Did Skarphedin speak this verse alive or
dead?'

'I won't make any guesses about that,' said Flosi.

'Let's go looking,' said Grani, 'for Skarphedin and for the other
men who burned to death here.'

'No!' said Flosi, 'and only fools like you would say that, when men
must be gathering forces all over the district. Whoever stays around
here now will be so frightened that he won't know which way to run,
and so my advice is that we all ride away at once.'

Flosi and all his men went quickly to their horses.

Flosi said to Geirmund, 'Is Ingjald home at Keldur?'

Geirmund said that he thought he was.

'That man,' said Flosi, 'has broken his oath and all faith with us.'

Flosi said to the Sigfussons, 'What do you want to do with him? Do you want to let him go, or shall we go after him and kill him?'

They all answered that they wanted to go after him.

Flosi and all the others then sprang on their horses and rode away. Flosi rode out in front and headed for the Ranga and followed it upstream. He saw a man riding down on the other side of the river; he recognized him as Ingjald of Keldur. Flosi called to him. Ingjald stopped and headed towards the river.

Flosi spoke to him: 'You have broken your pledge to us, and for that you have forfeited your property and your life. Here are the Sigfussons, eager to kill you, but I can see that you were in a difficult position, and I'm willing to spare you if you give me self-judgement.'

Ingjald said, 'I'll ride to join Kari before I'll give you self-judgement. And my answer to the Sigfussons is that I am no more afraid of them than they are of me.'

'Just stay there,' said Flosi, 'if you're not a coward, and I'll direct a message your way.'

'I'll wait right here,' said Ingjald.

Thorstein Kolbeinsson, Flosi's nephew, rode up to him with a spear in his hand. He was one of Flosi's bravest and most admired men. Flosi grabbed the spear from him and hurled it at Ingjald. It came at him from the left and passed through the shield below the handle and split the shield in two; the spear passed through Ingjald's thigh just above the knee and stuck fast in the side-board of the saddle.

Flosi spoke to Ingjald: 'Well, did it hit you?'

'It hit me all right,' said Ingjald, 'but I call it a scratch, not a wound.'

Ingjald jerked the spear out of his leg and spoke to Flosi: 'Now you stay there, if you're not a softie' – and he hurled the spear back across the river. Flosi saw it coming straight at him; he turned his horse aside; the spear flew past his chest and missed him and hit Thorstein in the waist and he fell down dead from his horse. Ingjald galloped into the woods, and they didn't catch him.

Flosi spoke to his men: 'We have just suffered a great loss. From the fact that this happened we can see what bad luck we shall have. My advice now is that we ride back to Thrihyrning ridge. From there we can see which way men are riding in the district, for by now they must have gathered a large force, and they'll expect that from Thrihyrning ridge we rode east to Fljotshlid, and they'll expect us to ride north from there to the mountains and then to the eastern districts. Most of their men will ride that way, but some will ride east along the coast to Seljalandsmuli, even though they have less hope of finding us there. And now I propose this plan – that we ride up to the mountain Thrihyrning and wait there until the sun has passed from the sky three times.'

They did this.

131 | To return now to Kari: he went from the hollow to the place where he met Bard and they had the talk which Geirmund reported. From there Kari rode to Mord Valgardsson and told him what had happened, and Mord grieved greatly. Kari said there were more manly things to do than weep for the dead, and he asked him to gather men and bring them all to Holtsvad.

Then he rode off to see Hjalti Skeggjason in Thjorsardal. As he was coming along the Thjorsa river he saw someone riding after him in great haste, and Kari waited for the man; he saw that it was Ingjald of Keldur and that his thigh was all bloody. He asked Ingjald who had wounded him, and Ingjald told him.

'Where did you two meet?' said Kari.

'At the Ranga river,' said Ingjald, 'and he threw a spear across the river at me.'

'Did you do anything in return?' said Kari.

'I threw the spear back,' said Ingjald, 'and they said that it hit a man and killed him.'

'Don't you know who it was?' said Kari.

'It looked like Thorstein, Flosi's nephew,' said Ingjald.

'Bless your hands!' said Kari.

The two of them then rode to Hjalti Skeggjason and told him about the burning. He took this angrily and said that it was imperative that they ride after them and kill them all. He gathered forces and called up all available men, and then they rode with Kari to meet Mord Valgardsson at Holtsvad. Mord was already there with a large force. They split up for the search: some rode east along the coast to Seljalandsmuli, others up to Fljotshlid, and others went further north up to Thrihyrning ridge, from there down to Godaland, and then north to Sand. Some went to Fiskivotn and then turned back.

Others went along the coast to Holt and told Thorgeir what had happened and asked him whether Flosi and his men had passed by there.

Thorgeir spoke: 'I may not be a great chieftain, but Flosi would find a better plan than to ride past me in full view after he has killed my father's brother Njal and my cousins. Your only choice is to turn back, for you have searched much too widely. Tell Kari that he should ride here and stay with me, if he wishes, and if he doesn't want to come east I will take care of his farm at Dyrholmar, if he wishes. And tell him that I will support him and ride to the Althing. He must be aware that my brothers and I are the ones who will take action for the burning. We'll keep at this until we have sentences of outlawry, if we're successful, and blood revenge on top of that. I won't go with you now because I know that nothing will happen – they'll be extremely careful now.'

They rode back then and all met at Hof and talked about how they had brought shame on themselves for not having found them. Mord said that this was not so. Many of them urged that they should go to Fljotshlid and seize the farms of all those who had taken part in the deed, but the matter was referred to Mord. He said that this would be most ill-advised. They asked why he said that.

He answered, 'If their farms are untouched, they will come to visit them and their women, and then they can be hunted down in due course. Have no doubt that I will be loyal to Kari in every way, for I must look out for myself.'[1]

Hjalti told Mord to keep to his promise. Then he invited Kari to stay with him; Kari said that he would make that his first stop. They told him what Thorgeir had offered, and he said he would make use of that offer later and that he would take heart if there were many such men.

Then they all disbanded.

Flosi and his men saw everything that was going on from where they were in the mountain.

Flosi said, 'Let's take our horses and ride away – it's safe for us now.'

The Sigfussons asked whether it would be a good idea for them to go to their farms and oversee the work there.

'Mord is expecting you to visit your women,' said Flosi, 'and it's my guess that his advice is to let your farms remain untouched. My advice is that none of us separates from the rest and that you all ride east with me.'

They all agreed to follow that advice. They rode away, north of the glacier and then east to Svinafell. Flosi sent men off at once to gather provisions so that they would not be short of anything.

Flosi never boasted of what he had done, and no one ever detected any fear in him. He was at home that winter until Christmas.

132 | Kari asked Hjalti to go and look for Njal's remains – 'because everybody will believe what you say and think about them.'

Hjalti said he would gladly do that, and also bring Njal's remains to church. Fifteen of them rode off. They went east over the Thjorsa river and called others to join them, and eventually they had a hundred men, including Njal's neighbours. They reached Berg-thorshvol at noon.

Hjalti asked Kari where Njal would be lying, and Kari showed him; they cleared away a great deal of ash. At the bottom they found the ox-hide, shrivelled up from the fire. They lifted it off and underneath lay the two of them, unburned. They all praised God for this and thought it a great miracle. Then the boy who had lain between them was taken up, and one of his fingers, which he had stuck out from under the hide, was burned off. Njal was carried out, and then Bergthora. Everybody came to look at their bodies.

Hjalti spoke: 'How do these bodies seem to you?'

They answered, 'We'll wait for what you have to say.'

Hjalti spoke: 'I'll be frank about this. Bergthora's body is as I would have expected, though well preserved. Njal's countenance and body seem to me so radiant that I've never seen a dead man's body as radiant as his.'

They all agreed that this was so.

Then they searched for Skarphedin. The servants showed them where Flosi and his men had heard the verse spoken, where the roof had collapsed next to the gable wall, and Hjalti said they should dig there. They did and found the body of Skarphedin; he had been standing up against the gable wall, and his legs were burned off almost up to the knees, but the rest of him was unburned. He had bitten into his upper lip. His eyes were open and not swollen. He had driven his axe into the gable wall so hard that half the blade was buried, and it had not lost its temper. Then he was carried out, with the axe.

Hjalti picked up the axe and said, 'This is not an ordinary weapon, and few men will be able to use it.'

Kari said, 'I know the man who should use it.'

'Who is that?' said Hjalti.

'Thorgeir Skorar-Geir,' said Kari, 'whom I consider the best man in that family now.'

Skarphedin was then stripped of his clothes; they had not been burned away. He had folded his arms in a cross, with the right arm above, and they found two marks on him, one between his shoulders and the other on his chest, and in both places a cross had been burned, and people thought he had probably burned these marks himself. Everybody said that it was easier to be in the presence of the dead Skarphedin than they had expected, for no one was afraid of him.

They looked for Grim and found his remains in the middle of the hall. Opposite him they found Thord Freed-man, under the side wall, and in the weaving-room they found the old woman Saeunn and three more men. Altogether they found the remains of eleven people. They carried the bodies to church.

Then Hjalti rode home, and Kari went with him. Ingjald had an infection in his leg and he went to see Hjalti, and he cured it, but Ingjald always limped after that.

Kari rode to Asgrim at Tunga. Thorhalla had already arrived home and she had told of the burning. Asgrim welcomed Kari with open arms and said that he should stay there for the next year; Kari said he would. Asgrim invited everybody who had been living at Bergthorshvol to stay with him. Kari said that this was a good offer – 'and I accept it on their behalf.' The whole household then moved over there.

Thorhall Asgrimsson was so moved when he was told that his foster-father Njal was dead and that he had been burned in his house that his whole body swelled up and blood gushed from both ears, and it did not stop and he fell in a faint, and then it stopped. After that he stood up and said that this had not been manly of him – 'but I wish I could take vengeance against the men who burned Njal in his house for what just happened to me.'

The others said that no one would consider that shameful, but he said that he could not stop people from talking.

Asgrim asked Kari what support he could count on from those on the east side of the rivers. Kari said that Mord Valgardsson and Hjalti Skeggjason would give as much help as they could, and also Thorgeir Skorargeir and his brothers. Asgrim said that this was a strong force.

'What help are we to have from you?' said Kari.

'Everything I have,' said Asgrim. 'I'll risk my life for this.'

'Do so,' said Kari.

'I have also brought Gizur the White into the matter,' said Asgrim, 'and I asked him how we should proceed.'

'That's good,' said Kari. 'What did he suggest?'

Asgrim answered, 'He suggested that we lie low until the spring, and then ride east and start legal proceedings against Flosi for the slaying of Helgi, and summon neighbours and give notice at the Thing of the suit for the burning, and summon the same neighbours to serve on a panel. I asked Gizur who should prosecute the case for the slaying, and he said that Mord should prosecute, even if he didn't like it – "he should have the heaviest lot, because in this whole matter the worst things have come from him. Kari must show anger towards him whenever they meet, and that, along with another plan of my own, will bring him round," said Gizur.'

Kari said, 'We shall follow your advice as long as we can and you are willing to lead us.'

Of Kari it is said that he was unable to sleep at night. Asgrim woke up one night and heard that he was awake.

Asgrim said, 'Aren't you sleepy at night?'

Kari spoke a verse:

15.

Sleep shuns my eyes, Ull
of the elm-string, all night;   *elm-string*: bow; its *Ull* (a god): warrior
I recall the man
who craved shields set with rings.   *man who craved shields*: warrior
In autumn the blazing
sword-trees burned Njal at home;   *sword-trees*: warriors
since then the harm done me
has dwelt in my mind.

Kari spoke of no one as often as he did of Njal and Skarphedin. He never spoke ill of his enemies, and he never made threats against them.

133 | To tell now about Flosi at Svinafell: he was sleeping badly one night. Glum Hildisson tried to wake him up, and it took a long time before Flosi was awake. He asked Glum to bring Ketil of Mork.

Ketil came there.

Flosi said, 'I want to tell you about a dream I had.'[1]

'Go ahead,' said Ketil.

'I dreamed,' said Flosi, 'that I was at Lomagnup and went outside and looked up at the peak. It opened, and a man came walking out of the peak, and he wore a goatskin and held an iron staff in his hand. He called out as he walked and called to my men – some first, some later – and he named them by name. First he called Grim the Red and Arni Kolsson. Then it was strange – I dreamed that he called Eyjolf Bolverksson and Ljot, the son of Hall of Sida, and about six

other men. Then he was quiet for a while. Then he called another
five of our men, and among them were the Sigfussons, your brothers.
Then he called five more, including Lambi and Modolf and Glum.
Then he called three men. Finally he called Gunnar Lambason and
Kol Thorsteinsson.[2]

'After that he walked over to me. I asked him what news he had.
He said he would tell me. I asked him for his name; he called himself
Iron-Grim. I asked where he was going; he said he was going to the
Althing.

' "What are you going to do there?" I said.

'He answered, "First I shall clear the panel of neighbours, and then
the court, and then the battlefield for the battlers."[3]

'Then he spoke this:

16.

A hardy warrior	*hardy warrior*: Kari
will harry here soon;	
men will see on the ground	
many forts of brains;	*forts of brains*: skulls
singing of sword-play	
will sound in the hills;	
dew of blood will	
dampen many legs.	

'He struck downwards with his staff and there was a great crash.
Then he walked into the peak, and I was frightened. Now I want you
to tell me what you think this dream means.'

'I have a sense,' said Ketil, 'that all those men who were called are
doomed to die. I think it would be wise for us not to tell anyone
about this dream as matters now stand.'

Flosi said that it should be so.

The winter wore on and Christmas passed.

Flosi spoke to his men: 'I want us to leave here now; I think we
will have no more peace, and we should now go around and ask for
support. What I told you once will now prove true, that we will have
to beg at the knees of many men before all this is over.'[4]

134 | They all made ready to leave. Flosi was wearing trousers and stockings in one piece because he was planning to walk, and he knew that others would then find it easier to walk.[1] They went from Svinafell to Hnappavoll, and the next evening to Breida, from Breida to Kalfafell, from there to Bjarnarnes in Hornafjord, from there to Stafafell in Lon, and then to Hall of Sida at Thvotta. Flosi was married to Steinvor, Hall's daughter. Hall gave them a warm reception.

Flosi said to Hall, 'I want to ask, father-in-law, that you and all your thingmen ride to the Thing with me.'

Hall said, 'It's turned out just as the saying goes, that the hand's joy in the blow is brief. The very men in your company who were once pushing for trouble are now hanging their heads. But I'm duty-bound to lend you my support in any way I can.'

Flosi said, 'What advice do you have for me, as things are now?'

He answered, 'You must go north, all the way to Vopnafjord, and ask all those chieftains for help; you'll need help from them all before the Thing is over.'

Flosi stayed there for three nights and rested and then went east to Geitahellur and on to Berufjord and stayed there overnight. From there they continued east to Heydal in Breiddal. Hallbjorn the Strong lived there; he was married to Oddny, the sister of Sorli Brodd-Helgason, and Flosi was well received there. Hallbjorn asked many questions about the burning, and Flosi answered him in full detail. Hallbjorn asked how far into the northern fjords Flosi was planning to go. He said he was planning to go to Vopnafjord. Flosi then took a purse from his belt and said he wanted to give it to him. Hallbjorn accepted the money, but said that Flosi owed him no gifts – 'and yet I'd like to know how you want me to repay this.'

'I don't need money,' said Flosi, 'but I'd like you to ride to the Thing with me and support me in my affairs there, even though I have no claim on you either by marriage or by blood.'

Hallbjorn said, 'I promise to ride to the Thing with you and support you in your affairs, as much as if you were my brother.'

Flosi thanked him.

From there he rode to Breiddal heath and then to Hrafnkelsstadir. Hrafnkel Thorisson lived there; his father was the son of Hrafnkel, the son of Hrafn. Flosi had a good welcome there, and he asked Hrafnkel to ride to the Thing with him and give him support. Hrafnkel tried for a long time to excuse himself but finally promised that his son Thorir would ride with all their thingmen and offer the same support as the other godis from that district.

Flosi thanked him and left for Bessastadir. Holmstein lived there, the son of Bessi the Wise, and he welcomed Flosi warmly and Flosi asked him for support. Holmstein said that Flosi had paid him for support a long time ago.

From there they went to Valthjofsstadir. Sorli Brodd-Helgason, the brother of Bjarni, lived there. He was married to Thordis, the daughter of Gudmund the Powerful of Modruvellir. They had a good welcome there. In the morning Flosi raised the question whether Sorli would ride to the Thing with him, and he offered him money.

'I don't know about this,' said Sorli, 'as long as I don't know where Gudmund the Powerful, my father-in-law, stands – I'll take whatever side he takes.'

Flosi said, 'I can see from your answer that your wife rules here.'

Flosi rose and told his men to take their clothing and their weapons. Then they went away, and had gained no help there.

They went by the southern end of Lagarfljot lake and then north across the heath to Njardvik. Two brothers lived there, Thorkel the All-wise and Thorvald; they were the sons of Ketil Thrym, the son of Thidrandi the Wise, the son of Ketil Thrym, the son of Thorir Thidrandi. Their mother was Yngvild, the daughter of Thorkel the All-wise. Flosi had a good welcome there. He told them all about his reason for coming and asked for their support, but they turned him down, until he gave each of them three marks of silver for their support; then they agreed to help Flosi.

Their mother Yngvild was near them; she wept when she heard them promise to ride to the Althing.

Thorkel spoke: 'Why are you weeping, mother?'

She answered, 'I dreamed that your brother Thorvald was wearing a red tunic, and that it was as tight as if it had been sewed onto him. His leggings were red, too, and badly tied. It hurt me to look at him in such distress, but I could do nothing about it.'

They laughed at her and said that this was nonsense and that her silly talk would not stop them from riding to the Thing.

Flosi thanked them and went from there to Vopnafjord, to the farm Hof. Bjarni Brodd-Helgason lived there; his father Brodd-Helgi was the son of Thorgils, the son of Thorstein the White, the son of Olvir, the son of Eyvald, the son of Ox-Thorir. Bjarni's mother was Halla Lytingsdottir. Brodd-Helgi's mother was Asvor, the daughter of Thorir, the son of Porridge-Atli, the son of Thorir Thidrandi. Bjarni Brodd-Helgason was married to Rannveig Thorgeirsdottir; her father was the son of Eirik of Goddalir, the son of Geirmund, the son of Hroald, the son of Eirik Stiff-beard.

Bjarni welcomed Flosi with open arms. Flosi offered Bjarni money for his support.

Bjarni spoke: 'Never have I taken any bribe for my manhood or my support. But since you need help, I will act out of friendship and ride to the Thing and help you as I would my own brother.'

'Now you're placing the burden of debt in my hands,' said Flosi, 'but I expected something like this from you.'

Then Flosi went to Krossavik. Thorkel Geitisson was already a great friend of his. Flosi told him the reason for his visit. Thorkel said it was his duty to help him as much as he was able, and not give up his cause. Thorkel gave Flosi good gifts at their parting.

*

Then Flosi went south from Vopnafjord and into the Fljotsdal district and stayed with Holmstein Bessason and told him that everybody was ready to support him in his need except Sorli Brodd-Helgason. Holmstein said that what lay behind this was the fact that Sorli was not a violent man. Holmstein gave Flosi good gifts.

Flosi went up Fljotsdal and then south across the mountains to the Oxarhraun lava, then down Svidinhornadal and out along the west side of Alftafjord, and he did not stop until he came to Thvotta, to his father-in-law Hall. Flosi and his men stayed there for a fortnight and rested.

Flosi asked Hall what he would advise him on how to proceed and arrange things.

Hall spoke: 'My advice is that you and the Sigfussons ride home now and stay at your farm, and that they send men to look after their farms. When you ride to the Thing, ride all together and don't break up into small groups. Let the Sigfussons visit their women then. I will also ride to the Thing, with my son Ljot and all our thingmen, and give you as much help as I can muster.'

Flosi thanked him, and Hall gave him good gifts at their parting.

Flosi then left Thvotta, and there is nothing to say about the rest of his journey until he returned home to Svinafell. He remained at home for what was left of the winter and the summer, right up until time for the Thing.

135 | To tell now about Kari Solmundarson and Thorhall Asgrimsson: one day they rode to Mosfell to visit Gizur the White. He welcomed them with open arms, and they stayed there a long time.

Once when they were talking about the burning of Njal, Gizur said that it was a great piece of luck that Kari had escaped. Then this verse came from Kari's mouth:

17.
A whetter of axes,   *whetter of axes*: warrior
I went out in anger

from the alder's sweat   *alder's sweat*: smoke
in Njal's abode,
when the wild
woods of the sword   *woods of the sword*: warriors (Njal's sons)
burned there; listen!
I lament my loss.

Gizur said, 'It is natural that this is on your mind, and let's not talk about it any more for the time being.'

Kari said that he was going to ride home.

Gizur spoke: 'I'll give you some frank advice. You must not ride home, but ride away from here if you want. Go east all the way to Holt in the Eyjafjoll district, to Thorgeir Skorargeir and Thorleif Crow. They will have to ride west with you, since they have the duty of prosecuting this case. Thorgrim the Tall, their brother, should ride with them. Ride to Mord Valgardsson. Give him this message from me, that he is to take over the suit against Flosi for the slaying of Helgi. If he utters any objection to this, go into a rage and act as if you'll sink your axe into his head. Tell him also of my anger, if he plays hard to get. Tell him in addition that I will come for my daughter Thorkatla and bring her home with me – he won't be able to endure that, for he loves her like the eyes in his head.'

Kari thanked him for his plan. He did not raise the matter of support, for he knew that Gizur would act as a true friend there as well.

Kari rode east across the rivers to Fljotshlid and then east across the Markarfljot and on to Seljalandsmuli. They rode on east to Holt. Thorgeir welcomed them with great pleasure. He told them about Flosi's travels and how much aid he had gathered in the East Fjords. Kari said that Flosi had good reason to ask for help, since he had so much to answer for.

Thorgeir said, 'The worse it goes for them, the better for us.'

Kari told Thorgeir about Gizur's plan.

*

Then they rode west to the Rangarvellir to visit Mord Valgardsson; he welcomed them. Kari gave him the message from Gizur the White, Mord's father-in-law. Mord was quite reluctant; he said it would be harder to prosecute Flosi than ten other men.

Kari spoke: 'You're carrying on just as Gizur expected, for you are ill-favoured in every way – you're both frightened and fainthearted. Now you'll get what's coming to you – Thorkatla is to go home to her father.'

She started making preparations at once and said she had long been ready for them to part. Then Mord suddenly changed his attitude and his language and asked them not to be angry with him and took over the case at once.

Kari spoke: 'You have now taken over the case, so prosecute it fearlessly, for your life depends on it.'

Mord said he would put his whole heart into doing it well and manfully.

After that Mord summoned nine neighbours, all from close to the scene of the burning. Then he took Thorgeir's hand and named two witnesses – 'to witness that Thorgeir Thorisson turns over to me the homicide suit against Flosi Thordarson, together with all the evidence for the prosecution of this case, to prosecute him for the slaying of Helgi Njalsson. You are turning this suit over to me, to prosecute and to settle with full use of the evidence, just as if I were the rightful plaintiff. You are turning this over to me lawfully, and I take it over lawfully.'

Mord named witnesses a second time – 'to witness,' he said, 'that I give notice of a punishable assault by Flosi Thordarson, in which he inflicted on Helgi Njalsson a brain wound or internal wound or marrow wound which proved to be a fatal wound, and Helgi died of it. I give this notice before five neighbours' – and he named them all. 'I give this lawful notice; I give notice that the suit was turned over to me by Thorgeir Thorisson.'

Again he named witnesses – 'to witness that I give notice of a brain wound or internal wound or marrow wound caused by Flosi Thordarson, which proved to be a fatal wound, of which Helgi died at the place where Flosi Thordarson had made a punishable assault against Helgi Njalsson. I give notice of this before five neighbours' – then he named them all. 'I give this lawful notice; I give notice that the suit was turned over to me by Thorgeir Thorisson.'[1]

Then Mord named witnesses for a third time – 'to witness,' he said, 'that I call on these nine neighbours to the scene of the action' – and he named them all by name – 'to ride to the Althing and to form a panel of neighbours to determine whether Flosi Thordarson ran at Helgi Njalsson in a punishable assault at the place where Flosi Thordarson inflicted on Helgi Njalsson a brain wound or internal wound or marrow wound which proved to be a fatal wound, and Helgi died of it. I call on you for all the findings which the law requires you to make and which I ask you to make before the court and which are relevant to this case. I call on you with a lawful summons in your own hearing. I call on you in the case turned over to me by Thorgeir Thorisson.'

Mord named witnesses – 'to witness that I call on these nine neighbours to the scene of the action to ride to the Althing and to form a panel of neighbours to determine whether Flosi Thordarson wounded Helgi Njalsson with a brain wound or internal wound or marrow wound which proved to be a fatal wound, and Helgi died of it at the place where Flosi Thordarson ran at Helgi Njalsson in a punishable assault. I call on you for all the findings which the law requires you to make and which I ask you to make before the court and which are relevant to this case. I call on you with a lawful summons in your own hearing. I call on you in the case turned over to me by Thorgeir Thorisson.'

Then Mord said, 'Now the proceedings have been started, as you asked, and I want to ask you, Thorgeir, to come to me when you ride to the Thing, and then we'll ride together with our two groups of men and stay close together. My men will be ready by the beginning of the Thing, and I will be loyal to you in all matters.'

They were satisfied with all this and bound themselves by oaths not to abandon each other until Kari allowed it, and to risk their lives one for the other. Then they parted in friendship and arranged to meet at the Thing.

*

Thorgeir then rode back east, and Kari rode west over the rivers until he reached Asgrim at Tunga, who gave him a very warm welcome. Kari told Asgrim all about Gizur the White's plan and the start of the case.

'I expected him to do well,' said Asgrim, 'and he has shown it once again. And what do you hear about Flosi, over in the east?'

Kari answered, 'He went all the way to Vopnafjord, and almost all the chieftains there have promised to ride to the Althing and support him. They're also counting on help from the men of Reykjadal, Ljosavatn and Oxarfjord.'

They talked about this at length. And now it was close to the time for the Althing.

Thorhall Asgrimsson had such an infection on his leg that above the ankle it was as swollen and as thick as a woman's thigh, and he could not walk without a staff. He was large in build and mighty in strength, with dark hair and dark skin, controlled in his speech and yet hot-tempered. He was one of the three greatest lawyers in Iceland.

Now it was time to leave home for the ride to the Thing.

Asgrim spoke to Kari: 'Ride so that you're there at the beginning of the Thing and cover our booths, and my son Thorhall will go with you, for I know you will show him great kindness and concern with his injured foot. We have the greatest need for his help at this Thing. Twenty other men will ride with you.'

After that they prepared for their journey and then rode to the Thing and covered their booths and made everything ready.

136 | Flosi rode from the east, along with the hundred men who had been with him at the burning. They rode until they came to Fljotshlid. The Sigfussons spent the day looking after their farms, and in the evening they rode west across the Thjorsa river and slept there that night. Early the next morning they took their horses and rode on.

Flosi said to his men, 'Now let's ride to Asgrim at Tunga and make him see our ill will.'

They said that that would be good, and rode until they were a short distance from Tunga.

Asgrim was standing outside, and some of his men were with him; they saw the men as soon as they came in view.

Asgrim's men said, 'That must be Thorgeir Skorargeir.'

Asgrim spoke: 'I don't think so at all; these men are coming with laughter and merriment, but the kinsmen of Njal, men like Thorgeir, will never laugh until Njal is avenged. My guess is quite different, and you may find it unlikely – I think it's Flosi and the other burners, and that they are planning to make us see their ill will. Let's all go inside.'

They did so. Asgrim had the house swept, hangings put up, the tables set and food brought out. He set up extra seats facing the benches the whole length of the main room.

Flosi rode into the hayfield and told his men to dismount and go inside. They did this. Flosi and his men came into the room. Asgrim was sitting on the raised floor. Flosi looked at the benches and saw that every need had been prepared for.

Asgrim did not greet them, but said to Flosi, 'The tables are set so that food is at hand for those who need it.'

Flosi and all his men sat at the tables and placed their weapons against the walls. Those who found no place on the benches sat on the seats, and four men stood with their weapons in front of Flosi's seat while they were eating. Asgrim kept quiet during the meal but was as red as blood to look at. When they had finished eating, some of the women cleared the tables, and others brought water-basins for washing. Flosi was in no more of a hurry than if he had been at home.

A wood-axe was lying in a corner of the raised floor. Asgrim grabbed it with both hands and leaped up to the edge of the floor and swung at Flosi's head. Glum Hildisson happened to see what was coming, jumped up at once and grabbed the axe above Asgrim's grip and turned the blade towards him – Glum was a powerful man. Many others jumped up and were ready to rush at Asgrim. Flosi said that no one should harm him – 'for we pushed him too far, and he only did what he had to do, and showed that he is a very bold man.'

Flosi said to Asgrim, 'We'll part for now, safe and sound, and meet again at the Thing to deal with this whole matter.'

'So we will,' said Asgrim, 'and I only hope that by the time the Thing is over you'll be brought down a peg.'

Flosi made no answer. They went out and mounted their horses and rode away. They rode until they reached Laugarvatn and spent the night there. In the morning they rode on to Beitivellir[1] and stopped to rest. Many bands of men joined them there, Hall of Sida and all the men from the East Fjords. Flosi welcomed them warmly and told them of his journey and his dealings with Asgrim. Many praised Flosi and said he had acted bravely.

Hall spoke: 'I don't see it that way, for I think this was a very foolish move. They'll remember their grief even without fresh reminders, and men who press others so hard are only creating trouble for themselves.'

It was clear that Hall thought they had gone too far.

They all rode away from there until they reached the Upper Fields of the Thing, and there they drew their forces up and then rode down to the Thing. Flosi had arranged for the Byrgi booth to be covered[2] before he rode to the Thing, and the men from the East Fjords rode to their booths.

137 | To turn now to Thorgeir Skorargeir: he rode from the east with a large force. His brothers, Thorleif Crow and Thorgrim the Tall, were with him. They rode until they came to Mord Valgardsson at Hof and waited there until he was ready. Mord had gathered every man who could bear arms, and the brothers found him to be most resolute in every way.

They rode west until they crossed the rivers and then waited for Hjalti Skeggjason. He came when they had been waiting only a short time. They welcomed him warmly and then all rode together until they reached Reykir in Biskupstunga, and there they waited for Asgrim; he joined them there.

Then they rode west across the Bruara river, and Asgrim told them everything that had happened between him and Flosi.

Thorgeir said, 'I would like us to try out their manliness before this Thing is over.'

Then they rode until they reached Beitivellir. Gizur the White arrived there with a very large force. They had a long talk together. Then they rode to the Upper Fields and drew up all their forces and rode to the Thing. Flosi and all his men rushed for their weapons, and they were on the verge of fighting, but Asgrim and his band did not react and rode straight to their booths. The rest of the day was quiet, and there was no fighting between them.

Chieftains had come from all quarters of the land, and there had never been such a crowded Thing as far back as men could remember.

138 | There was a man named Eyjolf; he was the son of Bolverk, the son of Eyjolf the Grey of Otradal, the son of Thord Bellower, the son of Olaf Feilan. The mother of Eyjolf the Grey was Hrodny, the daughter of Skeggi from Midfjord, the son of Skin-Bjorn, the son of Skutad-Skeggi. Eyjolf was held in great respect and was so clever in the law that he was one of the three greatest lawyers in Iceland.[1] He was an unusually handsome man, big and strong and with every promise of becoming a good chieftain. He was fond of money, like the rest of his family.

Flosi went one day to the booth of Bjarni Brodd-Helgason. Bjarni welcomed him with open arms, and Flosi sat down beside him. They talked about many things.

Flosi said, 'What course shall we take now?'

Bjarni answered, 'It's a tight spot to get out of, but I think the best course is for you to find more support, for they're gathering men against you. I also want to ask, Flosi, whether you have any distinguished lawyer on your side, for you have two choices: one is to ask for a peaceful settlement, and this would be very good; the other is to defend your side legally – if there is a possible defence – though this may seem audacious. I think you must take this choice, because you have acted aggressively so far, and it would not do for you to falter now.'

Flosi said, 'Since you asked about lawyers, I can tell you at once that there is none in our band, and I can't think of any in the East Fjords apart from your kinsman Thorkel Geitisson.'

Bjarni spoke: 'We mustn't consider him; he's wise in the law, but he's also very cautious, and no one ought to count on him as a shield. But he'll stand by you as well as the best, for he's a very bold man. I can tell you that death will come to the man who pleads the defence for the burning, and I don't want that for my kinsman Thorkel. We'll have to look elsewhere.'

Flosi said he had no idea who the best lawyers were.

Bjarni spoke: 'There's a man named Eyjolf Bolverksson. He's the best lawyer in the West Fjords Quarter, and he will have to be paid a lot of money to take the case, but we won't be put off by that. Also, we must take our weapons to all legal proceedings and be extremely watchful, but never fight unless we have to defend ourselves. I'll go with you now to ask for help, for we can't afford to sit quiet.'

They left the booth and went to the men from Oxarfjord. Bjarni spoke with Lyting and Blaeing and Hroi Arnsteinsson, and he soon got what he wanted from them.

Then they went to see Kol, the son of Killer-Skuta, and Eyvind Thorkelsson, the son of Askel the Godi, and asked them for help. They were reluctant for a long time, but finally they accepted three marks of silver and joined their cause.

Then they went to the booth of the men from Ljosavatn and stayed there for some time. Flosi asked the Ljosavatn men for help, but they were difficult and hard to persuade.

Then Flosi spoke to them in great anger: 'You're a bad lot. You're pushy and unfair in your own district, but you won't help men at the Thing even when they need you. You'll be looked on with scorn and you'll be treated with reproach at the Thing if you ignore the shameful treatment which Skarphedin dealt to you Ljosavatn men.'[2]

Flosi talked to them a second time, privately, and offered them money for their support and beguiled them with flattery. Finally they promised their support and became so resolute that they said they would even fight for Flosi, if need be.

Bjarni said to Flosi, 'Well done! You're a great chieftain and a brave, firm man, and you don't let anything stop you.'

Then they left and went west across the Oxara river to the Hlad booth. They saw that many men were standing outside the booth. There was one who had a scarlet cloak over his shoulders, a gold band around his head and a silver inlaid axe in his hand.

Bjarni said, 'This is good luck – here's Eyjolf Bolverksson.'

They went up to Eyjolf and greeted him. Eyjolf recognized Bjarni at once and welcomed him. Bjarni took Eyjolf by the arm and led him up to the Almannagja gorge. He told Flosi and his men to follow behind. Eyjolf's men went along with him. They were told to stay up on the edge of the gorge and keep watch from there.

The others went on until they came to a path which led down from the upper edge of the gorge. Flosi said this would be a good place to sit and have a wide view. They sat down; there were four of them, and no more.

Bjarni said to Eyjolf, 'We've come to see you, friend, because we very much need your help in all ways.'

Eyjolf said, 'There is a good choice of men here at the Thing, and it should be easy to find men who can give you more than I can.'

Bjarni spoke: 'That's not so, for you have many qualities that show that no man is greater than you here at the Althing. First of all, you're nobly born, as is everybody descended from Ragnar Shaggy-breeches. Your forefathers have always played a role in major events, both at the Thing and at home in their district, and they have always come out on top. Therefore it seems to us that you are as likely to win legal cases as your kinsmen.'

Eyjolf said, 'You speak well, but I hardly deserve this praise.'

Flosi spoke: 'You don't need to probe deeply to see what's on our mind: we want to ask you to support us in our case and go to court with us and look for points that might be used in our defence and argue them on our behalf – and stand by us in whatever may come up at this Thing'

Eyjolf jumped up in anger and said that no one should count on making him a puppet or risk-taker in matters he had no reason to be dragged into.

'I see now,' he said, 'what you were after with the flattery you aimed at me.'

Hallbjorn the Strong grabbed him and put him down between himself and Bjarni and spoke: 'A tree doesn't fall at the first blow, friend,' he said. 'Just sit here with us for a while.'

Flosi took a gold bracelet from his arm and spoke: 'I want to give you this bracelet, Eyjolf, for your friendship and support and to show you that I have no wish to deceive you. You had best accept this bracelet, for there's no man here at the Thing to whom I have given such a gift.'

The bracelet was so large and so well made that it was worth twelve hundred ells of striped homespun. Hallbjorn pulled it up Eyjolf's arm.

Eyjolf spoke: 'It seems quite proper to accept the bracelet now that you are being so kind. And you can count on me to take over your defence and do whatever is necessary.'

Bjarni said, 'Now you're both doing very well. And there are other men here, namely Hallbjorn and myself, who are qualified to witness that you're taking over the case.'

Eyjolf stood up, and Flosi too. They shook hands. Eyjolf took over from Flosi the defence and any other actions that might arise from it, for a defence can turn into a prosecution.[3] Then Eyjolf took over all the evidence to be used in the prosecution, whether it was to be presented in the Quarter Court or the Fifth Court. Flosi transferred the case lawfully, and Eyjolf took it over lawfully.

Then he spoke to Flosi and Bjarni: 'Now I have taken over this case, as you requested, but I want you to keep this a secret to begin with. If it goes to the Fifth Court you must be especially careful about saying that you gave money for my support.'

Flosi and Bjarni and all the others stood up. Flosi and Bjarni went to their booths, and Eyjolf went into Snorri the Godi's booth and sat down beside him. They talked of many things. Snorri the Godi grabbed Eyjolf's arm and turned up the sleeve and saw that he was wearing a large gold bracelet.

Snorri said, 'Was this ring purchased or given?'

Eyjolf was flustered and dumbstruck.

Snorri said, 'I see plainly that you got it as a gift – may this bracelet not be the cause of your death!'

Eyjolf jumped up and walked away and did not want to talk about it.

When he saw Eyjolf getting up, Snorri spoke: 'It's quite likely that by the time the courts are over you will know what gift you have accepted.'

Eyjolf then went to his booth.

139 | To return now to Asgrim Ellida-Grimsson and Kari Solmundarson: they met with Gizur the White, Hjalti Skeggjason, Thorgeir Skorargeir and Mord Valgardsson.

Asgrim spoke: 'There is no need to be secretive, for the only men here now are those who know they can count on each other. I want to ask if you know anything about the steps taken by Flosi and his men. It strikes me that we may need to think once more about our own plans.'

Gizur the White answered, 'Snorri the Godi sent a man to tell me that Flosi received much support from men in the North, and that his kinsman Eyjolf Bolverksson accepted a bracelet from somebody and was keeping it a secret – and Snorri said that it was his guess that Eyjolf Bolverksson has been chosen to argue for the defence in the case, and that's why the bracelet was given.'

They all agreed that this must be so.

Gizur spoke to them: 'My son-in-law Mord has taken on a case which must seem to everybody the most difficult of all – the prosecution of Flosi. I want you now to divide the other suits among yourselves, for it will soon be time to give notice of legal actions at the Law Rock. We also need to ask for more support.'

Asgrim replied, 'We'll do as you say, but we want to ask you to be with us on our quest for support.'

Gizur said he would do so.

Then Gizur picked out all of their wisest men to go with him.

Among them were Hjalti and Asgrim and Kari and Thorgeir Skorargeir.

Gizur said, 'Let's go first to the booth of Skafti Thoroddsson.'

Then they went to the booth of the men from Olfus. Gizur was in front, then Hjalti, then Kari, then Asgrim, then Thorgeir, and then Thorgeir's brothers. They entered the booth. Skafti was sitting on the cross-bench. When he saw Gizur he rose to meet him and welcomed him and his companions warmly and asked Gizur to sit beside him. Gizur sat down.

Gizur said to Asgrim, 'Present Skafti with our request for support, and I'll add whatever I see fit.'

Asgrim said, 'We have come to seek help and support from you, Skafti.'

Skafti said, 'You found me hard to persuade the last time, when I wasn't willing to take on your problems.'

Gizur said, 'It's a different matter now – a suit is being brought on behalf of the farmer Njal and his wife Bergthora, both of whom were burned to death without cause, and for the three sons of Njal and many other good men. You certainly do not want to go on refusing support to your kinsmen and in-laws.'[1]

Skafti answered, 'It was my resolve then – when Skarphedin told me that I had smeared tar on my head and cut out turf to put over me, and when he said that I was so frightened that Thorolf Loftsson had to carry me onto his ship in flour sacks and thus bring me to Iceland – that I would never take part in any action over his death.'[2]

Gizur said, 'There's no point in bringing up such things now, since the man who said that is dead. Surely you'll stand by me, even if you won't do so for others.'

Skafti replied, 'This case has nothing to do with you, unless you insist on getting mixed up in it.'

Gizur became angry then and said, 'You are not at all like your father – though he was thought to be sly, he was always ready to help others when they most needed him.'

Skafti said, 'We have different temperaments. You think of yourselves as men who have shared in mighty deeds – you, Gizur the

White, when you attacked Gunnar at Hlidarendi, and Asgrim because he killed his foster-brother Gauk.'[3]

Asgrim replied, 'Few bring up the better if they're aware of the worse.[4] Many would say that I didn't kill Gauk any sooner than I was forced to. There's reason for you not to help us, but there's no reason to throw insults at us. I hope that you'll be greatly dishonoured by this case before the Thing is over, and that no one compensates you for your shame.'

Gizur and his companions then rose and went away to the booth of Snorri the Godi and went inside. Snorri was sitting on the cross-bench. He recognized the men at once and stood up to meet them and said they were all welcome and gave them places to sit beside him. Then they asked each other what events were being talked about.

Asgrim spoke to Snorri: 'My kinsman Gizur and I have come to ask you for support.'

Snorri answered, 'You speak of something about which you have good reason to speak, since you are taking action for the death of your relatives. We received much good counsel from Njal, though few men remember that now. But I don't know what kind of support you think you need most.'

Asgrim replied, 'We think we'll need it most if we have to fight at this Thing.'

Snorri spoke: 'It's true that you would be at great risk then. Your prosecution of the case will no doubt be very forceful, but so will their defence, and neither side will give in to the other. You won't put up with this and you'll attack them, and indeed you will have no other choice, for they want to pay for their killings by shaming you, and for your loss of kinsmen by humiliating you.'

It was easy to see that he was egging them on.

Gizur said, 'You speak well, Snorri. You're at your best and most like a leader when it most counts.'

Asgrim said, 'I want to know what help you'll give us if things go as you say.'

Snorri spoke: 'I will make a gesture of friendship to you, upon which all your honour will depend. I won't go to court, but if you fight here at the Thing, only attack them if you're sure of yourselves, for you have great champions against you. If you find yourselves overwhelmed, then pull back towards us, for I'll have my men drawn up and ready to help you. If it turns out differently and they retreat, my guess is that they'll run for shelter into the Almannagja, and if they reach it you'll never be able to get at them. I'll make it my task to draw up my men before them and block them from reaching shelter, but we won't pursue them, whether they head north or south along the river. Then, when you've slain about as many of their men as I think you can afford to pay compensation for without losing your godords and your homes, I'll rush up with all my men and separate you. Then, if I've done all this for you, you must follow my orders.'

Gizur thanked him warmly and said this was just what they needed. Then they all went out.

Gizur said, 'Where shall we go now?'

Asgrim answered, 'To the Modruvellir booth.'

They went there next.

140 | When they came to the booth they saw Gudmund sitting and talking with his foster-brother Einar Konalsson, a wise man. They entered and went up to Gudmund; he welcomed them and cleared the booth so that they could all sit. Then they asked each other for news.

Asgrim spoke: 'There's no need to whisper what I have to say – we've come to ask for your firm support.'

Gudmund answered, 'Have you met with any other chieftains?'

They answered that they had met with Skafti and Snorri the Godi, and in a low voice they told him how it had gone with each of them.

Gudmund spoke: 'The last time we met I was small-minded and made myself difficult. I'll be as easy now as I was unyielding then. I, together with all my thingmen, will go to court with you and give you as much help as I can, and fight on your side, if necessary, and risk my life with yours. I'll pay back Skafti by seeing to it that his son, Thorstein Hare-lip, fights along with us; he won't dare go against my wishes, since he's married to my daughter Jodis. Skafti will then try to stop the fighting.'

They thanked him and talked for a long time so softly that others could not hear them. Gudmund asked them not to beg at the knees of any other chieftains; he said it was small-minded – 'Let's give it a try with the men we have now. Have your weapons with you at all legal proceedings, but for the time being don't fight.'

They all left and returned to their booths, and for a time this was known to only a few men. The Thing continued.

141 | One day men went to the Law Rock, and the chieftains placed themselves so that Asgrim Ellida-Grimsson, Gizur the White, Gudmund the Powerful and Snorri the Godi were up above, by the Law Rock, and the men from the East Fjords stood down below. Mord Valgardsson stood next to Gizur the White, his father-in-law. Mord was exceptionally clever with words. Gizur told him to give notice of the suits for homicide, and to speak loudly enough to be heard clearly.

Mord named witnesses – 'I call for witness that I give notice of a punishable assault by Flosi Thordarson, in which he assaulted Helgi Njalsson at the place where Flosi Thordarson assaulted Helgi Njalsson and inflicted on him an internal wound or brain wound or marrow wound which proved to be a fatal wound, and Helgi died of it. I declare that he deserves full outlawry for this offence, not to be fed, nor helped on his way, nor given any kind of assistance. I declare all his property forfeit, half to me and half to the men in the quarter who have the legal right to his forfeited property. I give notice of this homicide suit to the Quarter Court in which this case should be heard according to law. I give this lawful notice; I give notice in the hearing of all at the Law Rock. I give notice of the prosecution of Flosi Thordarson for full outlawry, to take place at this session. I give notice that the suit was turned over to me by Thorgeir Thorisson.'

There was much talk at the Law Rock about how well and boldly Mord had spoken.

Mord spoke for a second time: 'I call on you to witness that I give notice of a suit against Flosi Thordarson for having wounded Helgi Njalsson with an internal wound or brain wound or marrow wound which proved to be a fatal wound, and Helgi died of it at the place where Flosi Thordarson had run at Helgi in a punishable assault. I declare that you, Flosi, deserve full outlawry for this offence, not to be fed, nor helped on your way, nor given any kind of assistance. I declare all your property forfeit, half to me and half to the men in the quarter who have the legal right to your forfeited property. I give notice of this suit to the Quarter Court in which this case should be heard according to law. I give this lawful notice; I give notice in the hearing of all at the Law Rock. I give notice of the prosecution of Flosi Thordarson for full outlawry, to take place at this session. I give notice that the suit was turned over to me by Thorgeir Thorisson.'

Then Mord sat down. Flosi listened carefully but never said a word.

Thorgeir Skorargeir stood up and named witnesses – 'I call for witness that I give notice of a suit against Glum Hildisson for taking kindling and igniting it and placing it inside the house at Bergthorshvol, when they burned Njal Thorgeirsson and Bergthora Skarphedinsdottir and all the people who died there. I declare that he deserves the sentence of full outlawry for this offence, not to be fed, nor helped on his way, nor given any kind of assistance. I declare all his property forfeit, half to me and half to the men of the quarter who have the legal right to his forfeited property. I give notice of this suit to the Quarter Court in which this case should be heard according to law. I give this lawful notice and I do it in the hearing of all at the Law Rock. I now give notice of the prosecution of Glum Hildisson for full outlawry, to take place at his session.'

Kari Solmundarson brought suits against Kol Thorsteinsson and Gunnar Lambason and Grani Gunnarsson, and people commented on how wonderfully well he spoke.

Thorleif Crow brought suits against all the Sigfussons, and his brother Thorgrim the Tall brought suits against Modolf Ketilsson and Lambi Sigurdarson and Hroar Hamundarson, the brother of Leidolf the Strong. Asgrim Ellida-Grimsson brought suits against Leidolf, Thorstein Geirleifsson, Arni Kolsson and Grim the Red, and they all spoke well. Other men gave notice of their suits, and this took the greater part of the day. Then people went back to their booths.

Eyjolf Bolverksson went with Flosi to his booth. They walked to the east side of the booth, and Flosi asked whether he saw any grounds for defence against these suits.

'None at all,' said Eyjolf.

'What are we to do now?' said Flosi.

'It's a tight spot,' said Eyjolf, 'but I'll suggest a plan to you. You must give up your godord and place it in the hands of your brother Thorgeir, and then declare yourself the thingman of Askel Thorketils-son the Godi, from up north in Reykjadal. If they don't find out about this it may do them some damage: they will bring their suit in the East Quarter Court when they should bring it in the North Quarter Court – although they won't know this. Then they will be liable to an action in the Fifth Court for bringing a suit in another court than the correct one.[1] We will prosecute, but only as a last resort.'

Flosi said, 'It may be that we have been repaid for the bracelet.'

'I don't know about that,' said Eyjolf, 'but I will give you such help in legal matters that people will say that no more could have been done. Now you must send for Askel, and Thorgeir must join you at once, and another man with him.'

Thorgeir arrived shortly; he took over the godord. Then Askel came there. Flosi declared himself to be his thingman. This was known to nobody but them.

142 | Everything was quiet until the time for the courts to begin. Both sides made ready and armed themselves; both sides had put markings on their helmets.[1]

Thorhall spoke: 'Don't be too hasty, and do everything as correctly as you can. If you get into any difficulty let me know at once, and I'll give you advice.'

Asgrim and the others looked at him, and Thorhall's face was like blood to look at, and great gusts of hail gushed from his eyes. He asked for his spear to be brought; Skarphedin had given it to him and it was a great treasure.

As they walked away Asgrim spoke: 'My son Thorhall was not in good spirits back there in the booth, and I don't know what will be his next step. Now let's go to Mord Valgardsson and act as if only his suit mattered, for it's a greater thing to catch Flosi than many of the others.'

Asgrim sent a messenger to Gizur the White and Hjalti and Gudmund the Powerful, and they all met and went at once to the East Quarter Court. They came to it at the south side. Flosi and his men, and all the men from the East Fjords who had joined him, went to the north side of the court; men from Reykjadal and Oxarfjord and Ljosavatn were also with Flosi. Eyjolf Bolverksson was there too.

Flosi leaned towards him and said, 'This bodes well; it may be that your guess was not far off.'

'Keep quiet about that,' said Eyjolf. 'The time may come when we'll have to use that trick.'

Mord Valgardsson named witnesses and asked for a casting of lots for those who were prosecuting suits for full outlawry in the court, to determine who should prosecute or present his suit first, who second and who last. He made this lawful request of the court so that the judges could hear it. The lots were drawn and it fell to Mord to be the first to present his suit.

He named witnesses for the second time – 'I call for witness that I may remove any mistakes from my pleading, whether from saying too much or from error. I claim the right to correct all my wording until my entire suit is in correct form.[2] I name these witnesses for myself or for others who may need to use or benefit from this testimony.'

Then Mord spoke: 'I call for witness that I request Flosi Thordarson, or any other man who has taken over his legal defence from him, to listen to my oath-swearing and the presentation of my suit and all the evidence for the prosecution which I plan to bring against him. I make this lawful request before the court, so that the judges can hear it from one end of the court to the other.'

Mord continued: 'I call for witness that I swear this oath by the

Book, a lawful oath, and I declare before God that I shall do my best to prosecute this suit as truthfully and fairly as I know how and in accordance with the law, and that I will meet all the requirements of the law, as long as I am at this Thing.'

Then he spoke these words: 'I named Thorodd as witness, and Thorbjorn as second witness, that I gave notice of a punishable assault by Flosi Thordarson at the place where Flosi Thordarson ran at Helgi Njalsson in a punishable assault, when Flosi Thordarson wounded Helgi Njalsson with an internal or brain or marrow wound which proved to be a fatal wound, and Helgi died of it. I declared that he deserved full outlawry for this offence, not to be fed, nor helped on his way, nor given any kind of assistance. I declared all his property forfeit, half to me and half to the men in the quarter who have the legal right to his forfeited property. I gave notice of this to the Quarter Court in which this suit should be heard according to law. I gave this lawful notice; I gave notice in the hearing of all at the Law Rock. I gave notice of the prosecution of Flosi Thordarson for full outlawry, to take place at this session. I gave notice that the suit was turned over to me by Thorgeir Thorisson. In giving notice I used the same words which I have now uttered in presenting my case. I refer this case for full outlawry, stated as I stated it when I gave notice before, to the East Quarter Court, in the presence of Jon.'[3]

Mord spoke: 'I named Thorodd as witness, and Thorbjorn as second witness, that I gave notice of a suit against Flosi Thordarson for having wounded Helgi Njalsson with an internal or brain or marrow wound which proved to be a fatal wound, and Helgi died of it at the place where Flosi Thordarson had previously run at Helgi Njalsson in a punishable assault. I declared that he deserved full outlawry for this offence, not to be fed, nor helped on his way, nor given any kind of assistance. I declared all his property forfeit, half to me and half to the men in the quarter who have the legal right to his forfeited property. I gave notice of this to the Quarter Court in which this suit should be heard according to law. I gave this lawful notice; I gave notice in the hearing of all at the Law Rock. I gave notice of the prosecution of Flosi Thordarson for full outlawry, to take place at this session. I gave notice that the suit was turned over to me by

Thorgeir Thorisson. In giving notice I used the same words which I have now uttered in presenting my case. I refer this case for full outlawry, stated as I stated it when I gave notice before, to the East Quarter Court, in the presence of Jon.'

Then the witnesses to Mord's notice went before the court and spoke these words, with one of them reciting their testimony and both of them expressing assent, that 'Mord named Thorodd as witness, and me as a second witness; my name is Thorbjorn' – then he gave his father's name. 'Mord named us as witnesses that he gave notice of a punishable assault by Flosi Thordarson when he ran at Helgi Njalsson at the place where Flosi Thordarson wounded Helgi Njalsson with an internal or brain or marrow wound which proved to be a fatal wound, and Helgi died of it. He declared that Flosi deserved full outlawry for this offence, not to be fed, nor helped on his way, nor given any kind of assistance. He declared all his property forfeit, half to himself and half to the men in the quarter who have the legal right to Flosi's forfeited property. He gave notice of this to the Quarter Court in which this suit should be heard according to law. He gave this lawful notice; he gave notice in the hearing of all at the Law Rock. He gave notice of the prosecution of Flosi Thordarson for full outlawry, to take place at this session. He gave notice that the suit was turned over to him by Thorgeir Thorisson. In giving notice he used the same words for presenting the suit which we have now uttered in our testimony. We have now given our witness correctly and we are both in agreement on it. We refer this testimony of Mord's notice, stated just as he stated it when he gave notice, to the East Quarter Court, in the presence of Jon.'

They gave their testimony of the notice a second time, mentioning the wounds first and the assault second and keeping all the other wording the same. They referred this testimony to the East Quarter Court, stated just as Mord stated it when he gave notice.

Then the witnesses to Mord's taking over the prosecution went before the court, and with one of them reciting their testimony and both of them expressing assent declared that Mord Valgardsson and Thorgeir Thorisson had named them as witnesses that Thorgeir Thorisson had turned over to Mord Valgardsson the prosecution for homicide against Flosi Thordarson for the slaying of Helgi Njalsson – 'he turned the suit over to him with all the evidence for the prosecution which should accompany the suit. He turned over to him the right to prosecute or to settle with full use of the evidence, just as if he were the rightful plaintiff. Thorgeir turned this over lawfully, and Mord took it over lawfully.'

They presented their testimony of the taking over of the suit to the East Quarter Court in the presence of Jon, just as Thorgeir and Mord had called on them to testify. They had all their witnesses swear oaths before they presented testimony, and the judges as well.

Mord Valgardsson named witnesses – 'to witness,' he said, 'that I call on the nine neighbours whom I summoned concerning the suit I have brought against Flosi Thordarson to take seats on the west bank of the river, and I call on the defence to challenge this panel. I make this lawful request before the court, so that all the judges can hear it.'

Mord named witnesses a second time – 'to witness that I call on Flosi Thordarson, or any other man who has taken over his legal defence from him, to challenge this panel which I have placed together on the west side of the river. I make this lawful request before the court, so that the judges can hear it.'

Again he named witnesses – 'to witness,' he said, 'that all the first steps pertaining to this suit have now been taken – requesting that the oath be heard, swearing the oath, presenting the suit, witnessing the notice, witnessing the taking over of the prosecution, requesting the neighbours to be seated, and asking for the panel to be challenged. I call on these witnesses to confirm the steps which have now been taken and also to confirm that I will not have given up the prosecution even if I should leave the court to seek evidence or for any other reason.'

Flosi and his men then went to where the panel of neighbours was sitting. Flosi said to his men, 'The Sigfussons will know whether the neighbours who have been summoned here are legitimate.'

Ketil of Mork answered, 'One of these neighbours held Mord Valgardsson at his baptism, and another one is his second cousin.'

They explained the relationship and swore to it by oath.

Eyjolf named witnesses that the panel should stay in place until it had been invalidated. Then Eyjolf named witnesses a second time – 'to witness,' he said, 'that I dismiss both these men from the panel' – he named them, and their fathers – 'on the grounds that one of them is second cousin to Mord and another has a religious bond with him, as a result of which he should be dismissed. The two of you are now disqualified from the panel on legal grounds, since a lawful dismissal has been executed on you. I dismiss you according to the rules of the Althing and the law of the land. I dismiss you in the case turned over to me by Flosi Thordarson.'

Everyone present spoke up and said that Mord's case was disqualified; they all agreed that the defence was stronger than the prosecution.

Asgrim said to Mord, 'It's not all in their favour yet, though they think they are way ahead. Someone must go to my son Thorhall and see what he suggests.'

A trusty messenger was sent to Thorhall to tell him exactly what had been happening in the case and how Flosi and his party thought that they had disqualified the panel.

Thorhall spoke: 'I'll see to it that this will not destroy your suit, and tell them not to believe that it will, in spite of the trickery against them, for that great sage Eyjolf has overlooked something. Go back as quickly as you can and tell Mord Valgardsson to go to court and name witnesses that their dismissal is invalid' – and then he told him in detail how they should proceed. The messenger returned and told them Thorhall's suggestion.

Then Mord Valgardsson went to court and named witnesses – 'to witness that I invalidate the dismissal made by Eyjolf Bolverksson. My grounds are that he dismissed them for reasons that pertain not to the original plaintiff but only to the person pleading the case.[4] I name these witnesses for myself or for anyone who may have need of this testimony.'

Then he brought this testimony before the court. He went to where the panel of neighbours was sitting and said that the ones who had stood up should sit down again, and he declared them valid members of the panel. Everyone said that Thorhall had done a great thing;

everyone now thought the prosecution was stronger than the defence.

Flosi said to Eyjolf, 'Do you think that this was according to law?'

'I think so, definitely,' he said, 'and we clearly overlooked this. But we'll keep trying.'

Then Eyjolf named witnesses – 'to witness,' he said, 'that I dismiss these two men from the panel' – he gave their names – 'on the grounds that you are lodgers and not property owners. I will not allow you to sit on the panel, because a lawful dismissal has now been served on you. I dismiss you from the panel according to the rules of the Althing and the law of the land.'

Eyjolf said he would be very surprised if this could be invalidated. Everyone then said that the defence was stronger than the prosecution; everyone praised Eyjolf highly and said that no one could match his cleverness at law.

Mord Valgardsson and Asgrim then sent a messenger to Thorhall to tell him how things stood. When Thorhall heard this he asked whether these neighbours owned property or whether they were indigent.

The messenger said that one of them lived off milch animals, both cows and ewes, and that the other owned a third of the land on which they both lived and provided his own food; he and the man who leased the land owned one hearth together, and one shepherd.

Thorhall said, 'It will be the same for them as before – they have overlooked something and I will quickly invalidate what they have done, in spite of Eyjolf's big words about how correct this was.'

He told the messenger in full detail how they should proceed. The messenger returned and told Mord and Asgrim the plan which Thorhall had suggested.

Mord went before the court and named witnesses – 'to witness that the dismissal made by Eyjolf Bolverksson is invalid, because he dismissed men from the panel who have a legitimate right to be there. Any man who owns three hundreds or more in land has the right to sit on a panel of neighbours, even though he does not live off milch animals; and any man who lives off milch animals has the right to sit on a panel of neighbours, even though he owns no land.'[5]

He had this testimony presented to the court. Then he went to where the neighbours were sitting and told the two to sit down and declared them valid members of the panel of neighbours. A great shouting and crying went up, and every one said that the cause of Flosi and Eyjolf had been much shaken, and they agreed that the prosecution was stronger than the defence.

Flosi said to Eyjolf, 'Is this correct?'

Eyjolf said he had not the wisdom to know this for a fact. Then they sent a man to Skafti the Lawspeaker to ask him whether it was correct. He sent word back that this was indeed the law, though few knew it. This was reported to Flosi and Eyjolf.

Eyjolf then asked the Sigfussons about the other neighbours who had been summoned. They said there were four who had been wrongly summoned – 'because other men, who live closer to the scene of the action, are sitting at home.'

Eyjolf then named witnesses that he was dismissing all four of these men from the panel, and he spoke the correct language for dismissal.

Then he spoke to the rest of the neighbours: 'You are duty-bound to apply the law fairly to both sides. Now you must go before the court when you are called and name witnesses that there is an obstacle to your pronouncing a finding, namely that only five of you are correctly summoned, when there ought to be nine. If Thorhall can find a way out of this he can win any case.'

It was apparent in all this that Flosi and Eyjolf were being very boastful. Talk went around that the suit for the burning was quashed and that the defence was now stronger than the prosecution.

Asgrim said to Mord, 'They can't know that they have anything to boast about until we've seen Thorhall. Njal said that he taught Thorhall the law so well that he would prove to be the greatest lawyer in Iceland if he were put to the test.'

Then a man was sent to Thorhall to tell him how things stood and about Flosi and Eyjolf's boasting and the talk among everyone that the suit for the burning was quashed.

'That's fine,' said Thorhall, 'but they won't gain any honour from this. Go and tell Mord to name witnesses and to swear an oath that the majority of the panel was correctly summoned. He must then have this testimony presented to the court, and he will thus save the case for the prosecution; he will be sentenced to pay three marks for each man who was wrongly summoned, but that matter may not be prosecuted at this session,' he said. 'Go back now.'

The messenger went back and repeated every detail of what Thorhall had said.

Mord went before the court and named witnesses and swore an oath that the majority of the neighbours had been correctly summoned. He declared that he had thus saved the case for the prosecution – 'our enemies will have to build their reputation on something other than that we made a big mistake.'

There was much talk about how well Mord was handling the case, and people said that Flosi and his men were simply using trickery and guile.

Flosi asked Eyjolf whether this was correct, and he said he did not know for sure and that the lawspeaker should resolve the matter. Thorkel Geitisson went on their behalf and told the lawspeaker how things stood and asked whether what Mord had claimed was possibly correct.

Skafti answered, 'There are more great lawyers around than I thought. I must tell you that this is so correct in every point that no objection can be brought against it. But I thought that only I knew this detail of the law now that Njal is dead, for I was sure that he was the only one to know it.'

Thorkel went back to Flosi and Eyjolf and told them that this was good law.

Mord Valgardsson went before the court and named witnesses – 'to witness,' he said, 'that I request that the neighbours whom I called on in the suit which I brought against Flosi Thordarson announce their findings, whether for or against. I make this lawful request in the court, so that the judges can hear it from one end of the court to the other.'

Mord's panel of neighbours went before the court; one of them announced their findings and all of them gave assent, and he spoke: 'Mord Valgardsson called on nine of us freemen; five of us are standing here now, and four have been dismissed. Testimony has been brought against the four who should have made this announcement with us. The law requires us now to announce our findings. We were called on to declare whether Flosi Thordarson ran at Helgi Njalsson in a punishable assault at the place where Flosi Thordarson wounded Helgi Njalsson with an internal or brain or marrow wound, which proved to be a fatal wound, and Helgi died of it. He called on us to declare our findings as the law requires and which he wanted brought before the court and which pertain to this case; he called on us lawfully; he called on us so that we could hear him; he called on us in the case turned over to him by Thorgeir Thorisson.

'Now we have all sworn oaths and made a correct finding and agreed on it: we have found against Flosi and we find him guilty as charged. We nine neighbours give our finding thus stated in the East Quarter Court, in the presence of Jon, as Mord called on us to do. This is the finding of all of us.'

They gave their finding a second time and mentioned the wounds first and the assault second; all the rest of the language was as before. They found against Flosi and found him guilty as charged.

Mord Valgardsson went before the court and named witnesses that the neighbours whom he had called on in the suit which he brought against Flosi Thordarson had announced their findings and found him guilty as charged. He named these witnesses for himself or for those 'who may need to use or benefit from this testimony.'

Mord named witnesses a second time – 'I call for witness that I invite Flosi Thordarson, or any man who has taken over his legal defence, to present his defence in the suit which I have brought against him, since all evidence for the prosecution which legally pertains to the suit has now been brought forth – all testimony and the panel's findings presented and witnesses named to the announcement of the findings and to all the matters brought forward. But if anything arises in their lawful defence which I might use in my prosecution, I reserve the right to do so. I make this lawful request before the court, so that the judges can hear it.'

'It makes me laugh, Eyjolf,' said Flosi, 'to think how they will wince and scratch their heads when you present your objection.'

143 | Eyjolf Bolverksson went before the court and named witnesses
– 'to witness that here is a legitimate objection in this case –
that you prosecuted in the East Quarter Court a suit which should
have been prosecuted in the North Quarter Court, because Flosi has
declared himself a thingman of Askel the Godi. Here are two witnesses who were present and will testify that Flosi first turned over
his godord to his brother Thorgeir and then declared himself a
thingman of Askel. I name these two witnesses for myself or for those
who may need to use or benefit from this testimony.'

Eyjolf named witnesses a second time – 'I call for witness that I
invite Mord, who is prosecuting this suit, or any of the plaintiffs, to
listen to my oath and to the presentation of the defence which I shall
bring forth and to all the evidence which I shall bring forth; I make
this lawful request before the court, so that the judges can hear it.'

Eyjolf named witnesses once more – 'I call for witness that I swear
this oath by the Book, a lawful oath, and I declare before God that I
shall defend this suit as truthfully and fairly as I know how and in
accordance with the law, and that I will meet all requirements of the
law which pertain to me, as long as I am at this Thing.'

Eyjolf spoke: 'I name these two men as witnesses that I present this
legitimate objection, that the suit was prosecuted in a different quarter
court from the one where it belonged. I claim that this invalidates their
suit. I present the defence, thus stated, to the East Quarter Court.'

Then he had all the testimony brought forth which pertained to
the defence, and after that he named witnesses to all the evidence
pertaining to the defence which had so far been presented.

Eyjolf named witnesses – 'I call for testimony that I forbid the
judges to make a judgement in the suit presented by Mord and his
allies, because a legitimate objection has now been presented to the
court. I forbid you according to a lawful, incontestable, full and
binding right of prohibition, as I am entitled by the rules of the
Althing and the law of the land.'

Then he called on the court to judge his defence.

Asgrim and his allies presented the other suits for the burning, and
these suits took their course.

144 | To tell now about Asgrim and his allies: they sent a man to Thorhall to tell him how things stood.

'I was too far away,' said Thorhall, 'for the case wouldn't have taken this turn if I'd been present. Now I see their tactic: they're going to summon you to the Fifth Court for violation of Althing procedure. They are also going to create a division in the court over the suit for the burning and prevent it from being judged, for their scheme is to shrink from no evil whatsoever. Go back as quickly as you can and say that Mord is to summon both Flosi and Eyjolf for having brought a money payment into the proceedings,[1] and that he should demand a sentence of lesser outlawry. Then he must summon them with a second summons for bringing testimony that had nothing to do with the case,[2] and in this they violated Althing procedure. Tell them that I say that if two sentences of lesser outlawry are pronounced against the same man, he must then be judged a full outlaw. You must bring your suits first, so that you may prosecute them and have them judged first.'

The messenger went away and told Mord and Asgrim. Then they went to the Law Rock. Mord Valgardsson named witnesses – 'I call for testimony that I summon Flosi Thordarson for having paid money to Eyjolf Bolverksson, here at the Thing, for his help. I declare that he deserves the sentence of lesser outlawry for this charge, not to be helped on his way or given asylum unless the life-ring and sustenance fee are paid at the confiscation court[3] – otherwise he is a full outlaw. I declare all his property forfeit, half to me and half to the men in the quarter who have the legal right to his forfeited property. I summon this case before the Fifth Court, where this case should be heard according to law. I summon it now for prosecution and full punishment. I make this legal summons; I make this summons in the hearing of all at the Law Rock.'

With a similar summons he summoned Eyjolf Bolverksson on the charge of accepting the money; he also summoned this case before the Fifth Court.

He summoned Flosi and Eyjolf a second time, on the charge of bringing testimony into the Althing that was not relevant to the parties involved, and for having thus violated Althing procedure. He demanded a sentence of lesser outlawry against them for this, too. Then they went away to the Law Council; the Fifth Court was in place there.

When Asgrim and Mord had left, the judges were not in agreement on what judgement to give, for some wanted to judge in favour of Flosi, and others in favour of Mord and Asgrim. They had to declare the court divided.[4] Flosi and Eyjolf stayed on there while the summoning was going on.

A little later Flosi and Eyjolf were told that they had been summoned at the Law Rock to the Fifth Court, each of them twice.

Eyjolf said, 'It was bad luck for us to stay on here while they were first with their summoning. Thorhall's cleverness is evident in this – no man is his match for intelligence. Now they'll be able to prosecute their case first in court, and this is a big gain for them. Still, let's go to the Law Rock and start our case against them, even though it won't help us much.'

They went to the Law Rock then, and Eyjolf summoned them for violation of Althing procedure. Then they went to the Fifth Court.

To return to Mord: when he and Asgrim came to the Fifth Court, Mord named witnesses and requested that they listen to his oath-swearing and to the presentation of his suit and to all the evidence for the prosecution which he intended to bring forth against Flosi and Eyjolf. He made a lawful request to the court, so that the judges could hear it from one end of the court to the other.

In the Fifth Court co-swearers had to confirm the oaths, and they also had to swear oaths themselves.

Then Mord named witnesses – 'I call for witness that I swear a Fifth Court oath – I pray God to help me in this life and the next – that I shall prosecute this suit as truthfully and fairly as I know how and in accordance with the law. I hold Flosi to be guilty of this charge, insofar as there is substance behind it, and I have not brought money into the court to gain help in this suit, and I will not do so. I have not received money and I will not do so, either for a lawful or an unlawful end.'

Mord's two co-swearers went before the court and named witnesses – 'to witness that we swear this oath on the Book, a lawful oath – we ask God to help us in this life and in the next – that we pledge our honour that we consider that Mord will do his best to prosecute this suit as truthfully and fairly as he knows how, and that he has not brought money into this court to gain help in this suit, and he will not do so. He has not received money and he will not do so, either for a lawful or an unlawful end.'

Mord had called on nine men who lived near Thingvellir to hear the suit.[5] Then Mord named witnesses and presented the four charges which he had made against Flosi and Eyjolf, and he used the same words in his presentation of the suit that he had used in his summoning. He presented these suits for lesser outlawry to the Fifth Court in the same words he had used when he summoned them.

Mord named witnesses and invited the nine neighbours to take seats on the west bank of the river. Then he named witnesses and invited Flosi and Eyjolf to challenge the panel. They went up to challenge the panel and examined it and were unable to find fault with any of them, so they went away and were ill-pleased.

Mord named witnesses and asked the nine neighbours he had called on to announce their findings, whether for or against. Mord's panel went before the court, and one of them announced their findings and all expressed assent. They had all sworn the Fifth Court oath, and they found Flosi guilty as charged and found against him. They presented their findings in this form to the Fifth Court in the presence of the man before whom Mord had declared his suit. Then they announced all the findings that they were obliged to announce, for all the charges, and this was lawfully done.

Eyjolf Bolverksson and Flosi looked for a way to fault the proceedings, but they found none.

Mord named witnesses – 'I call for witness that these nine neighbours whom I have called on in the suits which I brought against Flosi Thordarson and Eyjolf Bolverksson have presented their findings and have found these men to be guilty as charged.'

He named these witnesses to this.

Again he named witnesses – 'I call for witness,' he said, 'that I invite Flosi Thordarson, or any other man who has taken over his defence for him, to begin his defence, for now all the evidence for the prosecution has been presented: requesting that the oath be heard, swearing the oath, reciting the charges, giving witness to the summoning, inviting the neighbours to be seated, asking for the panel to be challenged, announcing the findings of the panel, and naming witnesses to these findings.'

He named these witnesses to the evidence which had been presented.

Then the man in whose presence the suits had been presented rose and summed up the case. He first summed up how Mord asked them to listen to his oath and to the presentation of his suit and to all the evidence for the prosecution. He next summed up how Mord and his co-swearers swore their oaths. Then he summed up how Mord presented his suit, and he spoke in such a way that he had in his summary every word which Mord had used in the presentation of his suit and in his summoning – 'and Mord presented the suit to the Fifth Court in the same words which he had used when he summoned them.'

Then he summed up how they brought testimony to the summoning, and he repeated every word which Mord had used in his summoning and which they had used in their testimony – 'and now I have repeated them', he said, 'in my summary. The witnesses gave their testimony to the Fifth Court in the same words which he had used when he summoned them.'

Then he summed up how Mord invited the neighbours to take their seats; next he summed up how he invited Flosi, or any man who had taken over his defence for him, to challenge the panel. Then he summed up how the neighbours went before the court and announced their findings and declared Flosi to be guilty as charged – 'the nine neighbours announced their findings, thus stated, to the Fifth Court.'

Then he summed up how Mord named witnesses to the fact that the findings were announced, and then summed up how Mord named witnesses to the evidence presented and asked for the defence to raise objections.

Mord named witnesses – 'I call for witness,' he said, 'that I forbid Flosi Thordarson, or any other man who has taken over his defence for him, to raise objections, since all the evidence for the prosecution has now, with this summing-up and recitation of the evidence, been brought forth.'

Then the man who did the summing-up summed up this testimony.

Mord named witnesses and asked the judges to judge the case.

Then Gizur the White said, 'You will have to do more than this, Mord, because four dozen men have not the right to make a judgement.'

Flosi said to Eyjolf, 'What are we to do now?'

Eyjolf answered, 'It's a tight spot to get out of, and we had best wait, for I suspect they are going to make an error in the prosecution: Mord asked for a judgement in the case at once, but they must first remove six men from the court; then they must invite us, before witnesses, to remove another six, but that we won't do. Then they will have to remove another six men, but they will overlook this detail. Their whole case will be invalid if they don't remove six, because three dozen is the right number to make judgement.'[6]

Flosi said, 'You are a clever man, Eyjolf, and few can equal you.'

Mord Valgardsson named witnesses – 'I call for witness that I remove six men from the court' – and he named them all by name – 'I deny you seats in the court, and I remove you according to the rules of the Althing and the law of the land.'

After that he invited Flosi and Eyjolf, before witnesses, to remove another six men from the court, but they chose not to do so. Mord then asked for the case to be judged. When the case had been judged, Eyjolf named witnesses and declared the judgement, and their whole suit, invalid. He pointed out that three-and-a-half dozen had made the judgement, whereas it should have been three dozen – 'we shall now bring charges against them in the Fifth Court and have them declared outlaws.'

Gizur the White said to Mord, 'You overlooked something very important when you made this slip. This is very bad luck. What shall we do now, my kinsman Asgrim?'

Asgrim said, 'We must send a man to my son Thorhall and find out what advice he has for us.'

145 | Snorri the Godi found out how the lawsuits were going. He drew up his men between the Almannagja gorge and the Hlad booth, after he ordered what they were to do.

To turn now to Thorhall: a messenger came to him and told him how things stood, how they would all be outlawed and how their suits for homicide had all been quashed. When Thorhall heard this he was so upset that he could not speak a word. He sprang out of his bed and seized his spear, Skarphedin's gift, with both hands and drove it through his leg. Flesh and the core of the boil clung to the spear when he had cut open his leg, and a gush of blood and a flow of pus poured like a stream across the floor. He then walked out of the booth without a limp and moved so fast that the messenger could not keep up with him, all the way to the Fifth Court. There he came across Grim the Red, Flosi's kinsman, and as soon as they met Thorhall thrust at him with the spear and pierced his shield and split it in two, and the spear passed through him so that the point came out between his shoulders. Thorhall threw him off the spear, dead.

Kari Solmundarson caught sight of this and spoke to Asgrim: 'Here comes your son Thorhall, and he has already killed a man – it would be a great shame if he alone had the courage to avenge the burning.'

'That shall not be,' said Asgrim. 'Let's attack them.'

Shouts were heard through all their forces, and then a war-cry went up. Flosi and his men turned to face them and they urged each other on eagerly.

To turn now to Kari Solmundarson: he went to face Arni Kolsson and Hallbjorn the Strong. When Hallbjorn saw him he swung his sword at him and aimed at his leg, but Kari leaped into the air and Hallbjorn missed him. Kari turned to Arni Kolsson and swung at him and hit him on the shoulder and split his shoulder bone and collar bone and cut right down into his chest. Arni fell dead at once. Then he swung at Hallbjorn and hit the shield and passed through it and cut off Hallbjorn's big toe. Holmstein threw his spear at Kari, but he caught it in mid-air and sent it back, and that was the death of one of Flosi's men.

Thorgeir Skorargeir came up to Hallbjorn the Strong and made such a lunge at him with one hand that Hallbjorn fell over and had a hard time getting to his feet, and then he fled. Thorgeir next met up with Thorvald Thrym-Ketilsson and at once swung at him with the axe Battle-hag which had belonged to Skarphedin. Thorvald took the blow on his shield, but Thorgeir split the entire shield and the upper point of the blade hit his chest and went into his body, and Thorvald fell at once, dead.

To turn now to Asgrim and his son Thorhall: with Hjalti and Gizur the White they made an assault on Flosi and the Sigfussons and the other burners. The fighting was fierce, and the outcome was that Asgrim and his side pressed so hard that Flosi's side turned away. Gudmund the Powerful and Mord Valgardsson and Thorgeir Skorargeir attacked the men from Oxarfjord and the East Fjords and Reykjadal; the fighting was fierce there too. Kari Solmundarson came up to Bjarni Brodd-Helgason; he grabbed a spear and thrust it at him, and it hit his shield. Bjarni jerked his shield to the side – otherwise the spear would have gone through him. He swung his sword at Kari and aimed at the leg; Kari pulled his leg back and turned on his heel, so that Bjarni missed him. Then Kari swung back at once. A man stepped in and brought his shield in front of Bjarni. Kari split the shield from top to bottom, and the point of his sword hit the man in the thigh and tore open his whole leg; he fell down at once and was maimed for as long as he lived. Kari then grabbed the spear in both hands and turned to Bjarni and thrust it at him, and Bjarni saw no other choice but to fall sideways away from the thrust, and when he got back on his feet he ran away.

Thorgeir Skorargeir then attacked Holmstein Bessason and Thorkel Geitisson; the outcome of this was that Holmstein and Thorkel turned away. There was much jeering at them from Gudmund's men.

Thorvard Tjorvason from Ljosavatn received a great wound; his arm was pierced, and men thought that Halldor, the son of Gudmund the Powerful, had thrown the spear. Thorvard never received compensation for that wound as long as he lived.

The crush of men was great. Though a few of the things that happened are told here, there were many more for which no stories have come down.

Flosi had told his men that they should try to reach shelter in Almannagja gorge if they were overpowered, for there they could only be attacked on one side. But the band of men under Hall of Sida and his son Ljot had retreated in the face of the attack by Asgrim and his men, and they were going down along the east side of the Oxara.

Then Hall spoke to Ljot: 'This is a terrible business, my son – the whole Thing fighting. I want us to ask for help to keep the two sides apart, even though we might be blamed for this by some people. Wait for me at the end of the bridge, while I go to the booths to get help.'

Ljot spoke: 'If I see that Flosi and his men need help from us, I will run to them at once.'

'You must do what you like,' said Hall, 'but I beg you to wait for me.'

Then it happened that Flosi's men broke out in flight, and all of them fled to the west side of the Oxara, and Asgrim and Gizur the White and all their forces went after them. Flosi and his men retreated between the Virki booth and the Hlad booth. Snorri the Godi had drawn up his men so tightly there that they could not go that way.

Snorri the Godi called to Flosi, 'Why are you in such a rush? Who's chasing you?'

Flosi said, 'You're not asking this because you don't know the answer. Could it be you who's keeping us from reaching shelter in Almannagja?'

'I'm not keeping you,' he said, 'but I know who is, and I'll tell you, without being asked, that it's Thorvald Kroppinskeggi and Kol.'

Both these men were dead and had been the worst sort of men.

Snorri the Godi spoke again, to his own men: 'Go at them now with sword and with spear, and drive them away from here. They'll only hold out a short while when the others attack from below. But don't pursue them – just let them have it out with the others.'

Skafti Thoroddsson's son was Thorstein Hare-lip; he was fighting alongside his father-in-law Gudmund the Powerful. When Skafti heard this he went to Snorri the Godi's booth and was planning to ask Snorri to go along with him to separate the fighters. But just before he reached the door of Snorri's booth the fighting reached its peak. Asgrim and his men were coming up from below.

Thorhall said, 'There's Skafti Thoroddsson now, father.'

Asgrim said, 'I see that, son' – and he quickly cast his spear at Skafti and hit him just below the thickest part of the calf and pierced both legs. Skafti fell at the blow and could not get back up. The only thing the men near him could do was to drag him, laid out flat, into the booth of a certain sword-sharpener.

Asgrim and his forces were advancing so fast that Flosi and his men turned south along the river to the Modruvellir booth. A man named Solvi was outside one of the booths; he was boiling meat in a large cauldron and had just taken the meat out, but the cauldron was boiling at its strongest. Solvi caught sight of the East Fjords men as they fled – they had almost come up to him.

Solvi spoke: 'What? Are they all cowards, these men from the East Fjords who are fleeing here?' he said. 'Even Thorkel Geitisson is running, and a lot of lies must have been told about him – many have said that he's all valour, but no one's running faster than him now.'

Hallbjorn the Strong was near him and said, 'You won't get away with saying that we're all cowards.' He grabbed him and lifted him up high and plunged him head first into the cauldron. Solvi died at once. The pursuers then came towards Hallbjorn and he had to keep fleeing.

Flosi cast his spear at Bruni Haflidason and hit him in the waist, and that was his death. He had been one of Gudmund the Powerful's men.

Thorstein Hlennason pulled the spear out of the wound and threw it at Flosi and hit him on the leg; Flosi's leg was badly wounded and he fell down, but got back up at once.

They retreated towards the Vatnsfjord booth. Ljot and Hall were crossing from the east side of the river with all their men. When they came to the lava a spear was thrown from Gudmund's side and hit Ljot in the waist; he fell dead at once, and it was never found out who had done this killing.

Flosi and his men retreated past the Vatnsfjord booth. Thorgeir Skorargeir said, 'There's Eyjolf Bolverksson, Kari. Reward him for accepting the bracelet.'

Kari said, 'That's not far from what I've been thinking' – and grabbed a spear and threw it at Eyjolf; it hit him in the waist and went through him. Eyjolf fell down dead at once.

Then there was a lull in the battle. Snorri the Godi arrived with his men and Skafti, and they went at once between the two sides; then they were unable to fight. Hall joined them and also wanted to separate them. A truce was declared for the duration of the Thing. The bodies were laid out and brought to the church, and the wounds of those who were hurt were bound up.

The next day men went to the Law Rock. Hall of Sida stood up and called for silence, and it was given at once.

He spoke: 'Hard things have happened here, both in loss of life and in lawsuits. I'll show now that I'm a man of no importance. I want to ask Asgrim and the other men who are behind these suits to grant us an even-handed settlement.'

He went on with many eloquent words.

Kari spoke: 'Even if all the others settle, I shall never settle, because you will want to set these killings against the burning, and we won't stand for that.'

Thorgeir Skorargeir said the same.

Then Skafti Thoroddsson stood up and spoke: 'You would have done better, Kari, not to have run away from your in-laws than to hold back from a settlement now.'

Kari then spoke this verse:

18.
If I ran, warrior,
why rebuke me?
The weapon-storm pounded,
by my power, on shields.
Long, slender swords
sang loud, while you,
red-bearded softie,
ran to your booth.

Kari spoke another verse:

19.

When warriors lacked
the will to stop fighting,
Skafti the poet was pinned
scared behind his shield,
and the cooks dragged
this dauntless hero
flat on his back
to the juggler's floor.

Kari spoke a third verse:

20.

Men who mount the sea's elk   *sea's elk*: ship, *mount*ed by sailors
have mocked the burning of Njal
and of Grim and of Helgi –
they did a great wrong;
and now in the heather-decked
hills of the hog   *hills of the hog*: allusion to Svinafell (Flosi's home)
all goes otherwise
after the Althing.

There was great laughter. Snorri the Godi smiled and spoke in a
low voice, yet in such a way that many heard him:

21.

Skafti would shorten the fight,
but then Asgrim shot his shaft;
Holmstein fled unwillingly,
Thorkel was forced to fight.

Now they laughed even louder.

Hall of Sida spoke: 'All men know what sorrow the death of my
son Ljot has brought me. Many will expect that payment for his life
will be higher than for the others who have died here. But for the
sake of a settlement I'm willing to let my son lie without compensation
and, what's more, offer both pledges and peace to my adversaries. I

ask you, Snorri the Godi, and others among the best men, to see to it that a settlement is reached between us.'

Then he sat down, and much good was spoken about his words, and everybody praised his good will.

Snorri the Godi stood up and made a long and wise speech and asked Asgrim and Gizur and the others who were behind the case to accept a settlement.

Asgrim spoke: 'I resolved, after Flosi forced his way into my house, that I would never accept a settlement with him, and yet now, because of your words, Snorri, and those of other friends of mine, I will not hold back.'

In the same way Thorleif Crow and Thorgrim the Tall said that they would accept a settlement and urged their brother Thorgeir Skorargeir to settle also, but he held back and said he would never part from Kari.

Then Gizur the White said, 'Now Flosi must decide for his part whether he wants to agree to a settlement that some men will not be a part of.'

Flosi said he wanted to settle – 'the fewer good men I have against me,' he said, 'the better I like it.'

Gudmund the Powerful spoke: 'I for my part offer my hand in promise of compensation for the slayings that occurred here at the Thing, provided that the suits for the burning are not left out.'

Gizur the White and Asgrim and Hjalti spoke the same way, and under these terms a settlement was made.

It was referred by handshake to a panel of twelve men. Snorri the Godi was in charge of the arbitration and other good men were with him. The slayings were weighed against each other, and the imbalance was settled by payment. They also arbitrated the suits for the burning. Threefold compensation was to be paid for Njal, and twofold for Bergthora. The slaying of Skarphedin was weighed equally against the slaying of Hoskuld the Godi of Hvitanes. Twofold compensation was to be paid for both Grim and Helgi. There was to be single compensation for all the others who were burned.

No payment was awarded for the death of Kari's son Thord.

Flosi and the rest of the burners would have to leave the country, but not be obliged to leave that summer unless they wanted to, and if they did not go by the time three years had passed, he and the rest of the burners would become outlaws for life, and their outlawry would be proclaimed either at the Spring Assembly or the Autumn Assembly, whichever men preferred.

Flosi was to stay abroad for three years. Gunnar Lambason, Grani Gunnarsson, Glum Hildisson, and Kol Thorsteinsson were never to have the right to return.

Flosi was asked if he wanted to be paid for his own wound, but he said he would not use his own body to make money. Eyjolf Bolverksson's death was not to be compensated for, on account of his unfairness and wrong-doing.

All this was then agreed on by handshake, and never broken.

Asgrim and his men gave Snorri the Godi good gifts; he had won great respect from this case. Skafti was not compensated for his wound. Gizur the White and Hjalti and Asgrim invited Gudmund the Powerful to visit them. He accepted the invitations and each of them gave him a gold bracelet. Gudmund then rode back north and had the praise of all men for the way he acted in this affair.

Thorgeir Skorargeir asked Kari to come with him, but first they rode north with Gudmund as far as the mountains. Kari gave Gudmund a gold brooch and Thorgeir gave him a silver belt, both excellent treasures, and they parted in great friendship. Gudmund rode on to his home up north, and he is now out of the saga. Kari and Thorgeir rode south from the mountains and down to Hreppar and from there to Thjorsa.

To turn now to Flosi: all the burners rode east to Fljotshlid. Then Flosi told the Sigfussons to look after their farms. Flosi heard that Thorgeir and Kari had ridden north with Gudmund, and they took this to mean that Kari and Thorgeir were going to stay up north. The Sigfussons then asked if they might go east to the Eyjafjoll district to collect money which was owed to them at Hofdabrekka. Flosi gave them permission but begged them to spend as little time there as possible. Then he rode up past Godaland and to the mountains and north of the glacier Eyjafjallajokul; he did not stop until he had come home to Svinafell.

To tell now about Hall of Sida: when he had allowed his son's slaying to go without compensation, and did this for the sake of a settlement, everyone assembled at the Althing paid him compensation, and it came to no less than eight hundred ounces of silver, four times the usual amount. All the others who had been with Flosi got no compensation for their losses and they were not at all pleased at that.

The Sigfussons stayed at home two days, and on the third they rode east to Raufarfell and stayed overnight there. They were fifteen in number and had no fear for their lives. From there they rode east late in the day and planned to reached Hofdabrekka in the evening. They made a stop in Kerlingardal and there they fell into a deep sleep.

146 | To tell now about Kari: that same day he and his companions rode east across the Markarfljot and then on eastward to Selja-landsmuli. There they came across some women.

The women recognized them at once and said to them, 'You're not as light-hearted as the Sigfussons, but you're still quite careless.'

Thorgeir said, 'What makes you talk about the Sigfussons? What do you know about them?'

They answered, 'They spent last night at Raufarfell and plan to reach Myrdal this evening. It did us good, though, to see that they were in fear of you and asked when you would be coming home.'

The women then went on their way, and Kari and Thorgeir gave the spur to their horses.

Thorgeir said, 'What do you have in mind now? Do you want us to ride after them?'

Kari said, 'I won't stand in the way of that.'

Thorgeir said, 'How shall we go about this?'

'I don't know,' said Kari, 'because it often turns out that men slain only with words live a long life. But I know how you want to go about it – you want to take on eight of them, but still that's less of a feat than when you lowered yourself into a gorge with a rope and killed seven men.[1] You and your kinsmen are like that, always wanting to do something outstanding. I can do no less than stay with you in order to be able to tell the story. Let's ride after them, just the two of us, for I can see that this is your plan.'

They rode east on the upper road and did not pass Holt, for Thorgeir did not want his brothers to be blamed for whatever might happen. Then they continued east to Myrdal, and there they came across a man with peat baskets on his horse.

He said, 'You don't have enough men, my friend Thorgeir.'

'What does that mean?' said Thorgeir.

'It means,' he said, 'that there might be some prey around here. The Sigfussons rode by and will be dozing all day in Kerlingardal, because they don't plan to go any further than Hofdabrekka this evening.'

Then they rode their separate ways.

Thorgeir and Kari rode east on Arnarstakk heath. There is nothing to say about their trip until they came to the river Kerlingardalsa; it was high. They rode along the river, for they saw some saddled horses up there. They rode up to them and saw some men sleeping in a hollow, and their spears were standing upright just above them; Thorgeir and Kari took the spears and threw them into the river.

Thorgeir said, 'Do you want us to wake them up?'

Kari answered, 'Why ask? You've already decided not to attack sleeping men and kill them shamefully.'

Then they shouted at them. The sleepers awoke and jumped up and grabbed their weapons. Kari and Thorgeir did not attack them until they were armed. Thorgeir Skorargeir rushed at Thorkel Sigfusson. Another man came at Thorgeir from behind, but before he could get in a blow Thorgeir swung Battle-hag with both hands so fast and hard that on his back-swing the hammer of the axe hit the head of the man behind him and smashed his skull into small pieces; he fell down dead at once. And when he swung the axe forward it came down on Thorkel's shoulder and chopped off his arm.

Against Kari came Mord Sigfusson and Sigurd Lambason and

Lambi Sigurdarson. Lambi came at him from behind and lunged at him with his spear. Kari caught sight of him and leaped up and parted his legs wide as the lunge came; the spear went into the ground, and Kari landed on the shaft and broke it in two. He had a spear in one hand and a sword in the other, but no shield. He lunged at Sigurd Lambason with his right hand. The spear hit him in the chest and came out between his shoulders; he fell down dead at once. With his left hand he swung at Mord Sigfusson and hit him on the hip, and cut through it and the backbone as well. He fell forward and was dead at once. After that he turned on his heel like a top and went at Lambi Sigurdarson, and Lambi took the only way out and rushed off.

Then Thorgeir turned to face Leidolf the Strong, and each swung at the other at the same moment, and Leidolf's blow was so strong that it cut off the shield where it hit. Thorgeir had swung his axe with both hands, and the lower point hit the shield and split it in two and the upper point split the collar bone and tore deep down into his chest. Kari came over and cut off Leidolf's leg at mid-thigh. Leidolf fell down dead.

Ketil of Mork said, 'Let's run for our horses. We cannot hold out against these overpowering men.'

They ran to their horses and leaped on their backs.

Thorgeir said, 'Do you want us to chase them? We can still kill a few more.'

Kari answered, 'The one riding last, Ketil of Mork, is a man I don't want to kill, since our wives are sisters, and he has always played very fair with us.'

They mounted their horses and rode until they arrived home in Holt. Thorgeir made his brothers go east to Skogar – they had another farm there – because he didn't want them to be called truce-breakers.[2]

Thorgeir and Kari kept a great many men with them after that, never fewer than thirty in fighting form. There was much joy there. It was thought that Thorgeir had gained in stature from this, and Kari too. People kept alive the story of their pursuit, when the two of them attacked fifteen men and killed five of them, and put the rest to flight.

To return now to Ketil and the others: they rode as hard as they could until they reached Svinafell, and they told that their journey had not been smooth.

Flosi said this was to be expected – 'and this should be a warning to you never to travel like that again.'

Flosi was a very jovial man and an excellent host, and it was said that he was endowed with most of the qualities of a great chieftain. He stayed at home that summer, and the winter too.

After Christmas that winter Hall of Sida came from the east with his son Kol. Flosi was glad at his coming, and they often talked about the lawsuits; Flosi said that they had already paid dearly. Hall said that he had expected things to turn out the way they did. Flosi asked him what course he thought best to take.

Hall answered, 'I advise you to make a settlement with Thorgeir, if you have a chance, but he will be difficult about any settlement.'

'Do you think that the slayings will end then?' said Flosi.

'I don't think so,' said Hall, 'but you will have fewer men to deal with if Kari is alone. And if you don't settle with Thorgeir it will be your death.'

'What settlement shall we offer him?' said Flosi.

'One that will seem hard to you,' said Hall, 'but it's one that he'll accept. He'll only be willing to settle if he doesn't have to pay for what he's done, and if he receives his share of the compensation for Njal and his sons – one third.'[3]

'That's a hard settlement,' said Flosi.

'It's not a hard settlement for you,' said Hall, 'because you're not obliged to take action for the slaying of the Sigfussons; that's up to their brothers, and it's up to Hamund the Lame to take action for the slaying of his son.[4] But you can make a settlement with Thorgeir, for I'll ride with you, and he'll give me some kind of welcome. None of those involved in this dispute will dare to remain on their farms in Fljotshlid if they stay out of the settlement, for that will be their death – as is to be expected, given Thorgeir's temperament.'

Then the Sigfussons were sent for; the matter was put to them, and the outcome, thanks to Hall's persuasion, was that they agreed with everything that Hall proposed and were willing to make a settlement.

Grani Gunnarsson and Gunnar Lambason said, 'It will be easy – if Kari is left on his own – to make him no less afraid of us than we are of him.'

'Don't speak like that,' said Hall. 'You'll find it a bad bargain if you take him on, and you'll have to pay dearly before you're finished.'

Then they talked no more about it.

147 | Hall of Sida and his son Kol, six men altogether, rode west over Lomagnupssand and further west across Arnarstakk heath, and did not stop until they came to Myrdal. There they asked whether Thorgeir was home at Holt, and the people there said that he was and asked where Hall was heading.

'To Holt,' he said.

They said he was on a good errand. Hall stayed there a little while and rested their horses. After that they took their horses and rode to Solheimar in the evening and were there overnight.

The next day they rode to Holt. Thorgeir was outside with Kari and their men and they spotted Hall: he was riding in a black cape and carried a small axe inlaid with silver. When they came into the hayfield Thorgeir went to meet them and helped Hall off his horse, and both Kari and Thorgeir kissed Hall and led him between them into the main room and seated him in the high seat on the cross-bench and asked for news about many things. He was there overnight.

In the morning Hall brought up the matter of a settlement with Thorgeir and told him what terms they were offering him, and he explained it all in pleasing and well-meant language.

Thorgeir answered, 'You must know that I have not wanted to accept any settlement with the burners.'

'That was quite different,' said Hall. 'Then you were in a rage to kill, but you've accomplished much in the way of killings since then.'

'That's true,' said Thorgeir. 'What settlement are you offering to Kari?'

Hall said, 'He will be offered honourable terms if he's willing to settle.'

Then Kari spoke: 'I beg you to make a settlement, my friend Thorgeir, for your part in all this should not be better than good.'[1]

He answered, 'It seems to me a bad thing to settle and separate from you, unless you accept the same settlement that I do.'

'I am not willing to settle,' said Kari. 'Even though I can say that we've avenged the burning, I have to say that my son is unavenged, and I plan to take that upon myself alone and do what I can.'

Thorgeir was unwilling to settle, until Kari said he would be displeased with him if he did not. Thorgeir then gave his hand on a truce with Flosi and his men until the peace meeting, and Hall did the same on behalf of Flosi and the Sigfussons, as they had empowered him. Before they parted, Thorgeir gave Hall a gold bracelet and a scarlet cloak, and Kari gave him a silver necklace with three gold crosses on it. Hall thanked them kindly for the gifts and rode away with very great honour and did not stop until he came to Svinafell; Flosi welcomed him.

Hall told Flosi all about his journey and his talk with Thorgeir, and how Thorgeir was not willing to settle until Kari stepped in and said he would be displeased with him if he did not, and how Kari was not willing to make peace himself.

Flosi spoke: 'Few men are like Kari, and what I would wish most is to have a character like his.'

Hall and his party stayed there for a while. Then, at the time fixed for the settlement meeting, they rode west to Hofdabrekka, as had been agreed between them. Thorgeir came there from the west to meet them.

They discussed the settlement, and everything went as Hall had said. Thorgeir made the stipulation that Kari should be allowed to stay with him whenever he wanted – 'and neither side should harm the other at my home. And I don't want to have to collect the compensation money from each of you separately; I want you, Flosi, to be responsible for collecting the money from your followers, and I also want complete adherence to the agreement over the burning that was made at the Thing. And I want you to pay me my third.'

Flosi readily agreed to all this. Thorgeir did not remit the orders of exile or district banishment.[2]

Then Flosi and Hall rode back east.

Hall said to Flosi, 'Keep to all the terms of this settlement, my son-in-law – the exile and the pilgrimage to Rome[3] and the compensation payments. You will be regarded as a brave man, in spite of the fact that you landed in this terrible business, if you carry out all these things manfully.'

Flosi said he would do so.

Hall then rode east to his home, and Flosi rode home to Svinafell. He stayed there for a time.

148 | To tell now about Thorgeir: he rode home from the peace meeting. Kari asked whether the settlement had been worked out; Thorgeir said that they were fully reconciled. Then Kari wanted to take his horse and ride away.

Thorgeir said, 'You don't have to ride away, because it was stipulated in our settlement that you should stay here whenever you wanted.'

Kari said, 'That cannot be, kinsman, for if I do any killing they'll claim at once that you are allied with me, and I don't want that. What I do want is for you to take over my property in trust and assign it to yourself and my wife Helga Njalsdottir and my daughters. Then it cannot be seized by my adversaries.'

Thorgeir agreed to what Kari wished from him, and then he took over Kari's property in trust.

Then Kari rode away; he had two horses, his weapons and clothes, and some silver and gold. He rode west past Seljalandsmuli and up along the Markarfljot all the way to Thorsmork. Three farms are there, all with the name Mork. In the middle one lived a man named Bjorn, called Bjorn the White; he was the son of Kadal, the son of Bjalfi. Bjalfi had been the freed slave of Asgerd, the mother of Njal and Holta-Thorir. He was married to a woman named Valgerd; she was the daughter of Thorbrand, the son of Asbrand. Her mother was named Gudlaug, and she was the sister of Hamund, the father of

Gunnar of Hlidarendi. She was married to Bjorn for his money and did not love him much, and yet they had children together. They had enough of everything at their farm. Bjorn was a man given to self-praise, and his wife hated that. Bjorn was sharp-sighted and swift of foot.

Here it was that Kari came for hospitality, and they received him with open arms; he was there overnight.

In the morning he and Bjorn talked together. Kari said, 'I'd like you to take me in – I sense that I am in good hands with you. I would like you to be with me on my travels, because you're keen-sighted and swift, and I suspect that you have great courage.'

Bjorn answered, 'I won't question my keen eyesight or my courage or my other manly qualities. You must have come here because you had no other place to turn. But at your request, Kari,' said Bjorn, 'I won't treat you the same as ordinary men. I shall certainly help you in everything you ask.'

His wife heard this and spoke: 'May trolls take your swaggering and strutting,' she said. 'You shouldn't try to fool both yourself and Kari with such deceit and nonsense. I'll gladly give Kari food and other good things which I know will be of use to him. But don't count on Bjorn for bravery, Kari, for I'm afraid he may not turn out to be as reliable as he claims.'

Bjorn answered, 'You've often poured scorn on me, but I trust myself well enough to know that I won't take to my heels for anybody. The proof of this is that few men pick a fight with me – because no one dares!'

Kari stayed there in hiding for a time, and few knew about it. People thought that he had ridden north to see Gudmund the Powerful, since Kari told Bjorn to tell his neighbours that he had met Kari on the move and that he was on his way up to Godaland and from there to Gudmund the Powerful. This spread over all the country.

149 | To tell now about Flosi, who spoke to the burners, his companions: 'We can't allow ourselves to sit still any longer. We have to think about going abroad and paying compensation and carrying out our part of the settlement as honourably as we can. Let each of us take passage wherever it seems best.'

They asked him to take charge.

Flosi said, 'We'll ride east to Hornafjord, for there's a ship waiting there owned by Eyjolf Nose, a man from Trondheim. He wants to get married, but can't have the woman unless he settles down here. We'll buy his ship from him, since we have little wealth but many men – it's a big ship and will carry us all.'

Then they concluded their talk.

A little later they rode east and did not stop until they came to Bjarnarnes in Hornafjord. There they found Eyjolf, for he had been a guest there that winter. Flosi was welcomed there, and they stayed the night. In the morning Flosi brought up the purchase with the skipper; he said he was not against selling it as long as he got what he wanted for it. Flosi asked him what kind of payment he wanted. The Norwegian said he wanted land, and nearby, and he told him everything about his agreement with the farmer. Flosi said he would work with him to secure the marriage, and then buy the ship from him. The Norwegian was pleased at that. Flosi offered him land at Borgarhofn. Then the Norwegian had a talk with the farmer, with Flosi standing by. Flosi put in a word, and the marriage agreement was made.

Flosi turned over the land at Borgarhofn to the Norwegian and shook hands on the purchase of the ship. He also got twenty hundreds in homespun from the Norwegian, as part of the bargain.

Flosi then rode back. He was so well liked by his men that he could have any goods from them as a gift or on loan, whatever he wanted. He rode home to Svinafell and stayed there for a while. Flosi sent Kol Thorsteinsson and Gunnar Lambason east to Hornafjord; they were to stay there with the ship and get it ready, set up booths, pack the homespun in sacks and gather supplies.

*

To turn now to the Sigfussons: they told Flosi they would ride west to Fljotshlid to see to their farms and bring homespun and whatever else they needed from there – 'there's no need to guard against Kari now, since he is up north.'

Flosi answered, 'I am not sure from such stories whether the truth is being told about Kari's movements. I've seen stories collapse that came from closer sources than these. My advice is that you travel in a large group and split up rarely, and be as alert as you can. And you, Ketil – remember the dream I told you, which you asked that we keep secret, for there are many in your company now who were called out in that dream.'[1]

Ketil spoke: 'All things in the lives of men will come to their fated end – but your warning is well meant.'

They said no more about this.

Then the Sigfussons and the men who were to go with them got ready; they were eighteen in all. They rode away, but before they left they kissed Flosi. He said that there were some riding off whom he would never see again. They did not let this stop them, and rode on their way.

Flosi had said that they should fetch his goods at Medalland and carry them east, and do the same at Landbrot and in the Skogar district. They rode to Skaftartunga and then up into the mountains and north of Eyjafjallajokul glacier, then down into Godaland and through the woods at Thorsmork.

Bjorn of Mork spotted the men riding along and went at once to meet them, and they greeted each other. The Sigfussons asked about Kari Solmundarson.

Bjorn answered, 'I met Kari, but that was some time ago. He rode north to Gasasand and planned to go to Gudmund the Powerful, and it seemed to me that he was rather afraid of you and felt very isolated.'

Grani Gunnarsson said, 'He'll have more to fear later – he'll find that out when he comes within our range. We're not afraid of him at all now that he's on his own.'

Ketil told him to be silent and stop the big talk.

Bjorn asked when they would be coming back.

'We'll stay in Fljotshlid close to a week,' they said – and then they gave him the day when they would be riding to the mountains; at this they parted. The Sigfussons rode to their farms, and their people at home were glad to see them. They stayed there one week.

Bjorn came home and met Kari and told him all about the movements of the Sigfussons and their plans. Kari said he had shown him great friendship and loyalty in this.

Bjorn answered, 'I knew that if I promised a man my help it would make a difference.'

His wife said, 'Things can be pretty bad, even if you're not a traitor.'

Kari stayed there six days after this.

150 | Kari spoke to Bjorn: 'Now we'll ride east across the mountains and down into Skaftartunga and travel on the sly through the district of Flosi's thingmen, for I'm planning to take passage abroad from Alftafjord.'

Bjorn said, 'That's a risky undertaking, and not many men besides you and me would have the courage for it.'

His wife spoke: 'If you let Kari down, you might as well know that you'll never come into my bed again. My kinsmen will divide the property between us.'

Bjorn answered, 'It's more likely, dear wife,' he said, 'that you'll have to think of some other grounds for divorce, because I'm going to bring evidence of what a champion and man of prowess I can be in battle.'

That day they rode east into the mountains north of the glacier, but never rode on the common path, and then down into Skaftartunga and above all the farms as far as the Skafta river, and there they led their horses into a hollow and kept on the lookout and placed themselves so that no one could see them.

Then Kari said to Bjorn, 'What shall we do if they ride down from the mountain at us?'

Bjorn answered, 'Aren't there two choices? Either ride away north along the slopes and let them ride past us, or else wait in case any of them fall behind, and then attack them?'

They discussed this at length, and Bjorn declared one moment that he would flee as fast as possible, and the next moment that he would stay and fight it out. Kari found this very amusing.

To turn now to the Sigfussons: they rode from their homes on the day they had mentioned to Bjorn. They came to Mork and knocked on the door and wanted to see Bjorn, and his wife went to the door and greeted them. They asked at once for Bjorn. She said that he had ridden down to Eyjafjoll and east past Seljalandsmuli and then on east to Holt – 'because he has money owed to him there.'

They believed this and knew he had money to collect over there. Then they rode east to the mountains and did not stop until they came to Skaftartunga, and from there they rode down along the Skafta and rested their horses at the place where Kari and Bjorn expected they would. Then they split up: Ketil of Mork, with eight other men, rode east to Medalland, and the rest lay down to sleep and noticed nothing until Kari and Bjorn came at them.

A small point of land projected into the river. Kari went to it and told Bjorn to stand behind him and not put himself forward, and give him as much support as he could.

Bjorn answered, 'I never expected to have anyone be a shield for me, but as things are now, you must decide. Anyway, with my brains and speed I can still cause our enemies no little harm.'

The others stood up and ran at them, and Modolf Ketilsson was the fastest and thrust his spear at Kari. Kari had his shield before him, and the spear landed on the shield and stuck in it. Kari twisted the shield so that the spear broke; in the meantime he had drawn his sword and swung it at Modolf. Modolf struck back. Kari's sword struck the hilt and glanced off onto the wrist and cut off Modolf's hand, and it fell to the ground with his sword, and Kari's sword ran on into Modolf's side and between the ribs. He fell then and was dead at once.

Grani Gunnarsson grabbed his spear and threw it at Kari, and Kari brought his shield down swiftly so that it stuck in the ground and caught the spear in the air with his left hand and threw it back at Grani, and then picked up the shield with the same hand. Grani had his shield before him. The spear hit the shield and went right through it and hit Grani's thigh just beneath the crotch and passed through it into the ground, and he could not get loose from the spear until his companions pulled him away and carried him into a hollow and fenced him round with shields.

A man dashed forward and came at Kari from the side and tried to cut off his leg. Bjorn swung at him and cut off his hand and then dashed back behind Kari; they were not able to harm him. Kari sliced with his sword at this man and cut him in two at the waist.

Then Lambi Sigurdarson ran at Kari and swung at him with his sword. Kari caught the blow with the flat of his shield, and the sword did not bite. Kari lunged with his sword at Lambi's chest so that it went out between the shoulders; that was his death.

Then Thorstein Geirleifsson ran at Kari and tried to come at him from the side. But Kari caught sight of him and sliced with his sword across the shoulders so that he cut the man in two. A little later he dealt a death blow to Gunnar of Skal, a good farmer.

Bjorn had wounded three men who had tried to strike Kari, but he never put himself forward enough to be at risk; he was not wounded in this fight, and neither was Kari, but all those who got away were wounded. They jumped on their horses and rushed out into the Skafta as fast as they could, and were so frightened that they never stopped at a farm, and they did not dare to report what had happened. Kari and Bjorn shouted at them while they were rushing away. They rode east to the Skogar district and did not stop until they came to Svinafell. Flosi was not at home when they came up, and so no hunt was made for Kari and Bjorn from there. Everyone thought the Sigfussons' journey a complete disgrace.

Kari rode to Skal and gave notice that he had done the slayings. He told of the death of the head of the household[1] and the other four, and of Grani's wound, and he said it would be best to bring him to some house if he were to live. Bjorn said that he had not bothered to kill him, though he deserved it, and they answered that few men's corpses were rotting because of him. Bjorn said he now had the chance to make as many of the men of Sida rot as he wanted.

They said that that would be hard to live with. He and Kari then rode off.

151 | Kari asked Bjorn, 'What shall we try now? I want to test your brains.'

Bjorn answered, 'Do you think that a lot depends on our being very clever?'

'Yes, certainly,' said Kari.

'Then it's quickly decided,' said Bjorn. 'Let's fool them all as if they were dumb giants. Let's pretend to ride north to the mountains, and as soon as a hill comes between us, let's turn back and come down along the Skafta river and hide in whatever seems the safest place while the pursuit is hot – if they follow us.'

Kari answered, 'That's what we'll do – in fact, I'd already planned that.'

'And you'll find out,' said Bjorn, 'that I don't falter in bravery any more than in brains.'

He and Kari rode, as they planned, down along the Skafta until it branched to the east and to the south-east. They went along the middle branch and did not stop until they came to Medalland and a swamp called Kringlumyri. It has lava all around it.

Kari told Bjorn to watch the horses and be on the lookout – 'I feel a drowsiness coming on.'

Bjorn watched the horses and Kari lay down and slept only a short while before Bjorn woke him. He had brought their horses up and they were standing close by.

Bjorn spoke: 'You really need me. A man with less courage would have run away from you, because now your enemies are riding at you. You had better make yourself ready.'

Kari went under an overhanging rock.

Bjorn said, 'Where am I to stand?'

Kari answered, 'There are two choices before you. One is for you to stand behind me and hold a shield to protect yourself, if it can be of any use. The other is to get on your horse and ride away as fast as you can.'

'I won't do that,' said Bjorn. 'There's much against it. First, it could happen, if I rode off, that people with vicious tongues might start saying that I ran away from you out of cowardice. Second, I know what a great catch they must consider me – two or three of them would ride after me, and then I'd be of no use or help to you. So I'd rather stay with you and defend myself as long as fate allows.'

They did not have long to wait before some pack-horses were driven across the swamp, and there were three men with them.

Kari said, 'They don't see us.'

'Let them ride on,' said Bjorn.

These men rode on, but then another six men came riding along, and they all leaped at once off their horses and attacked Kari and Bjorn. Glum Hildisson was first to rush at Kari and he thrust at him with his spear. Kari drew back on one foot and Glum missed him, and the spear hit the rock. Bjorn saw this and quickly hacked the point off Glum's spear. Kari swung his sword from where he had pulled back and hit him at the top of the thigh and cut off his leg. Glum died at once.

Then the two sons of Thorfinn, Vebrand and Asbrand, rushed at him. Kari ran at Vebrand and drove his sword through him, and then he chopped both of Asbrand's legs from under him. Kari and Bjorn were wounded in this exchange.

Ketil of Mork rushed at Kari and thrust at him with his spear. Kari threw his leg up and the spear went into the ground; Kari jumped on the shaft and broke it in two.

Kari grabbed Ketil in his arms. Bjorn rushed up at once and was about to kill Ketil.

Kari spoke: 'Hold still. I will spare Ketil – and even if it happens again, Ketil, that I have power over your life, I'll never kill you.'

Ketil said nothing and rode off after his companions and told what had happened to those who had not already heard. They passed this on to the men of the district, and they quickly gathered a large band of armed men and went along all the streams, so far north into the mountains that they spent three days searching. Then they turned back and all the men went home, but Ketil and his companions rode east to Svinafell and reported what had happened. Flosi made little of what they had gone through, but said it was not certain that things would now end – 'there is no one in our land now who can match Kari.'

152 | To return to Kari: he rode out on the sands and brought the horses to a bank covered with lyme-grass, and they cut grass for them so they would not die of hunger. Kari made such a close estimate that he rode away from there just as Ketil and the others were giving up the search. He rode up through the district that night and then into the mountains and then back on the same route which they had ridden east. They did not stop until they came to Mork.

Then Bjorn spoke to Kari: 'Now you must be a true friend in the presence of my wife, for she won't believe a word I say, and this means a lot to me. Pay me back now for the good support I've given you.'

'I will,' said Kari.

Then they rode up to the farm. The wife asked how things had gone and welcomed them warmly.

Bjorn answered, 'Our troubles have grown a little, old girl.'

She said nothing and smiled. Then she said, 'How did Bjorn turn out with you?'

Kari answered, 'Bare is the back of a brotherless man: Bjorn turned out very well. He injured three men, and was wounded himself. He was supportive to me in every way he could be.'

They stayed there three nights. Then they rode to Thorgeir at Holt and told him in private what had happened, for no news had come there yet. Thorgeir thanked Kari, and it was clear that he was pleased at the news. He asked Kari what remained undone of the things he meant to do.

Kari answered, 'I plan to kill Gunnar Lambason and Kol Thorsteinsson, if I have a chance. Then we will have killed fifteen men, including the five that you and I killed together.[1] But I have a favour to ask you.'

Thorgeir said he would grant whatever he asked.

Kari said, 'I want you to take this man into your protection – his name is Bjorn, and he was with me at the killings. Change farms with him and give him a fully stocked one close to you here, and hold your hand over him so that no vengeance is directed at him. This should be an easy matter for a chieftain like you.'

'I'll do it,' said Thorgeir.

He gave Bjorn a fully stocked farm at Asolfsskali, and he took over the farm at Mork. Thorgeir himself brought Bjorn's household and possessions to Asolfsskali. He arranged a settlement for all of Bjorn's disputes and reconciled him fully to his enemies, and Bjorn was now thought to be much more of a man than before.

Kari rode away and did not stop until he came to Asgrim Ellida-Grimsson. He gave Kari a hearty welcome, and Kari told him all the details of the slayings. Asgrim was pleased. He asked what Kari planned next. Kari said that he planned to go abroad in pursuit of the others and track them down and kill them, if he could. Asgrim said that there was no man like him for bravery. He stayed there for a few nights.

Then he rode to Gizur the White, and Gizur welcomed Kari with open arms. Kari stayed there a while. He told Gizur that he was going to ride out to Eyrar. Gizur gave Kari a fine sword at their parting. Then Kari rode down to Eyrar. He took passage with Kolbein the Black, a man from Orkney and a life-long friend of his, and a very bold man. He welcomed Kari with open arms and said that the same fate awaited them both.

153 | To tell now of Flosi: he and his companions rode east to Hornafjord. Most of his thingmen went with them. They carried their goods and other supplies east with them and all the things they needed to take along. Then they fitted out their ship. Flosi stayed with the ship until it was ready. As soon as they had a good wind they put out to sea. They had a long passage and bad weather, and they went way off course.

One day they were struck by about three huge waves, and Flosi said that they were near land and that these were breakers. The fog was thick and the weather turned so bad that a heavy storm came over them. They did not know what was happening until they were driven ashore during the night; their lives were spared, but the ship shattered into pieces and they were not able to save their goods. They had to look for a place to keep warm.

The next day they went up on a hill. The weather was good. Flosi asked those who had travelled abroad before whether they recognized this land. There were two men who recognized it and said that they had come to Mainland in Orkney.

'We could have made a better landing,' said Flosi, 'for Helgi Njalsson, whom I killed, was the follower of Earl Sigurd Hlodvisson.'

They looked for a hiding-place and pulled up moss to cover themselves and lay there for a while, but before long Flosi said, 'Let's not lie here any longer and wait for the natives to discover us.'

Then they got up and talked over plans.

Flosi spoke: 'Let's turn ourselves over to the earl. We have no other choice, for he has our lives in his hand anyway, if he wants to take them.'

They went away from there. Flosi said that they should not tell anybody about what had happened or about their journey until he told it to the earl.

They went on until they met men who directed them to the earl. They went before the earl, and Flosi and all his companions greeted him. The earl asked what men they might be. Flosi gave his name and told what district of Iceland he came from. The earl had already heard of the burning and realized at once who these men were.

He then asked Flosi, 'What can you tell me about my follower Helgi Njalsson?'

'This,' said Flosi – 'that I struck off his head.'

The earl ordered them all to be seized, and this was done. Just then Thorstein, the son of Hall of Sida, came up. Flosi was married to Steinvor, Thorstein's sister. He was one of Earl Sigurd's followers. When he saw Flosi being arrested, he went before the earl and offered all his possessions for Flosi's life. The earl was very angry and for a long time very determined. Eventually, at the request of other good men along with Thorstein – for he was surrounded by friends, and many stepped forward to plead with him – the earl agreed to a settlement and made peace with Flosi and all his companions.

The earl kept to the custom of powerful men and let Flosi enter his service in the place that Helgi Njalsson had filled. Thus Flosi became the follower of Earl Sigurd, and he soon earned his great affection.

154 | To turn now to Kari: he and Kolbein put out to sea from Eyrar half a month after Flosi and his companions left Hornafjord. They had a good wind and were only a short while at sea. They made land at Fair Isle, between Shetland and Orkney. A man named David the White received Kari. He told Kari everything he knew about Flosi's travels. He was a close friend of Kari's, and Kari stayed with him that winter. They heard from west in Mainland of all the things that were going on there.

To tell now about Earl Sigurd: he invited Earl Gilli of the Hebrides, his brother-in-law, for a visit; Gilli was married to Sigurd's sister Hvarflod. A king also came there, named Sigtrygg, from Ireland. He was the son of Olaf Kvaran, and his mother's name was Kormlod. She was a very beautiful woman, but her best qualities were those over which she had no control, and it was commonly said that her character was evil insofar as she had control over it.

Brian was the name of the king to whom she had been married, but they were divorced. He was the best of all kings; he had his seat at Kincora.[1] His brother was Ulf Hraeda, a mighty champion and warrior. Brian had a foster-son named Kerthjalfad. He was the son of King Kylfir, who had fought many battles against King Brian and then fled the country and became a monk. When King Brian made a pilgrimage to Rome he met King Kylfir, and they were reconciled. King Brian then adopted his son Kerthjalfad, and he loved him more than his own sons. Kerthjalfad was grown up at this point in the story and was the boldest of men.

Dungad was the name of one of Brian's sons; another was Margad and the third Tadk – we call him Tann; he was the youngest. The two older sons of King Brian were fully grown and the bravest of men.[2] Kormlod was not the mother of Brian's children. She had become so spiteful towards him after their divorce that she wanted very much to see him dead.

King Brian pardoned outlaws three times for the same crime, but if they did it again he let them be dealt with according to law, and from this it can be seen what sort of king he was.

Kormlod pressed her son Sigtrygg hard to kill King Brian. She sent him to Earl Sigurd to ask for help in this. Sigtrygg arrived in Orkney before Christmas. Earl Gilli had come there too, as was written above.

The seating was arranged so that the king sat in the middle on a high seat, with one of the earls on each side. Sigtrygg and Gilli's men sat on the inner side, and on Earl Sigurd's side, towards the entrance, sat Flosi and Thorstein Hallsson. The hall was full.

King Sigtrygg and Earl Gilli wanted to hear about everything that had happened at the burning and also about what had happened since. Gunnar Lambason was called on to tell the story, and a chair was set up for him to sit on.

155 | To tell now about Kari and David and Kolbein: they came unnoticed to Mainland and went ashore at once, while a few men guarded their ship. They walked up to the earl's residence and came to the hall at drinking time. It happened that Gunnar was telling his story just then, and Kari and his companions listened to him from outside. It was Christmas Day.

King Sigtrygg asked, 'How did Skarphedin bear up during the burning?'

'Very well, to begin with,' said Gunnar, 'but by the end he was weeping.'

He slanted his whole account and lied about many details. Kari could not stand this; he rushed in with his sword drawn and spoke this verse:

22.
Men bold of battle
boast of the burning of Njal,
but have you heard

how we harried them?
Those givers of gold   *givers of gold*: men (the burners)
had a good return:
ravens feasted
on their raw flesh.

Then he rushed along the hall and struck Gunnar Lambason on the neck; the head came off so fast that it flew onto the table in front of the king and the earls. The tables and the clothing of the earls were all covered in blood.[1]

Earl Sigurd recognized the man who had done the killing and spoke: 'Seize Kari and kill him.'

Kari had been one of the earl's followers and was extremely well liked by everyone. No one rose, in spite of what the earl had said.

Kari spoke: 'Many men would say, lord, that I did this deed for you, to avenge one of your followers.'[2]

Flosi spoke: 'Kari did not do this without reason. He has not made peace with us, and he did what he had to do.'

Kari walked away, and he was not pursued. He went with his companions to his ship. The weather was good. They sailed south to Caithness and went ashore at Freswick to a worthy man named Skeggi and stayed with him a long time.

To tell now about Orkney: they cleaned off the tables and carried out the dead body. The earl was told that Kari had sailed south to Scotland.

King Sigtrygg spoke: 'That was a rugged fellow, who acted so daringly and didn't look to the consequences.'

Earl Sigurd answered, 'There's no man like Kari for bravery.'

Flosi then took over and told the story of the burning; he spoke fairly of everybody, and his account was trusted.[3]

King Sigtrygg then brought up the purpose of his visit with Earl Sigurd and asked him to join him in battle against King Brian. The earl held back for a long time, but eventually agreed on one condition: that he marry Sigtrygg's mother and then become king of Ireland if they killed Brian. Everyone tried to prevent Sigurd from joining them, but without avail. So they parted on these terms: Earl Sigurd promised to take part in the expedition, and King Sigtrygg promised him his mother and the kingdom.[4] It was arranged that Earl Sigurd would come to Dublin with all his army on Palm Sunday.

Sigtrygg then went south to Ireland and told his mother that the earl was joining them, and also what he had promised in return. She showed pleasure at this, but said that they would have to gather much more support. Sigtrygg asked where that might come from.

Kormlod answered, 'There are two Vikings lying off the Isle of Man, with thirty ships, and they are so fierce that no one can withstand them. One is called Ospak, and the other Brodir.[5] Go find them, and spare nothing to make them join you, whatever they ask.'

Sigtrygg went to look for the Vikings and found them off Man. He brought up the purpose of his trip at once, but Brodir held back all support until King Sigtrygg offered him the kingdom and his mother. But this was to be kept quiet so that Earl Sigurd would not hear of it. Brodir too was to come to Dublin by Palm Sunday.

Sigtrygg went back and told his mother.

After that Brodir and Ospak talked together. Brodir told Ospak all that he and Sigtrygg had said and asked him to join him in battle against King Brian; he said that there was much at stake. Ospak said he did not want to fight against such a good king. They both became angry and divided their forces: Ospak had ten ships, and Brodir twenty.

Ospak was a heathen and the wisest of men. He drew up his ships inside the sound, and Brodir was at the outside. Brodir had been a Christian and an ordained deacon, but he had cast aside the faith and become a renegade and sacrificed to heathen spirits and was very skilled in sorcery. He had armour which no steel could bite. He was both big and strong and had such long hair that he tucked it under his belt; it was black.

156 | It happened one night that a great noise broke out above Brodir and his men, so that they all awoke and sprang up and put on their clothes. Along with the noise a rain of boiling blood came down on them. They protected themselves with shields, but many men

were scalded. This wonder lasted until daybreak. On each ship one man died. Then they slept during the day.

The next night the noise came again, and again they all sprang up. Swords leaped out of their sheaths, and axes and spears flew up in the air and fought. The weapons attacked the men so hard that they had to protect themselves, but many were wounded, and on each ship one man died. This wonder lasted until daybreak. Again they slept the following day.

The third night the noise came as before. Ravens flew at the men, and it seemed that their beaks and claws were of iron. The ravens attacked them hard, but they defended themselves with swords and protected themselves with shields. This went on until daybreak. Again one man died from each ship. Again they slept for a time.

When Brodir awoke he drew a heavy breath and told his men to get a boat and said he wanted to see his foster-brother Ospak. He and some of his men stepped into the boat. When he came to Ospak he told him of all the wonders that had appeared to him, and asked him to tell him what they meant. Ospak would not tell him until he made a pledge of peace with him. Brodir promised him peace, and yet Ospak delayed until nightfall, because Brodir never killed at night.

Then Ospak spoke: 'When blood rained down on you, it meant that you will shed the blood of many men, both your own blood and that of others. When you heard a great noise, it meant that you will witness the breaking-up of the world – you will all die soon. When weapons attacked you, it meant you will be in a battle. When ravens attacked you, it meant that the fiends whom you trusted will drag you down to the torments of hell.'

Brodir was so angry that he was not able to speak and went back at once to his men and had them block the sound with his ships and fasten them to the shore with ropes and planned to kill Ospak and all his men in the morning.

Ospak saw all their preparations. Then he vowed to accept Christianity and go to King Brian and stay with him until death. He devised the plan of covering all his ships and poling them along the shore and cutting the ropes of Brodir's ships, and those ships then drifted into each other while the men slept.

Ospak and his men sailed out of the fjord and then west towards Ireland and did not stop until they came to Kincora. Ospak told King Brian everything that he had found out and took baptism from him and placed himself in his hands.

King Brian then gathered men from all over his realm, and this army was to come to Dublin in the week before Palm Sunday.

157 | Earl Sigurd Hlodvisson prepared to sail from Orkney. Flosi offered to go with him, but the earl would not have that, because Flosi still had to make his pilgrimage to Rome. Flosi offered fifteen of his men for the expedition, and the earl accepted this, while Flosi went with Earl Gilli to the Hebrides.

Thorstein Hallsson went along with Earl Sigurd, together with Hrafn the Red and Erling of Stroma. The earl did not want Harek to come along, but said he would be the first to be told what happened.[1]

The earl came with all his army to Dublin on Palm Sunday. Brodir had already arrived with his men. Brodir tried through sorcery to find out how the battle would go, and the prediction was that if the battle were fought on Good Friday, Brian would be killed but have the victory, and if they fought before Good Friday, all those who were against Brian would be killed. Then Brodir said that they should not fight before Friday.

On Thursday a man rode up to them on an apple-grey horse, with a throwing-spear in his hand. He spoke at length with Brodir and Kormlod.

King Brian had already brought all his army to the town. On Friday the army came out of the town, and both sides drew themselves up for battle. Brodir was on one flank, and King Sigtrygg on the other. Earl Sigurd was in the centre.[2]

As for King Brian, he did not want to fight on Friday, and so a shield wall was thrown up around him and the army was drawn up in front of him. Ulf Hraeda was on the flank facing Brodir, and on the other flank were Ospak and the sons of King Brian, facing Sigtrygg, and in the centre was Kerthjalfad, and in front of him the banners were being carried.

The ranks went at each other. The fighting was very fierce. Brodir went through the enemy force and killed everybody who was in his way, and no steel could bite him. But then Ulf Hraeda came up against him and thrust at him three times so hard that Brodir fell down each time and could scarcely get back on his feet. When he finally picked himself up he fled into the woods.

Earl Sigurd had a hard fight with Kerthjalfad. Kerthjalfad came on so fiercely that he killed everybody in his way. He cut his way through Earl Sigurd's ranks right up to the banner and killed the banner-bearer. The earl then found another man to carry the banner. The battle became fierce again. Kerthjalfad dealt this man a death blow, and then those around him, one after the other.

Earl Sigurd asked Thorstein Hallsson to carry the banner. Thorstein was ready to take it.

Then Amundi the White said, 'Don't carry the banner – everybody who does gets killed.'

'Hrafn the Red,' said the earl, 'you carry the banner.'

'Carry that devil of yours yourself,' answered Hrafn.

The earl said, 'Then it's best that the beggar and his bag go together,' and he took the banner off the pole and stuck it between his clothes. A little later, Amundi the White was killed. Then the earl was pierced through by a spear.

Ospak had fought his way through the whole flank of the army. He was badly wounded and both of Brian's sons were dead. King Sigtrygg fled before him. Then his whole force broke into flight. Thorstein Hallsson stopped to tie his shoe-string while the others were fleeing. Kerthjalfad asked him why he wasn't running away.

'Because I can't reach home tonight,' said Thorstein – 'my home's out in Iceland.'

Kerthjalfad spared him.

Hrafn the Red was chased out into a river and there he thought he saw Hell down below and devils trying to drag him down to them.

He spoke: 'This dog of yours has run twice to Rome, Apostle Peter, and would run there a third time if you let him.'

Then the devils turned him loose, and he got across the river.

Brodir saw that King Brian's forces were chasing the fugitives and that there were only a few men at the shield wall. He ran out of the woods and cut his way through the shield wall and swung at the king. The boy Tadk brought his arm up against it, but the blow cut off the arm and the king's head too, and the king's blood fell on the stump of the boy's arm, and the stump healed at once.

Then Brodir called loudly, 'Let word go from man to man – Brodir killed Brian.'

They ran after those who were chasing the fugitives and told them of the fall of King Brian. Ulf Hraeda and Kerthjalfad turned back at once and formed a circle around Brodir and his men and hemmed them in with branches; Brodir was then taken prisoner. Ulf Hraeda cut open his belly and led him around an oak tree and in this way pulled out his intestines. Brodir did not die until they were all pulled out of him.[3] All of Brodir's men were killed too.

Then they took King Brian's body and laid it out; the king's head had grown back on the trunk.

Fifteen of the burners fell at Brian's battle. Halldor Gudmundarson and Erling of Stroma also fell there.

On the morning of Good Friday, in Caithness, this happened: a man named Dorrud walked outside and saw twelve people riding together to a women's room, and then they disappeared inside. He went up to the room and looked in through a window that was there and saw that there were women inside and that they had set up a loom. Men's heads were used for weights, men's intestines for the weft and warp, a sword for the sword beater, and an arrow for the pin beater. The women spoke these verses:[4]

23.(1.)
A wide warp
warns of slaughter;
blood rains
from the beam's cloud.   *beam's cloud*:
                   the threads hanging from the crossbeam on a loom
A spear-grey fabric   *spear-grey fabric*: battle ranks

is being spun,
which the friends
of Randver's slayer   *Randver*: son of Ermanric (fourth century),
                                       hanged or killed by Odin himself;
                                       friends of his *slayer*: valkyries
will fill out
with a red weft.

(2.)
The warp is woven
with warriors' guts,
and heavily weighted
with the heads of men.
Spears serve as heddle rods,
spattered with blood;
iron-bound is the shed rod,
and arrows are the pin beaters;
we will beat with swords
our battle web.

(3.)
Hild sets to weaving,   [the names are of valkyries]
and Hjorthrimul
and Sanngrid and Svipul,
with swords drawn.
Shafts will splinter,
shields shatter;
the dog of helmets
devours shields.   *dog of helmets*: sword

(4.)
We wind and wind   [image refers to winding up the woven fabric
                                       on the loom beam]
the web of spears   *web of spears*: battle

which the young king
has carried on before.
Let us go forth
amongst the fighters
when our dear ones
deal out blows.

young king: Sigtrygg

(5.)
We wind and wind
the web of spears,
and then stand by
our stalwart king.
Gunn and Gondul,
who guarded the king,
saw the bloody shields
of the brave men.

(6.)
We wind and wind
the web of spears,
there where the banners
of bold men go forth;
we must not let
his life be lost –
valkyries decide
who dies or lives.

(7.)
The men who inhabited
the outer headlands
will now be leaders
in the lands.
I declare the mighty king
doomed to death.

men: the Vikings

mighty king: Brian

The earl has fallen
in the face of the spears.

earl: perhaps Sigurd Hlodvisson

(8.)
And the Irish will
endure an evil time
which will never lessen
as long as men live.
Now the web is woven
and the war-place reddened;
the lands will learn
of the loss of men.

(9.)
Now it is gruesome
to gaze around,
as blood-red clouds
cover the sky;
the heavens will be garish
with the gore of men
while the slaughter-wardens
sing their song.

slaughter-wardens: valkyries

(10.)
Our pronouncement was good
for the young prince;
sound of mind
we sing victory songs.
May he who listens
learn from this
the tones of spear-women
and tell them to men.

young prince: Sigtrygg

spear-women: valkyries

(11.)
Let us ride swiftly
on our saddle-less horses
hence from here,
with swords in hand.

The women then pulled down the cloth and tore it to pieces, and each of them kept the piece she was holding in her hand.

Dorrud then went away from the window and back home, and the women climbed on their horses and rode away, six to the south and six to the north.

A similar event occurred to Brand Gneistason in the Faroe Islands.

At Svinafell in Iceland blood appeared on the priest's cope on Good Friday, and he had to take it off.

At Thvotta river on Good Friday a priest thought he saw a deep sea next to the altar, and he saw many terrifying sights in it, and it was a long time before he was able to sing mass again.

In Orkney this happened: Harek thought he saw Earl Sigurd together with some other men. Harek took his horse and rode to meet the earl, and people saw them come together and ride behind a hill. They were never seen again, and no trace of Harek was ever found.

Earl Gilli in the Hebrides dreamed that a man came to him and gave his name as Herfinn, and said he had come from Ireland. The earl asked him for news, and Herfinn spoke this:

24.
When swords screamed in Ireland
and men struggled, I was there;
many a weapon was shattered
when shields met in battle.

The attack, I hear, was daring;
Sigurd died in the din of helmets
after making bloody wounds;
Brian fell too, but won.

din of helmets: battle

Flosi and the earl talked at length about this dream.

A week later Hrafn the Red came to them and told them all about Brian's battle, about the death of the king and Earl Sigurd and Brodir and all the Vikings.

Flosi spoke: 'What can you tell me about my men?'

'They all died there,' said Hrafn, 'except for your brother-in-law Thorstein, but he was spared by Kerthjalfad and is now with him. Halldor Gudmundarson died.'

Flosi told the earl that he was going away – 'we have to make our pilgrimage to Rome.'

The earl told him to go as he wished and gave him a ship and whatever else they needed, and much silver. Then they sailed to Wales and stayed there a while.

158 | To turn now to Kari: he told Skeggi that he wanted him to find him a ship, and Skeggi gave him a fully manned longship. Then Kari and David and Kolbein went aboard. They sailed south along the Scottish fjords. There they met men from the Hebrides. They told Kari what had happened in Ireland, and also that Flosi a nd his men had gone to Wales. When Kari heard this he told his companions that he wanted to go south to Wales and find them. He asked that those who wanted to part company with him should do so; he would not deceive anyone about the fact that he considered his sorrows to be still unavenged. All his men chose to stay with him. He then sailed south to Wales and they pulled into a sheltered inlet.

That morning Kol Thorsteinsson went into the town to buy silver. He had the most vicious tongue of all the burners. Kol had spent much time with a wealthy woman, and it was all but fixed that he would marry her and settle there.

That morning Kari went into town, too. He came to the place where Kol was counting the silver. Kari recognized him. He rushed at him with drawn sword and struck at his neck, but Kol was still counting silver and his head uttered the number ten as it flew from the body.

Kari spoke: 'Tell Flosi that Kari Solmundarson has killed Kol Thorsteinsson. I give notice that I did the slaying.'

Then he went to his ship and told his companions about the slaying. They sailed back north to Berwick and pulled the ship ashore and went to Whitbury in Scotland and spent that winter with Earl Melkolf.

To turn now to Flosi: he went and took the body of Kol and laid it out and spent much money on his burial. Flosi never spoke harshly of Kari. From there he sailed south across the Channel and then began his pilgrimage and walked south and did not stop until he came to Rome. There he was treated with such great honour that he received absolution from the Pope himself, and he gave much money for that.

He returned by the eastern route[1] and stopped in many towns and presented himself to powerful men and received honours from them. He spent the following winter in Norway and received from Earl Eirik a ship for the journey to Iceland. The earl also gave him much flour, and many other men showed him honour.

Then he sailed to Iceland and landed at Hornafjord. From there he went home to Svinafell. He had then fulfilled all his part in the settlement, both the exile and the payments.

159 | To tell now about Kari: the following summer he went to his ship and sailed south across the Channel and began his pilgrimage in Normandy and walked south and received absolution and returned by the western route[1] and took over his ship in Normandy and sailed north across the Channel to Dover in England. From there he sailed west to Wales and then north along the coast of Wales and on to the Scottish firths, and did not stop his journey until

he came to Skeggi, at Freswick in Caithness. Then he turned the cargo vessel over to Kolbein and David. Kolbein sailed this ship to Norway, while David stayed behind on Fair Isle.

Kari spent that winter at Caithness. During the winter his wife died in Iceland.

The next summer Kari prepared to go to Iceland. Skeggi gave him a cargo vessel, and there were eighteen of them on board. They finished their preparations late, but put out to sea. They had a long passage, but at last they reached the promontory Ingolfshofdi, and there the ship was shattered into pieces; their lives, however, were spared.

The snow was falling thickly. Kari's men asked him what they were to do, and he said that it was his plan to go to Svinafell and put Flosi's magnanimity to the test. They walked to Svinafell through the snowstorm.

Flosi was in the main room. He recognized Kari at once and jumped up to meet him and kissed him, and then placed him in the high seat by his side. He invited Kari to stay there for the winter. Kari accepted.

They made a full reconciliation. Flosi gave Kari the hand of his brother's daughter, Hildigunn, who had been the wife of Hoskuld the Godi of Hvitanes. They lived at Breida to begin with.

People say that the end of Flosi's life came when he had grown old and went abroad to find wood for building a house and spent the winter in Norway. The next summer he was late in his preparations. Men talked about the bad condition of the ship. Flosi said that it was good enough for an old man doomed to die, and he boarded the ship and put out to sea, and nothing was ever heard of the ship again.

These were the children of Kari and Helga Njalsdottir: Thorgerd, Ragnheid, Valgerd and Thord who was burned at Bergthorshvol. The children of Hildigunn and Kari were Starkad and Thord and Flosi. Flosi's son was Kolbein, who was the most distinguished man in that line.

And here I end the saga of Njal of the burning.

Notes

Chapter 1

1. *Dala-Koll*: His name means Koll from the Dalir or 'Dales' district. This sudden shift of scene from the flat south-west coast of Iceland to the eastern valleys which feed into Breidafjord is unusual in the sagas.

Chapter 2

1. *Sixty hundreds*: The Old Germanic 'hundred' signifies one hundred and twenty; thus the figure which Mord proposes as his part of the dowry is 60 × 120 = 7,200 ells of homespun. Hrut is to add half of this amount, an additional 3,600. An amendment in a late-thirteenth-century lawbook reveals that the figure shows Mord to have been a very rich man: 'Here in Iceland no one may give a maiden or woman a larger bride-price than sixty hundreds, even if these men are rich, and never more than a fourth part of his goods' *Jónsbók*, ed. Ólafur Halldórsson (Copenhagen: S. L. Møller, 1904), p. 70. A cow was worth between 72 and 100 ells of homespun in twelfth and thirteenth-century Iceland.

2. *two hundred marks if he got it all*: There were two means of exchange in medieval Iceland, homespun cloth and refined silver. There were eight ounces of silver in a mark, and six ells of homespun were worth one ounce of silver. The total amount of Hrut's estate in Norway is thus 240 × 8 × 6 = 11,520 ells of homespun, which exceeds the amount decided on in the marriage agreement.

3. *Hern Islands*: A group of islands off Hordaland in the west of Norway.

Chapter 3

1. *Harald Grey-cloak ... in the east*: Harald Grey-cloak was king of Norway from 961 to 965. His mother Gunnhild was the widow of Eirik Blood-axe, who ruled Norway from 930 to 935. Here she is said to be the daughter of Ozur Toti, but it is more likely that she was the daughter of King Gorm of Denmark. Many stories were told of her harshness, her skill in magic and her fondness for men. Konungahella was near present-day Göteborg in Sweden.

Chapter 4

1. *"guests"*: A special group of followers at the king's court, charged with internal spying and killing the king's enemies.

Chapter 5

1. *Hakon, foster-son of King Athelstan*: Hakon the Good preceded Harald Grey-cloak as king of Norway, from 935 to 961; he had been fostered by King Athelstan of England.

Chapter 6

1. *'You're pulling against a powerful man'*: The metaphor is of a tug-of-war; it appears in several other sagas and is common in modern Icelandic.
2. *the king*: Some manuscripts have 'Gunnhild' here.
3. *six weeks before winter*: Around the middle of September. The wedding was originally scheduled (in Ch. 2) for early August two years before.

Chapter 7

1. *Sigmund Ozurarson*: Nothing is known of this Sigmund or the favours Unn has shown him, but since he refers to Hrut as his kinsman he may be the son of Ozur, Hrut's uncle.
2. *men's door*: This seems to have been the main door (of two or three) and a

place where various legal ceremonies took place. The travel directions which Mord gives to Unn in the following sentence are meant to avoid the usual route which would start by going south rather than east.

3. *divorced*: There are two divorces in the saga. This one, from the woman's side, consists of a threefold series of declarations (at the bed, at the door, and at the Law Rock) and may well represent early Icelandic law; the threefold process is treated as important in Ch. 24. The other divorce, from the man's side, occurs in Ch. 34 and is a much simpler procedure, a single declaration.

Chapter 8

1. *he set the figure at ninety hundreds . . . three marks*: Mord is asking, legitimately, for the sixty hundreds provided by himself as dowry and the thirty hundreds added by Hrut (see Ch. 2). The fine is for failure to pay promptly.

2. *episode*: So read most manuscripts, but Reykjabók has a word meaning 'conflict' here.

Chapter 9

1. *foster-father*: Although the term *fóstri* (usually translated 'foster-father/son/ brother') is used of Thjostolf, he was not so much Hallgerd's foster-father as simply a man who looked after her as she was growing up.

2. *paid no compensation for them*: The refusal to pay compensation for slayings, to make reasonable amends for an unjust act, is a sure sign of a wicked and intractable character.

Chapter 12

1. *Ljot the Black, her kinsman*: Like Sigmund Ozurarson in Ch. 7 and Jorund the Godi in Ch. 8, this character is brought on stage without prior introduction and is, like Sigmund, not known elsewhere.

2. *Reykjanes*: It is not explained why Osvif, Thorvald's father, is to be found at Reykjanes rather than at Fell, his residence in Ch. 9, but we may guess that he moved there after his son's marriage.

3. *'Osvif's personal spirits are coming this way'*: Svan, with his second sight, has a vision of the personal spirits of Osvif and his men. Such visions were often marked by sleepiness, and this explains his yawning.

4. *The nose is near to the eyes*: A proverb which asserts the duties that go along with family ties. The sense here is 'what involves those close to us involves us as well'. The proverb will be uttered again by Ketil of Mork in Ch. 112.

Chapter 13

1. *Three brothers ... owned that farm together*: Glum, who will play the largest role of the three brothers in this saga, is the only one who is not known from other sources. Thorarin was the second Icelandic lawspeaker, from 950 to 969.

2. *Engey and Laugarnes in the south*: Laugarnes is part of the modern capital city of Reykjavík, and the island Engey, uninhabited, lies in Faxafloi bay just north of the city.

3. *one oath does not invalidate all oaths*: A proverbial saying which means that what happens once, even though done badly like an oath violated, need not be repeated.

Chapter 14

1. *my father's mother ... Sigurd Fafnisbani*: Compare the genealogy given for Hoskuld in Ch. 1, which does not go back this far. Sigurd Fafnisbani (Sigurd the slayer of Fafnir) is a great hero in the Eddic poetry and the *Saga of the Volsungs*; he corresponds to Siegfried in the medieval German epic *Das Nibelungenlied* and in Wagner's operatic cycle *The Ring of the Nibelung*.

2. *sprinkled with water*: A pagan ceremony resembling, but not related to, Christian baptism.

Chapter 16

1. *I don't want to follow in the footsteps of your slaves*: This is intemperate speech, for Glum's servants are certainly not slaves. The Icelandic word used for them elsewhere is *húskarlar*, 'house-men', and the same term was used for men in the Norwegian king's court.

Chapter 17

1. *The only bad company comes from home*: A proverbial phrase which also appears in other sagas. Although the contexts are different, one might compare Matthew 10: 35–6: 'For I have come to set a man against his father, and a daughter against her mother, and a daughter-in-law against her mother-in-law; and a man's foes will be those of his own household' (RSV), and James Joyce, *Ulysses* 9.812–13 (Gabler edition): 'A man's worst enemies come from house and family.'

Chapter 19

1. *Gunnar . . . Sandholar*: For Gunnar's relation to Unn see the beginning of the saga, where Mord Gigja, Unn's father, is the son of Sighvat the Red. She is thus Sighvat's granddaughter, and here we learn that Gunnar, through his mother Rannveig, is the great-grandson of Sighvat. According to *The Book of Settlements*, it was Sigmund, the son of Sighvat, who was slain at the Sandholar ferry (see translation by Pálsson and Edwards, p. 131). This Sigmund is unknown in *Njal's Saga*.

2. *Uni the Unborn*: 'Unborn' means born by Caesarean delivery rather than by the normal way. Uni is one of the settlers of Iceland, and his father Gardar is considered the discoverer of Iceland in some versions of *The Book of Settlements* (see p. 17 of the English translation by Pálsson and Edwards) and in Theodoricus Monachus, *The Ancient History of the Norwegian Kings* (London: Viking Society for Northern Research, 1998), p. 6.

Chapter 26

1. *Asgrim slew Gauk*: This is referred to again in Ch. 139, where Asgrim is taunted for having slain his foster-brother Gauk. An entry in the early-fourteenth-century manuscript Möðruvallabók indicates that there existed a 'Saga of Gauk Trandilsson' and that the scribe planned to copy it into that manuscript immediately after *Njal's Saga*. But the copy was not made, and the saga is lost.

Chapter 29

1. *Earl Hakon Sigurdarson ruled the realm*: He ruled in Norway from 975 to 995.

Chapter 31

1. *King Harald Gormsson was staying there*: King of Denmark, nicknamed 'Blue-tooth'; he died around 986 after a reign of perhaps forty years.

Chapter 33

1. *I'm very demanding when it comes to men*: Hallgerd's response is deliberately ambiguous: (*a*) she is demanding in her choice of men; (*b*) she makes many demands on men.

Chapter 34

1. *He was Gunnar's uncle*: Thrain's father Sigfus was the father of Gunnar's mother, Rannveig. See the beginning of Ch. 19 and Genealogical Tables 1 and 2. Thrain and his brothers (the Sigfussons) are not known outside this saga.
2. *Thorgerd and Helga*: In Ch. 20 it was said that Njal had three daughters, but only these two are named and play a role in the saga.
3. *Hoskuld*: This Hoskuld is the natural son of Njal (see Ch. 25), and not to be confused with Hoskuld Dala-Kollsson, the father of Hallgerd. It has often been noticed that the seating arrangement, with Njal and his family on one side of Gunnar, and the Sigfussons and their allies on his other side, foreshadows the major conflict in the saga.

Chapter 35

1. *you have gnarled nails on every finger*: Some scholars believe that such deformed nails, probably a fungus growth, were taken as a sign of nymphomania, in which case Hallgerd is accusing Bergthora of a tendency which

she herself will best exemplify, at least according to Skarphedin's insult in Ch. 91 where he calls Hallgerd 'either a cast-off hag or a whore'.

Chapter 39

1. *Asgerd*: Njal's mother; see the genealogy in Ch. 20.

Chapter 41

1. *there was close kinship between him and Sigmund*: See Genealogical Table 2; Sigmund's father was the brother of Gunnar's grandfather. This Sigmund is not known from other sources than this saga.

Chapter 44

1. ... *all of them malicious*: The slanderous nature of Hallgerd's remarks and Sigmund's verses (unrecorded here) cannot be exaggerated. First, Njal's strong point, his wisdom, has been impugned. Second, the epithets for both Njal and his son are a slur on their manhood: 'Old Beardless' is an insulting reference to a physical characteristic of Njal, and 'Dung-beardlings' implies that his sons can only have beards by putting dung on their faces.

Chapter 45

1. *red elf*: Skarphedin is making fun of Sigmund's dyed clothing, playing on the more common dark (or malicious) elves.
2. *you'll be on your back*: The literal meaning of the Icelandic is 'you'll fall into your mother's kin'. Compare Charles the wrestler in *As You Like It*, I. ii: 'Come, where is this young gallant that is so desirous to lie with his mother earth?'
3. *He was compensated for long ago*: What Gunnar means is that Sigmund got what was coming to him for having defamed Njal and his sons.
4. *No one was ever ... without right to compensation*: Anyone who repeated the slander would immediately be outside the law (i.e. an outlaw), and thus could be slain by anyone without fear of reprisal.

Chapter 46

1. *There was a man ... a great chieftain:* This impressive genealogy, which agrees with that in *The Book of Settlements*, looks back to Norway (Gizur's maternal grandfather Bodvar was a 'hersir' or local leader in Norway, as was his ancestor Bjorn Buna) and forwards beyond the time frame of the saga: Isleif Gizurarson was the first bishop of Iceland, 1056–80. Thord Beard (Thord Skeggi), Gizur's great-grandfather, was a settler in the south-west of Iceland.

2. *A man named Geir ... from Mosfell:* Ketilbjorn the Old, a settler himself, was a son-in-law of the settler Thord Beard. Geir the Godi and Gizur the White were thus related: both are grandsons of Ketilbjorn the Old.

Chapter 47

1. *a man named Otkel ... were brothers:* Otkel's grandfather Hallkel was the brother of Ketilbjorn, the grandfather of Gizur the White and Geir the Godi; this relationship with Otkel explains why Gizur and Geir support him, and eventually turn against Gunnar.

2. *Lambi Sigurdarson:* Lambi has not been mentioned before, but he is the son of Sigurd Sigfusson who was mentioned in Ch. 34; he is therefore Thrain Sigfusson's nephew.

3. *The men of Mosfell:* This refers primarily to Otkel and his brothers Hallkel and Hallbjorn the White and his son Thorgeir, as well as Otkel's friend Skammkel, although Mosfell was in fact the farm of Otkel's powerful kinsman, Gizur the White.

Chapter 49

1. *I know some things ... that neither of you knows:* Mord has apparently learned about the food served at Hlidarendi to Gunnar's guests from Sida (see previous chapter).

2. *your grandfather Hallkel, who was a great hero:* See the duel referred to at the beginning of Ch. 47. By referring to this Hallkel, who was the brother of Ketilbjorn the Old, Skammkel is reminding Otkel of his kinship with Gizur and Geir.

Chapter 50

1. *what you must have already decided ... best for all*: The advice given by Gizur and Geir is not specified, but presumably it was to give Gunnar self-judgement. In any case, it is not reported truly by Skammkel, and the reader is in the same position as those who heard Skammkel's report, of not knowing what Gizur and Geir really advised.

2. *Summons Days for the Althing*: Summonses had to be made at least four weeks before the meeting of the Althing in late June.

Chapter 51

1. *there's more to judge now*: In the interval since Gunnar offered to judge the case himself (in Ch. 49) he has had to endure the indignity of a legal summons.

Chapter 52

1. *Runolf, the son of Ulf Aur-Godi*: Although he is presented here as if for the first time, Runolf was mentioned in Ch. 34 as a guest at the wedding of Gunnar and Hallgerd.

Chapter 53

1. *You must report this ... against the dead*: Kolskegg assumes that Gunnar will kill Otkel.

Chapter 56

1. *There was a man named Skafti ... in all matters*: Skafti Thoroddson was lawspeaker from 1004 to 1030 and is usually treated with great respect, but not in this saga, where he is treated with mockery. A key to his unpopularity may lie in Ari Thorgilsson's statement (in *The Book of the Icelanders*, Ch. 8): 'In his day many chieftains and great men were outlawed or exiled for manslaughter or assault as a result of his power and authority.'

2. *There are some slayings . . . found guilty*: Even if Otkel is, as Gunnar charges, guilty of outlawry, the other men whom Gunnar killed were not, and in those cases he is guilty.

3. *there is a charge of full outlawry . . . as I say*: Njal seems to have in reserve a complaint he can bring against Geir; he shows similar resourcefulness in Ch. 64.

Chapter 59

1. *that was the name given to the boy*: This child, Hoskuld Thrainsson, the son of Thrain Sigfusson, will play a crucial role in the saga. He is not known outside of *Njal's Saga*. The only other character whose birth is reported together with the naming is Hoskuld's mother Thorgerd (Ch. 14). In both cases Hallgerd chooses a name from her father's side.

2. *Olaf Peacock*: The son of Hoskuld Dala-Kollsson and the Irish princess Melkorka; he figures prominently in *The Saga of the People of Laxardal*.

Chapter 60

1. *Njal and my friend Helgi*: The ties between Njal and his son Helgi and Asgrim Ellida-Grimsson are strong: in Ch. 27 it was told that Helgi Njalsson married Asgrim's daughter and that Njal fostered Asgrim's son Thorhall.

Chapter 64

1. *Steinvor*: She was introduced in Ch. 58 as the wife of Egil and the mother of their three sons, all now slain. She is also the sister of Starkad, who lost two sons in the fight with Gunnar at Knafaholar.

Chapter 65

1. *choose Kol as the slayer . . . this is lawful*: The actual slayer of Hjort was the Norwegian Thorir (see Ch. 63), but the law permitted the citing of another man, as Njal here asserts.

2. *his brothers-in-law*: Gunnar's brothers-in-law (Hallgerd's brothers) are Olaf, Thorleik and Bard. They were mentioned at the end of Ch. 1, and Olaf

(Peacock) befriended Gunnar in Ch. 59; he will do so again in Chs. 70 and 75.

Chapter 66

1. *Hjalti Skeggjason of Thjorsardal*: Hjalti Skeggjason is introduced abruptly here. He is mentioned widely in early texts, and although *Njal's Saga* does not say so, *The Book of Settlements* tells that he is the son-in-law of Gizur the White; this should place him on the side of Gunnar's enemies.

Chapter 69

1. *heaviness came over them and they could do nothing but sleep*: Being overcome by sleep while *en route* to a fight is a literary motif in the sagas. The sleep may be accompanied by a dream, as with Gunnar in Ch. 62, or may provide a pause in which the party being attacked can gather forces, as in this case.

Chapter 71

1. *Ormhild, Gunnar's kinswoman*: Ormhild is mentioned in *Njal's Saga* only in this chapter; from *The Book of Settlements* we know that she is the daughter of Gunnar's sister Arngunn and Hroar the Godi of Tunga – see Ch. 19.

Chapter 72

1. *it was called 'wound rain ... great battles*: 'Wound rain' is another word for 'blood rain', which occurs frequently as an omen of death in Old Icelandic literature, very likely under Irish influence. For similar omens, see Chs. 127, 156 and 157. The Olvir to whom Gunnar refers here is Olvir of Hising, who helped him in Sweden (see Ch. 29).

Chapter 73

1. *a second time*: The second notice has to do with the wound, whereas the first had to do with the assault. The filing of such distinct complaints in cases of homicide is in accord with early Icelandic law, which the language of this passage follows closely. See *The Laws of Early Iceland*, p. 148, and Chs. 135 and 141–2 of this saga.

Chapter 74

1. *They went there . . . that this was so*: Again in Ch. 142 a panel of nine members is reduced to five, but there it is because four members are disqualified. Here the point seems to be that a panel for the prosecution (nine men) can become a panel for the defence if four members are eliminated.

2. *Gunnar and Kolskegg were to go abroad . . . the slain Thorgeir*: Gunnar is declared an outlaw in the next chapter for breaking this agreement, but he is not at this point an outlaw, although the arbitrated three-year exile is similar to that of lesser outlawry. Under official outlawry, Gunnar could be killed with impunity by anyone at all for failing to go abroad; under this arbitrated settlement only the kinsmen of Thorgeir Otkelsson would have licence to kill him.

3. *Gunnar gave no indication that he thought this settlement unfair*: In fact the settlement is unfair, as these words imply. Njal had just shown that Gunnar was not the aggressor in the battle. Njal could have gone on to win acquittal for Gunnar, but instead chose to allow the case to be arbitrated, probably thinking of what would be best for Gunnar in the long run.

Chapter 75

1. *'Lovely is the hillside . . . I will ride back home and not leave'*: In *Alexanders saga*, translated into Icelandic by Bishop Brand Jonsson in the late thirteenth century from the long twelfth-century Latin poem *Alexandreis* by Walter of Chatillon, Alexander is also moved towards a fateful decision by a beautiful view; the fact that the phrase 'pale fields' occurs in both texts has led some scholars to claim a direct literary borrowing by the author of *Njal's Saga*.

2. *'I made a promise . . . I shall keep this promise'*: The incident Hjalti refers to was recounted in Ch. 66.

Chapter 77

1. *'Then I'll recall ... for a long or a short time'*: Gunnar had slapped Hallgerd in Ch. 48, over the matter of the stolen cheese, and she promised at that time to pay him back. Earlier she had been slapped by her first husband, Thorvald (Ch. 11) and by her second husband, Glum (Ch. 16).

2. *Thorvald the Sickly ... Hestlaek in Grimsnes*: This slaying will be reported in Ch. 102.

Chapter 78

1. *how Gunnar behaved after the slaying of your kinsman Sigmund*: In Ch. 45, after Skarphedin killed Gunnar's relative Sigmund Lambason, Gunnar restrained himself from seeking compensation, until eventually Njal persuaded him to do so.

Chapter 80

1. *All the facts were weighed.... they were fully reconciled:* The self-judgement granted to Hogni by Mord was set at the same value as the penalties levied against Skarphedin and Hogni for the slaying of Starkad and Thorgeir.

2. *the case between Geir the Godi and Hogni:* Geir must have brought a separate suit against Hogni for the slaying of his son Hroald.

3. *Hogni ... is now out of the saga:* In spite of this statement, Hogni appears again in Chs. 93 and 109.

Chapter 81

1. *King Svein Fork-beard:* King of Denmark from 986 to 1014.

2. *the Varangian guard:* An élite corps of Scandinavians and other foreigners in close attendance on the Byzantine emperor.

Chapter 83

1. *Melkolf*: Possibly Malcolm II (1005–34).

Chapter 85

1. *Mainland*: The modern name for Icelandic *Hrossey* (Horse island), the main island in Orkney.

Chapter 88

1. *Thorgerd Holda-bride*: Thorgerd and her sister Irpa (mentioned shortly after) were semi-divine figures associated with the family of the earls of Lade.
2. *Thrain ... was not certain what the earl would place highest*: Thrain is not sure whether the confidence he has already earned with the earl, by killing Kol, will cause the earl to trust him now in the matter of Hrapp.

Chapter 89

1. *the tribute money*: The earls of Orkney owed tribute to Norway, and it was mentioned in Ch. 86 that Kari would be carrying this tribute money from Earl Sigurd to Earl Hakon.

Chapter 91

1. *the effect of every action is two-sided*: Njal shared this same proverbial wisdom with his wife in Ch. 44; it indicates his awareness, central to the meaning of the saga, that blood vengeance is not a definitive resolution of a conflict.
2. *we must put out such a wide net*: The meaning of this metaphorical expression, based on net-fishing, is that they must proceed with care and patience.
3. *cast-off hag*: The unusual word translated here as 'cast-off hag', Icelandic *hornkerling*, appeared in Ch. 35, when Hallgerd refused Bergthora's request to move aside for Thorhalla Njalsdottir. Skarphedin recalls that fateful scene and asserts that Hallgerd is indeed what she earlier said she was not.

4. *pay him a red skin for his grey one*: A proverbial way of saying 'make someone shed (red) blood for the shabby (grey) treatment he gave'.

Chapter 92

1. *'That's what you said the other time . . . but then you were hunting men'*: The 'other time' that Njal refers to was the similar scene at the end of Ch. 44.
2. *to help Hogni*: Skarphedin helped Hogni avenge his father, Gunnar of Hlidarendi, in Ch. 79.

Chapter 93

1. *They decided that Ketil . . . to agree to peace*: A section of the Codex Regius text of the *Grágás* ('Grey-goose') lawbook deals with the division of compensation for a slaying among the members of the kin group, and the wording here seems to reflect those provisions. See 'The Wergild Ring List', in *Laws of Early Iceland*, pp. 175–85. Dividing the compensation money becomes an issue on three occasions in this saga (with Lyting in Ch. 98, with Amundi in Ch. 106, and with Thorgeir Skorargeir in Chs. 146–7), but normally in the family sagas there is only talk of a lump payment of compensation.

Chapter 95

1. *There was a man named Flosi . . . daughter of Herjolf the White*: Flosi Thordarson, the last major character to be introduced in the saga, has a rich ancestry with parallels in *The Book of Settlements*. Noteworthy antecedents are the Norwegian hersir Bjorn Buna and the settler Helgi the Lean.

Chapter 96

1. *There was a man named Hall . . . Thidrandi Geitisson*: Hall of Sida's genealogy, traced back to a Norwegian earl, indicates his importance. He will play no strong role in the plot, but will stand out as an advocate of peace and reconciliation and one of the most noble characters in the saga.

2. *whom Kari was to slay in Wales*: The slaying of Kol Thorsteinsson by Kari will take place in Ch. 158. Other cases of anticipation of an event to be narrated later occur in Ch. 77 (Thorvald the Sickly) and Ch. 101 (Glum Hildisson).

3. *Thidrandi, whom, it is said, the dísir killed*: The story alluded to here is told in the saga of Olaf Tryggvason in the fourteenth-century Icelandic manuscript *Flateyjarbók* (vol. i, pp. 419–21 of the 1860–68 edn.), just prior to the story of Thangbrand's mission to convert Iceland. The young Thidrandi, contrary to the advice of a seer, went outside one night and encountered nine women in black riding from the north with swords, who struck him mortally in spite of nine women in white on white horses who came riding from the south. The event was interpreted to signify the coming change of faith, the nine women (*dísir*) in black being personal spirits of Thidrandi's family who were unhappy about what was to come. This story of a young man who goes outside at night and experiences supernatural beings on horseback resembles the story of Hildiglum in Ch. 125 of *Njal's Saga*. For an English translation of 'Thidrandi Whom the Goddesses Slew', see *Eirik the Red and Other Icelandic Sagas*, translated by Gwyn Jones (Oxford: Oxford University Press, 1961), pp. 158–62.

4. *There was a man named Thorir . . . Thorgrim the Tall*: Holta-Thorir and his three sons were mentioned in Ch. 20, where it was specified that he was the brother of Njal. The sons of Holta-Thorir will later be responsible for avenging the burning of Njal. Skorargeir's proper name is Thorgeir.

Chapter 97

1. *the relationship . . . is very precarious*: Flosi is referring to the fact that Njal's sons killed Hoskuld's father Thrain Sigfusson, and the possibility that the peaceful settlement made for Thrain's death (in Ch. 93) could be broken.

2. *Skafti Thoroddsson*: According to Ari Thorgilsson's *Book of the Icelanders*, written in the early twelfth century, Skafti was responsible for the establishment of the Fifth Court, usually dated around 1004. This chapter of *Njal's Saga* presents a deviant and unlikely version; see Glossary under 'Fifth Court'.

3. *cases involving the offer or acceptance of payment for assistance in legal suits*: In this saga, though not in *Grágás*, payment for legal service is equated with a bribe to a witness or judge. This will become an issue in Ch. 144 with Eyjolf Bolkverksson, who in Ch. 138 accepts a gold bracelet when he agrees to act as lawyer for Flosi.

4. *bought land at Ossabaer . . . and settled there*: Ossabaer is about ten kilometres

from Bergthorshvol. Hildigunn's stipulation above that she and Hoskuld live in the east (i.e. at Svinafell) after their marriage has been ignored, probably because of Hoskuld's deep trust in Njal; see the comment he makes after Hildigunn's stipulation.

Chapter 98

1. *Hoskuld Njalsson.* It is important to keep the two Hoskulds apart: Hoskuld Thrainsson, Njal's foster-son, is now at Lyting's feast with his relatives (his father was a Sigfusson); Hoskuld Njalsson, the victim in this passage, is Njal's natural son with Hrodny. As a Njalsson, he is an enemy to the Sigfussons, since his half-brother Skarphedin killed Thrain Sigfusson.

2. *I have not received compensation for my brother-in-law Thrain.* As the husband of Thrain's sister and not related to Thrain by blood, it is to be expected that Lyting did not receive a share of the settlement money for the slaying of Thrain; see Ch. 93.

3. *that other woman.* The Icelandic word which Hrodny uses for Bergthora, *elja,* means concubine or a woman who shares a man with another woman. In this extreme situation the concubine Hrodny is indulging in heavy sarcasm at the expense of the legitimate wife Bergthora.

4. *His nostrils are still open.* It was the custom in the north to close the eyes, mouth and nostrils immediately after death.

Chapter 99

1. . . . *they'll keep to whatever I decide*: Compare a similar conversation between Njal and Gunnar, in Ch. 43.

Chapter 100

1. *Olaf Tryggvason.* King of Norway from 995 to 1000.

Chapter 101

1. *the sign of the cross.* The Icelandic word is *prímsigning,* from Latin *prima signatio,* a rite preliminary to baptism.

Chapter 102

1. *Hall, who was then three years old*: Hall (Thorarinsson) lived from 995 to 1089 and fostered the historian Ari Thorgilsson (1068–1148) at Haukadal from 1075 to 1089. In Ch. 9 of his *Book of the Icelanders* Ari writes, 'Hall, who was both of good memory and truthful, remembered that he was baptized and that Thangbrand baptized him when he was three years old, one year before Christianity was made law here.'

Chapter 104

1. *Hjalti Skeggjason was outlawed for mocking the gods*: On account of the verse he uttered in Ch. 102 calling Freyja a bitch and Odin a dog. In the same chapter it is said that he went abroad, and thus he was sentenced to outlawry *in absentia*.

Chapter 105

1. *Thorgeir . . . Thorkel the Long*: In other sources Thorgeir the Godi of Ljosavatn is the son, not the grandson, of Thorkel.

2. *Thorgeir spread a cloak over his head . . . and no one spoke to him*: This and the detail of Hall's payment of money to Thorgeir, just above, have been especially intriguing to scholars of the Conversion. Did Hall bribe Thorgeir? Did they agree beforehand that Christianity should be adopted? Did Thorgeir lie under the cloak for an entire day in order to ascertain the will of his gods – or simply to prepare his speech? These and further questions cannot be resolved here.

3. *'This will be the foundation of our law . . . no punishment'*: Some of the language here echoes the Conversion account in *The Book of the Icelanders*, Ch. 7. Only in this saga are the exposure of children and eating horse-flesh banned, in addition to pagan worship, at the time of the Conversion. In the parallel account in *The Book of the Icelanders*, for example, only pagan sacrifice is banned.

Chapter 106

1. *I have received no compensation.* Amundi is a parallel case to Lyting in Ch. 98. Neither had a strong claim to compensation according to early Icelandic law, Lyting as a sister's husband, Amundi as an illegitimate son.

Chapter 107

1. *people have stopped being my thingmen and gone over to Hoskuld.* Mord and Valgard have two good reasons to resent Hoskuld: his new assembly place at Hvitanes has replaced the old one at Thingskalar, and he has attracted many of Mord's thingmen to himself. In commonwealth Iceland men were free to select their own godi; they were not required to support the one living closest.

Chapter 108

1. *neither side took a decision unless the other agreed.* This phrase echoes, with heavy irony, the similar phrase used at the end of Ch. 97 describing the close amity between Hoskuld Thrainsson and the Njalssons, the very amity that Mord is now seeking to destroy.

Chapter 109

1. *'I don't think they can be blamed for that,' said Hoskuld.* Mord has just implied that the Njalssons provoked Amundi into killing Lyting (Ch. 106), and Hoskuld correctly denies that they were involved.

2. *I don't want that*: It is common in the sagas for a hero to turn down an offer of safety when in great danger, and in this case there is a verbal echo which links son to father: Hoskuld's father Thrain uttered nearly the same words in Ch. 92, shortly before he was killed.

3. *He had also fostered Thorhall ... one of the three greatest lawyers in Iceland.* The adoption of Thorhall, whose legal skills will soon become useful, was also reported in Ch. 27, where he was called the greatest lawyer in Iceland. Thorhall will be called one of the three greatest lawyers in Iceland again in Ch. 135, and in Ch. 142 we learn that Njal predicted he would be the greatest lawyer in Iceland, if put to the test (as he is in that chapter).

Chapter III

1. ... *that will cause serious damage to their case*: Mord's audacious scheme is that if he acts as plaintiff the suit will be invalid once it is revealed that he was in fact one of Hoskuld's slayers. Thorgerd, it should be remembered, is Hoskuld's mother and the widow of Thrain Sigfusson.

Chapter 112

1. *the nose is near to the eyes*: See note 4 to Ch. 12 above.

Chapter 116

1. *our day-meal*: Chief meal of the day but eaten around nine in the morning.
2. *Arnor Ornolfsson ... at the Skaftafell Assembly*: This fight is recorded in *The Book of Settlements*, in the Icelandic Annals under the year 997, and in *The Saga of the Sons of Droplaug*, with the difference that the avenging sons are Kolbein and Flosi, not Kolbein and Egil.
3. *Cold are the counsels of women*: This phrase also appears in *The Saga of Gisli* and *The Saga of the People of Laxardal*. Its use by Chaucer's Nun's Priest ('Wommennes conseils been ful ofte colde') indicates that it may have been a common proverb.
4. *as red as blood, as pale as grass, and as black as Hel itself*: The threefold simile, providing three of the 148 similes counted in the Sagas of Icelanders, gives powerful emphasis to Flosi's overwrought state. 'Hel' is the Old Norse word for both the goddess of death and the place of the dead, corresponding to the Greek Hades. The word has been adapted in English for the Christian concept of Hell as a place of eternal punishment.
5. *when I married you to my brother's daughter ... in all things*: This wedding and this promise have not been mentioned, nor indeed has Thraslaug, Flosi's niece and wife of Ingjald. Ingjald, Thraslaug and Hrodny do not appear in any sources other than this saga.

Chapter 119

1. *My sister Jorunn will not expect me to avoid helping you*: Gizur's sister Jorunn is Asgrim's mother.

2. *You're Skafti Thoroddsson . . . in his flour sacks*: Skarphedin's insult against one of the most prominent and respected Icelanders of the early eleventh century (see note 1 to Ch. 56 and note 2 to Ch. 97 above) is effective: Skafti not only disguised himself and escaped in an undignified way, he also associated with slaves and had a strip of turf, usually raised for a solemn purpose such as swearing brotherhood or an ordeal, cut in order to conceal himself. Skafti remembers this insult in Ch. 139, when he refuses aid for a second time, and Gizur the White compares him unfavourably with his father. In the battle at the Althing (Ch. 145) Skafti is wounded through the calf and dragged into the booth of a sword-sharpener, and the saga writer states specifically that he receives no compensation for this wound. This treatment of an important lawspeaker as vain, cowardly and ineffectual is reminiscent of the insults directed by Broddi Bjarnason against some leading chieftains, including Skafti, in *Olkofri's Saga*. The story contained in Skarphedin's insult is not recorded elsewhere.

3. *you need to be avenging your father rather than predicting my fate*: Snorri's father Thorgrim was slain by Gisli Sursson, the outlaw hero of *Gisli Sursson's Saga* (see Ch. 16 of that saga). Vengeance in this case was complicated, because Gisli, the slayer, was the brother of Snorri's mother Thordis; Skarphedin's insult is therefore unfair. Snorri's response, that he has heard this insult before, may indicate that the saga author know *Olkofri's Saga*, where Broddi says the same thing to Snorri.

4. *It would be more fitting . . . from your home*: Svanlaug and this story are not known elsewhere.

5. *Thorkel Bully . . . you deserve blame for that*: The slander of Gudmund to which Skarphedin may be referring appears in *The Saga of the People of Ljosavatn*, Ch. 19, as an explicit accusation of homosexuality: 'I imagine your ass has slaked itself at many streams, but I doubt it has drunk milk before.'

6. *He was the son . . . Hallbjorn Half-troll*: This genealogy repeats the one given for Thorkel's father in Ch. 105.

7. *Balagardssida*: This is thought to refer to the south-west coast of Finland.

8. *a creature half-man, half-beast*: The Icelandic word for this centaur-like creature is *finngálkn*, which does not appear in any other family saga. Thorkel's adventures with this creature and with the flying dragon are more typical of the legendary and romantic sagas. Only in one other family saga, *The Saga of Bjorn, Champion of the Hitardal People*, Ch. 5, does a man kill a flying dragon.

Chapter 120

1. *It's never happened ... such a filthy thing*: This insult combines the likely and the outrageous. In Ch. 2 of *The Saga of the People of Ljosavatn* Thorkel and his brothers oppose their father Thorgeir (the lawspeaker who decided in Ch. 105 above that Iceland should be Christian). The charge of eating the mare's rectum has nothing to do with the prohibition against eating horse flesh; the sense is that only someone as low as Thorkel Bully could eat such food, with a hint at his avarice. The small household at his farm Oxara is mentioned in Ch. 13 of *The Saga of the People of Ljosavatn*.

2. *I had this axe in my hand ... to catch me*: See the account of this killing in Ch. 92.

Chapter 122

1. *I felt that the sweetest light of my eyes had been put out*: The phrase 'light of my eyes', more than any other in the saga, has religious echoes, as in Tobit 10: 4: '*lumen oculorum nostrorum*'. In the life of St Alexis appears '*lumen oculorum meorum*' (*Acta Sanctorum*, XXXI, p. 252). In both cases a mother is lamenting the death (or presumed death) of a son. The additional word 'sweet' in this phrase appears only in one other place in the sagas of Icelanders, in Thorstein Eiriksson's prophecy about Gudrid's descendants (among whom were bishops) in Ch. 5 of *The Saga of the Greenlanders*: 'you will live a long life together, and have many descendants, promising, bright and fine, sweet and well-scented.' The combination of sweetness and brightness in that passage, as in *Njal's Saga*, may go back to Psalm 18: 10–11 (Vulgate), where the commandments of the Lord are said to enlighten the eyes and to be sweeter than honey. Sweetness was associated with sanctity in the Middle Ages.

2. *when I helped your kinsman ... Hall the Red*: This story is not told elsewhere, but Thorgrim is mentioned in *Thorstein Sidu-Hallson's Saga* and his father, Stout-Ketil, appears in a number of sources.

Chapter 123

1. *the farmers' churchyard*: *Grágás* mentions a farmer's churchyard at Thingvellir, where such payments were made. It is not known where this churchyard (or church) was.

2. *a silk robe ... on top of the pile*: The robe, though costly, was apparently suitable for either sex and thus gave Flosi an excuse to take offence. Njal may have added these gifts as a gesture of good will, but some readers have suspected that he was deliberately provoking Flosi and in effect sealing his own doom. The fact that he is silent when Flosi asks (twice) who put the robe on the pile can be taken to support this view; if the gift was innocent, why not acknowledge it?

3. *black trousers ... more need of these*: The insult lies either in the fact that these trousers were women's trousers, or that they were men's trousers which Flosi, with his woman's nature, needed badly.

4. *he uses you as a woman every ninth night*: Similar insults about a man being a woman every ninth night appear in *Thorstein Sidu-Hallson's Saga*, Ch. 3, and *The Saga of Ref the Sly*, Ch. 7. The Svinafell troll, presumably a semi-human creature who lived at Svinafell, is mentioned only here. The seriousness of the insult can be measured by the Old Norwegian Gulathing Law: 'No one is to make an exaggerated utterance about another or a libel. It is called an "exaggerated utterance" if someone says something about another man which cannot be, nor come to be, nor have been: declares he is a woman every ninth night or has borne a child or calls him *gylfin* (some sort of unnatural monster). He is outlawed if he is found guilty of that.' Cited in '*Níð* and the Sacred,' by Preben Meulengracht Sørensen, in *Artikler: Udgivet i anleding af Preben Meulengracht Sørensens 60. års fødselsdag 1. marts 2000* (Aarhus: Norrønt Forum, 2000), p. 79.

5. '*They can never prosecute us, according to the laws of the land*': What this means is unclear. Skarphedin seems to think that because of the legal mistake committed (deliberately) by Mord, it will be too late to initiate the legal process once more.

Chapter 124

1. *the Lord's Day which falls eight weeks before winter*: Sunday at the end of August, a good time for a long ride in the Icelandic highlands, with the ground hard but not snow-covered.

Chapter 126

1. *Sand*: Lomagnupssand, as Flosi indicated in Ch. 124. Today it is called Skeidararsand. The 'Sand' in the next paragraph is Mælifellssand. The main feature of Flosi's route is that it passes to the north of Eyjafjalla glacier, rather than along the usual route, close to the southern coast.

Chapter 129

1. *one fate should await us both*: This phrase, with slight variations, appears four other times in chapters close to the burning (119, 123, 124 and 130), thus lending a sense of fate to that event. The clause also appears after the burning, at the end of Ch. 152.

Chapter 130

1. *Thord Freed-man*: Presumably the son of Thord Freed-man's son and Gudfinna – see Ch. 39.
2. *Gunn of gold . . . cried out*: The translation of the second half of this stanza is conjectural, as these lines have not been satisfactorily interpreted. The first four lines refer to a woman, presumably Skarphedin's wife Thorhild, who will grieve over her husband's death. The fact that there is no mention of the burning does not necessarily mean that the poem was originally composed for another occasion.

Chapter 131

1. *Have no doubt that I will be loyal . . . for myself*: Mord was an enemy of the Sigfussons for his part in the slaying of Hoskuld Thrainsson, and thus he is forced to align himself with Kari.

Chapter 133

1. '*I want to tell you about a dream I had*': The dream which Flosi is about to recount, in which a figure comes out of a mountain and calls out, in groups, the names of men about to die, has a literary source in the following passage from the *Dialogues* of Gregory the Great, which were known in medieval Iceland: 'A steep mountain towered high above the monastery, and a deep chasm lay beneath it. When omnipotent God had decided to reward the venerable Anastasius for his labours, a voice was heard one night crying out from the top of the cliff in prolonged tones saying: "Anastasius, come!" And when this had been said, seven other monks were likewise called by name. For a short while, however, the voice which had been heard fell silent, and then it called the eighth monk. Since the community had clearly heard this, no one doubted that death was approaching those whose names had been called. Thus within a few days first the most revered Anastasius passed away, and the others also in the same order in which their names had been called from the top of the mountain. That brother whose name had been preceded by a moment of silence lived on for a few days after the others had died and then he too passed away. Thus it was clearly shown that the silence which interrupted the voice signified a brief period of life.' Migne, *Patrologia Latina*, 77, col. 185; the English translation is taken from Einar Ólafur Sveinsson, *Njáls Saga: A Literary Masterpiece*, p. 206.

2. *First he called ... Kol Thorsteinsson*: The names called out anticipate the deaths of Flosi's men: Grim the Red and Arni Kolsson are killed in the beginning of Ch. 145; later in that chapter come the deaths of Eyjolf and Ljot 'and about six other men'. For the others see n. 1 to Ch. 152. The only discrepancy between this prophecy and later events is that Glum is not killed in a group of five, as here, but in the group of three killed in Ch. 151.

3. "*First I shall clear the panel ... for the battlers*": These words look ahead to the battle at the Althing in Ch. 145. The translation attempts to capture the rhetorical zeugma in the original, where the single verb *ryðja* ('clear') is used in two different senses with two different kinds of objects, first in a legal sense with 'panel' and 'court' and then in its original literal sense with 'battlefield'.

4. *What I told you once ... before all this is over*: Flosi had predicted this in Ch. 117.

Chapter 134

1. *Flosi was wearing trousers ... easier to walk*: This is obscure, but the idea seems to be (1) that such a garment makes walking easier, and (2) that if Flosi walks, many men of lesser rank will be inclined to join him. Presumably there were not enough horses for everybody.

Chapter 135

1. *I give notice ... Thorgeir Thorisson*: See n. 1 to Ch. 73.

Chapter 136

1. *Beitivellir*: 'Grazing fields', a grassy area between Laugarvatn and Thingvellir where they rested and let their horses graze before the final stretch to Thingvellir.
2. *Flosi had arranged for the Byrgi booth to be covered*: The Byrgi booth seems to have belonged to Flosi and the men from Svinafell. It is mentioned in other sources and tradition associates it with a definite place at Thingvellir.

Chapter 138

1. *There was a man named Eyjolf ... in Iceland*: Eyjolf Bolverksson's family is prominent, and his brother(?) Gellir Bolverksson was lawspeaker on two occasions, but Eyjolf is not known outside this saga. Thorhall Asgrimsson is also referred to as one of the three greatest lawyers, on three occasions – see note 3 to Ch. 109 above. The third is presumably the lawspeaker, who at that time was Skafti Thoroddsson. The designation of both Thorhall and Eyjolf as among the three greatest lawyers anticipates the legal battle between them in Chs. 142–4.
2. *the shameful treatment ... you Ljosavatn men*: This refers to Skarphedin's insult to Thorkel Bully in Ch. 120, when the Njalssons and Asgrim were going around asking for support at the Althing.
3. *a defence can turn into a prosecution*: An alliterative saying in the Icelandic, referring to the way that the defendants in a lawsuit sometimes turn into prosecutors, if they find an error in the prosecution. This will in fact happen

in Ch. 144, when Flosi's side, the defendants, will bring charges against the plaintiffs for procedural violations.

Chapter 139

1. *in-laws*: Gizur was married to Skafti's sister.

2. *when Skarphedin told me . . . over his death*: Skarphedin said these things to Skafti in Ch. 119.

3. *Asgrim . . . killed his foster-brother Gauk*: This was also referred to in Ch. 26; see n. 1 to that chapter.

4. *Few bring up the better if they're aware of the worse*: A proverb expressing the fact that when you want to insult someone you do not choose the least offensive thing about him.

Chapter 141

1. *I'll suggest a plan to you . . . the correct one*: Eyjolf 's trick, though taken seriously by the author (see Ch. 143), cannot have been valid, since Flosi's change of thing allegiance will come *after* the suit has already been brought in the correct quarter.

Chapter 142

1. *both sides had put markings on their helmets*: This is the only time in the family sagas that this motif occurs; the marking of helmets, so that one warring party can be distinguished from the other, sets the stage for the large-scale battle which will erupt in Ch. 145.

2. *I claim the right to correct all my wording until my entire suit is in correct form*: Although most of the legal formulas in these passages can be found in Old Icelandic laws, there is no precedent for this appeal to the right to eliminate mistakes in wording. The importance of using the correct wording in a legal pronouncement lay behind Njal's ruse in Ch. 22 (carried out by Gunnar in Ch. 23), and in *The Saga of Hrafnkel Frey's Godi*, Ch. 10, for example, it is reported that Sam prosecuted his suit against Hrafnkel 'in a faultless and powerful presentation'.

3. *in the presence of Jon*: 'Jon' was a common blank name in legal formulas, much like 'John Doe' in American legal usage. This conspicuously Christian

name is an anachronism; 'Jon' would not have been in legal usage in the early eleventh century.

4. *he dismissed them for reasons ... pleading the case*: Thorgeir Thorisson (Njal's nephew) is the original plaintiff, but he turned over the case to Mord Valgardsson. A relationship between a panel member and Thorgeir would be a breach of rules; a relationship to Mord is insignificant.

5. *Any man who owns three hundreds ... owns no land*: Here the saga reflects early Icelandic law; see Miller, *Bloodtaking and Peacemaking*, p. 117, for a translation of the relevant passage.

Chapter 144

1. *for having brought a money payment into the proceedings*: Flosi's hiring of Eyjolf as a lawyer with a gold bracelet (Ch. 138) is considered in this saga to be an illegal bribe, though the formula used, 'bringing money into court', applies only to the bribing of judges. There is no indication in early Icelandic law that hiring legal services was forbidden.

2. *testimony that had nothing to do with the case*: It is not clear what this testimony is.

3. *confiscation court*: This was held two weeks after a pronouncement of outlawry, usually at the man's house, to deal with property matters. The payments mentioned here gave the right to safe passage out of the country. The life-ring payment was one mark in silver, an eighth of which (one ounce) was the sustenance fee.

4. *They had to declare the court divided*: Decisions by the Quarter Courts (thirty-six judges in each) had to be unanimous; in case of a split vote, as here, judgement was referred to the Fifth Court, where a simple majority could decide. On the establishing of the Fifth Court in order to resolve such impasses, see Ch. 97.

5. *Mord had called on nine men ... to hear the suit*: Neighbours to Thingvellir were chosen because the misdemeanours Mord is now charging Flosi and Eyjolf with took place at the Althing at Thingvellir.

6. *Their whole case will be invalid ... to make judgement*: See Ch. 97 for the stipulation that the Fifth Court had to be reduced from forty-eight to thirty-six members in order to make judgements.

Chapter 146

1. *when you lowered yourself into a gorge ... and killed seven men:* This episode, from which Thorgeir earned his nickname 'Skorargeir' (Gorge-spear), has not come down to us in any medieval source, though the author seems to assume that his audience would know it. An attempt to recreate the episode appears in the nineteenth-century *Saga of Holta-Thorir* (Holta-Thorir was the father of Thorgeir and the brother of Njal).

2. *Thorgeir made his brothers go east ... truce-breakers:* Thorgeir does not want his brothers Thorleif Crow and Thorgrim the Tall to be associated with his continuing vengeance against the burners, since they agreed to the settlement over the burning (see Ch. 145).

3. *one third:* In Ch. 145 it was agreed that the compensation for Njal would be threefold (i.e. 3 × 200), and twofold for Grim and Helgi, a total of 1,400. Hall seems to be saying that Thorgeir would have to have an equal share with his brothers, which would come to an additional 700 ounces. But the meaning of Hall's statement is not certain. See Glossary under 'compensation' for the rates paid in this saga.

4. *his son:* Leidolf the Strong. Thorgeir had killed both Leidolf and Thorkel Sigfusson in the skirmish reported earlier in this chapter.

Chapter 147

1. *your part in all this should not be better than good:* Kari is saying that what Thorgeir has done so far in the way of revenge is 'good', but that to be 'better' would mean more killing, and Kari does not want that for Thorgeir.

2. *the orders of exile or district banishment:* In Ch. 145 Flosi was sentenced to stay abroad for three years ('lesser outlawry', in effect), while Gunnar Lambason, Grani Gunnarson, Glum Hildisson and Kol Thorsteinsson were given permanent exile ('full outlawry'). The exile sentence here could refer to Flosi, for the same word is applied to his sentence directly afterwards, but 'district banishment' does not seem to fit the cases of permanent exile and must refer to other sentences fixed after the battle at the Althing.

3. *the pilgrimage to Rome:* It was not mentioned before that Flosi's sentence included a trip to Rome.

Chapter 149

1. *remember the dream I told you . . . in that dream*: See Flosi's dream in Ch. 133.

Chapter 150

1. *the death of the head of the household*: The head of the household at Skal, a farm apparently close to the scene of the battle, was the 'good farmer' Gunnar, slain just above; this man appears only here.

Chapter 152

1. *Then we will have killed fifteen men . . . killed together*: The victims of Kari's revenge correspond to Flosi's dream in Ch. 133 – though not all the names were given there, and Kari does not here count the men slain at the Althing, presumably because that large-scale battle, initiated by Thorhall, was not an act of personal revenge. Here is the scorecard of those slain:

Slain by Kari and Thorgeir (Ch. 146) – second group in Flosi's dream:
  1. unnamed
  2. Thorkel Sigfusson
  3. Sigurd Lambason
  4. Mord Sigfusson
  5. Leidolf Hamundarson
Slain by Kari in company with Bjorn (Ch. 150) – third group in Flosi's dream:
  6. Modolf Ketilsson
  7. unnamed
  8. Lambi Sigurdarson
  9. Thorstein Geirleifsson
  10. Gunnar of Skal
Slain by Kari in company with Bjorn (Ch. 151) – fourth group in Flosi's dream:
  11. Glum Hildisson
  12. Vebrand Thorfinnsson
  13. Asbrand Thorfinnsson
Still to be slain – fifth group in Flosi's dream:
  14. Gunnar Lambason (Ch. 155)
  15. Kol Thorsteinsson (Ch. 158).

Chapter 154

1. *Brian was the name of the king . . . Kincora.* This marks the beginning of the 'Brian episode' (Chs. 154–7), which recounts events in Ireland culminating in the battle of Clontarf (1014). Gilli is known only from this saga, but Sigtrygg (d. 1035), Olaf Kvaran (d. 981), Kormlod (d. 1030), and Brian are attested historical figures. The character of Kormlod (Irish Gormflaith) and her plan to have Brian killed correspond to the Irish sources. She was first married to Olaf Kvaran, Sigtrygg's father; her third marriage, which ended in divorce, was to King Brian, who died at Clontarf.

2. *Brian had a foster-son named Kerthjalfad . . . the bravest of men.* Kylfir is not otherwise known, but the three sons of Brian as well as Kerthjalfad (Irish Toirdhelbach) are known from Irish sources, where Kerthjalfad is Brian's grandson, the son of Margad. Ulf Hraeda's Norse name makes him an unlikely brother to Brian, but it has been suggested (by J. H. Lloyd, *New Ireland Review,* 1907, p. 52) that 'Ulf hraeda' is merely a corruption of 'Murchad', one of the sons of Brian. Working against this theory is the fact that the name 'Margad' in this passage must represent Murchad. Contrary to what the saga says, Kormlod was the mother of one of Brian's sons, Dungad (Donnchad).

Chapter 155

1. *The tables . . . were all covered in blood.* This scene resembles Ch. 118 of Snorri Sturluson's *Saga of Saint Olaf,* in which Asbjorn Sigurdarson comes to an island where King Olaf is celebrating and overhears Thorir Sel telling how Asbjorn held up when Thorir cleared his ship. 'Thorir said, "He held up pretty well, but when we took his sail he wept." And when Asbjorn heard this he drew his sword at once and rushed into the hall and swung at Thorir. The blow hit him on the neck; the head fell on the table in front of the king, and the body fell at his feet. The tablecloths were covered with blood, both above and below.'

2. *one of your followers:* Kari is referring to Helgi Njalsson.

3. *Flosi then took over . . . his account was trusted.* This scene must be understood in the light of the beginning of Ch. 130, where Gunnar Lambason leaped on the wall of the burning house, saw Skarphedin inside and asked if he were crying. Skarphedin denied that, but admitted that his eyes were smarting (from the smoke). Here the same Gunnar Lambason declares outright that Skarphedin was crying, and Kari cuts off his head for this. Flosi, though not

an eye-witness to that earlier scene, presents an unbiased version of what happened, and is believed because of his stature as a man of honour.

4. *King Sigtrygg promised him his mother and the kingdom*: The kingdom which Sigtrygg offers to Earl Sigurd along with his mother's hand – and later, with remarkable diplomacy, offers to Brodir – is the Norse kingdom of Dublin, of which Sigtrygg himself was king.

5. *Brodir*: Known in the Irish sources as Brodar, but Ospak (with his Norse name meaning 'Un-wise') is not known and might have been invented to provide a contrast with Brodir. Ospak is a pagan who recognizes the goodness of King Brian, refuses to fight him, and eventually joins him and is baptized – a typical Conversion narrative. Brodir on the other hand is a Christian, even a deacon, who becomes a pagan, fights against the saintly king and receives divine retribution.

Chapter 157

1. *together with Hrafn the Red ... what happened*: The names Hrafn the Red, Erling of Stroma and Harek are otherwise unknown. The mention of Harek in particular gives the impression that the author is working from another source which he abridged. The same can be said about the man on an apple-grey horse who appears a few lines later, a blind motif as it stands in this saga. One remembers perhaps the supernatural figure on a grey horse in Ch. 125, though the man who talks to Brodir and Kormlod here is likely to be an ordinary man.

2. *the army came out of the town ... in the centre*: The army that came out was the combined army of the Norse and Leinstermen. Dublin was a Norse city-state. According to Irish sources, Sigtrygg (Sitric) remained in the stronghold of Dublin during the battle.

3. *Brodir was then taken prisoner ... they were all pulled out of him*: The torture and killing of Brodir, an apostate Christian, recall the evisceration of two earlier apostates, Judas and Arian, as recorded in religious literature. See Thomas D. Hill, 'The Evisceration of Bróðir in "Brennu-Njáls saga"', *Traditio*, 37 (1981), pp. 337–44.

4. *these verses*: This poem usually goes by the name 'Darraðarljoð' (Song of Dorrud). Thomas Gray (1716–71) translated it as 'The Fatal Sisters', referring to the valkyries who sing the song and weave the fabric which corresponds to the battle of Clontarf (called 'Brian's battle' here). The poem is based on the similarities between weaving on a loom and fighting on a battlefield, and even the terminology is similar: the word 'shaft' in stanza 3, for example,

suggests both the heddle rod on a loom and a spear shaft. The valkyries are engaged in two activities simultaneously: weaving a fabric made of men's intestines and describing (even directing) the battle.

Chapter 158

1. *the eastern route*: By way of Switzerland and Germany.

Chapter 159

1. *the western route*: By way of France.

Plot Summary

The twin peaks of *Njal's Saga*, the death of Gunnar (Ch. 77) and the burning of Njal (Chs. 129–30), suggest a two-part division, and indeed it has been thought that the author worked with two main sources, now lost, a 'Gunnar's Saga' and a 'Njal's Saga'. Such a division is obvious and reasonable, and provides interesting parallels and contrasts, but does not do justice to the vastness and complexity of the saga, or to the fact that its two chief figures are not introduced until Chs. 19 and 20. Gunnar dies in Ch. 77, and Njal dies thirty chapters before the end of the saga. Other attempts to divide the saga have resulted in three sections (Gunnar's death, Njal's death, Kari's revenge) or as many as eleven. All such attempts are arbitrary, and in the summary analysis that follows the lines drawn attempt to follow the natural breaks, the rises and falls in the text.

Chs. 1–18 deal with three different narrative strands: Hrut's betrothal and marriage to Unn, and their divorce (Chs. 2, 6–8); Hrut's adventures abroad and his amorous encounter with Queen Gunnhild, who puts a spell on him which makes it impossible for him to satisfy his wife sexually (Chs. 2–6); and Hallgerd Hoskuldsdottir's first two marriages, one forced and unhappy, the other voluntary and happy, both of which end with the husband's death at the hands of her troublesome foster-father Thjostolf (Chs. 9–17). Hrut distinguishes himself as a splendid warrior abroad and a wise adviser to his hapless brother Hoskuld at home, but Unn and Hallgerd have a more far-reaching influence on the course of the saga. In the curiously split first chapter, these two women, one from the south and the other from the west of Iceland, are introduced and juxtaposed. Of Unn we learn merely that she is the daughter of the law expert Mord and that she is the best marriage prospect in the district. Of the young Hallgerd we learn that she has long hair and is beautiful – and has thief's eyes (an accurate prophecy, see Ch. 48). In the final chapter (18) of this group, the shortest in the saga, we learn that Unn's father Mord has died (this neatly balances his introduction in Ch. 1 and provides a frame for the section); his attempt to regain Unn's dowry has failed, and she quickly squanders the wealth she has inherited. The section thus ends with one divorced and impoverished woman and another woman who has, directly or indirectly, caused the deaths of two husbands.

Chs. 19–34 cover Gunnar Hamundarson's life up to and including his wedding. The introduction of new characters, Gunnar in Ch. 19 and Njal in Ch. 20, seems to mark a fresh beginning, but in fact – and this is typical of *Njála* – the apparent closure of the previous section was only a setting for further complications. Gunnar himself will advance the thwarted careers of both women. He aids his kinswoman Unn to regain her dowry from Hrut (Chs. 21–4), by employing an unnecessarily elaborate scheme devised by Njal, and when this legal approach fails, by challenging Hrut bluntly to a duel, just as Hrut had challenged Mord in Ch. 8. His success in regaining the dowry raises Unn's standing in the marriage market (though the saga does not say so), with immediate results: in Ch. 25 a 'devious and unpopular man' named Valgard comes into the saga and marries her. Of their son Mord it is said that 'he will be in this saga for a long time' and that 'he was bad to his kinsman, and to Gunnar worst of all'. This comes as harsh irony after the conclusion of the previous chapter, when Gunnar took no payment from Unn but stated that he would count on support from her and her kinsmen. In another of the harsh juxtapositions of which the author is fond, the rest of Ch. 25 and Chs. 26–7 introduce Njal's sons and describes the marriages arranged for them, as if to say that the Njalssons as well as Gunnar will be the objects of Mord Valgardsson's malice. And so it proves.

The journey abroad of Gunnar and his brother Kolskegg (Chs. 29–31) is the perfect model of its type: Gunnar wins not one but two sea battles against Vikings and is favourably received by two rulers, in Norway and in Denmark. But like other journeys abroad in this saga, it leads to trouble at home: in the fateful meeting at the Althing (Ch. 33), Gunnar's newly acquired fame and splendour attract the eye of Hallgerd, and they become engaged – quite against the wishes of Njal, who predicts that 'Every kind of evil will come from her when she moves east.' The wedding takes place in Ch. 34 and is remarkable for two things: (1) The seating arrangement, with Gunnar flanked on one side by the Sigfussons (his mother's brothers) and others who will plague him, and on the other side by Njal and his sons – this foreshadows later disaster, in particular the clash between the Njalssons and the Sigfussons; (2) the unexpected interruption when Thrain Sigfusson divorces his wife and becomes engaged to Hallgerd's daughter (by her second marriage), Thorgerd Glumsdottir.

Chs. 34–45, beginning with Bergthora's pointed insult to Hallgerd at a feast at Bergthorshvol, tell of six reciprocal killings of members of the households at Hlidarendi (Gunnar's home) and at Bergthorshvol, prompted by the two wives and carried out while their husbands are away at the annual Althing. Hallgerd initiates the killings, and Bergthora takes vengeance, and the stakes become higher and higher, the last pair of victims being the beloved foster-father of the Njalssons, Thord, and a kinsman of Gunnar's named Sigmund. At the last stage, after Sigmund has killed Thord and exacerbated matters by composing verses (at the prompting of Hallgerd) which question the manhood of Njal and his sons, the Njalssons themselves take vengeance, killing both Sigmund and his companion Skjold. The killings put an increasing strain on the friendship between Gunnar and Njal, but impressively in each case the one whose wife caused the killing offers 'self-judgement' to the other (allowing him to fix the amount to be paid in compensation), and they remain friends. Ch. 45 concludes this murderous feud with the announcement that Njal and Gunnar agreed that they would always resolve any difficulty that should arise – but there is still Hallgerd to deal with, and people less well-disposed than Njal.

Chs. 46–81. Chs. 46–7 again mark a new beginning, with the introduction of new characters: the prominent Gizur the White and Geir the Godi, their wealthy but unimpressive kinsman Otkel, and Otkel's shameless friend Skammkel (the first element of his name is homonymous with the word for 'shame'). For good measure we are also reminded of the lurking presence of Mord Valgardsson and his envy of Gunnar. The whole of Chs. 46–81, leading to the death of Gunnar and concluding with the vengeance taken for him, may be taken as a single section, but the quasi-conclusions and new characters along the way give grounds for dividing it into sub-sections.

Chs. 46–51: A food shortage forces Gunnar to offer to buy hay and food from Otkel, but he – following the malicious prompting of Skammkel – refuses him. Never one to endure a slight, Hallgerd sends a slave Melkolf, whom Gunnar had bought from Otkel, to steal butter and cheese from Otkel and burn down his shed. He does so, but inadvertently leaves his knife alongside a river on his return to Hlidarendi. When Gunnar learns of the theft, he slaps Hallgerd in the presence of guests. Otkel and Skammkel ask Mord to look into the matter, and with a bit of detective work Mord discovers that the theft was instigated by Hallgerd. Gunnar makes generous offers of compensation, but Skammkel sees to it that he is refused, wilfully misrepresenting the opinions of Gizur and Geir on the subject and advising Otkel to serve a summons for theft on Gunnar. When Skammkel's lie is exposed, Gizur and Geir manage to make peace with Gunnar by offering him self-judgement, 'and for a while everything was quiet'.

In Chs. 52–6 more characters, allies of Otkel, are introduced, and on a journey east Otkel's horse runs out of control and Otkel accidentally rides towards Gunnar while he is sowing grain in his field, striking him on the ear with his spur. Gunnar, already offended by the summons, now takes further offence, and Skammkel makes things even worse by claiming that Gunnar wept when he was struck by Otkel's spur. Gunnar and his brother Kolskegg attack Otkel and his party on their return from the east, and kill all eight of them in a battle by the Ranga river (Ch. 54). Geir the Godi brings charges of manslaughter against Gunnar at the Althing, but at Njal's urging the matter is submitted to arbitration. Gunnar pays the fee levied against him by the arbitrators, and comes away from the affair with honour.

Chs. 57–66. More new characters: Starkad of Thrihyrning and Egil of Sandgil, each with three aggressive sons. Gunnar is lured into a horse fight, his horse against Starkad's, at which his horse's eye is put out by Thorgeir Starkadarson and Kol Egilsson. Gunnar and Kolskegg and a third brother, Hjort, are ambushed at Knafaholar by the men of Thrihyrning and Sandgil; they kill fourteen of the attackers, but Hjort is slain and buried in a mound at Hlidarendi. In the ensuing lawsuit Njal advises Gunnar and Mord advises his opponents; the matter is put up to arbitration, and once again Gunnar pays compensation and comes away with his honour enhanced.

Chs. 67–77 round off this series of provocations, clashes and settlements. Njal had prophesied to Gunnar in Ch. 55 that if he ever killed two members of the same family it would lead to his death. He has already killed Otkel, and now Mord, who has learned of this prophecy, conspires with Thorgeir Starkadarson to see to it that Gunnar kills Otkel's son Thorgeir. Thorgeir Starkadarson feigns friendship with Thorgeir Otkelsson and persuades him to attack Gunnar. Their first attempt is thwarted by Njal, who arranges an arbitrated settlement by which the Thorgeirs have to pay Gunnar for the attempt on his life. But they try again and ambush Gunnar and Kolskegg along the Ranga river, and this time achieve the desired effect: Gunnar kills Thorgeir Otkelsson. The killing is arbitrated at the Althing, and Gunnar and Kolskegg are to go abroad for three years. Njal warns him against breaking the settlement, and Gunnar promises not to, but in the most celebrated scene in the saga (Ch. 75), the departing Gunnar looks back at his farm Hlidarendi, comments on its beauty, and decides to return home, alone. Kolskegg goes abroad and never returns. The mass attack at Hlidarendi inevitably follows. When Gunnar's bowstring breaks and he asks Hallgerd for two locks of her hair to replace it, she recalls the slap on the cheek (Ch. 48) and refuses. He is finally overcome, largely out of sheer exhaustion.

Chs. 78–81 form the aftermath to the killing of Gunnar. Njal admits that since Gunnar died as an outlaw, no legal action is possible. Skarphedin Njalsson and Hogni Gunnarsson, goaded by the sight of the slain Gunnar sitting in his burial mound and chanting a verse about not yielding, execute blood vengeance against Starkad and his son Thorgeir and two others. With Njal's aid, these killings are arbitrated at a district assembly. The statements that Geir the Godi and Hogni Gunnarsson are 'now out of the saga' mark an ending to the Gunnar section of the saga.

Chs. 82–94 cover the parallel and then converging adventures abroad of Thrain Sigfusson and two of the Njalssons, Helgi and Grim, and the consequences back in Iceland. Thrain is well received by Earl Hakon of Norway because of his close kinship with Gunnar of Hlidarendi, and in Gunnar's fashion he defeats a Viking force at sea (Gunnar, though, won *two* sea battles against Vikings). The journey of Grim and Helgi is more perilous: they have bad weather and are attacked by Vikings. But just when the fight looks hopeless they are aided by a fleet of ships led by Kari Solmundarson, whose sudden appearance in Ch. 84 is surely the most glorious introduction of a character in the saga. Kari takes Grim and Helgi to Earl Sigurd of Orkney, and they become his followers and help him against enemies in Scotland. Another Icelander, called Killer-Hrapp, has a different kind of voyage abroad: he leaves Iceland because he has killed a man, he cheats his skipper out of payment, he seduces the daughter of his host Gudbrand of Dalarna and he burns down a temple owned jointly by Gudbrand and Earl Hakon. The earl declares him an outlaw and puts a price on his head. The three voyages intersect when Hrapp flees to Lade (the earl's seat, close to Trondheim), where both Thrain and the Njalssons are preparing to set sail. Thrain betrays his loyalty to Earl Hakon by concealing Hrapp on his ship, and he sails away, leaving Grim and Helgi to bear the brunt of the earl's anger, from which they barely escape with their lives. Again, Kari helps them, and on their return to Iceland Kari marries their sister Helga. Hrapp, on the other hand, spends most of his time with Hallgerd, Gunnar's widow.

The Njalssons make vain attempts to obtain redress from Thrain for his treatment of them in Norway, but all they receive are insults, including the same derogatory epithets from Hallgerd as in Ch. 44 when she dubbed Njal

'Old Beardless' and his sons 'Dung-beardlings'. This inevitably leads to an attack on Thrain and his party as they return from a visit in the east (reminiscent of Ch. 54) and the most memorable killing in the saga, when Skarphedin splits Thrain's head with his axe while skimming by him on the ice at the edge of the Ranga river (Ch. 92). Njal makes a settlement with Ketil of Mork for the slaying, and in addition offers to foster Thrain's son, Hoskuld Thrainsson.

Chs. 95–97 bring the last of the chief players on the stage, the formidable chieftain Flosi Thordarson, his niece Hildigunn Starkadardottir and his father-in-law Hall of Sida. Njal tries to arrange a marriage between his foster-son Hoskuld Thrainsson and Hildigunn, but she declines on the grounds that Hoskuld is not a godi. Njal responds (quite contrary to the historical record) by persuading the lawspeaker Skafti Thoroddsson and the Law Council to establish a court of appeal, the Fifth Court, for which new godis will be needed, and he arranges for Hoskuld to be one of them. The suit for Hildigunn's hand is brought up again; this time she agrees, and the wedding feast is held. Hildigunn and Hoskuld settle at Ossabaer, not far from Bergthorshvol.

Chs. 98–9 and Ch. 106 illustrate how legal settlements never settle things. Lyting, married to the sister of Thrain Sigfusson, feels dissatisfied because he was not included in the settlement for Thrain (in fact he was not so entitled) and takes blood revenge, killing the illegitimate son of Njal, Hoskuld Njalsson. Hoskuld's mother Hrodny transports the body to Njal and asks Skarphedin to take vengeance. Skarphedin and his brothers attack Lyting and his brothers and kill the brothers, but Lyting escapes. Hoskuld Thrainsson comes to Njal with an offer of self-judgement, and Njal accepts two hundred ounces in silver for the slaying of Hoskuld. In Ch. 106 Hoskuld Njalsson's blind son Amundi comes to Lyting's booth at a local assembly to ask for compensation. Lyting refuses, and Amundi miraculously gains his sight long enough to kill him.

Chs. 100–105 contain an account of the Conversion of Iceland, coinciding in many ways with Ari's *Book of the Icelanders* and *Kristni saga* (The Saga of Christianity). Chs. 100–103 tell of the sometimes violent preaching mission of a Saxon named Thangbrand sent out by King Olaf Tryggvason. Hall of Sida is the first to be converted, and Njal is another who accepts the new faith. But Thangbrand returns to Norway and tells King Olaf of the hostility he faced, and the king is so angry that he plans to kill all the Icelanders within his reach. Gizur the White and Hjalti Skeggjason, however, offer to go out to Iceland and spread the faith. The climax comes at the Althing in Ch. 105, when a battle seems likely, but Hall of Sida, speaking for the Christians, asks a pagan godi,

Thorgeir of Ljosavatn, to make the decision. After lying with a cloak over his head for a whole day, Thorgeir proclaims that there must be one faith – the Christian faith – and the dispute is settled peaceably.

Chs. 107–23 begin with the return of Valgard the Grey, Mord's father, to Iceland. He astutely sizes up the changed political situation – the new godi Hoskuld Thrainsson has diminished the power of Mord's godord – and proposes as a remedy that Mord spread slander between the Njalssons and Hoskuld which will lead to the slaying of Hoskuld. Mord does as his father advises, and is successful: in Ch. 111 the Njalssons, together with Kari and Mord, slay Hoskuld while he (like Gunnar in Ch. 53) is sowing grain in his field. Hoskuld offers no resistance and dies saying 'May God help me and forgive you.' Njal is so grief-stricken at the news that he says he would rather have lost two of his sons than Hoskuld, and he predicts that the slaying will lead to his death and that of his wife and all his sons.

The duplicitous Mord initiates legal proceedings against the Njalssons, calculating that when it is revealed that he inflicted one of the wounds, the case will be invalidated. Flosi sets out for the Althing with a large force of men and stops at Ossabaer, the home of his widowed niece Hildigunn. In one of the most emotional scenes in this saga and the best goading scene in all the sagas (Ch. 116), Hildigunn places on Flosi's shoulders the bloody cloak in which Hoskuld was slain and charges him to accept nothing less than blood vengeance. At the Althing the Njalssons, with the help of Asgrim Ellida-Grimsson, enlist the support of Gizur the White, Gudmund the Powerful of Modruvellir in the north, and Gudmund's brother Einar of Thvera. Other men whose booths they visit, however, refuse to give their support (Chs. 119–20).

When Thorhall Asgrimsson, on the side of his foster-father Njal, declares the suit invalid because of Mord's involvement in the slaying, Njal seeks for an arbitrated settlement. Flosi agrees, and each side chooses six arbitrators; their decision is that the compensation for the death of Hoskuld Thrainsson should be six hundred ounces of silver (three times the normal amount). Njal and his sons collect the money and bring it to the Law Council, and Njal places a robe and a pair of boots on top of the money. Flosi arrives, and in a scene of great tension – he senses an insult in Njal's gifts – asks who placed the robe there. No reply. He asks again. Skarphedin asks him who he thinks might be responsible, and Flosi explodes with a vile insult to Njal, calling him by the ugly and well-worn epithet 'Old Beardless'. Skarphedin, who showed himself a master of insults in Chs. 119–20 when they were seeking help, accuses Flosi of being 'the sweetheart of the troll at Svinafell' – and all hopes for peace are ended.

In **Chs. 124–30** Flosi gathers a hundred men to attack the Njalssons at home, vowing that 'we'll ride to Bergthorshvol in full force and attack the Njalssons with fire and iron, and not leave until they're all dead' (Ch. 124). The atmosphere is laden with portents: an old woman at Bergthorshvol curses a pile of chickweed, saying that it will eventually be ignited to burn Njal in his house (Ch. 124); a man named Hildiglum has a vision of a man as black as pitch setting fire to mountains by throwing a torch (Ch. 125); Njal himself has a vision of the destruction of the hall (Ch. 127). When Flosi and his men arrive, Njal has his sons go inside even though their chances are better outside, and in spite of Skarphedin's prediction that Flosi will use fire. After some heavy fighting Flosi realizes that he will indeed have to resort to fire. He offers the women and children and Njal free exit, and most leave, but Njal and Bergthora and Kari's son Thord remain inside and lie down together. The others continue the fight. In the fire eleven members of the household die; Helgi Njalsson is beheaded by Flosi as he tries to escape dressed as a woman. Unsuspected by the other side, and to their great dismay when they hear of it, Kari Solmundarson makes his escape in the smoke.

Chs. 131–45. The first chapters (131–7) describe the gathering of forces for an unsuccessful attempt to hunt down Flosi, Flosi's enlistment of support (Ch. 134), and preparations for the forthcoming legal contest at the Althing. There are two interludes, the removal of the burned bodies in Ch. 132 (those of Njal and Bergthora and the boy Thord are miraculously unburned) and Flosi's dream in Ch. 133. In Ch. 138, at the Althing, Flosi enlists the legal services of Eyjolf Bolverksson, 'one of the three greatest lawyers in Iceland', and pays him with a gold bracelet. On the other side, Mord has taken over the prosecution from Thorgeir Skorargeir (Njal's nephew), and he is to be assisted by the Njal-trained Thorhall Asgrimsson, confined to his booth with an infected leg. In Chs. 139–40 Gizur the White gains support from Snorri the Godi and Gudmund the Powerful against the men who burned Bergthorshvol.

The legal procedures themselves begin with long and repetitive recitations of legal formulas – caviar to the general – followed by a strenuous to-and-fro argument about the validity of the panel chosen to reach a preliminary finding, with Mord sending a messenger to Thorhall for advice in each case. When Mord and Thorhall have finally won their point, Eyjolf pulls his trick: Flosi has secretly become a thingman of a godi from the north, which means that the case has been prosecuted in the wrong quarter court (Ch. 143). Thorhall's response is to summon Flosi and Eyjolf for having given and received payment for legal services. They present this charge before the Fifth Court, as is proper, since it involves violation of Althing procedure.

But then Eyjolf tricks them into overlooking a technicality, one that was spelled out by Njal when he proposed the Fifth Court in Ch. 97 – that the number of judges must be reduced from forty-eight to thirty-six before a judgement can be rendered. When Thorhall hears about this (beginning of Ch. 145) he is so angry that he drives his spear into his leg to let the infection flow out, makes his way to the Fifth Court and kills the first man on Flosi's side that he meets, a kinsman of Flosi. Thus begins the greatest full-scale battle of the saga, ironically at a hallowed place where men were forbidden to fight.

Chs. 145–59. After the battle, Ch. 145 continues with efforts at peace initiated by the ever-temperate Hall of Sida. He persuades Snorri the Godi to head an arbitration panel of twelve men, who deliver verdicts on compensation and punishment. Flosi is to leave the country for three years, and some of the others responsible for the burning (henceforth referred to as 'the burners') for life. Kari and Thorgeir Skorargeir refuse to be party to the agreement, but after a time, when they have killed five of the burners, Thorgeir agrees to a settlement with Flosi (Ch. 147). Kari, whose son Thord was uncompensated after being burned at Bergthorshvol, continues his course of vengeance alone, except for the company of the blustering Bjorn the White (Chs. 148–52), whose presence offers welcome comic relief. At the end of Ch. 152 Kari tells Thorgeir that thirteen of the burners have been killed (see note 1 to Ch. 152) and that he plans to kill two more. He does this abroad, killing Gunnar Lambason in Orkney (Ch. 155) and Kol Thorsteinsson in Wales (Ch. 158), both by sudden decapitation. For the first killing he incurs the wrath of Earl Sigurd, until Flosi speaks up for him and says 'he did what he had to do'.

Chs. 154–7 contains an Icelandic version of the battle of Clontarf (called 'Brian's battle' in the saga), fought outside Dublin on Good Friday 1014, between the Christian King Brian and heathen forces led by Earl Sigtrygg of Dublin. Its relevance to the story of *Njal's Saga* is slight, apart from the fact that Earl Sigurd of Orkney died on the heathen side, along with fifteen of the burners. The account of the battle, in which Brian fell but his enemies were defeated, is followed by a number of miraculous visions in different northern countries, the most famous of which is the *Song of Dorrud*. The only long poem in the saga (eleven stanzas), it tells of a man named Dorrud at Caithness, witnessing through a window the weaving of a bloody web (signifying the battle) by twelve valkyries.

The final two chapters (158–9) return to a more sober world and record the pilgrimages to Rome undertaken by Flosi, and then by Kari. Two years after Flosi returned to his farm at Svinafell, Kari sails to Iceland and is shipwrecked at Ingolfshofdi. He and his men walk from there to Svinafell, where there is instant reconciliation between the two opponents. As a seal of the reconciliation, Kari, whose wife Helga Njalsdottir had died, marries Flosi's niece Hildigunn, whose first husband Hoskuld had fallen under the blows of the Njalssons and Kari.

Veidilausa
Kaldbak
Kaldbakshorn
Svanshol (Svan)
Hunafloi
Ljotardal
Bjarnarfjord

Steingrimsfjord

Hagi
(Gest Oddleifsson)

Reykjanes

Hrutafjord

Bjarneyjar

Breidafjord

Laxardal heath

Hjardarholt (Olaf Peacock)
Laxardal
Hoskuldsstadir (Hoskuld)
Thrandargil
Hrutsstadir
Haukadal
(Hrut)

Holtavarda heath

Nordurardal

Hvita river

Varmalaek (Glum)
Lund
Reykjadal
Skorradal

Faxafloi bay

Borgarfjord

Engey
Laugarnes
(Hallgerd)

▨	600 m
▤	300 m
☐	0

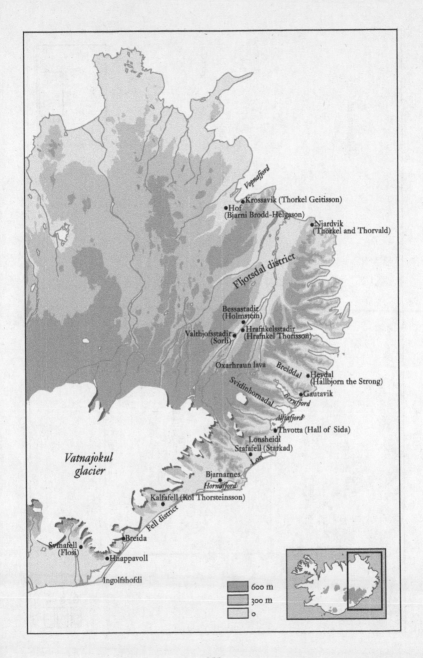

Vopnafjord

Krossavik (Thorkel Geitisson)
Hof
(Bjarni Brodd-Helgason)
Njardvik
(Thorkel and Thorvald)

Fljotsdal district

Bessastadir
(Holmstein)
Valthjofsstadir
(Sorli)
Hrafnkelsstadir
(Hrafnkel Thorisson)

Oxarhraun lava
Breiddal
Svidinhornadal
Heydal
(Hallbjorn the Strong)
Berufjord
Gautavik

Alftafjord
Thvotta (Hall of Sida)

Lonsheidi
Stafafell (Starkad)

Vatnajokul
glacier

Lon

Bjarnarnes
Hornafjord
Kalfafell (Kol Thorsteinsson)

Fell district

Svinafell
(Flosi)
Breida
Hnappavoll

Ingolfshofdi

600 m
300 m
0

355

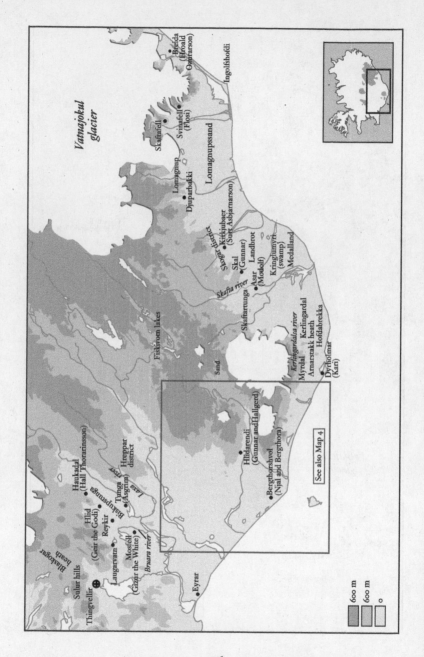

Vatnajökul glacier

Breida (Hroald Özurarson)

Ingólfshöfdi

Svínafell (Flosi)

Skaftafell

Lomagnup
Djúparbakki

Lomagnupssand

Skogar district
Kirkjubaer (Surt Asbjarnarson)
Skal (Gunnar)
Asar Landbrot (Modolf)
Kringlumyrt (swamp)
Medalland

Skafta river

Skaftartunga

Kerlingardalsa river
Myrdal Kerlingardal
Amarstakk heath
Hofdabrekka
Dyrhólmar (Kari)

Fiskivotn lakes

Sand

Hildarendi (Gunnar and Hallgerd)

See also Map 4

Bergthorshvol (Njal and Bergthora)

Haukadal (Hall Thorarinsson)
Hreppar district
Hlíd (Geir the Godi)
Reykir
Tunga
Bishopstunga
Ásgrím
Laxa river

Biaskogar heath
Sulur hills
Thingvellir
Laugarvatn
Mosfell (Gizur the White)
Bruara river

Eyrar

600 m
600 m
0

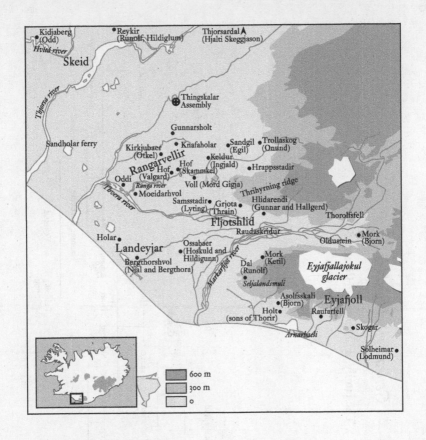

Genealogical Tables

1. The family of Gunnar of Hlidarendi

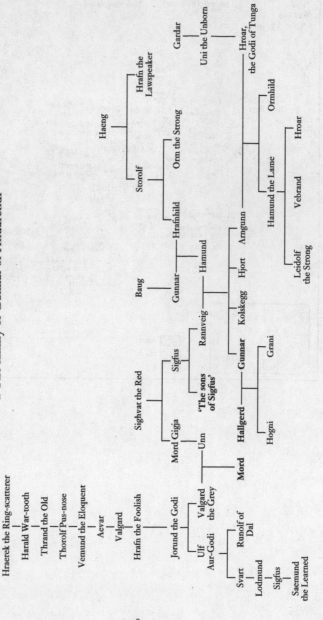

2. The sons of Sigfus

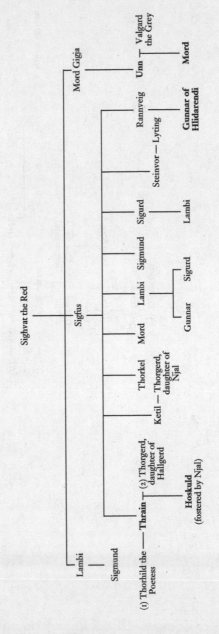

359

3. Hallgerd's family

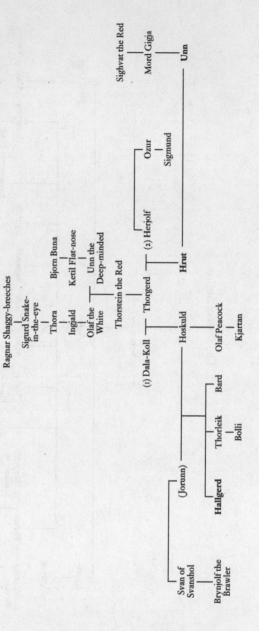

4. The Family of Njal and Bergthora

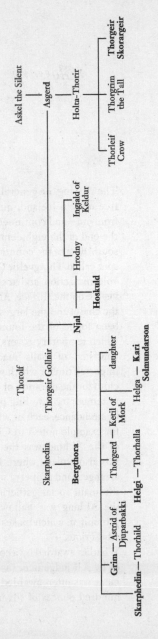

Glossary

Althing

The Althing, or general Thing (assembly) of all the free men in Iceland, met for two weeks every June from 930 – and continued in some form or other until the end of the eighteenth century. It was held in the south-west of the country at a spectacularly beautiful spot called Thingvellir ('assembly plains'), shaped by volcanic action and tectonic forces whose effect is visible on the surface. At the meeting place, between the chasm and the largest lake in Iceland, traces have been found of the foundation walls of booths, over which temporary covers could be raised. The booths consisted of walls made of turf and stone and imported timber which were covered with homespun cloth for the duration of the Althing in order to serve as temporary dwelling places for the various groups in attendance, each of which had its own booth – see for example note 2 to Ch. 136. The primary business of the Althing was the settling of disputes, but it was also a place where friends met, marriages were arranged, and property was exchanged. It was in effect the main social gathering of the year. The site of the Althing was hallowed, and fighting there was prohibited, which makes the battle in Ch. 145 especially serious.

compensation

Whether awarded by a court or by a mutual arbitrator or by self-judgement (as in Chs. 36–45), a cash payment was often awarded to the offended party. One hundred ounces of silver was normal compensation in the sagas and was the amount paid for Atli in Ch. 38 and Brynjolf in Ch. 40. In this saga, however, two hundred ounces seems to be the norm; see the payments for Thord Freed-man's son (Ch. 43) and Hoskuld Njalsson (Ch. 99), as well as the statement in Ch. 123 that the payment for the slaying of Hoskuld Thrainsson is to be 'triple compensation ... six hundred ounces of silver'. One character in the saga, Ljot Hallsson, gets fourfold compensation, specified as eight hundred ounces (Ch. 145); in this unusual case the money comes from voluntary contributions after Ljot's father, Hall of Sida, renounces any claim to compensation in order to bring about peace after the battle at the Althing.

duel   The Icelandic word *hólmganga* means 'going to the island', probably because the area prescribed for the fight formed a small 'island' with clearly defined boundaries; it might also refer to the fact that small islands were originally favoured sites for duels. The rules stipulated that the two duellists strike blows in turns, the seconds protecting the principal fighters with shields. Shields hacked to pieces could be replaced up to three times. If blood was shed, the fight could be ended, and the wounded man could buy himself off for three marks. No duels are fought in *Njal's Saga*, but two challenges to a duel are made, and refused (Chs. 8 and 24).

Fifth Court   Around 1005 a Fifth Court was established as a kind of court of appeal to hear cases which were unresolved by the quarter courts. Details of the court's constitution and functions are described accurately in Ch. 97, but both the time (before rather than after the Conversion in the year 1000) and the person responsible (Njal rather than Skafti Thoroddsson) are out of accord with other historical sources.

foster-child/parent   Children were often brought up by foster-parents, who received either payment or support in return. Fosterage was thus important as a form of alliance, though fostered children were part of the family circle and the emotional bonds could be very strong,

as between Njal and his foster-son Hoskuld Thrainsson. The term 'foster-' was also used for the relationship between household servants and the children
they helped to raise. *Njála* has two such foster-fathers,
the homicidal Thjostolf who brought up Hallgerd
(Chs. 9–17) and the beloved Thord Freed-man's son
who brought up the Njalssons (Chs. 39–42).

full outlawry   Outlawry for life, permanent outlawry. One of the
terms applied to a man sentenced to full outlawry
was *skógarmaður*, which means literally 'forest man',
even though in Iceland there was scant possibility of
his taking refuge in a forest. Full outlawry simply
meant banishment from civilized society. It also
meant the confiscation of the outlaw's property to pay
the prosecutor, cover debts and sometimes provide an
allowance for the dependants he had left behind. A
full outlaw, according to the formula in this saga, was
'not to be fed, nor helped on his way, nor given any
kind of assistance'. He had lost all goods, and all
rights. Wherever he went he could be killed without
legal redress. According to one legal codex from
Norway, it was 'as if he were dead'.

godi   (Icelandic *goði*) A local chieftain who had legal and
administrative responsibilities in Iceland. It was a
unique office, without precedent in Norway or exact
parallel elsewhere. The origin of the office may lie in
pagan religious duties, as the name (related to 'god')
seems to indicate, but as time went on the godi's
role became mainly secular. There were originally
thirty-six godis, and after the division of the country
into quarters in 965 there were thirty-nine; nine more
were added when the Fifth Court was established.
The godis were responsible for convening local
assemblies (three in each quarter, four in the North
Quarter) and were obliged to attend the Althing,
where they appointed members of the quarter courts
and sat on the Law Council. The first godis were
chosen from the leading families who settled Iceland
between 870 and 930. Neither Gunnar nor Njal is a
godi, though they are prosperous farmers.

godord   The authority and rank of a godi, including his social and legal responsibilities towards his thingmen. A godord could be sold or inherited or divided or temporarily loaned out; it was not an elective office.

halberd   (Icelandic *atgeirr*) The weapon seems to have resembled a halberd, even though no specimens of this combination of spear and axe have been found in archaeological excavations in Iceland. Gunnar's halberd, the only one in this saga, has magical powers (see Ch. 30).

hersir   A local leader in western and northern Norway; his rank was hereditary. It is likely that the hersirs were originally those who took command when the men of the district were called to arms.

homespun   For centuries wool and wool products were Iceland's chief exports, especially in the form of strong and durable homespun cloth. It could be bought and sold in bolts or made up into items such as homespun cloaks. There were strict regulations on homespun, as it was used as a standard exchange product and often referred to in ounces, meaning its equivalent value expressed as a weight in silver. See notes 1 and 2 to Ch. 2.

horse-fight   A popular sport among the Icelanders, which seems to have been practised especially in the autumn. Two horses were goaded to fight against each other until one was killed or ran away. Understandably, emotions ran high, and horse-fights commonly led to feuds, as in Ch. 59.

hundred   A 'long hundred' or one hundred and twenty, reflecting the early custom of counting by twelve rather than by ten. The expression, however, rarely refers to an accurate number, rather a generalized 'round' figure.

Law Council   The legislative assembly at the Althing made up of the godis, for the purpose of reviewing and passing legislation.

Law Rock   The raised spot on the slope at the Althing at Thingvellir, where the lawspeaker is thought to have recited the law code, and where public announcements and speeches were made.

lawspeaker   The Icelandic word *lögsögumaður* means literally 'the man who recites the law', referring to the time before the advent of writing when the lawspeaker had to learn the law by heart and recite one-third of it every year. If he was unsure about the text, he had to consult a team of five or more 'lawmen' who knew the law well. The lawspeaker presided over the assembly at the Althing and was responsible for the preservation and clarification of legal tradition. He could exert influence but was in no sense the ruler of the country.

lesser outlawry   This differed from full outlawry in that the lesser outlaw was only banished from society for three years. Furthermore, his land was not confiscated, and money was put aside to support his family, which made it possible for him to return later and continue a normal life. When leaving the country he was allowed to stop at three farms on a direct route to the ship which would take him abroad. Anywhere else he was fair game and could be killed without redress. He had to leave the country and begin his sentence within three summers after the verdict, but once abroad he regained normal rights.

panel   A kind of jury that delivered a verdict on the facts, motives and/or circumstances behind a case. They were not as important as witnesses, but could still carry a great deal of weight, especially if there were no witnesses to a particular action. The panels were composed of 'neighbours' to the scene of the incident or the home of the accused. Nine-man panels were called for more serious cases, five-man for less important ones. The verdict was by majority decision.

quarter   Administratively, Icelandic was divided into four quarters based on the four cardinal directions.

Quarter Court   Four quarter courts were established at the Althing in *c.* 965. The godis appointed thirty-six men to each of the quarter courts, whose decisions had to be unanimous.

self-judgement   To grant self-judgement is a legal procedure in which – in lieu of third-party arbitration – the offender allows the offended person himself the right to determine the amount of compensation to be paid.

shieling
A roughly constructed hut in the highland grazing pastures away from the farm, where shepherds and cowherds lived during the summer. Milking and the preparation of various dairy products took place here, as did other important farm activities like the collection of peat and charcoal burning.

Spring Assembly
The local assembly, held each spring. There were thirteen in all and they were the first regular assemblies to be held in Iceland. Lasting four to seven days between 7 and 27 May, they were jointly supervised by three godis. The Spring Assembly had both a legal and an economic function. It included a court of thirty-six men, twelve appointed by each of the godis, where local legal actions were heard, while major cases and those which could not be resolved locally were sent on to the Althing. In its other function it was a forum for settling debts, deciding prices and the like. Godis probably used the Spring Assembly to urge their followers to ride to the Althing. There were also autumn gatherings at the same locations.

Thing
See Althing.

thingman/men
Every free man and landowner was required to serve as a thingman ('assembly man') by aligning himself with a godi. He would either accompany the godi to assemblies and other functions or pay a tax to cover the costs of those attending. A man was not obliged to be the thingman of the nearest godi, and he could change his allegiance whenever he wished. This option becomes the basis of a legal ruse devised by Eyjolf Bolverksson in Ch. 141 and employed by him, without success, in Ch. 143. See also Ch. 107, n. 1.

Index of Characters

This index lists all the characters in Njal's Saga except those who appear only in genealogies. Kings and earls and certain key figures from the saga world are included, as well as the gods named in the verses. The index follows the Icelandic naming convention of the patronymic (-*son* or -*dottir*). Most names of fathers take the ending -*s* or -*ar* before being combined into patronymics (*Njalsson, Starkadarson*) while those ending in -*i* change this to -*a* (*Helgason*). Nicknames are included and many characters are also identified by their place of residence, status or relation to important figures in the saga. The name of the father is included in parentheses after the patronymic where clarification is useful, either because several characters bear the same name (e.g. *Hoskuld*) or when the name undergoes a vowel change when combined (e.g. *Mord*, but *Mardardottir*).

THE ILIAD

Homer

'Look at me. I am the son of a great man. A goddess was my
mother. Yet death and inexorable destiny are waiting for me'

One of the foremost achievements in Western literature, Homer's
Iliad tells the story of the darkest episode in the Trojan War. At
its centre is Achilles, the greatest warrior-champion of the Greeks,
and his refusal to fight after being humiliated by his leader
Agamemnon. But when the Trojan Hector kills Achilles' close
friend Patroclus, he storms back into battle to take revenge –
although knowing this will ensure his own early death. Interwoven
with this tragic sequence of events are powerfully moving descriptions of the ebb and flow of battle, of the domestic world inside
Troy's besieged city of Ilium and of the conflict between the gods
on Olympus as they argue over the fate of mortals.

Originally translated by E. V. Rieu
Revised and updated by Peter Jones with D. C. H. Rieu
Edited with an introduction and notes by Peter Jones

ISBN: 978 0 14 044 794 1

THE ODYSSEY

Homer

'I long to reach my home and see the day of my return. It is my
never-failing wish'

The epic tale of Odysseus and his ten-year journey home after the
Trojan War forms one of the earliest and greatest works of Western
literature. Confronted by natural and supernatural threats – ship-
wrecks, battles, monsters and the implacable enmity of the sea-god
Poseidon – Odysseus must test his bravery and native cunning to
the full if he is to reach his homeland safely and overcome the
obstacles that, even there, await him.

E. V. Rieu's translation of *The Odyssey* was the very first Penguin
Classic to be published, and has itself achieved classic status. For
this edition, Rieu's text has been sensitively revised and a new
introduction added to complement his orignial introduction.

Translated by E. V. Rieu
Revised translation by D. C. H. Rieu
with an introduction by Peter Jones

ISBN: 978 0 14 044 911 2

THE SONGS OF THE SOUTH

An Ancient Chinese Anthology of Poems by Qu Yuan and Other Poets

'From of old things have always been the same:
Why should I complain of the men of today?'

Chu chi (*The Songs of the South*) and its northern counterpart, *Shi jing*, are the two great ancestors of Chinese poetry and contain all we know of its ancient beginnings. *The Songs of the South* is an anthology first complied in the second century AD. Its poems, originating from the state of Chu and rooted in Shamanism, are grouped under seventeen titles. The earliest poems were composed in the fourth century BC and almost half of them are traditionally ascribed to Qu Yuan. Covering subjects ranging from heaven to love, work to growing old, regret to longing, they give a penetrating insight into the world of ancient China, and into the origins of poetry itself.

Translated with an Introduction and Notes by David Hawkes

ISBN: 978 0 14 119 870 5

THE AENEID

Virgil

'Some of us looked in awed wonder at that massive horse ...
which was to be our destruction'

Aeneas the True – son of Venus and of a mortal father – escapes
from Troy after it is sacked by the conquering Greeks. He undergoes many trials and adventures on a long sea journey, from a
doomed love affair in Carthage with the tragic Queen Dido to a
sojourn in the underworld. All the way, the hero is tormented by
the meddling of the vengeful Juno, Queen of the Gods and a bitter
enemy of Troy, but his mother and other gods protect Aeneas from
despair and remind him of his ultimate destiny – to found the
great city of Rome. Reflecting the Roman peoples' great interest
in the 'myth' of their origins, Virgil (70–19 BCE) made the story
of Aeneas glow with a new light in his majestic epic.

Translated with an introduction by W. F. Jackson Knight

ISBN: 978 0 14 044932 7

METAMORPHOSES

Ovid

'Her soft white bosom was ringed in a layer of bark, her hair was
turned into foliage, her arms into branches'

Ovid's sensuous and witty poems brings together a dazzling array
of mythological tales, ingeniously linked by the idea of transfor-
mation – often as a result of love or lust – where men and women
find themselves magically changed into new and sometimes extraor-
dinary beings. Beginning with the creation of the world and ending
with the deification of Augustus, Ovid interweaves many of the
best-known myths and legends of ancient Greece and Rome, including Daedalus and Icarus, Pyramus and Thisbe, Pygmalion, Perseus
and Andromeda, and the fall of Troy. Erudite but light-hearted,
dramatic and yet playful, the *Metamorphoses* has influenced writers and artists throughout the centuries from Shakespeare and
Titian to Picasso and Ted Hughes.

A new Verse Translation by David Raeburn
with an Introduction by Dennis Feeney

ISBN: 978 0 14 044 789 7

THE AGE OF ALEXANDER

Plutarch

'It is my task to dwell upon those details which illuminate the
workings of the soul'

The *Parallel Lives* of Plutarch are cornerstones of Western literature, and have exerted a profound influence on writers and
statesmen since the Renaissance, most notably Shakespeare. This
selection of ten biographies spans the period from the start of the
fourth century BC to the early third, and covers some of the most
important figures in Greek history, such as the orator Demosthenes
and Alexander the Great, as well as lesser-known figures such as
Plato's pupil Dion of Syracuse. Each *Life* is an important work of
literature in itself, but taken together they provide a vivid picture
of the Greek world during a period that saw the collapse of Spartan
power, the rise of Macedonia, the conquests of Alexander and the
wars of his successors.

Translated by Ian Scott-Kilvert and Timothy E. Duff
With an introduction and notes by Timothy E. Duff

ISBN: 978 0 14 044 935 8

THE TALE OF GENJI

Murasaki Shikibu

Written in the eleventh century, this exquisite portrait of courtly life in medieval Japan is widely celebrated as the world's first novel – and is certainly one of its finest. Genji, the Shining Prince, is the son of an emperor. He is a passionate characeer whose tempestuous nature, family circumstances, love affairs, alliances, and shifting political fortunes form the core of this magnificent epic.

Edited and translated by Royall Tyler

ISBN: 978 0 14 303 949 5

INFERNO

Dante

'And nothing, where I now arrive, is shining'

Dante's *Inferno* describes his descent into Hell midway through his life with the Roman Virgil as his guide, and is unparalleled in its depiction of the tragedy of sin. It is a work inspired by a profound confidence in human nature, yet also expresses Dante's horror at the way individuals can destroy themselves and each other, creating Hell on Earth. A response to the violent society of thirteenth-century Italy, the *Inferno* reveals the eternal punishment reserved for sins such as greed, self-deception, political double-dealing and treachery. Portraying a huge diversity of characters culminating in an horrific vision of Satan, it broke new ground in the vigour of its language and its storytelling. It has had a particular influence on Modernist writers and their successors throughout the world.

Translated and edited with an introduction, commentary and notes by Robin Kirkpatrick

ISBN: 978 0 14 044 895 5

THE CANTERBURY TALES

Geoffrey Chaucer

'Now as I've drunk a draught of corn-ripe ale,
By God it stands to reason I can strike
On Some good story that you all will like'

In *The Canterbury Tales* Chaucer created one of the great touch-stones of English literature, a masterly collection of chivalric romances, moral allegories and low farce. A story-telling competition within a group of pilgrims from all walks of life is the occasion for a series of tales that range from the Knight's account of courtly love and the ebullient Wife of Bath's Arthurian legend to the ribald anecdotes of the Miller and the Cook. Rich and diverse, *The Canterbury Tales* offers us an unrivalled glimpse into the life and mind of medieval England.

Translated by Nevill Coghill

ISBN: 978 0 14 042 438 6

MONKEY

Wu Ch'êng-ên

'Dear Monkey! He set out on his cloud trapeze, and in twinkling
he had crossed those two hundred leagues of water'

Monkey depicts the adventures of Prince Tripitaka, a young
Buddhist priest on a dangerous pilgrimage to India to retrieve
sacred scriptures accompanied by his three unruly disciples: the
greedy pig creature Pigsy, the river monster Sandy – and Monkey.
Hatched from a stone egg and given the secrets of heaven and
earth, the irrepressible trickster Monkey can ride on the clouds,
become invisible and transform himself into other shapes – skills
that prove very useful when the four travellers come up against
the dragons, bandits, demons and evil wizards that threaten to
foil them in their quest. Wu Ch'êng-ên wrote *Monkey* in the mid-
sixteenth century, adding his own distinctive style to an ancient
Chinese legend, and in so doing created a dazzling combination
of nonsense and profundity, slapstick comedy and spiritual
wisdom.

Translated by Arthur Waley

ISBN: 978 0 14 044 111 6

DON QUIXOTE

Miguel de Cervantes

'Didn't I tell you they were only windmills? And only someone
with windmills on the brain could have failed to see that!'

Don Quixote has become so entranced by reading romances of
chivalry that he determines to become a knight errant and pursue
bold adventures, accompanied by his squire, the cunning Sancho
Panza. As they roam the world together, the ageing Quixote's
fancy leads them wildly astray. At the same time the relationship
between the two men grows with fascinating subtlety. Often considered to be the first modern novel, *Don Quixote* is a wonderful
burlesque of the popular literature its disordered protagonist is
obsessed with.

Translated with an introduction and notes by John Rutherford

ISBN: 978 0 14 044 909 9